FALCON

THE QUIET PROFESSIONALS | BOOK 3

RONIE KENDIG

SHILOH RUN PRESS

An Imprint of Barbour Publishing, Inc.

© 2015 by Ronie Kendig

Print ISBN 978-1-62416-319-7

eBook Editions:
Adobe Digital Edition (.epub) 978-1-63409-379-8
Kindle and MobiPocket Edition (.prc) 978-1-63409-380-4

This book is a work of fiction. Names, characters, places, and incidents are either products of the author's imagination or used fictitiously. Any similarity to actual people, organizations, and/or events is purely coincidental.

For more information about Ronie Kendig, please access the author's website at the following Internet address: www.roniekendig.com.

Cover Design: Kirk DouPonce, DogEared Design

Published by Shiloh Run Press, an imprint of Barbour Publishing, Inc., P.O. Box 719, Uhrichsville, Ohio 44683, www.shilohrunpress.com

Our mission is to publish and distribute inspirational products offering exceptional value and biblical encouragement to the masses.

 Member of the
Evangelical Christian
Publishers Association

Printed in the United States of America.

DEDICATION

To those who serve in the intelligence community,
protecting Americans and their freedoms.

ACKNOWLEDGMENTS

My husband, Brian—Thank you for letting me pester you with
one scenario after another, enduring my irritation when you didn't
magically produce a perfect scenario or when I didn't like one you
suggested. You're my hero!

Keighley Kendig—My darlin' girl whose passion for all things anime and
manga helped me create a unique history for my characters. Thank you!

Ryan & Reagan—Thanks for enduring many on-your-own meals while
I fought to get this book done!

My agent, Steve Laube—You encouraged and protected me so I could
get this story written. Thank you, Agent-Man!

Robin Miller—Thank you, dear friend, for being a champion, cheer-
ing and challenging me as I worked feverishly to finish this novel. God
blessed me with you!

Narelle Mollet and Shannon McNear—You ladies have tirelessly read
every word I've written, encouraged me through waning courage, and
cheered me on to the finish!

Rapid-Fire Fiction Task Force—My own team of warriors and cham-
pions. You ladies make all the difference in the world.

Ironmance Group—Thank you for your prayers, your support, encouragement and wisdom! I treasure you ladies!

LITERARY LICENSE

In writing about unique settings, specific locations, and invariably the people residing there, a certain level of risk is involved, including the possibility of dishonoring the very people an author intends to honor. With that in mind, I have taken some literary license in *Falcon*, including renaming some bases within the U.S. military establishment, creating sites/ entities that do not otherwise exist, and other aspects of team movement/integration. Also, some elements of the story are pure entertainment and, as with any work of fiction, demand a level of suspension of disbelief. Writing about a potential threat to our American military personnel can be tricky, and those experts within that field cannot divulge too much information. Therefore, to protect our heroes, some elements of the story about the cybersecurity threat have been left intentionally and partially vague. I have done this so the book and/or my writing will not negatively reflect on our military community and its heroes. With the quickly changing landscape of the combat theater, this seemed imperative and prudent.

GLOSSARY OF TERMS/ACRONYMS

ACU—Army Combat Uniform
AHOD—All Hands On Deck
ANA—Afghan National Army
CECOM—Communications-Electronics Command
CID—Criminal Investigations Department
DIA—Defense Intelligence Agency
IED—Improvised Explosive Device
ISAF—International Security Assistance Force
Klick—Military slang for *kilometer*
M4, M4A1—Military assault rifles
MARSOC—Marine Special Operations Command
MRAP—Mine-Resistant Ambush-Protected vehicle
MRE—Meals Ready to Eat
MWD—Military Working Dog
NVG—Night-Vision Goggles
ODA—Operation Detachment Alpha
OEF/OIF—Operation Enduring Freedom/Operation Iraqi Freedom
PCS—Permanent Change of Station
RPG—Rocket-Propelled Grenade
RTB—Return To Base
SAS—Special Air Service (Foreign Special Operations Team)
SATINT—Satellite Intelligence
SCIF—Secure computer used by the military
Sitrep—Military abbreviation for *situation report*
SOCOM—Special Operations Command

CHARACTER LIST

Brian "Hawk" Bledsoe (Staff Sergeant)—Raptor team member; coms specialist

Brie Hastings (Lieutenant)—General Burnett's administrative officer

Cassandra Walker (Lieutenant)—works for DIA's National Military Joint Intelligence Center

Chris Riordan (Lieutenant Commander)—Navy SEAL officer

Ddrake—Explosives Detection Dog; German shepherd

Dean "Raptor Six" Watters (Captain)—Raptor team commander

Eamon "Titanis" Straider (SAS Corporal)—Raptor team member; Australian; engineering specialty

Grant Knight (Sergeant)—Ddrake's handler; temporarily assigned to Raptor team

Kiew Tang—executive assistant to Daniel Jin

Lance Burnett (General)—Raptor's commanding officer; attached to Defense Intelligence Agency

Meng-Li Jin /Daniel Jin—Chinese businessman

Mitchell "Harrier" Black (Sergeant First Class)—Raptor team member; combat medic

Ramsey (General)—Brigadier general; commander of U.S. Army Joint Special Operations Command

Sajjan Takkar—CEO of Takkar Corp.

Salvatore "Falcon" Russo (Warrant Officer)—Raptor team member; aka team "daddy"; expert in ops/intel

Todd "Eagle" Archer (Staff Sergeant)—Raptor team member; weapons expert; team sniper

Tony "Candyman" VanAllen—former Green Beret on Dean Watters's team

SUNDRY CHARACTERS

Boris Kolceki—expert computer hacker
Fariz Al-Bayati—teen caught up in combat zone
Fekiria Haidary—ANA helicopter pilot; Zahrah Zarrick's cousin; Hawk's girlfriend
Nina Laurens Takkar—Sajjan's wife; Timbrel's mother
Phelps (Lieutenant General)—Associate Director for Military Affairs
Schmidt—Navy SEAL on Riordan's team
Timbrel VanAllen—Tony's wife
Zahrah Zarrick—Fekiria's cousin; Dean's girlfriend; missionary teacher
Zmaray: "The Lion"/Lee Nianzu— assassin, terrorist

SPECIAL FORCES SOLDIER
(AUTHOR UNKNOWN)

I was that which others did not want to be.
I went where others feared to go,
and did what others failed to do.
I asked nothing from those who gave nothing,
and reluctantly accepted the thought
of eternal loneliness should I fail.
I have seen the face of terror,
felt the stinging cold of fear,
and enjoyed the sweet taste of a moment's love.
I have cried, pained, and hoped,
but most of all, I have lived times
others would say are best forgotten.
At least someday, I will be able to say
I was proud of what I was. . .
A Special Forces Soldier

CHAPTER 1

Fire ruptured the black veil of night. A pillar of orange and yellow roared upward, thirty meters, leaving a trail of smoke, ash, and debris in its wake. Metal groaned and heaved, collapsing in exhausted defeat. Screams ripped the air, their primal howl propelling him across Kandahar Airfield.

Warrant Officer Salvatore "Falcon" Russo sprinted with every ounce of strength he had toward the burning inferno that had been the U.S. Army's Communications-Electronics Command building. The very building that held the key to unearthing the mole and those responsible for the attacks against the U.S. military's super-secure network.

Gunfire popped amid the crackling growl of the blaze. Behind him the thud of boots reassured him that Raptor team was hot on his heels.

He shoved past a group of soldiers and airmen ogling the scene. Irritation skidded through him.

"Stop staring and start helping!" he shouted and kept moving toward the garish scene.

Hastily abandoned vehicles, debris, and moaning victims turned the parking lot into an obstacle course. Sal navigated through it, gaze locked on the facility. Injured stumbled from sections not yet fully consumed by the fire or decimated by the initial blast. A soldier hustled from amid the flames, his arm hooked around another soldier.

"What's the sitrep?" Sal asked.

After helping the woman to the ground, her hands bloodied an angry red, the man straightened, his ash-smudged face shaded with shock as he studied the burning structure. "Uh. . .not good." He swiped a hand along his forehead, leaving a dark streak. Blood. "Probably ten or twenty still. . .inside. . .inside our area. I d—don't know about the other." He swayed.

Eamon "Titanis" Straider appeared behind him, catching the guy by the shoulders and easing him down. "Careful, mate. You took a blow to the head." The Australian SAS corporal knelt over the man, cradling his head as the man relaxed on the ground.

Sal pivoted, gauging the best way to help. He spotted a fire tech grabbing some gear from a water tanker and rushed over to him. "What can I do?"

"Stay out of the way! It's too hot. The building's unstable."

"But there are people in there."

"Our men are on scene. If you go in there, that's just one more body we're digging out later." Three sets of firefighters struggled against the blaze that felt angry and personal.

Turning away, Sal bit back his frustration. Able to help yet unable to help. A shriek of pain drew his attention to the field of injured. Triage. Ambulances loaded wounded. He heard medics talking about sending some off base to the NATO hospital because they were quickly maxing out medical capabilities here.

Across the base, a chopper descended as an ambulance raced toward it. Para-jumpers—PJs—were responsible for providing emergency and life-saving services to airmen, soldiers, and civilians in both peacetime and combat environments.

Captain Dean Watters jogged toward him with a thrust of his chin, asking without words what was happening.

"They don't—"

A loud cracking mingled with a tinkling sound that snapped Sal's gaze toward the building. Near the fully engulfed area, a chair clattered across the ground. Sal looked to the window, which was now shattered. A man teetered precariously on the sharp glass, trying to haul himself free.

He stumbled.

Sal launched himself toward the injured airman. Even before he reached him, the bloody situation knotted Sal's gut. Amputation by explosive. Below the knee, the guy's leg was missing. Blood pooled around the guy's stump.

On his knees, Sal ripped out his combat application tourniquet.

"Hey," Dean shouted. "We've got an Alpha over here!" He bent over the man. "Stay with us. Okay?"

The airman groaned.

"I'm going to check on him," Dean said, pointing to another person laid out a few yards away.

Sal continued working, sliding the C-A-T up around the guy's leg, tightening the strap, and securing it back on itself, blocking out the sticky warmth coating his hands now. He then used the free winder and tightened it until the blood flow slowed. With a hemorrhaging loss like this, it didn't surprise him that the flow didn't completely stop. He tugged off his belt and used it as a secondary tourniquet.

The airman let out a feral howl then bit down and arched his back. He slumped like a limp rag with a pitiful moan.

"Hey," Sal said, checking for more injuries. "Where are you hurting?"

Only another low moan.

"Hey." Sal shook his shoulder. "What's your name?"

"J–Jason."

"All right, Jason. Tell me where you're hurting."

"Everywhere. . .my leg." Jason rolled his head side to side, now whimpering. "Give me something and knock me out, man."

That was exactly what they didn't want. Had to keep him conscious till the PJs or medical staff took over. "What happened, Jason? Do you know?"

Boots pounded toward them.

"Jason, can you tell me what happened?"

The airman whimpered. "Blue on Green. . .blue. One of. . .ours—" His eyes rolled.

"Jason! Hey!"

Two PJs moved in with a stretcher, and Sal backed away to let them do their job and get Jason to the hospital within the golden hour. He glanced at his hands then wiped the blood on his tac pants. Not the most sanitary method, but in combat situations, time was against them.

He squatted before the woman. "Hey, where are you hurting?"

She sighed, tears trickling down her cheeks, marking dark rivulets against her skin. She shook her head. More tears sped down.

Shock.

"Hey." Sal touched her shoulder then let his hand slide down her arm to surreptitiously assess her for injuries and a blood check. "What's your name?"

Unblinking, she stared at the building.

Sal cut into her line of sight. But she still wasn't seeing him.

"She injured?"

Depended on the definition of *injured*. Some wounds weren't visible—the notorious kind that inflicted more trauma on the mind than the body. Sal looked up at Mitchell "Harrier" Black, Raptor's medic, and shook his head. "Shock."

Harrier moved on.

A clipped, incessant crackling—not hard like the fire, but softer— sifted through the chaotic night to Sal's awareness. The woman's moans pulled his attention back. He wrapped his arms around hers and tried to draw her up. "Let's move you to safety." Away from the gruesome scene.

The staccato noise broke into his awareness again. This time louder. More insistent.

Sal glanced over his shoulder. Twenty feet away, he spotted Sergeant Grant Knight running after his military working dog, Ddrake, an impressive German shepherd who worked off-lead. Ddrake vanished around the side of the CECOM building.

Suddenly Knight pulled up straight. Drew his weapon and aimed in the direction his dog had vanished.

Knight and Ddrake needed backup. With one last look to the woman, Sal touched her shoulder. "Move to the fence." He pointed her toward safety then took off toward the MWD/handler team.

"On your knees, on your knees," Knight shouted, his weapon trained on someone. "Now or I will give my dog the command to take you."

In a wide arc, Sal rounded the corner, pulling his M4 up. There, not more than fifteen feet away, a man wearing an Afghan National Army uniform stood in a standoff, half poised to run.

Sal took a bead on the hostile. "What's going on?" he asked Knight, backing him up.

"Ddrake hit on him." Knight hadn't relaxed. "He's PEDD. Something's wrong."

Patrol Explosives Detection Dog. That meant Ddrake detected the scent of explosives on this man. Or a similar chemical scent.

A secondary hit? Sal tightened his shoulders. Considering the burning building beside them. . .

"*Blue on Green*. . ." Jason's earlier words speared his mind. The code for attacks on American troops by their trained allies, the ANA. Like this man in front of them.

His heart shoved into his throat. "Down! Down on your knees, hands up," Sal shouted in Pashto, Dari, then Farsi.

The man reached for something.

Sal couldn't wait any longer. Couldn't risk another attack. He coiled his finger against the trigger.

"No shoot," the man shouted, thrusting his hands in the air.

No way he'd relax. Not now and end up in a billion pieces. "Hands!" Sal inched closer.

The man pitched forward, a tiny explosion ripping through his chest.

"Shooter! Taking fire!"

—m—

Kandahar Airfield, Afghanistan
25 March—1735 Hours

Suffocating and fierce, a wave of heat roiled across her shoulders.

Lieutenant Cassandra Walker cried out and pressed lower to the cement floor, living her childhood nightmares of dying in a fire. She coughed against the thick smoke clogging her lungs. Might as well have sandpaper in her eyes—the ash rubbed and burned, forcing her to blink rapidly. She tried to see. Futile against the blanket of smoke. The inferno seemed to have a demonic presence, pursuing her as she sought escape.

Eyes closed, she let her fingers direct her as she probed the floor, which was still a bit cool. She crawled forward, listening not to the thundering panic of her own pulse but to the howl of the fire and the cackle of the flames. As if they mocked her. She'd rushed over here away from *him*. Away from the searing truth Sal had thrown at her. Right into this scalding nightmare.

"Nothing needs to be said. You know what you did. So do I. . . I never want to hear anything from you again. . ."

She pushed forward, but her fingers grazed the warmed surface of a filing cabinet. Scrambling around it, she kept moving. Had to get out. A few more paces and she hit a wall. Fear morphed into panic as a deep groaning vibrated against the floor.

Cassie hesitated, listening. Daring to look up. Like some Hollywood CGI image, the roof glowed beneath the power of the flames. A center section bowed inward. *Oh snap.* Her stomach dropped as the ceiling seemed to grope for her.

She threw herself to the side, struggling to remember the layout. Where the doors were. Where the exits had been located. *C'mon—you got here because of your wits. Now, use them!*

Whoosh! The beam's impact blasted hot air across her face. Fanned the flames, which rushed up the walls, surrounding her.

She scrabbled backward.

Thumped into something. She glanced down, but the thick black smoke proved an impenetrable barrier. Fingers tracking across the— hands! Someone's hands. "Hey!" she shouted—inhaling a lungful of smoke. A coughing fit wracked her. She doubled over, leaning to the person's chest. She shook them and shifted around. Something thumped against her hand. Instinctively, her fingers coiled around it. A water bottle!

Grabbing it, she started untucking her shirt. Ripped a stretch off. Doused it with water and tied it around her face. It'd buy her a little time.

She bent to the person again. "Hey," she said, more carefully this time, nearly pressing her nose to theirs.

Only then did she register the eyes. The brown eyes. The *dead* brown eyes.

With a cry, she clambered backward. Lowered her face to the floor, fighting back a pitiful sob. *God, I gave this to You back then. Will I never live it down?* She'd hoped to talk to him, at least ask his forgiveness, but

Sal wouldn't talk to her. Now, she'd die with his anger following her into the grave?

"Walker," came a distant voice.

She lifted her head. Where had that come from? "Here!"

A form swam amid the smoke, on all fours.

She didn't care who it was. As long as it was someone. Someone *alive*.

When the familiar face solidified, Cassie froze. "What are *you* doing?" It was ludicrous to look around. But she did. "You *can't* be here."

He hooked her arm around his shoulder and held her wrist as he guided her to the right, away from the dead body.

Exhaustion and smoke inhalation weighted her limbs. "If they see you—"

"Don't talk."

She let her head lob against his shoulder, surprised to find him wearing a fire-resistant jacket. Where had he gotten that from? Though it felt like an eternity, they finally navigated into a hall that had less smoke. When he lessened his hold, she stumbled.

His grip tightened, hoisting her up. Twenty feet ahead, she could barely make out a door. Oh! And above—an exit sign. Her heart leapt. Almost there! Almost able to feel the cool breeze on her face. Filling her lungs. She shot him a look as he reanchored his arm around her waist. He nodded. Took a step.

A steel joist crashed through the ceiling, delivering a greedy stream of fire.

Pain spiked through Cassie's temple. Blazed across her shoulder, followed by a trail of strange warmth. She felt herself falling backward. Thrust out a hand to steady herself, but only met hot air. She landed with a soft thud against him. He grunted but was already coming back up.

On her feet, she followed his lead, clambering over the hot joist. An electrical wire hissed and popped at them like an angry copperhead.

"Hurry!" he shouted.

Cassie threw herself forward, terrified of being buried alive in this burning furnace. As she launched toward him, a prick of pain sliced up her leg. She ignored it and caught his hand. He hooked her closer and barreled into a door.

Momentum carried her face-first into a sidewalk. She shoved her hands out to break her fall. Rocks and pebbles dug into her palms. She hauled in a deep breath. *Air! Sweet air!* Her lungs seized, still struggling with the smoke that had filled them. Another gagging-coughing fit pitched her to the ground.

"Walker!" someone shouted from her left. Boots thudded toward her. "Oxygen! We need oxygen!" A hand came to her back. "We didn't know you were in there."

Captain Watters.

She clutched her chest, willing it to loosen its fist hold on her breathing as she looked up at him.

He cupped her elbow. "Let's get away from the building."

Cassie nodded and pushed to her feet. The world tilted and swayed.

He lifted her and hurried her to a wall. With more care than she expected from Sal's captain, he guided her to the ground as an airman rushed up behind him with an O_2PAK.

Watters went to a knee and extended the mask toward her. "Careful, you're bleeding."

Cassie blinked, barely remembering the pain after the joist. She touched the throbbing spot above her right temple then to the stinging in her shoulder. Both sticky with her blood.

"Where do you hurt?" the medic asked, opening his kit.

"Just my head and shoulder."

"Who came out with you?" Watters looked around, his brow etched with concern.

Surprise spiraled through Cassie as she followed his gaze, not entirely shocked that her rescuer had vanished. She shook her head. "A firefighter, I think," she spoke around the mask. "He had on"—she waved her hand at her torso—"a protective jacket." That much was true. But he wasn't a firefighter. And nobody could know he'd been on this base.

"You didn't see him?"

She shook her head again, though his knotted brow and scowl warned that he didn't believe her. "Too much smoke."

The airman reached into his med kit. "Let me check that cut."

Grateful for the diversion, Cassie nodded. Angled toward him.

"He has to be around here somewhere," Captain Watters said.

"Think he went back in?" another soldier asked—only then did she see Sergeant Brian "Hawk" Bledsoe join them.

Cassie's gaze struck the building. He hadn't gone back inside, had he? That would be. . .idiotic. He'd die. But even as she looked at the burning building, she couldn't shake the horrible feeling that he'd done just that. *He's not that stupid.*

With only one wall remaining upright, the CECOM building resembled a steel giant kneeling in defeat.

"If he did," Captain Watters said, "he's not coming out."

As if to prove his point, the giant collapsed in on itself, surrendering with a hot breath of fury.

"Taking fire!" someone shouted from across the parking lot. "We're taking fire!"

CHAPTER 2

Kandahar Airfield, Afghanistan
25 March—1745 Hours

Do you see the shooter?"

Sal shifted, pressing his shoulder against the hull of a Jeep sitting in the parking lot of the burning CECOM building and scanned the distance. It wasn't like Kandahar Airfield was small and jammed up against the city. There was distance—the airport sat ten miles southeast of Kandahar City. The base was massive, hosting a couple hundred aircraft. Maintained by the U.S. Armed Forces and the ISAF, it also had a smaller, dedicated portion to the Afghan Armed Forces' base and an even smaller portion for the Afghan Air Force.

Whoever was firing on them had to be *on* the base—and was it his imagination or were those shots coming from the AAF's location?

"I got nothing," he said.

The man they'd caught lay dead in a pool of his own blood. CECOM was burning. American soldiers and Afghan allies were dying. This mess had to stop.

He shot a look to Knight, who had taken cover behind a portable building. "We need to end this."

Knight nodded. "Ddrake and I will find them." He turned to his intense German shepherd, who stood ready and willing to work. After his handler spoke a quiet command to him, Ddrake turned and started his methodical stalking of the scent. Weapon cradled in both hands but held down, Sal trailed the MWD team away from CECOM. Experience had sharpened his trust in the K9 units, in their ability to track down trouble and their fierce loyalty to protect their pack. It's why he'd requested a team for Raptor.

Dirt crunched beneath his boots as they skirted one building after another, Ddrake systematically making his way toward what had once been a thriving center of downtime—the Boardwalk. Most shops had closed down, a few rebellious, stubborn ones lingering as the troop count had been drastically scaled back.

Ddrake trotted on, his breathing almost staccato as he hauled in air and processed the scents at the back of his throat, tasting as much as smelling what lingered in the air.

They were sitting ducks out here, with most of the base personnel embroiled in the chaos at CECOM. Sal slowed, his gaze sweeping back and forth. The hairs on the back of his neck prickled. What he wouldn't do to have his M4A1 carbine with its modified trigger he'd done with an off the shelf kind and overhauled. That beat a handgun in a firefight any day and every day.

He rolled his shoulders and swallowed, telling himself the enemy wasn't as well trained. They were more frantic. More desperate. They made mistakes.

Still. A carbine went a long way in making him feel more secure.

"Falcon!" came a hissed voice.

He pivoted, bringing his weapon up.

Dean and Todd "Eagle" Archer jogged toward him, both carrying weapons and a vest. Dean tossed him the tac vest. Sal threaded his arms through it and secured the straps before accepting the assault rifle.

"What've you got?" Dean asked Knight.

"Nothing yet. But he's tracking." Knight kept moving, following his dog.

Sal resumed his course, this time with Eagle and Dean in tow. That felt better. Right. Even though he had his issues with Dean. Friends could handle that though. And Dean was a bigger man than to let differences get in the way of doing the job or the mission.

Sal wished he could be like that.

At a juncture of two portable buildings, Ddrake suddenly back-tracked. Lowered his snout and hauled in hard.

Hawk and Titanis caught up with them as the German shepherd sorted the scents. Sal scanned their surroundings, thinking through what could be in the area. "Less than half a klick to the airfield."

"Even less to the Afghan Air Force base," Titanis added.

Sal focused on that area. After the president had announced the U.S. withdrawal and scaled back efforts, there'd been a lull in attacks then there seemed to be a vicious uptick in Blue-on-Green attacks. What infuriated him were the innocent civilians who wanted the protection against the Taliban but were caught in the middle and suffering because of the swell of violence.

"He's got something!"

Sal swung around as the two bolted down the darkened alley between the buildings. Ddrake went right. Knight followed.

"Stay with them!" Dean shouted.

Known for his gift of speed, Sal sprinted behind them, his boots digging into the half-dirt, half-pebbled ground. He rounded the corner just as Ddrake sailed over a barricade. Even as he watched Knight throw himself at the wall, Sal slung his weapon over his shoulder. Knight cleared it, but not as easily as the dog.

Sal jumped against the wall. His feet hit. He palmed the cement bricks and vaulted over. He landed with a thud and shifted to the side, going to a knee. Assessed. Knight and Ddrake were circling a small car.

"Back! Get back!" Sal could just see that thing blowing sky-high and taking the MWD team with him.

"Ddrake, heel!" Knight slapped his left thigh twice and the dog immediately circled back, turned, and sat against Knight's leg, looking up at his handler happily. "I can see supplies, but it doesn't look like a bomb."

Sal kept his weapon trained out, staring down the sight as the others grouped up.

Dean dropped over the wall next, followed by Hawk and Eagle. Approaching cautiously, Dean eyed the interior of the car. Keyed his mic. "Command, this is Raptor Six Actual. We are just north of the blast well and found some chemicals. Let's get Hazmat out here."

"Shooters?" Hawk asked.

"Nothing yet. I can have him track." Knight shrugged.

"He can decipher between human and chemicals?"

"Ddrake tracks chemicals, but whoever carried those"—he pointed to the car—"they'll have that scent on them. Ddrake can find them."

"Let's do it."

The words had no sooner left Sal's mouth than a wall of growling, snarling teeth and fur flew into the air. With a beastly growl-snap, Ddrake bolted into a dark sliver of space between a shack and the perimeter fence.

"He saw som—"

A primal scream howled through the night.

Running, Sal shouted to Dean and pointed. "South! South." He and Knight rushed up to the opening maw of the shadowed space that had devoured Ddrake.

Screams mingled with Ddrake's growls—which sounded like they were issued against a mouthful of flesh.

"Ddrake, out!"

Ddrake gave one more shake of his neck before disengaging his teeth. After another low growl that sounded a lot like some night ghoul, he returned to his handler's side.

"On your knees," Sal shouted, edging in with his SureFire blasting bright white at the guy.

Blood spurted from the arm wounds inflicted by Ddrake. An AK-47 peeked out from beneath the portable unit. Sal nudged it out of reach with his boot.

Dean shimmied in behind the guy. "Take him back to Command. We'll interview him there."

They cuffed the man without incident and led him back toward the main base where lights had been cut and an ominous sense of dread hung over the place.

The door to the JSOC building opened. General Lance Burnett stepped out with Brassie Cassie and Lieutenant Hastings.

"Caught him near the explosives with a weapon." Sal ignored Cassie. Or tried to. His rising anger told him he wasn't winning the war this time.

"Ddrake detected him as a threat," Knight said. "He took him down."

"Get him cleaned up and we'll—"

Something splatted Sal's face. He wiped at it as his gaze struck Burnett's chest. Blood spurted from a wound. The general collapsed to his knees.

Cassie yelped as she and Hastings reached for the general.

Dean dove toward them. "Down! Down!"

CHAPTER 3

Kandahar Airfield, Afghanistan
25 March—1800 Hours

Sticky, warm blood squished between her fingers, forcing Cassie to press harder against the chest wound.

"Knight, get him in a holding cell inside," the captain ordered the MWD handler, who nodded, hooked the guy's arm, and pushed him into the building.

"Augh!" Sal said as he assessed the general. "There's too much blood."

"Guess this is a bloody mess," General Burnett mumbled and tried to laugh.

"Yeah, leave it to you." Sal's words held a hint of humor but his expression didn't. "We have to get you to the hospital. Now." He almost met Cassie's gaze.

"Titanis." Dean removed his shirt and balled it. "Find a vehicle."

The big Aussie took off as Dean lifted Cassie's hand for a second and stuffed the shirt under her fingers. "Hold that. Push." His large hands dwarfed hers and pushed down. "Harder."

Cassie nodded, ignoring the squeamish protest of her stomach.

"Sir." Sal leaned down at the general, who stared up at the ceiling of stars. "Stay with us."

Brie Hastings crouched over him. "You're too mean to die."

"Got that right," he said around a cough.

Panicked blue eyes met Cassie's. "H–he—"

Sal held two fingers to the general's neck. "Pulse is thready."

"Always thought my heart would get me." General Burnett's mouth quirked in a half smile. He coughed again. "Son of. . .cowards. Couldn't. . .face me."

Cassie shoved her focus to Sal, desperate for them to save the general before. . .before he died. The handler jogged back out. "I put in a call. CECOM tied up the ambulances. But triage is expecting him." Rocks crunched and popped as a vehicle swung to a stop near them.

"Lift him." Sal hooked his arms beneath the general's legs as the captain carefully lifted his head. "Keep his legs higher to slow blood flow."

With Knight and Titanis, the two men maneuvered the general to the back of the truck. Cassie stayed with them, nausea roiling as she kept the pressure on his wound.

The captain and Sal situated the general as Cassie went down. Steel digging into her knees, she held both hands over the gunshot wound. But no matter how hard she pressed, the blood kept spilling out. "I can't stop it," she cried out, hearing the panic and not caring.

"Go!" Sal shouted, clamping his hands over Cassie's.

"Moving him traumatized the wound," Dean yelled over the wind and engine noise as they barreled toward the base hospital.

Though it wasn't a large distance, the trip took longer than Cassie wanted. He didn't have an endless supply of blood. Even with Sal's hands on hers, it seemed blood still seeped around the edges of the ever-widening circle.

She stiffened, seeing a stream roll down the general's chest and pool at the hollow of his throat.

"C'mon," Sal yelled.

Titanis seemed to obey, whipping the truck up to the hospital that was already abuzz. The early bombing victims would complicate this.

The doors burst open, Hawk leading two orderlies and a stretcher.

"Hawk, here!" The captain leapt from the truck, waving them over. The medical team rushed toward them.

Sal shifted beside her, pushing to his feet but bending in half to keep their hands in place. "Can't stop the bleeding."

Two nurses climbed up, replacing Brie, who had hovered at the general's head the whole time. They laid the stretcher out next to him.

"Roll him toward you," the doctor said. "On three. One. . .two. . .roll!"

Sal, Cassie, and Brie rolled the general's body to the side as the medical team slid the stretcher into place. They eased him back down and within seconds, they slid the general out of the truck bed.

Adrenaline racing through her veins, hands covered in blood, Cassie followed the medical team and Raptor into the hospital.

Captain Watters recapped the incident, the medical situation, and stalked the team back toward the prep bays, which were all full. Sal remained with his general and captain, though they hung back to stay out of the way so the medical team could work their magic.

Cassie held back, her hands trembling. Her heart feeling as if it pumped peanut butter. General Burnett. . .

"Please save him," a voice whispered.

Read her thoughts. Her silent plea to God.

"He can't die."

This time, the words snapped Cassie out of her stupor. She looked to the side and found Brie Hastings, hands slightly less bloodied than her own, covering her mouth, mumbling.

"He'll be okay." Cassie didn't know why she said it. Somehow, she knew the words weren't true. General Burnett probably wouldn't make it. He'd lost too much blood. An artery had been nicked. But Brie had been one of her few allies since arriving in Afghanistan a few weeks ago. And she hated to see anyone looking or sounding desperate or scared.

Brie met her gaze but said nothing. Instead she turned. Started for the door.

"Brie," came a deep, quiet voice.

Titanis hurried after her, touching Cassie's shoulder as he did. As if to comfort her. She had worked with the general, but she didn't know him. Not the way these people did. But he was a good man. A good leader.

"Would you like to wash?" A nurse motioned toward a large bin-style sink.

Cassie glanced at her hands. Right. With a mute nod, she stumbled that way.

"Antiseptic soap here," the nurse said, motioning to the wall-mounted bottle. "Towel there. Put it in the bin when you're done."

Another silent nod and Cassie was washing her hands. Scrubbing.

Would he make it? She'd never been in a situation like that, having to stop a man's death with her bare hands. If he died—

Sal will blame me

Again.

Her eyes slid closed. The din of running water blended with the hum of shouted orders, curtains slinking across metal rods, and the ominous *whoosh* of medical personnel running back and forth.

"He's flatlining."

Cassie jolted at the voice beyond the wall. She flipped off the faucet and dried her hands, a strange venom pulsing though her veins, urging her to leave the building. Away from death. Away from blame. She didn't want to be here if General Burnett died. Didn't want to watch him die. Or hear him die. She just. . .couldn't.

She discarded the towel in the receptacle and eased back into the main hall. A quick look revealed an arc of tactical shirts forming a protective barrier around the bay that held the general.

Sal stood with his back to her, his concern and loyalty evident in the ever-watchful guardian, maintaining watch over his fallen general. He shifted, shaking his head. Started to turn—and his gaze skidded in her direction.

Cassie pivoted away. She didn't need his scathing rebuke. His hatred. Not this time. Not after tonight.

—∞—

Kabul, Afghanistan
25 March—1830 Hours

Applying pressure to an individual could be fruitless. Unless one used the right kind of pressure. And right now, that's what he had to find out about this impudent man. Sajjan Takkar stood removed but present. Active but inactive. A posture of power. He needed this man to know who was in charge. Since they'd dragged him here a few days ago, they'd managed to learn nothing that Sajjan's own intelligence ring hadn't already provided.

Waris laid out the kit of needles and serums.

"Y–you're joking, right?" Sweat beaded the man's brow. "You know all you have to do is throw money at me and I'll squeal like a stuck pig."

Sajjan unfolded his arms and walked toward the twenty eight-year-old hacker. "Mm, yes. You would. And you have, but what would you say?"

"Whatever you want me to say."

"Indeed." That was the problem. "I do not want to hear what you think I want to hear." He clipped his words to show irritation, though he wasn't irritated yet. Determined, yes. Focused, even more so. "I want the truth."

"What is truth? How do you define truth?" A smile quivered above the man's lips. "Right? I mean. Let's be real here. You want to know who hired me. Who paid me. But why—why would you want to know that? You're not American. They don't help you. I mean, who do they help, ya know?"

Sajjan walked a slow circle around the room. His phone chirruped and he tugged it from the pocket as Waris loaded a vial of gold liquid into the syringe. "Keep me informed."

Once the door behind him hissed shut, he took the call. "Sabir, what can I do for you?"

"There has been an attack. A bold, brazen attack against the American base in Kandahar."

Sajjan started for the private elevator. "You know this how?"

"Dozens of their wounded are here."

At the NATO hospital.

"I am hearing whisperings that someone is paying the Taliban to be more open in their attacks."

"I hear the same," Sajjan said gravely.

"We must stop this." Sabir's voice was rushed, quiet. "All these years of hard work—even if you do not agree with American policy, this—*this* is not good for Afghanistan. For business."

"I agree." It was why he had worked so hard in the last decade to be an ally on many fronts, not to one government over another but for the good of Afghanistan. For the good of his mother's people. "Let me know if you hear anything."

"Will you deal with this?" The question was as pleading as it was demanding.

"You know me, Sabir."

A shaky breath carried through the line. "Of course. Of course, I do. Thank you." Sabir's nervous anticipation and desperate hope to see the violence quiet down in the regions carried through the phone. After watching what happened with Iraq and ISIS, the threat against any freedom and free enterprise hung in the balance.

"Do not thank me. We must do this together." Sajjan ended the call as he entered the elevator then slid his key into the slot and rode to the top floor. Stepping into his office, he heard terse conversation in the foyer of his penthouse apartment. In particular, he heard Nina's voice. A primal instinct to protect her pushed him across the lush office to the door. He moved into the open area slowly to gain perspective before injecting himself.

Dressed in a silk kaftan and hijab, Nina stood as elegantly and poised as ever. It was a testament to her that she wore the scarf out of respect for the people of his country. He appreciated the gesture of his American wife who, having been influential in Hollywood after a stunning career, certainly did not have to spend her better years tucked away from the glamour and glitz on the other side of the world. Yet she insisted. And he was glad for it. She was a breath of fresh air with her strong views, confident manner, and beauty.

The man standing with her just beyond the entryway was Aamir al Wahidi, an imam hired by the community to not only lead them in prayer but provide counsel. While Sajjan never sought the imam's advice, it had been given. Often.

Nina held her hands out, palms up. "I am so sorry, Mr.—"

Sajjan moved forward, not willing that his wife should have to make an excuse. Not on a night like this.

"Ah." Nina's eyes brightened as she met his gaze. Relief flickered through her brown irises as she inclined her head. "Here you are."

Sajjan wrapped an arm around Nina's waist and kissed her temple, making sure the imam understood this significant gesture that Nina may be his wife, but she was more than that as well—friend, confidant, business partner. "Forgive me for being late." He shifted to the imam and inclined his head. "*Salaam,* Aamir."

"Salaam." Aamir inclined his covered head.

"*Haleh shoma chetor hast?*" Here, it would be an insult or slight to get right down to business as was so often done in American and other business circles. Which was why he'd asked how the imam was doing—to show courtesy and respect.

Aamir, dressed in the traditional *khet partug,* a tunic slightly tightened at the waist and loose pants with plenty of pleats, bowed again. It was the *karakul* hat that marked the man with some level of pride, marked his leadership within the community. But Sajjan would not fault him for it as he himself still wore the turban of the Sikh.

He motioned toward Sajjan's office. "We should speak."

Ignoring the slight at not asking after *his* family, Sajjan nodded to Nina, acknowledging her with a warm smile as she slipped down the hall to where her daughter no doubt waited with her husband and dog. Sajjan led the way into the office, flicking on the light as he entered. "Your disregard for my family speaks to the urgency, it would seem."

"Please," Aamir said, motioning behind Sajjan. "Close the door."

He would ignore the man's slight in telling him what to do in his own home. "It is an honor to have you in my home." A subtle reminder to the man of his position here.

"There has been an attack," Aamir said with a hiss. "Against the Americans."

Interesting that he left out the location. "Where?"

"Kandahar."

"Isn't that under Bahram?"

"Bah!" Aamir spun and stalked toward a chair. "You and I both know Bahram is unfit to lead."

"Do I?" Sajjan strolled to the window and stared down on the city.

"Do not play games with me, Sajjan."

Sliding his hands into the pockets of his suit pants, Sajjan turned. "Then do not play with me. You have ignored courtesy and impugned a friend." He let a handful of breaths eek out in a calming measure before continuing. "What is your point today, friend?"

"The attack was not by our people."

Sajjan said nothing because he wasn't surprised by the words. There had been an undercurrent of tyranny in current events. And he'd recently confirmed the source of that influx of hatred and violence had been birthed or perpetuated from within the walls of this tower. Beneath his very nose.

And he would deal with it. Once he had what he needed.

"You suspect. . .whom?" Sajjan asked, arching an eyebrow as he played the innocent. "Who else but the Taliban would carry out such an attack that serves no purpose when the Americans are already withdrawing?"

Reason had never worked with those emboldened by religious fervor. Or a herd mentality. He had been as frustrated as he had been inspired by his mother's people.

"I do not have an answer for this," Aamir said, as if it was abhorrent that Sajjan would ask him.

"Then why are you here, Aamir? I am a busy man—"

"You have the power to influence people, to get to the bottom of this and stop it."

"And why would I want that?"

Aamir lifted his chin only a degree. Enough for the arrogance and true purpose behind his visit to be revealed. "We must all work for a stronger Afghanistan."

"Of course." Sajjan waved a dismissive hand. "Is that not what I am doing here, building the first skyscraper in Kandahar? Bringing industry and money to the city that gave birth to the Taliban? What else would you have me do?"

Aamir leaned forward. "Talk to your sources. Find out who is behind this."

"*My* sources?" Sajjan feigned ignorance. "Aamir, you give me too much credit. My sources are business and money—"

"I trust that you will do what is possible to help our country." Aamir stood, straightening his *khet*. "Please, we must. For peace. As Allah wills it."

"Of course." As if that saying sanctioned whatever the individual said. Surely he did not expect Sajjan to believe this was for peace, for Allah.

Aamir swallowed. Gave a shaky smile then started for the door. "I knew I could count on you, Sajjan. You are faithful. Just as your father."

A twinge of anger spat through Sajjan's veins at the mention of his father, a tactic designed to play on his sympathies. He squelched the thought of slamming this impudent man through the walls. Instead he guaranteed the man's removal from his home by following Aamir out. After their good-byes, he wandered back to the living area, his mind heavy with the implications of the imam's words. His insistence of Sajjan's help.

Across the marble floor, a flicker of movement stilled him.

Dressed in an Army tactical shirt and pants that hid his prosthesis, Nina's son-in-law sat on the sofa, elbows propped on his knees, fingers threaded. Intelligence lurked behind those pale green eyes. Tony held his gaze for a second then looked down.

Ah. "You heard."

Tony shrugged. "He's not exactly quiet."

With a sigh and bob of his head, Sajjan sat opposite the young man who'd entered his life like a storm and hadn't let up. But today, right now—the taut lips. The intensity. "You're angry."

"Absolutely. That attack"—he pointed to the south with flared nostrils—"was against *my* brothers." His lip curled as he thumped a hand on his chest. "And that man knows something about it."

Sajjan rubbed his well-trimmed beard, thinking. "Yes, I believe he does."

"What are you going to do about it?"

Sajjan considered the young man. At least twenty years his junior but with no less fervor or willingness to play the intelligence game. "Me?" He gave a cockeyed nod, smiling at Tony VanAllen. "I'm going to recruit help."

EAMON

Rich. As sole heir of his father's fortune, which had a net worth of over two billion dollars, Eamon Straider grew up lacking nothing. Except meaning.

Powerful. Primed and prepped to walk in the shoes of his father, who served as prime minister of Australia, commissioned by the governor-general.

War hero. With his own Australian SAS team, he'd earned two Victoria Crosses, which was why he'd tattooed one over his heart. He loved the joint special forces, working with foreign elite warriors like himself. And he had a special place for certain Americans, especially those with Raptor, but his loyalty would never waver from his homeland.

He'd attained every single goal he'd set for himself, save one: marriage. Being a warrior didn't lend itself well to building a family and being a part of the family. But if his father could do it, perhaps Eamon could. Someday.

He strode toward the JSOC building carrying the heavy burden of bad news. Captain Watters had offered to deliver the news, but they both knew that Eamon had developed. . .something with Lieutenant Hastings. He should be the one to convey the tragic news.

Inside, he made his way toward the general's office, noting the lone lamp light burning at the end of the hall. That would be her desk. He held straight and didn't let himself falter.

A strange, strong odor stung the air. It smelled like antiseptic. He glanced around. Was someone cleaning?

"Oh."

Eamon pivoted toward the soft voice. His gut tightened, but this time for a different reason.

Lieutenant Brie Hastings stood there in uniform, the ACUs doing nothing to camouflage her figure. But it was her smile, those soft blue eyes, that had him paying more attention than he should. Especially now.

He finally noticed the red around her eyes. And the way she rubbed and folded her hands quickly. That was what he smelled. Antiseptic. But the stink of it was strong. How much had she used?

"I—I couldn't get the blood off." Her voice pitched as she went to her desk and dropped into her chair. "Did you. . .see him? Is he. . . ?"

The way her voice cracked again, her eyes pleading with him, broke his resolve. He eased toward the chair at the corner of her desk. Sat on the edge. Looked at his boots. Couldn't. . .

"He's dead. Isn't he?"

Swallowing, he met her gaze. Gave a curt nod. "The bullet nicked a main artery. Lodged in his heart. There. . .there wasn't anything they could do."

Her chin quivered as her eyes drifted away, filling with tears. "He's gone." A shudder pulled her straight. The grief and brokenness vanished in a strange wave of resolve as Brie pushed to her feet. "Excuse me. I have to contact Command."

"Hey—"

"They need to know right away that he's gone."

"Brie," Eamon said, taking long strides to catch up with her fast pace down the hall. "Brie, wait." He caught her arm. Tugged her around.

"Please." Her word squeaked into a whisper as her blue orbs flicked to his chest.

A wall of protective instincts rose up in him as awareness muddied the waters. Her athletic build still seemed dwarfed when they stood close. He touched her shoulder. "Brie, it's okay to grieve."

A tear broke free. Spilled down her tawny cheek. She shook it away. "No, it's not." She met his gaze, strength she'd mustered from somewhere deep filling her features.

Eamon angled in, concerned. "He—"

"I can't." Vulnerability skated across her pretty face. "Not now." She drew in another shaky breath, her hands trembling. "I have to..."

"Brie."

She cupped a hand over her mouth as a sob escaped.

Eamon's arms went around her shoulders, tugging her close, but she went rigid. Though she let out a few choked sobs, she kept that tight control in place before finally stepping out of his hold.

She gave a nod-shake. "Sorry. Thank you. I..." She looked down the hall. "Oh no." Her brow twisted into a knot. "His wife..."

"No, leave that for the Army."

"But she's his wife! She should know he's gone."

"Yes. And she will. But if you call her—who will be there to hold her as she comes to grips with his death? Let's leave that to special services to make sure someone is there to help her through this."

She gave a curt nod. "Of course. You're right." Brie swallowed. "That's why you came to me."

True. He'd known of Brie's special relationship with the general and didn't want her to find out alone. Or by anyone else. "He was like a father to you, so—"

"Yes." Determination flitted into her eyes. "Yes, he is"—she shook her head—"*was*. Which is why I need to honor him by pushing on, finding his murderer."

Eamon inched closer, itching to hold her. Make everything right. She was tough, strong, determined, and focused. There was a reason Burnett had her as his aide, and it was the same reason that had drawn Eamon into her net, too.

Shoulders squared, hair in that meticulous bun, Brie nodded. "Thank you, Titanis." She sighed. "I have work to do. If you'll excuse me."

"Of course." He tucked away his misplaced thoughts. The ones that had him feeling like a scolded schoolboy. A billion dollars, a yacht, a powerful father, an outstanding military service record. But the one area he desperately wanted to succeed...instead, he walked into a landmine field of rejection.

CHAPTER 4

Grief was the vicious enemy of progress.

Sal sat in the squeaky chair at his desk, elbows on his knees. Head down. Barely visible from his position, the office down the hall sat ominously closed up. It seemed to epitomize death with the way it alone sat darkened when all other lights glowed and tinkled.

When Burnett was around, the door was open and more than just the lights glowed. Hope. Progress. Sal lowered his gaze, remembering the general. Remembering his caustic wit that could be easily taken as mean. But to those who knew him, he was a balls-to-the-walls kind of guy. Gut it up and get it done. He didn't put up with crap, and he didn't dish it out either. With Lance Burnett came solid, honest, hardworking ethics. Sal had lost an anchor in life. He knew if he got off center, the general would yank his butt back in line. Give him what for and tell him to straighten up or ship out.

Now he was gone. Murdered on a tragic, deadly night. Right in front of his own soldiers. Right out his office door, practically.

"Who do you think will replace him?" Hawk asked, boots propped on the legs of his chair and head against the wall.

Sal leaned back with a heavy sigh. He didn't even want to think about that. Denial did nothing except prevent forward momentum, yet the idea of facing new brass, new leadership, when they needed to nail this terrorist who'd attacked Raptor and Kandahar Airfield. . . "Just better be someone good."

"Hooah." Hawk dropped forward in the chair, noticeably changed since his trek through the snow-riddled mountains. He had settled into himself, and Sal somehow felt the loudmouthed guy earned some respect and space. "Someone who knows what's going on."

"They will." Quiet and firm, Dean's words pulled Sal's gaze to where the captain sat, face awash in the blue haze of his computer screen.

"What're you reading?" Sal asked.

"Reports from the attack."

Sal glanced at his own desk, at the files stacked up. He'd gone through them a couple of times already, looking for anything that provided a tip on the deadly attack against CECOM. Found nothing. "What about the prisoner?" He could put a little of his frustration to rest by introducing his fists to the guy's face.

Dean yawned as he slumped back and checked his watch. "Should have an answer by fourteen hundred."

"We should've already had *immediate* access." Sal pushed to his feet. "Why did Ramsey stall us anyway?"

"DIA's interviewing him."

Interviewing. That was a nice word for what actually happened in those meetings.

"Let's hope it's an aggressive talk," Hawk said with a gleam, one that matched what Sal felt.

And that scared him to be this keyed up. This ready to cram a rocket down someone's gullet.

The front door swung inward, throwing bright afternoon light across the Command building. In stormed a bevy of brass—more than one might see at a range. Sal straightened, giving respect to the officers who streamed in.

"Captain," General Ramsey stepped from behind a colonel and extended a hand to Dean. He was a good ten to fifteen years younger than Burnett and had a truckload of intensity about him. Probably why he was balding and gray.

"What is that smell?" Hawk muttered, his gaze flicking to the newcomers hanging near the door. SEALs—squids. Riordan. Schmidt—the one who'd fought Hawk at the hookah bar. And a handful of others.

Sal gave Hawk a warning look to keep the tone neutral with officers on deck. But when he turned, Cassie had joined the group. He hated himself for thinking it, but he'd been hoping that she'd vanish with Burnett gone.

"Captain, if we could have a word with you and your team." Ramsey moved toward the briefing room without waiting for a reply, the officers and squids following him like a wake of rotten fish.

"Guess we're about to get answers," Hawk muttered as he sidled up to Dean and Sal.

Harrier, Titanis, and Knight were with them now, too.

"This feels wrong." Sal couldn't shake the feeling no matter how hard he tried.

"Keep it calm," Dean said, giving everyone a firm look. "Discuss later. Just hear them out."

"Who keeps bringing the stale fish into the house?" Hawk complained as he made his way into the room, shouldering past the SEALs and taking a seat.

Inside the crowded briefing room, Sal remained near the door. And to his chagrin, so did Cassie. He set his jaw and trained his attention on General Ramsey.

"It's been a rough couple of days. We're all ticked off about General Burnett's murder, and we're not going to let that go unanswered."

"Hooah," Hawk murmured.

"But we need chain of command established. For the foreseeable future until we get someone else in place, Raptor, you'll report to me."

It made sense, mostly, for them to answer to Ramsey, but somehow, it stuck in Sal's gut. Why it bothered him, he couldn't tell.

"I'm also keeping the JSOC pairing of Raptor and Riordan's team."

That's why.

Sal shifted and resisted the urge to fold his arms over his chest, a sign of disrespect. He skated a look at Dean, whose stony expression gave nothing away about his feelings.

Dean might be stoic, but he wasn't an unfeeling sort. It's what made him a good team leader. Made him a man Sal respected, even when they disagreed. Yet he couldn't read what the captain thought about this. Not all men were as gifted at hiding their feelings as Dean. Sal envied that.

He'd never been able to hide what he felt.

"With what's on the line, It's no time to make sweeping changes," Ramsey said. "We'll keep things as Burnett had them. Captain, I'll need you liaising with Command more than ever. Russo, you'll manage the team and coordinate with your captain and Commander Riordan."

Sal nodded. "Yes, sir." He swallowed the bile in having to coordinate with Riordan. But they'd do what they had to in order to complete the mission.

"Lieutenant Hastings, until further notice, keep working intel about this terrorist who's hit." General Ramsey's gaze shifted—right at Sal. "You'll stay with the team, too."

Why wouldn't I? He'd just told—

"Yes, sir." Cassie's soft voice, lilting with her Southern roots, drifted over Sal's shoulder. "Thank you, General."

Son of a french-fried biscuit! The general had been talking to Cassie.

"Mr. Russo, as team leader, you'll need to work closely with Walker to make sure she has the most recent, up-to-date intel."

So much for hoping she'd be gone. Out of his sight. Out of his life.

Ramsey angled toward the colonel at his left. "Am I missing anything?"

The full bird shook his head.

"Okay." Ramsey pursed his lips, his shoulders relaxing a fraction. "Questions?"

"Sir," Dean spoke up. "We'd like access to the prisoner we secured the night of Burnett's murder."

"Of course you would." He nodded and looked at the colonel again. "Get that cleared."

"Sir," the colonel said with a nod.

"Thank you, gentlemen—and ladies." General Ramsey exited, the other brass trailing him. But not the SEALs.

Dean slapped his shoulder. "I'll catch up with you. I need a word with Ramsey."

"Something wrong?"

"Too much."

"Hooah," Sal mumbled as the captain made his way out.

Riordan strutted toward Sal. Stuffed a hand toward him. "Guess we'll be working together again."

Sal shook the hand. "Guess so."

"Let's meet at the Boardwalk to talk."

"It's shut down," Harrier said, joining them.

Riordan's dark eyes sparked with amusement. "Perfect place for a quiet talk. Away from ears."

After a quick check of his watch, Sal nodded. "Fifteen hundred at the Boardwalk."

"Sixteen," Riordan countered. "We have things to follow up on first."

Sal nodded. That sounded a lot like they wanted a plan in place that didn't include Raptor. Which made sense since Sal planned to do the same thing.

The squids followed Riordan out, and Raptor tightened up around Sal. He had to admit, he was sick of this. All of it. Fighting some invisible ghost in the network. A ghost that seemed to have grown corporeal and spat bullets at them. But that Riordan wanted to talk away from eyes and ears gnawed at him. What did he know? Or did he have an idea of who might be behind this? Either way, Raptor couldn't afford to shirk this opportunity.

"Sir?" Harrier asked.

Sal patted his shoulder. "Shower up and grab some grub. Meet at my tent at fifteen hundred."

Tonight had altered everything—life. Getting saddled with Walker when he had to keep his mind on this mission, not on hating her, Sal felt a suffocating weight pressing on him.

He logged off his system but sagged toward his chair—movement out of the corner of his eye stopped him. Pushed him straight. He tried to hold back the flinch at the blond hair and blue eyes. She was watching him, probing in that formidable way of hers. She always found the holes in his armor. Always got under his skin.

"What?" he bit out.

"I hope we can work together. . .peaceably."

His gut churned. "You nuked any chance of that four years ago." Sal turned and left the quiet hum of the Command building.

God had seen fit to torment him. It wasn't enough for Vida to pay for his sins. Now he had to live and breathe the same air as the woman responsible for killing her.

—✺—

Boris
26 March—1335 Hours

Seriously. Do they think this will work? I mean, I'm here. They're here. But there's no point in this. I have no information to surrender. And— yes, I know they're not easily dissuaded. This dude has some serious determination lurking in his big, dark eyes.

But that, that is *nothing* compared to what this minion has going on. I mean, I swear Jason Bourne's creator takes cues from this guy. It's terrifying.

"I mean it. I don't know anything. It was all kept sterile." The pain throbbing through my fingers is horrific. I just want it to stop. I need it to stop. Can't think. The whole thing with these spy games is to figure out what your opponent wants most. And give it to them.

Not literally, of course. Because then what power do you have? None. You're at the bottom of the dung heap, with them tromping over your rotting corpse. You're dead. No, you keep that information close to your heart and your weakness closer. If they find your weakness, they find the information.

He's moving toward me again, all calm and stoic. Like some stone-coldhearted piece of work.

And he is. Trust me.

"I ain't got nothing man. Plucking out my nails"—a whimper trickles through my words. I'd like to say it's on purpose but I'm not that good—"won't produce what I don't know."

That's what I have to make them believe. Because if I give up the goods, then it's over. I'm over. And we all know, I can't let that happen.

Imagine if I can endure this. Get free—there's always hope because we all know that everyone has a price—then get back to Mr. Big Money himself and *cha-ching*! I'm in and richer than ever.

And my name is written in the stars of the cyberverse. I'll be notorious.

Mr. Big Whig enters now. "What has he told you?"

"Lies."

"No—no, they're not. It's true. I don't know anything. They didn't tell me."

The man at the utensil tray smirks. "See? He thinks we will believe him."

The man in the slick olive suit and turban stares at me with what can only be described as an icy glare. "Change his mind."

EAMON

He had better things to worry about, but the blue eyes of a certain lieutenant nagged to the point of distraction. Eamon submitted his report from the attack then headed down the hall. Burnett's death had shaken her up, but she'd warrioved on as only Brie could. He could relate. It'd been the same for him when his mother had died. She'd looked after him while his father politicked and made his billions.

He wouldn't make the same mistake. Wouldn't abandon a family to make money. Something gone in a flash.

Voices slowed him. As the senior administrator for the generals, Brie probably had a lot of work, and no doubt had to coordinate with Ramsey and Ames. Eamon checked around the corner.

Brie hunched over her desk, arms folded on paperwork she was looking at. But leaning over from behind her and pointing at one of the documents—Riordan. They were...close. Cozy. The SEAL, Eamon hated to admit, was handsome and gregarious. That latter trait was one Eamon lacked. He'd had to protect too much for most of his life to be outgoing and boisterous.

Brie laughed at something the commander said.

A strange feeling bumped Eamon's confidence out of line. Had he read her wrong? He'd thought she liked him. She let Riordan a lot closer than she'd let him. He lowered his hand, which had been poised to rap on the door. He glanced at her once more then pivoted. His boot squeaked as he stepped away, much like the pinch in his chest.

"Titanis?"

He stopped. Hesitated then stepped back. "Sorry." He glanced between them, hoping his displeasure wasn't evident on his face. "I can come back later."

Brie sat back in her chair with a smile. "No, it's okay," she said, waving him in. "Actually, I need to talk to you."

With a nod, Eamon tucked aside the bruise of jealousy and entered, hovering across from Brie at her desk.

"I'll check back with you later." After a conciliatory nod to Eamon, Riordan left the office.

Eamon watched the commander then turned his attention back to Brie.

She arched an eyebrow. "You okay?"

He lifted a shoulder. "Sure."

"You looked ticked."

Not exactly successful at burying his feelings. Though she was right, Eamon redirected. "You wanted to talk to me?"

Brie stood and closed the office door. "Yes," she said, returning to her seat. "Burnett was putting a plan in place when he died. I just heard from DIA and they have ordered me to pick up where he left off."

"If I can help. . ."

She grinned, and if she knew that smile could get anything out of him, she'd probably be the death of him. "I'm glad you said that. Because the general wanted you and me to go do some recon at Takkar Towers."

Eamon stilled. Recon with her? "Wouldn't Raptor be a better choice?"

Her grin widened. "No, because we'll be inside—civilian. We're going in as siblings who want to lease a condo in the residential tower."

"Wait," Eamon said, tripping over her words. "I'm trained for combat. Not espionage."

"Actually, you're trained for both, aren't you? I mean—SAS commandos need to know how to read and manipulate situations for their benefit, right?"

"Sure, but—"

"And you're less known to Takkar and his minions. Being Australian works for you."

"But you're not Australian."

"Right." Brie shook her head, confused. "So?"

"You said we'd go as siblings. You don't have an accent."

"I'll fake it."

Eamon sniggered. "A real Aussie against a fake one?"

With sagging shoulders and a puffed breath pushed out between pursed lips, Brie scratched the side of her head. "I was never good at faking them anyway. In high school, I was in a play and did the worst-ever rendition of a Southern accent, so I'd probably murder your language."

"Accent," he corrected.

"Have you heard how thick it is? Yours is more like its own language."

"Are you saying you don't like my accent?"

"It's sexy—I mean, fine." She ducked, crimson flooding her cheeks.

Sexy. A smirk pulled at his lips. So he *hadn't* read her wrong. But how far did her attraction to him go?

"Stop. Focus on this." She sliced her hands through the air. "So. We're. . .business partners."

"Partner is no good."

"Why?"

"Tower Two is residential. Tower One is commercial and corporate." He shrugged. "They'll want to know why we aren't leasing in One. Unless you have unlimited resources—"

"Ha. U.S. Army does not stand for Unlimited Supply Army." She sneered. "More like useless supply." Hands cradling her head as she leaned on her desk, she sighed heavily. "Fine." She straightened, as if bracing herself. "I'm your girlfriend."

His eyebrows winged up before he could stop.

Brie seemed to go rigid, her gaze locked on the documents. "The condo has three bedrooms, so we'll have our own rooms. Nothing funny."

Again, he arched an eyebrow. He might not watch a lot of movies, but he knew how flicks with arrangements like that ended. Apparently, by the crimson hue of her face and her unwillingness to look at him, so did she.

Finally she slapped her desk. "What?"

Eamon gave a slow shake of his head. This was the most twisted assignment he'd been handed. But he had to admit—he liked the idea of having time to get to know her better. However, it flustered her. He needed to redirect. "What are we looking for?"

She seemed to relax. "Burnett wanted someone he could trust on the inside trying to get information on Meng-Li Jin. Information that can't come from external recon. And with the way things have gone and Walker's information turning out to be limited, eyes inside is more important than ever. We need to know what he's doing. Plant some bugs and cameras. Monitor. See who's coming and going."

Eamon nodded.

"Do you have civvies?"

"Sorry?"

Her gaze swept his tall frame. "Normal clothes."

"I know what they are. I wondered why you'd asked."

"Put on your best duds, Titanis. We're hitting the Kandahar Ritz, aka Takkar Towers, tomorrow."

CHAPTER 5

Kandahar Airfield, Afghanistan
26 March—1400 Hours

Water dribbled across his shoulders, a long cry from the hot showers of home, but enough to scrub the Afghan sand from his skin. Sal roughed a cloth lathered with soap across his arms and abs. The bubbles sickeningly reminding him of the general's blood bubbling up between Cassie's fingers.

Sal swallowed and hung his head, closing his eyes and mind from the memory. He breathed deeply. Felt the swell of distant images flooding in, thickening the water around him. Drenching him in the blood of not only the general, but of Vida and Mario.

No!

Heaviness shoved his shoulders. Weighted his muscles. His heart.

Palming the wall of the cubicle shower, Sal pushed back against the oncoming torrent. Despite his resistance, it came. He gritted his teeth, knowing it was his punishment. His penance. His world, his mistakes, thrown in a blender. Words clashed with visages. Voices with people. Truth with guilt. Blurred. Mixed up.

"We'll finally be together."

Happiness. She'd been so excited.

Kisses. So many kisses. Passion. Losing control.

"You're such a good man. You honored my sister."

An explosion. A bang.

Sal snapped his head up, hauling in a ragged breath. Somewhere in the showers came the plodding of feet. Only then did he realize the bang had been a stall door in the unisex bathroom. Breathing hard, he shook off the memories.

46

He'd failed her. Failed him. Failed the general. Failed himself.

Balling his fists, he ground his molars against the anger. *She's dead!* Dead because of Cassie. The fury rose up like a volcanic explosion. He bit through the tears that demanded freedom. The pain that roiled like a tornado, whipping his life into a frenzy.

He banged his head against the prefab wall.

It's your fault she's dead!

So sweet. So trusting. He'd promised her. . .promised he'd take care of her.

Nobody should trust him. Candyman lost a leg because Sal hadn't protected him. General Burnett died right in front of him. Vida died because of him, because of his weakness.

He growled. Against the truth. Against the litany of condemnation. The pressure built within him. Demanding release.

Sal reached outside the curtain and tugged his Ka-Bar from its sheath. Trembling beneath the weight of his anger, he placed the blade against his lifted bicep. Soap slid down his forearm, over the scarred ridges.

"We can get married now!"

Hand fisted, muscles taut, Sal drew the blade across. *Freedom! Release!* Pain sluicing with release. He closed his eyes for a second then breathed out. Lifted the blade again and carved another. Watched the crimson line speed down his arm, chasing time. Chasing memories. Chasing pain.

He clenched his eyes tight.

Go away. Just. . .go away.

Steel glinted beneath a mixture of blood and water as it pinched his flesh with another line between good and evil. Right and wrong. Sin and redemption.

"Falcon!"

Sal blinked. Stilled. Swallowed hard as his pulse jammed.

"You in here?" Dean's voice was close.

"Yeah." Sal cleared his throat. Glanced at the Ka-Bar. At the blood on the floor, diluted by the water. Dean wouldn't understand. The guy had everything under control. Exuded authority and strength. He hadn't made stupid mistakes that cost lives. Hadn't convinced people to believe in him, trust him, then have their lives thrown under the bus of his idiocy.

Boots stomped closer. . .closer. . .

Sal swallowed harder. If Dean found out. . .if anyone found out, he'd end up with a psych eval. He could get put out.

He shook his head. Cassie would destroy yet another life. "Access to the prisoner came through. Need you over there now."

"On my way." Sal held his arm under the water. Rinsed his blade. Grabbed the keffiyeh, tore off a section, and tied it around his bicep. After drying off and dressing, he made his way to his bunk, verified he was alone as he stowed his gear, then removed the scarf and applied a line of wound sealer. Sal tensed through the stinging. He holstered his weapon and hurried to the detention facility.

"Captain Watters?" Sal asked the guard as he logged in.

"He—"

"Falcon."

Sal shot a look over his shoulder and spotted Dean at the end of the hall. He dropped the pen on the clipboard and trotted down the narrow corridor. "You talk to him yet?"

"Titanis is having a go," Dean said as they entered the fifteen-by-twenty room and folded his arms over his chest.

"Titanis?" Sal frowned. What was the Aussie doing here? Sal was second-in-command. Why had Titanis been chosen over him?

"I called him over after I found you. Thought he might have some persuasive methods—since he's not officially on the team, he might get away with things we might not."

Right. Not entirely true. But it'd be a distraction they could play with if questions arose.

Titanis hulked over the small-framed Afghan national. "Sorry, mate. We just don't believe you."

"It is true," the man snapped.

Shifting to the side, Titanis afforded Sal a view of the man. And anger spiraled up from the places he'd tucked it not ten minutes ago. It didn't look like anyone had touched the guy. Defiance oozed from the man's posture and words. Why wasn't blood dribbling from his lips and nose yet?

The thought gave Sal a start. *Bloodthirsty. . .*

"You had an assault rifle," Titanis went on. "You ran from my team. You shot at us."

The Afghan's lip curled. "You cannot prove it."

Titanis looked at Dean, who gave an almost-imperceptible lift of his chin.

Good. They'd step it up a little.

"Captain?"

Sal shifted as a man entered the cell and met Dean with a discerning gaze. He wasn't in uniform. Hair long around the ears and neck. Brawny. Tactical pants and shirt. All the marks of a Special Forces operator—and yet Sal didn't recognize him. SEAL? MARSOC?

"Can I help you?" Dean asked.

"If you'll call off your dingo"—he nodded toward Titanis—"I have work to do."

Sal exchanged a look with Dean.

Shoulders squared, Dean didn't move or answer for a few seconds. "And you are?"

"Running behind." The man had a bag in hand. It didn't look like anything official. More like something out of a thriller novel—leather satchel sagging heavily. Something inside it clinked and clanked.

"We have authorized access to this prisoner—he shot at my men. I'm not walking out of here."

"Then you can answer to Ramsey for holding up information demanded by DIA and POTUS."

POTUS? Since when? The president wanted to look good, not look at what was happening in the war theater.

Brawny gave a cheeky grin and swung his head toward the door. "If you'll excuse me. I believe you have a phone call with Ramsey."

Phone call my hairy backside. Sal shook his head. "You must think we're stupid. We walk out of here and you beat the crap out of him or kill him. Then our names are on the logs and we take the heat for this."

"Forget the heat," Dean said. "He's our prisoner. I need time with him."

Brawny considered Dean. "Sorry, Captain. Playtime's over." He looked to the door then back to Dean then Sal. "Leave. Now."

"Who gave you your orders?" Sal demanded.

"Ramsey."

Sal started for the guy, not believing him. Not buying this story. But Dean slapped a hand on his chest. Sal shot Dean a glare.

"We'll do it the right way." Dean and Titanis headed down the hall together.

Sal glowered at the Painful Query Master. Saw the gleam in the man's eyes. Knew that if he walked out of here, there was little chance they'd come back to a live prisoner. "I'm not leaving." Challenge set, Sal held his ground.

Though the man betrayed nothing in his mannerisms—no flaring nostrils, no balled fists, no clenched jaw—there was something, a glint, a flicker in his eyes, that dumped cold dread down Sal's spine. The man's gaze struck the empty hall then bounced back to Sal. "Your captain left. I'm sure you'll want to verify with Ramsey."

Right. Verifying with Ramsey meant Sal left the cell.

Get help. Check the log. Dean would check with Ramsey. Though it was the last thing he wanted to do, Sal turned and walked out.

—⁂—

Kandahar Airfield, Afghanistan
26 March—1445 Hours

Dean stalked to the Command building. They were beaten at every corner. Pushed back at each junction. Two steps closer to the truth. Five steps farther. It was time to stop playing the game with rules in place. Time to break out and end this.

He yanked open the door and stormed in. His conscience pinged, knowing that on a day prior to this one, he would've been storming to Burnett's office. But the general was gone. A great loss haunted the halls of Command now.

Behind him he heard the steady thumps of Sal's and Titanis's boots. The rhythm gave him courage. He rounded the corner and aimed for Ramsey's office.

Lieutenant Hastings emerged from the office, closing it behind her, as Dean shoved through the glass door. "Captain." Eyes wide, she gaped. "Can I help you?" Her gaze flicked to the door as Falcon and Titanis entered.

"I need a word with General Ramsey."

"He asked not to be disturbed."

"How long?" Dean asked, his frustration peaking.

Hastings once again glanced at Titanis. "I'm not sure. He said he had calls to make."

"Lieutenant, we need him. Someone just locked us out of talking with the prisoner."

"I—" She blinked. "What? Are you sure?" She lifted a paper from her desk. "I have your authorization to question him right here."

"Dean!" Sal jogged down the hall, his face twisted. "The guard's gone."

"What guard?"

"The gatekeeper for detention."

Dean drew back.

"We need to go in there," Sal said, pointing to the general's office. "Something's not right."

"Agreed." Dean nodded to the door. "Let him know we need to talk—now."

The lieutenant shrugged reluctantly. "I—"

Sal strode around her and went for the door. "We're short on time and answers." He rapped on the MDF barrier.

Dean stepped forward. "Falcon—"

But Falcon was already entering the office, interrupting a steady hum of phone conversation. "General, we—"

"Get out of my office!"

Dean reached for Sal, ready to haul him out of there. He'd gotten used to wrangling Hawk, but Sal?

General Ramsey slid a manila folder over a stack of papers, his expression a tangle of anger and frustration. "Captain—"

Might as well grab the bull by the horns. "Sir, with all due respect," Dean said, finding himself strangely confident. "You gave us exclusive access to the prisoner and we were—"

"I swear if you do not get out—"

"I want our access restored to the prisoner." Dean wouldn't waver now.

Red-faced and coming to his feet, Ramsey shouted, "I never revoked it!"

Dean stilled.

"So what are you doing in my office? Get in there and interrogate the crap out of that prisoner. Find out who sent him to kill Lance." His anger pushed the boundaries of rage. "So help me if you break in here again, I will have charges brought against you."

Dean frowned, skidded a confused look to Sal, who returned the expression. "Sir, we were shut out of the prison. Told to leave. He mentioned you."

"Me? I didn't have anything to do with this." Ramsey scowled as he plopped into his chair, hand resting on the folder. "Who was it?"

Titanis edged in, smoothing a hand over his beard. "Some mate who looked a lot like a spook."

"He said he had to get answers, told us to leave. That you ordered him in there."

"He had a leather satchel," Sal added. "I swear the guy had bloodlust in his eyes. He was going to get answers from that prisoner no matter what means—conventional or unconventional."

Ramsey's face drained of color. He faltered coming to his feet. He rushed around the corner of his desk. "Hastings, get the MPs to the detention facility!" He ran down the hall.

"Not good," Sal muttered.

Dean pivoted and ran after the general, busting through the front door, and beat a hard path to the detention area. He caught up with the general as he shoved into the building.

The desk remained unattended. "Specialist!" the general shouted but no one answered.

Dean stalked around the counter and pushed into the small office. The door thumped against a leg. "He's down!" He went to a knee. "He's alive but unconscious."

"The prisoner," Sal hissed.

Boots thudded down the hall, hauling Dean back out of the room. He sprinted toward the end of the hall. Watched the other three enter the last cell.

General Ramsey cursed. Loud. Several times.

The prisoner, hands cuffed behind his back, lay cockeyed in the chair. Blood trailed down his neck and shirt from a bullet wound in the head.

Titanis crouched beside him, fingers on his neck. He slowly shook his head. "Dead."

Pinching the bridge of his nose, Dean fought the wave of despair.

"Some work." Sal stood beside Dean. "He knew what he was doing." He pointed to the man's neck where a red dot glared at them. "Probably gave him some drug to make him spill his guts."

"Then he *does* spill the man's guts," Titanis said.

"I want to know who did this!" Ramsey shouted, turning as MPs jogged toward them. "Check the surveillance. Find out who this assassin was!"

"We saw him," Dean mumbled, thinking through the scenario. "He walked in as brazen as day and told us to leave."

Sal folded his arms. "Which means he's not worried about being caught."

"Probably drastically changed his appearance for our benefit." Titanis leaned against a table, his hands propped against the steel. "Makes me wonder. . ."

Dean nodded.

Sal crouched before the dead prisoner. "Our Afghan friend here knew something."

"Something so dangerous they couldn't risk us finding out." Dean straightened.

"You know what that means?" Sal had death in his eyes. Fierce determination mixed with a lethal concoction of thirst for vengeance. "We finish this—at all costs."

—⚬—

Kabul, Afghanistan
26 March—1545 Hours

"What are you doing with my HunkySoldierBoy?"

At the demanding question by his spunky stepdaughter, Sajjan slumped back in his leather chair. Timbrel VanAllen had every bit the beauty and wit of her mother, but with an added pound of combat-hardened attitude. He could only thank God that Nina didn't have that or he wouldn't have given her the time of day, let alone taken her as his bride. "You would be speaking of Tony."

"I'm pretty sure that's the only HunkySoldierBoy in existence."

He could not help but smile as she shrugged. "I am doing nothing with Tony." He held his hand toward the empty office.

"You can try your spy games on me, but I'm not cool with this if you're putting his life in danger." She had never been afraid of anything or anyone.

"If you are concerned for that, then I think you married the wrong man. Tony thrives on action, does he not?"

"Yes, but he's smart with it. . .normally."

"Your words wound me." Truly they did. Though his stepdaughter accepted his marriage to her mom, and though she gave voice to her acceptance of him, there lurked in her a hesitation. "You would suggest that he's not smart with me."

She narrowed her eyes and batted long brown hair from her shoulders. "Tony respects you. Admires you—"

"And you do not?"

Timbrel snapped her mouth shut. Considered him. "I wouldn't have let my mom marry you if I didn't. But I also know the games you play, the alliances you toy with. In fact, I'm not really sure any of us know where your allegiance rests."

Sajjan came out of his chair and eased around his desk to her side. "I am grateful for your respect and admiration, and I would ask that you let that guide you."

"I am. That's why I'm here." Undaunted. So like Nina.

"Daughter," he said softly, noting how the edges of her hard shell seemed to wilt beneath that word. "My allegiance is to my family first and my country second."

"And God?"

He lifted his chin, smiling down at her. "Above all others."

"So. Afghanistan before America." Defiance glinted in her

expression. "You realize Tony is American, I am American. So—"

He touched a finger to her lips.

She slapped it away, scowling.

"Trust me, Timbrel. But do not demand of me what you know I will not give, and at the same time, believe me when I say I would never intentionally put those in my family in harm's way."

She gave a curt nod. "Fine." Backed up a step. "I'll sic Beo on you if Tony gets hurt."

As if responding, the retired working dog growled from the shadows of a corner, and then the bullmastiff's nails clicked on the highly polished floor as he trotted out ahead of the firebrand. The door closed.

A low rumble of laughter came from the side office.

Sajjan turned toward the door. "You heard that?"

Tony VanAllen walked in, his chest out a little more than normal. His chin a measure higher. "I'd say I have nothing to fear with her watching my back."

"And you were worried about your back?"

"Not in the least," Tony said, his expression sparked with conviction.

He had chosen the former Special Forces soldier for good reason and after much deliberation. With all the years Sajjan spent working the tricky waters of politics in this volatile area, he could not be too careful. "What have you said to her of what we're doing?"

"Nothing. Timbrel just knows I'm working. And after what happened"—he patted his leg, indicating the prosthesis—"she's a little protective."

"A little?" Smiling, Sajjan returned to his desk. Scanned the recent encrypted reports. Heaviness weighted his optimism about turning this region around financially and politically. "I think we should plan for you to return to Raptor team as a contractor."

"Contractor—might as well send me in as the enemy." Tony rubbed the scruffiness around his jaw. "You think it's necessary, I'll go. But—can you get it set up?"

Sajjan gave him a look.

"Forget I asked—but seriously? Are you asking me to spy on my own brothers?"

CHAPTER 6

Kandahar Airfield, Afghanistan
26 March—1545 Hours

A storm blew into the Command building, a cluster of soldiers stalking past her cubicle. General Ramsey, Captain Watters, Titanis, and yes—Sal, trouped toward the rear of the building.

Cassie came to her feet.

Foreboding draped their countenances like a thick, heavy blanket. They were ticked. Determined. So much that they didn't even notice or acknowledge her. She moved to the edge of the cubicles, watching. Something was wrong. Very wrong.

Her phone buzzed. Not her work phone. But the other phone. Cassie scurried back to her desk, tugged open the drawer, drew out the black nondescript phone, and glanced at the ID. Gearney—her handler.

She coded in. Pressed the phone to her ear. "This is Lieutenant Walker with DIA." The words had to be spoken exactly in that order. She glanced around the room, verifying there wasn't anyone in proximity, which would determine what she said next. "How can I help you?"

"You're alone?"

"Yes." Cassie's gaze locked onto the crowd gathering around Ramsey's office door and the hum of conversation.

"We need you in Kabul. An asset will give you the packet."

Kabul? Cassie frowned and turned away from Ramsey's office. "Sir, something is happening here. I think—"

"Tomorrow, Walker. No questions. Just do it."

The phone went dead. Frustration coiled in Cassie's stomach and tightened. Tomorrow? With what was happening here? Were they insane? But she was a low-level analyst. A lackey. Barely had clearance for what they'd tasked her with.

She rolled her shoulders and stretched her jaw. Fine. She wouldn't be at the bottom of the stack forever. She'd prove herself. She'd gotten this far. Faster than most operatives.

But leaving the base when things were heating up so much, when she felt she could be of help, didn't make sense. She could guide the soldiers toward answers that would stop this insanity. She reached for the thin tendril of hope that she could redeem herself. Maybe then Sal would forgive her.

The thought squeezed the air from her lungs. His hatred was so palpable. Had, for so long, mirrored her own hatred of herself. The hatred that pushed her to contemplate suicide.

But then God threw her a lifesaver.

Cassie's landline rang. She lifted the handset. "Lieutenant Walker."

"So, you are in Afghanistan."

Heart thumping at the feminine Chinese voice filtering through her phone, Cassie leaned forward. "Kiew?" Disbelief colored her voice and her mind!

"So you remember." Her words held a smile in them.

"Of course I do," Cassie said through a laughing breath. "How could I forgot my China sister?"

"Or me my America sister."

Her laugh mingled with her friend's as the worries of the day seemed to flit away amid a rush of affection and endearment. "How. . . ?"

"I am here, too."

Cassie blinked again. "Here?" She looked around the somewhat-quiet area. Of course her friend didn't mean the base—she couldn't. "You mean Afghanistan?"

"Yes. On business."

"How crazy—how on earth did you find me here?"

"Look, I'm in between meetings and time is short. I just wanted to connect. When I heard you were here, I couldn't resist calling."

"Where are you?"

"Kabul."

"Kabul? But that's only a few hours away!"

Kiew laughed. "Crazy, isn't it? That we're both here—in another country yet closer than we've been since the year you were an exchange student. It's been too long since we got to see each other. E-mail and phone calls are nice but not the same."

"No kidding." Cassie gasped, remembering her earlier call. "Hey, I just remembered they're sending me that way for a meeting with a contractor. Do you think you could get away for lunch or something?" She couldn't shake the joy but something else was there. The wildness of it all.

"Oh, I'm not sure. My schedule is very tight."

Disappointment tugged at Cassie. "I bet. You've always been hard to get ahold of."

"Yes," Kiew mumbled, her tone shifting dramatically.

"I'm sorry. I wasn't blaming you."

"No, no, I understand."

"I'm just glad you called. You made my day. It's been pretty crazy and depressing here."

"Same here. Look," Kiew said firmly. "I will meet you for lunch."

Cassie brightened. "Really? Are you sure?"

"I will make time. Two o'clock?"

"Oh, I'll need to confirm the time—I'm not sure of my schedule yet." Cassie reached for a pen and paper. "What number can I reach you at?"

"I'm at a pay phone. I'll have to call you back."

"Oh. Okay." Strange, but that's the way things had always been with Kiew. She shrugged aside the surprise and disappointment. "I can confirm by tomorrow morning. Call my cell." After providing her number, Cassie hung up, smiling. Breathing a little deeper, a little more contentedly.

"...plan with Riordan for contingencies."

Cassie looked up as Sal's voice drew closer.

He stalked down the hall with Captain Watters, both of their faces taut with tension.

"Captain?"

Watters stopped and turned as Lieutenant Hastings hurried toward him with a handful of papers.

Cassie seized the opportunity. She went to Sal and touched his arm.

He jerked, his handsome face contorted not in pain. But anger. "What?"

"What happened? Everyone's—"

"Someone killed the prisoner." His brown eyes sparked with disgust. "Camera feed wasn't working while the man was in the facility murdering our only possibility of finding out who was behind the attack."

"The feed didn't work?"

"Coincidentally so." Sal wouldn't look at her.

She remembered the days when he couldn't *stop* looking at her. When those brown eyes teemed with admiration and attraction. Not repulsion or disgust.

The phone in Cassie's hand buzzed. She lifted her phone. "Excuse me." She stepped away and coded in, receiving the text: OUTSIDE, TWO MINUTES.

Her pulse sped. Slipping out and not drawing attention while Sal was within sight. . . She lifted her purse from the drawer and started for the side entrance. With a quick glance to verify Sal and his captain were enthralled in conversation with Hastings, Cassie pushed into the night. Almost seven o'clock. The thin veil of night had just draped across the base, but the stalwart lights served as sentries to ward off the darkness, the terrorists.

—m—

Though he might resent her and hold Vida's death against her, Sal knew Cassie Walker better than most people knew their best friends. And she had walked out of the Command building with concern and haste. What had that been about?

He collided with someone and turned. Froze. "Candyman?"

The man's grin was buried beneath a burly sandy-blond beard. "Glad to see you haven't forgotten me."

"What are you doing here?" Dean asked.

"Hastings called me in. Contracting me to work with Raptor because they're pulling Titanis for another gig."

Dean scowled. "When were they going to tell me about this?"

"Probably about now," Candyman said. "Sorry if I popped the lid early."

With a slap on the man's shoulder, Dean smiled. "No worries. Glad to have you onboard again. We're about to head out. You ready?"

The question was probably more about the prosthesis than about the man's preparedness. "Titanium-man reporting for duty, sir." Unflappable as always.

"Sal, talk to Riordan and let me know what he says." Dean broke away from Hastings. "I need to work with Ramsey and General Ames to get things sorted. We need some credible intel to work." He nodded to Candyman. "I'll find you after the meeting."

"Agreed." Sal jammed his hands in his pant pockets and headed out of the building with Candyman. "I knew that guy was bad meat. Never should've left that cell."

"What happened?"

"Spook got in and killed a witness." He left and the guy died. "We all knew something was wrong." Their boots crushed pebbles as they trudged across the gravel path from the Command building.

Sal hunched his shoulders. They desperately needed the tide to swing in their favor. "Too much going wrong," he mumbled, his periphery catching something.

To the left, two people stood between the USO building and a portable maintenance building. No. Sal slowed. Not just two people. A male and a female. About to divert his gaze, his mind registered the hair of the female. Her build and shape.

Cassie.

Something in his chest backfired like an RPG had hit center mass. The man touched the side of her face. Cassie ducked then glanced over her shoulder. Looked right at Sal.

Anger exploded through him.

She widened her eyes.

Whistling, Candyman nudged Sal. "D'you see that?"

"How could I not?" Sal churned the memory through his mind. So, Cassie hadn't changed. Was this guy her next victim?

"Crazy. I heard she was into you. Thought she had more class than that."

"Yeah, well, now you know." But as Sal made his way across the base to the Boardwalk to meet up with Riordan and the rest of Raptor, something tugged at his mind. Nagged at him.

"Hey." Eagle hustled up to him. "Something's up—oh! Candyman." The two shook hands and patted shoulders.

"Candyman's contracting," Sal said. "And we knew something was up."

Eagle was soon joined by Harrier and Hawk. "No, I mean with the SEALs." He bobbed his head toward the Boardwalk.

In the middle of an open area, Riordan stood alone beneath a lone lamp. Like a well-lit target. The gruesome reminder of Burnett's death made Sal hesitate to join the party. In a wide perimeter, Riordan's team stood around him.

"What's that about?"

"Dunno," Hawk said. "Knight's patrolling with Ddrake but none of them are talking."

Interesting. Obviously Riordan wanted to talk alone. "Okay, spread out." Sal started toward the SEAL commander.

"A little late, Falcon?" Riordan smirked. "Heard there was some excitement over at detainment."

"Someone killed the shooter we captured the other night." Sal glanced around the area, feeling exposed. Vulnerable.

"We needed to talk."

"Kinda figured that out," Sal said, spotting Knight and MWD Ddrake near some of the portable buildings that once held restaurants.

"Any thoughts on who killed your prisoner?"

Sal sighed. "A spook. Came in with too much information and got the job done before we could figure it out."

"Surveillance footage?"

"Down."

"Convenient."

"Agreed." Sal let out another long sigh. Then met Riordan's gaze. "So, we're here. You're here." He eyeballed the teams standing around, unsettled. "This is a lot of cloak-and-dagger stuff. What's going on?"

Head bowed, the late-twenties SEAL looked up through a terse brow as he nodded. His dark hair hung in straggly curls around a bearded face. Against his sun-darkened brow a white scar told of at least one battle the SEAL had seen. He looked like a homeless man, but those dark eyes betrayed him. Told Sal the man missed nothing. He took everything in like a supercomputer, processing and analyzing. Though he hated squids out of Green Beret duty, Sal had a keen respect for this one. Schmidt, with his white-blond hair and cocky attitude, was another fish altogether.

"I think you know things are a bit whacked."

"That's an understatement."

"I'm not entirely sure which of our COs we can trust."

Sal drew his gaze back to the commander, surprised at the comment. But it was one that had become painfully obvious in the last month as Osiris made impossible headway in his attack against the U.S. military.

"They've already attacked CECOM, and it'll be days, if not weeks, before we figure out what damage was done."

"I can just about guarantee the intel we gathered from that Tera Pass laptop is destroyed."

"It was a strategic, well-planned hit." Riordan scratched the side of his beard. "They got in when they shouldn't have."

"Then someone kills the only lead we have on the shooter and those responsible for the attack."

Riordan nodded. "I think you're starting to see where I'm coming from."

"I think I've been there for a while, just unwilling to accept what it meant." Accusing superiors of colluding with the enemy wasn't a charge made lightly.

"It's too well coordinated. Funny that your prisoner dies while the cameras are down."

"Hysterical," Sal said. "About as hysterical as watching my favorite general bleed out."

Riordan's expression hardened. "So, we know the same thing—this goes up the chain."

Balling his fists was all Sal could do with what he felt, a tangle of emotions he couldn't seem to sort through. "We need proof. Work it hard. Keep reports to Command vague. Enough to keep them off our butts about reporting in, but not enough for whoever is behind this to head us off."

"Or kill another friendly." Riordan tossed his chin, indicating behind Sal. "What about your team?"

"What about them?"

"How far do you trust them?"

Sal didn't like the question and threw it back at the SEAL. "More than I trust you."

Riordan smirked. "Okay, let's keep tabs. I'll give you what I know and keep you informed. I'd like you to do the same."

Sal nodded—and as he did, a glint somewhere caught his attention. He snapped his gaze to the right. To a shadowy spot beyond the USO building.

Riordan shifted. "What?"

He couldn't say why or what propelled him, but Sal took off running. He wasn't going to lose anyone to another sniper. Wasn't going to let anyone take out another of his team because he wasn't responsive enough.

Even as he bolted, he heard shouts and the teams rallying behind him—at the same time, he saw a shadow drop from the roof of the chow hall. A light beam struck the man.

Sal thanked God He'd made him fast. He sprinted. "It's the spook!"

EAMON

Takkar Towers, Kabul, Afghanistan

I can't believe you told him I'm your wife!"

Eamon locked the door, retrieved the weapon from his pack that he'd slung over his shoulder. He walked the condo, anticipating trouble, but not wanting to stress Brie any more than she already was. "It's Afghanistan. A man and a woman staying in the same condo would not only draw attention, but ire and possible outrage. Being American and here is trouble enough."

Fifteen hundred square feet with clean lines and Spartan furniture. No trouble crossing a room and avoiding obstacles. Easy to defend with only a short hall to negotiate. Bedrooms sat off the main living area and full-sized kitchen. A bathroom sat between the two smaller bedrooms and the master opposite. Yet it felt cramped. Maybe because every time he turned around, she was there. Right there.

He tossed his pack on the small bed of the first bedroom. "You can take the master." She'd have her own bathroom and privacy that way.

"Don't you think if someone comes in they'll figure out we don't sleep in the same bed?"

"No. I'll store my duds in the dresser in the master room. Bed will be made with hospital corners and no creases."

She crossed her arms. "You can do that?"

"Every day."

Amusement rippled through her tawny features, but she said nothing as she slipped into the bathroom. After suitcases were delivered, they settled in. First order of business—Eamon set up miniature cameras and microphones throughout the flat, tested each one, then set them to record through his laptop. As dusk fell in on the space and he flicked on the kitchen light, Brie worked alongside with her system, setting them to receive the same data and keeping in contact with her superiors.

They had a good system that flowed naturally. Eamon made contact with his command sergeant major, updating on his progress and purpose, now that they'd relocated the mission to the tower itself. For now, he left out that he was alone with the beautiful lieutenant.

"I hope you don't expect me to cook." Brie stood on the vinyl floor, arms crossed. She had these brightly colored pajama bottoms and a tank top on, her brown hair down. Comfortable and less military.

"Why? Are you a disaster in the kitchen?"

"My forte is soup."

Eamon shrugged and nodded.

"From a can."

He chuckled. "Good if we're going to survive the zombie apocalypse."

"You're mocking me."

"I am." He laughed. "But no worries. I'm actually a decent cook."

"You?" Brie came to the table and folded herself back into the chair, propping her leg on the edge of the vinyl cushion. "Seriously?"

Eamon worked to set up the temporary network. "I lived on my own and hated fast food, so I learned." He lifted a shoulder casually. "And in one of my phases of rebellion—"

"*One?* You had more than one?"

He gave her a glare. "I went to culinary school just to anger my father."

"Seriously? You know how to cook? Besides putting shrimp on the barbie?"

"My oath, I do." He smiled at her, amused that she found that interesting. "And apparently, I cook better than you."

Brie sat back with her hands up in surrender. "I gladly accept defeat." She waved him to the kitchen. "I want dinner in an hour."

He laughed as the system streamed data. "We need ingredients to do that."

"Is *that* how that works?" She sounded saucy as she hunched around her laptop.

"You seem a bit chuffed. Think you won one over on me?"

"I don't have to make dinner, do I?" Her eyes twinkled in triumph as she adjusted her computer in front of her. "No slaving housewife for this girl."

No. . .*housewife*. Was she saying she didn't ever want to get married? A strong, independent woman in the American Army. An officer. What family did she have? Was that what shaped her feelings about not being a housewife? It'd make sense the attractive lieutenant wanted a career more than she wanted a family.

He slapped his laptop closed, a little harder than he meant to. The thought of her not wanting to get married irked him. Which was stupid. He hadn't even invited her out yet. Marriage was on the other side of a long road, laden with minefield-quality traps—family, religious views, politics, history, money. . .

"You okay?"

"Sure." He looked at her. "Cameras are up and working."

"You went quiet," Brie said softly. "Did I upset you or something?"

"Takes a lot more than the fact you can't cook to offend me." He pushed from the table and stalked to the fridge. Opened it and saw shelves and the lone light glaring back. "Probably should hit a store or market before it gets dark."

"Let me grab a jacket, and I'll come with you."

Eamon donned his own coat, not because it was cold but because he wanted to conceal his weapon, and waited for her. "You're paying, right?" By "you" he meant the Americans. Since they were footing the bill for this condo-recon, that meant they paid for food, too.

Brie sauntered from the bedroom. "Don't you know the guy is supposed to pay for the date?"

"We're married, remember. Your money is mine. And my money is mine."

Brie struck his arm. "Hey."

He opened the door. Though they kept up a light banter as they headed out of the towers, it'd taken them three mikes fifty to make it to the open plaza that anchored the two high-rises. They hung a right out of Tower Two and climbed back into their car. No sense in walking and exposing themselves to more threats. A few blocks down, they found a small market. Eamon spotted a street-side vendor with cherries. He parked and climbed out.

Brie made her way around the different stands, eyeing the vegetables.

Eamon made his way to the vendor and bought a pound of cherries. From another, he bought yellow onions. Across the street, he found a butcher shop and managed to procure a pound of chopped lamb.

"Do we even have utensils?" Brie asked with a laugh.

"Probably not," Eamon said after paying. "We need a store to get some things."

They started toward a shop he'd seen a block away. Though Brie seemed very relaxed, he couldn't let down his guard. They might have a low-key mission, but danger was always present. And her life was in his hands.

Brie darted to a stand. "Pomegranates!" She lifted one and held it to her nose and inhaled deeply.

Glancing around, Eamon couldn't help but notice the way the locals were watching. Without trying to be obvious. It made his nerves buzz. He closed the gap between them.

"Here. Smell." Brie held it up.

Eamon craned his neck away. "Can't stand those things."

"What?" Brie's eyes went wide. "No." She nudged it closer. "Smell that! How can you not like pomegranates?"

Because my mate was killed in a pomegranate grove.

Unrelenting, Brie reached toward him. She tripped over his feet. Fell against him. Eamon wrapped an arm around her to make sure she didn't fall. "I'm buying pomegranates. I'll make you something."

His mind buzzed again—but not because of the locals watching. Because Brie was still in his arms. She straightened but didn't step out of his hold. She stayed. Against him. Warm. Curvaceous. Lighthearted.

He let his arm slide down around her waist. "You're not the full quid if you think I'm letting you in my kitchen."

She gasped in mock shock and looked up at him, exposing flushed cheeks. Hesitating and unmoving, she searched his face. But then looked away quickly—as if embarrassed—and paid for the fruit. Still, she stayed way closer than was appropriate. Triumph glistened in her eyes as she presented her purchase. "Who says it's your kitchen? And why can't I be in it?"

"You'll burn it down."

CHAPTER 7

Sal sprinted across the base, aiming for the alley he'd seen the spook vanish down. Son of a gun if he wasn't again chasing a target across the base. This was getting old. Determination shoved him forward.

"Stop him," Hawk shouted from behind.

No kidding, Sherlock.

"Command, this. . .is. . .Riordan, we have. . .spy. . ."

Sal barreled into the night-darkened shadows. Saw the spook ahead, aiming for the heavily trafficked HQ and USO buildings. If the guy made it into HQ, they'd never find him.

Throwing himself forward, Sal rounded a corner.

Rammed straight into someone.

A woman screamed.

Pain jarred through Sal's head as cement rushed up at him. He landed with a thud.

A gargled cry came beneath him.

He heard the unmistakable crack of skull on cement. The person he'd collided with had hit their head. Sal rolled to the side, disoriented.

Raptor team and the SEALs caught up. Glanced at him.

Pointing toward the alley, he said, "Go! Go!"

On a knee, he glanced at the woman. And froze.

Peeling herself off the sidewalk as she wiped at a dark stain on her blouse, Cassie groaned. Blood trickled down her temple. She reached for her head with another low moan. A foam cup rolled across the path.

"What were you doing?"

"*Me?* You were the one who—" Cassie tensed, hunching her shoulders as she grabbed her head. She swayed.

Guilt chugging through his veins, Sal caught her shoulders. "We had a lead on the spook." Why had she been in his path? Why her? Why couldn't it have been anyone else?

Tentative eyes came to his. "What? And now it's my fault that you didn't catch them. Right?" She blinked, wincing beneath a jab of pain it seemed.

Sal felt the anger rising. "You did knock me off the pursuit."

"Right. And I did that because I have nothing better to do than make your life miserable." She bent and snatched the foam cup from the ground. When she stood and took a step, her legs buckled.

Sal caught her again.

"Quite a knot," Harrier's voice boomed through the conversation as he returned. "Let me take a look."

"Did you get him?"

Shaking his head, Harrier edged in, used his finger and thumb to open Cassie's eyes wider. Asked her to track as he moved a finger back and forth in front of her. "Think you might have a concussion."

"A concussion?" Sal objected. "We just ran into each other."

"Her head hit the sidewalk." At Sal's skeptical look, Harrier shrugged. "Just telling you what I saw coming up the path."

"I'm fine." Cassie pushed Harrier's hands away.

"You should get that looked at," Harrier said.

"I said I'm fine." She pursed her lips and turned her gaze deliberately to Sal. "Sorry I messed up your high-speed chase. I didn't know getting coffee could be so dangerous." Though she smiled, her face had gone a shade paler with a tinge of gray.

"I'll walk you back," Sal heard himself saying.

Cassie stilled at the same time he did, apparently just as surprised as he was that the words had come from him. He saw in the quick moment a spurt of hope. Then it crashed. "No." She swallowed, touching the knot on her head. "I'm. . .I'll be fine."

She walked down the path, her gait a bit awkward.

"She shouldn't be alone, sir," Harrier mumbled. "She should be monitored to make sure she doesn't pass out or slip into a coma."

Sal wanted to curse. Wanted to rail and loudly object that Cassie wasn't hurt that bad. But the tug on his conscience was too great. "Let me know how she does."

"Excuse me for saying so, sir, but I've seen enough to know it should be you."

Sal snapped toward Harrier, but the medic was already moving in the opposite direction. "Son of a fried biscuit. . ." Sal started in Cassie's direction. He walked a little faster, his gut twisting as images of her collapsing and being rushed to the hospital clogged his mind.

But as he rounded the corner, he stopped short. The path lay empty. The parking lot, if you could call it that, was barren of cars. He scanned the buildings. Where had she gone?

He turned a circle. The Command building. Was she in there?

He remembered she'd spilled coffee. Maybe she was heading back there. He walked a little faster, stepped inside the building and checked her desk. Empty. A common theme.

Maybe her head had started hurting more. Maybe she went to rest.

Bad idea. If she was suddenly tired—surely Cassie knew not to lie down. A spurt of panic darted through his chest. He jogged toward her tent and stepped inside. It took a second for his eyes to adjust.

A flash of white yanked his gaze to the far right.

In that instant, he realized what his eyes had seen. He flung himself around with a curse. She was changing her shirt. He swallowed hard, seeing the curve of her back. Remembering the softness of her skin. . .

He pushed away from her and the memories.

"Sal."

Go. Don't stay.

But he couldn't move. Anchored by memories of what they'd had. What they'd shared.

Cassie was there, in front of him, tugging her hair out from under the collar of a clean shirt. The knot had already shaded to an angry red. Fingers reached to brush the blond strands from the drying blood.

Only when her lips parted did Sal realize it was his hand reaching for her face. He clenched his fingers into a fist. Froze. "Sorry." His voice was hoarse. Dry. *What are you doing?*

"Sorry," he repeated. "I wanted to make sure. . ." He hated himself for being weak. For standing here caring when Vida was six feet underground. "If you feel sleepy, go to the hospital." His words came out gruffer than he'd intended. But they had resolution. And he had no remorse for that. He took a step away.

"Sal, when will you stop hating me?"

"When Vida comes back to life."

"But even you said you didn't really love her."

The words were a blow to the back of his head. To his conscience. "But I committed to her. Promised her." He nailed her with a look that shot hot daggers. "And you sent her to her death."

"I made a mistake."

He snorted. "Is that what you call it? She's *dead*!"

"Yes, it's something I will live with for the rest of my life," she said, her voice eerily quiet. "I messed up because I was so crazy in love with you—"

"Don't put this on me!" Fury leapt through his chest. He backed away from her.

Cassie hung her head. Shook it. "I'm not, Sal." Her soft eyes came to his. "I'd do anything to undo what happened, what came out of my actions. But I can't. And I've made peace with God over it."

"God." Sal snorted again. "Never thought you were religious."

She tilted her head, blond hair slipping over her face. "I wasn't—and I'm not still. But in a very dark time in my life, He was there for me."

"I wouldn't know about that. He's never been there for me."

"Maybe you shut Him out, just like you do with everyone else you get mad at."

"This is stupid," Sal spat out. "I just wanted to make sure you were alive."

Her smile was soft. "Thank you. I am."

She was like a tidal pool, sucking in everything around it. He wasn't going down, not this time. Sal stalked out of the tent.

RONIE KENDIG

Kabul, Afghanistan
27 March—1320 Hours

Pain throbbed across her temple and down the back of her neck despite the three ibuprofen she'd taken climbing out of the car. Cassie crossed the open street in front of the thirteen-story building, the tallest in Kabul. A giant among the crumbling plaster sentries of the wounded city.

She stepped into the lobby of Takkar One, the larger of the two towers owned by Takkar Corp., breathing in a long, deep breath of chemically cooled air. A treat in this part of the world. The upper levels overhung the lobby, suspended surreally. Incredible architecture! Smiling, she made her way to Nina's, the first-floor restaurant where she'd agreed to meet Kiew. Wearing her uniform would be a screaming homing beacon for those wanting to harm Americans, so it was decided she'd wear slacks and a blouse.

Brushing her hair forward, she accidentally grazed the knot Sal had given her—a concussion with it. She'd had one before and knew the markers. But she hadn't wanted the fuss. Didn't want to incite Sal. A dart of pain responded to her touch.

"May I help you?" an attendant at a podium asked. Dressed in a smart little navy suit with a silk scarf draped around her face, the attendant smiled.

"I have a reservation with—"

"Miss Tang?"

Cassie started. "Yes."

"She's waiting for you."

"Oh." A weird feeling slithered through Cassie, but she shoved aside her misgivings. Today would be a fun day. A time of remembering and laughing. Long ago, they decided she and Kiew were twins separated at birth.

"This way," the woman said, as she sauntered around the podium and started for a secluded section of the restaurant.

Being a trained operative, Cassie did the perfunctory assessment of the setting. There were two visible exits—one at the front and one at the very back. Another entrance probably led to the kitchen or bathrooms and might provide another means of escape.

Suits littered the more secluded area, their condescension and arrogance as thick as steel-cut oatmeal. Doubt and discomfort slithered down her spine as she weaved through the white-draped tables with their amber glowing candles. A spiced scent rose on a tendril of smoke from each.

At the back, a cluster of well-placed ficus provided a natural barrier. Through the leaves, she caught sight of a brightly colored silk blouse. Kiew. Had to be.

"Miss Tang, your guest."

Cassie rounded the last ficus, excitement thrumming through her in anticipation of seeing her friend for the first time in seven years. She threw her arms out when she saw the round, beautiful face. "Kiew!"

But the woman before her sat stiff and unmoving. "Cassandra. So good to see you again."

Though she already laced an arm around Kiew's neck for a hug, Cassie knew she'd made a mistake. Cassandra. Not Yong, the Chinese equivalent of a "bubbling." But she swallowed her pride and tucked herself in the chair, noting the attendant still waiting. Kiew had always been reserved in front of strangers.

"A drink?" Kiew asked her, eyebrow arched.

"Water," Cassie said. "Please."

With an upturned nose, the attendant left.

Alone, Cassie grinned unabashedly. "This is awesome!"

Kiew still kept her hands in her lap, her composure rigid as steel. "It was good of you to meet me on such short notice."

Now Cassie hesitated. Things were. . .off. Maybe the indifferent behavior was because of the years they'd spent apart. But still, Kiew had been much nicer on the phone. "Of course—can't believe we're both in Afghanistan at the same time! And for me to be sent up here for business while you're here."

"Quite a coincidence."

Okay, enough. "What's wrong, Kiew?"

Kiew leaned away, her face an impassive mask of civility. "What could possibly be wrong?"

A waiter appeared like a gust of wind with her glass of water and a china cup of black tea for Kiew.

"I will have the bok choy. My guest will have the salmon and rice." Kiew gave Cassie a measured look. "You still like salmon, yes?"

"I love it." What she didn't love was the change in her friend. But Cassie had never been the confrontational kind—in fact, she'd walked a wide mile around conflict to avoid it. She laid the linen napkin across her lap and lifted the small water glass and sipped.

"How long have you been in Afghanistan?" Kiew asked as she raised her steaming tea.

"About three months."

"Aren't you scared?"

Cassie frowned. "Why would I be?"

"The attacks."

"How do you know about those?"

Kiew sniffed. "It is all over the news. Local outlets take great pride in the damage done to the Americans."

"I'm sure they do."

The chatter between them did not improve before the food arrived, forcing them into silent eating. Something was wrong. Or maybe Kiew had just changed. A lot. This wasn't the same girl she'd known and considered a blood sister. Sure, Kiew had always been quieter and more reserved than Cassie, but not cold and aloof.

"You have changed," Kiew finally said quietly.

Yes, that was true, too. "Life has. . .challenged me."

Kiew laughed. "That is a good way to put things."

"I could be angry and bitter about what I've been through, but in the end, that only makes me miserable." Cassie couldn't help but think of Sal's anger and bitterness. She could understand his anger, but what. . .what happened to Kiew? "What about you? How have you been?"

Kiew's gaze fell to the table and silence blanketed them. A chilled silence. "I'm. . ." She breathed in and then exhaled. "I have changed, too. Life has, as you say, *challenged* me." Her eyes sparkled and, for a brief moment, the old Kiew peeked from behind the reserved facade. "I am not sure, however, that I have conquered where it threw me."

Cassie set her plate aside. "I'm not sure I can say I've conquered it either, but I'm fighting to have the life I want." Why did Sal just leap into her mind with his handsome, brooding eyes? She had to change the subject. "So, what do you do for work? Do you travel a lot? Do you think we can see each other again?"

Kiew laughed again. Cassie remembered loving the sound, so much that she would make up things to say so Kiew would laugh. "One question at a time."

With bunched shoulders, Cassie grinned sheepishly. "Sorry. So— job. What are you doing here?"

The stony mask slipped back into place. "Protecting interests for my. . .boss."

The words seemed as carefully picked as plucking roses from a thornbush.

"That sounds. . .mysterious." Cassie wrinkled her nose. "When you were in school, you said people teased you because you were so smart."

"No." Kiew glanced down at the napkin she folded and smoothed. "I said, because I was too smart."

"There is no such thing as *too* smart. Crazy smart? Maybe." Cassie laughed. "That was you—I always envied your brain."

"And how happy you were."

Now it was Cassie's turn to look away.

"But I see that you are not quite as happy." Kiew considered her. "What happened? I see a wound behind those eyes, and I do not mean the injury on your temple."

Cassie's hand almost went to the knot. How ironic that the knot and her subdued happiness were both connected to the same person. "Things happened. I let my naïveté and gregarious nature get me in trouble." She lifted her chin. "But I bounced back." After years of heartache.

"What was his name?" Kiew asked, her voice thick with understanding.

"Trouble."

Kiew eyed her.

They both burst into laughter, drawing more than a few looks from the other patrons. Kiew tucked her head, making Cassie laugh more. Finally she caught her breath, though she felt a snigger tugging at her. "What about you? What was his name?"

"Me?" Kiew tried to look surprised.

"Yes, I can tell—"

"Miss Tang."

Kiew glared at the attendant, but then her gaze flicked to the side. Her normally pale face went white. She immediately set aside her napkin, lifted her small clutch from the floor, and stood. "If you will excuse me, Cassandra."

A northeasterly blast would've been warmer.

Cassie searched for the source of her friend's sudden change. Three men stood near the trickling fountain in the center of the room. One wearing a fierce expression and staring at Kiew. The man was none other than Daniel Jin.

A man broke away from their group and started toward her. Dread spilling into her stomach, Cassie eased back, hiding behind the foliage, willing herself to vanish.

"Miss Walker?"

Cassie couldn't move when she met the man's gaze.

"Please come with me."

EAMON

What do you call this again?"

"*Qorma-e-Aloo Baloo*," Eamon said as he finished the last of the dinner he'd prepared. "My mother loved it."

"She doesn't anymore? Maybe you should stop cooking it then."

Removing his plate to the sink gave him the chance to hide the pain of her teasing. "She died. Four years ago."

"Oh." When he turned around, Brie sat with her head bowed. "I'm sorry. I didn't mean—"

"No worries." He scrubbed the plate and dried it off then set it in the cabinet with the other furnished dishes. "I know you meant no harm."

She was at his side, a little of her serving still on the china. "Really, I'm sorry. My mom was a champion—raising five kids and homeschooling them."

Eamon took her dish and cleaned it, too.

Palms on the counter behind her, she pressed her back against it. "Do you have brothers or sisters?"

"No," he said with a sheepish grin. "Mom always thought I was enough to handle."

"Is she the one who taught you to clean up? You're like a househusband or something."

"My first flatmate was a slob. Disgusting habits. Drove me mad with the bugs it drew."

Brie stared at him as she stood there. He wiped the towel around the sink, hoping she'd break the silence. But she simply stared.

Eamon shifted toward her, a hand propped on the counter. He peered down into her blue eyes. "Do I have something between my teeth?"

Brie didn't look away. "No. You just look...different without your beard."

He dragged his fingers over his jawline. "Feels naked."

"It looks good."

Words like that, simple phrases, could be innocent. Or they could have hidden meaning. He was sick of trying to figure out clues. "Okay." He tossed down the towel. Planted his hands on either side of her and leaned in.

Surprise and something else slid into her expression as she eased back slightly.

"I'm not going to play games. Life is too short and I'm getting old. You intrigue me, Brie Hastings. Your character and professionalism speak loudly. You're beautiful and fascinating. I want to know if you feel the same way."

She hesitated, her gaze evading his until she finally ducked under his arm and moved to the table. "I really don't think this conversation is appropriate."

Eamon faced her, hands on his belt. *"Inappropriate?"*

"Yes," she said, nodding to the room around them. "We are on assignment."

"So?" If it weren't for the assignment, for the times they were put together on missions, he wouldn't have met her.

"And we're. . .alone."

Eamon drew up, affronted by her insinuation. She thought he'd take advantage of her while they were alone. "Brie—"

"No." She held up a hand. "I get it."

"I don't think you do." He tried to temper the frustration and indignation clawing through him. "My attraction to you started the first time I met you. It has nothing to do with being alone and wanting to take advantage—you don't seriously think that of me, do you?"

She averted her gaze, swallowing.

"Brilliant," he muttered.

"See?" She swallowed. "See why I felt it was inappropriate? You're upset now."

"Because you just called my character into question. I serve with honor. I live by that. When have you ever seen anything to the contrary from me?"

"Titanis, I only meant that opening this box now invites trouble."

Unbelievable. "Understood, Lieutenant Hastings." He stretched his jaw and worked to smother his frustration. "We have work to do." Moving to the table took a colossal effort, to not show agitation. He lifted a document on which they'd detailed tasks to accomplish from within Takkar One. "We need to walk the building. I'll head to the basement."

By the time he stood in the elevator, Eamon couldn't figure out what made him angrier—that she had accused him of trying to sleep with her, or that when he'd reset the button on their relationship, she didn't comment. Or when he walked out, she hadn't called him back. Apologized.

With his weapon in his side holster, Eamon made his way down to the basement with his camera and a whole lot of insult. He wanted to put his fist through a wall. How could she even think that? He'd never made a move. But she was right. It wasn't the right time. He'd missed that mark. Walking halls and planting more devices would clear his head. Put distance between his mistake and her reaction.

He glanced at the blueprint of the building on his secure phone and banked right as he stepped out of the elevator. Six paces brought him to a T-split, the walls nondescript, the ground bare cement. A blue sign indicated right for laundry and vending, left for maintenance and electrical. The drone of machines and industrial blowers pressed against his ears.

A door clanked open behind him. Eamon checked over his shoulder. A man strode from the door marked STAIRS and gave him a nod before banking left.

Eamon stood at the juncture, glancing down both sides. Light spilled out of two open doors to the right. And to the left, darkness had a fist hold. According to the engineering plans, the rooms down there would be of little interest. The maintenance and electrical were no more than closet sized. One in, one out. He wasn't sure which one the man had entered. But he must be cramped. Eamon would need to wait for the man to leave, or he'd show his hand here.

He headed toward the laundry-service area, sliding his thumb across his phone to the RECORD tab as his boot struck the light of the laundry room. Before he entered, he barely heard the *thump-whir-thump* of a machine and anticipated company.

The room was lined down the middle with industrial-sized

machines. Flanking them stood enormous tumbling dryers. A woman in a sleek black uniform and hijab stood at a table folding linens. She only afforded Eamon a perfunctory glance before returning to her task.

He backed out and headed toward the vending. There, he found a soda machine, the normal scrawl of Coke done in Arabic but unmistakable all the same. He deposited a crisp bill and bought one to give himself a reason for being down here. Beside that machine stood a snack dispenser.

Back in the hall, he returned to the juncture. He hadn't seen or heard the man come out, but with the din down here, it's possible he'd just missed it. But the doors were closed.

Angling his head to the side to see farther into the darkened corridor, Eamon felt a warning skid across his shoulders. Moving forward, he held the Coke low, gently shaking it, as he eased his hand back to his weapon.

Each step blackened the darkness until he couldn't see. No light seeping beneath doors. He released his weapon and lifted his phone once more. He used the ambient light from the display, which exploded like a beacon in the darkness.

He aimed the beam away from him. Traced the first door marked MAINTENANCE and followed the wall down to the last door. Electrical, no doubt. He tested the handle but it didn't budge. Not surprising. They wouldn't want someone wandering in and rewiring something.

Backing up, he made his way back to the maintenance closet. The door gave way easily. He flipped on the light and grunted when his expectations were met. Cramped and smelly, the closet offered a place to clean a mop—one that dangled over the built-in basin and silver knobs. Three large garbage receptacles lined up against the far wall. Floor slick with grime, the greatest irony.

Eamon reached for the light switch.

A bloodcurdling scream seemed to climb out of the walls. He froze, listening. The scream. . .it sounded distant. Yet close.

What. . .?

He deposited the soda on a shelf then rushed into the corridor, lifting his weapon.

But the screaming seemed partially muted now. Eamon turned a circle, taking in the lights, the variation of brightness, the hum of the air-conditioning unit. Slowly, he returned to the maintenance closet.

The screaming had stopped.

Or maybe it wasn't there at all. Maybe it was the shriek of a turbine or something. With all the machines and hum of electricity and groan of air units. . .

What if the electrical room wasn't an electrical room?

If that was someone screaming. . . He had a job to do.

Eamon moved back into the darkness. Found the door. He rammed his heel into the handle. Pain jarred through his leg and hip. The door didn't give. He repeated the move, this time harder. More deliberate.

The door flung open. Lights blinked and flickered along wall-to-wall electrical units. Eamon snapped up his weapon and aimed into the room, the lights giving adequate illumination for him to see the room had enough space for a man to stand, maybe squat, but nothing else. The walls couldn't be seen for the electrical hubs.

Maybe he *had* been hearing things.

Shaking it off, Eamon made his way to the elevators. He punched the call button and waited, but his gaze kept climbing the walls and ceilings, searching. Probing for an indication that he *had* heard someone screaming. But why would they have anyone down here?

His gaze hit the door to the stairs. The man had come from there. Then went down the hall. And vanished.

Two long strides carried him to the door. He pulled his weapon and punched the door open. Gun low, he stepped into the stairwell and propped the door open with his boot. He scanned right, traced the wall around to the next, then came around.

A blur flashed at him.

Pain exploded across his temple. Snapped his head back. Hit the wall. His vision swam. Warmth slid down his jaw. His legs twisted and tangled as he went down. Eamon scrambled, fought to stay alert.

On all fours, he shook his head, trying to clear it. Splotches of blood appeared on the floor. Just beyond his right hand, his weapon had skidded and hit the wall. He dove for it. Even as he did, he heard the door clap shut.

CHAPTER 8

Kabul, Afghanistan
27 March—1420 Hours

Look, I think there's been a misunderstanding."

"I doubt that," the man said as he guided her through the rear of the restaurant.

"How do you know my name?" She eyed the cement stairwell and swallowed hard. If he wanted to kill her, nobody would hear her. They could dispose of her body out back and nobody would be the wiser.

But she was trained for this.

If she could just think through her panic. Remember that her every move was being monitored. Which meant someone would come to her rescue, right?

No, she was on her own. That was made perfectly clear before she set foot in the country.

"What do you want with me?"

He shoved open a door and thrust her through it.

Cassie swung around, ready for a fight.

"You have the package?" He held out his hand.

She froze. Package? Her thudding heart caught up with her racing mind. This was her contact? But he'd been with— "The rain stays on the plain."

He rolled his eyes. "Only in the movies."

That wasn't the right response. At least not completely. "Which one?"

"Do you have it or not?"

FALCON

Fifteen Klicks North of Kandahar, Afghanistan
28 March—1635 Hours

Sal pressed his gut to the hard, rocky terrain and lifted the binoculars to his eyes. SATINT had spotted their spook heading out of the base and racing across Kandahar City to this remote village at the bottom of what appeared to be a dried-up streambed. Raptor peered down from the rim. He flipped to thermals and scanned the buildings. Set in a horseshoe formation, they effectively provided an advantage to those inside—only one point of infil and exfil. Pockmarks peppered the plaster structures, giving credence to the suspicion that this wasn't just a quiet, remote village, but one that harbored terrorists. And now, spooks.

A half-dozen heat signatures lurked behind the southernmost wall, which was also the back side of the largest building, presumably a two-story residence. One signature bent over something, laboring. Cooking? Two others were small—children. Another sat near the one laboring. And two were huddled in a corner. Six possible hostiles in all.

"Blue two," Sal said, indicating the position of the two in the corner, and passed the nocs to Hawk. "What do you think?"

Propped on his elbows, Riordan looked down at the scene. "One could be our guy."

Rocks crunched and popped as someone settled beside Sal. Dragging himself up to the ledge, Hawk returned from recon of the surrounding area. " 'Terp said a shepherd saw the spook head in there about three hours ago. Hasn't come out."

Their interpreter was a man who had Afghan parents but had been born in the States and joined up at eighteen. They trusted his word. Trusted that the target was in there. Hiding. Among skirts and children.

"I want this piece of dirt," Sal said. "Can't let him hurt the woman or children."

"He'll probably take them hostage," Hawk muttered.

"It's a risk," Riordan conceded.

But that spook had killed the Afghan shooter for a reason. Maybe the spook had taken out Burnett. The way he moved in and out of American installations bothered Sal. A lot. He had too much information to let him walk away.

"We don't have a choice," Riordan said. "He has answers we need."

"Reading my thoughts, squid." Sal smirked. "Be careful—I might think you're smart."

"You know how to think?" Riordan threw the caustic humor right back at Sal.

Sal smiled. "Okay, let's move in. Bring your team in from the north. We'll hit south." East and west were blocked by eight-foot walls. "Eagle will stay high and provide cover fire and take the guy out if he manages to slip past us."

Raptor swept down the side of the hill, buzzed with adrenaline. Knight and Ddrake went ahead, searching for IEDs or mines as they descended. With Hawk, Harrier, and Candyman behind him, Sal took a knee at the bottom where a ravine separated them from the road to the village. "Eagle, sitrep?"

"Clear," Eagle's voice rattled through the coms. "No movement inside."

With two fingers, he sent Candyman and Harrier forward. Sal hustled along the wall, using it for cover. Hawk brought up the rear. This was what he loved. Working with his team. Taking action. Delivering justice.

Hustling forward, M4 at the ready, Sal stacked up behind the others. Candyman moved inside the compound, scurrying to the right and pieing out as he moved to keep eyes on all forty-five degrees visible. Harrier went left and pied toward Candyman.

"Clear," Harrier subvocalized.

Sal rushed into the area, gliding past his men with ease and confidence. He went to a knee at the corner of the primary residence. Across the compound, beyond a rusting truck, Riordan and his team were sidling up to a dilapidated Toyota.

Sal waited for the pat on his shoulder that would signal his team's readiness. When it came, he keyed his mic. "In position." He'd have preferred to do this in the dark, with the lower risk of visibility, but they couldn't take the chance that the spook would get wind of their knowledge of his location and vanish.

Riordan and his men moved like a steady stream of shadows through the compound. "Eagle, report."

"Still clear."

A strange comfort came in the fact that if the situation demanded it, Eagle could shoot through a wall to take out a target. But they needed this guy alive. At least long enough to get the information they needed.

Even as he watched them, Sal was thankful for the addition of more skilled warriors working the same mission. But he wasn't sure how far he trusted Riordan. The guy. . .he seemed to know something he wasn't telling them. Or maybe he was the problem. Could Riordan be behind the attacks?

What if Riordan killed the prisoner?

Jarred by the thought, Sal almost missed the "in position" signal from the SEALs. He held up three fingers. Three. . .two. . .go!

Candyman shifted around. Stepped back and rammed his heel into the crumbling wood barrier. It splintered with a loud *crack*!

Sal rushed inside. "On your knees, on your knees!" He aimed at a woman huddled over two small children. Not cooking. Not working. Just. . .huddling. Sal kept moving, hustling toward the middle where they'd seen the two men in the corner.

On the other end of the residence, he heard Riordan shouting similar orders. They would work their way toward each other. Sal continued on, knowing Harrier or Hawk would tend to the woman and children.

Candyman was at his right, sweeping back and forth.

"Clear," Sal called as he moved through the room. The next area should be exciting. With a nod to Candyman, they breeched the next entrance.

Two large forms shifted to the far right.

Sal's heart jammed. He snapped his weapon toward them. Sucked in a breath—and then whipped his weapon down. Riordan.

"Where are they?" Riordan roared, pivoting and glancing back in the direction they'd inserted. "He's not there. My men cleared it."

"Same here." Frustration roiled through Sal. "Eagle, what do you have?"

"Nothing. No thermals. No visual."

Riordan cursed.

"Knight," Sal shouted, stomping back the way he'd come. "Bring in Ddrake. Find this sorry piece of crap!"

"On it," Knight's deep voice carried through the house. "Ddrake, seek seek seek!"

Sal caught sight of the German shepherd trotting around the room, his nose hauling in scents greedily. A staccato pant indicated he was processing scents at the very back of his nostrils and throat, tasting them.

Ddrake's nose dug into the dirt. He traced back and forth.

"Falcon, he's got something!"

He glanced at Riordan. "Tunnels."

CHAPTER 9

Her longtime friend was involved with Daniel Jin. Though it would've been a nice, creepy story to say the man who'd escorted her had beat her and forced her to promise not to mention who or what she'd seen, he simply escorted her out of the restaurant, demanded the package, then shut the door behind her.

She'd watched from another shop as Kiew and Daniel Jin marched to the elevator, accessing a restricted floor with a chained key. Then Cassie went to the hotel lobby on the second floor of Takkar Towers and checked in, per orders from on high. She really didn't appreciate having to stay here. To be out in the open.

Away from Sal.

"I had thought you would be long gone."

Cassie flinched at the soft voice, yanking her gaze from the mostly uneaten rice and lamb. "Kiew," she breathed as she pushed upward.

"Stay." Kiew slid into the seat beside her. "My assistant mentioned she saw you here. Sorry, I did not realize you were staying at the hotel."

With a heavy sigh, Cassie shrugged. "I've been told to wait here for an answer, but as with any military proceedings, answers are slow in coming." She glanced at her Timex. "And minutes are falling off the clock. I just hope they don't write me up for returning to the base late."

"It is so odd to think of you in the Army."

She smiled. "Being raised by a single mom, I had to get creative with education and career choices. I went into the Army hoping for a nice, fat GI Bill after I got out."

"But you're still in."

She gave another shrug. "I got to travel, they taught me skills I couldn't have acquired out there, and. . ." A pair of rich brown eyes flashed across her memory banks. She didn't want to admit she'd stayed in to be near Sal, though she'd PCSed far away from him.

"What was his name again?" Kiew's almond eyes were wise to the unspoken words as she leaned forward and touched Cassie's wrist. "He must have been quite handsome to distract you so much."

"Quite." He'd fit neatly into that "devastatingly handsome" category of her sister's Harlequin novels. Salvatore Russo had been more handsome and charming than any man she'd met before. When he took an interest in her, she'd felt certain her wildest dreams had come true. And for six months, they did.

"What was that?"

Cassie blinked, looking at her beautiful friend. "What?"

"You're sad now. What happened with this mystery man?"

It'd be easy to rehash this story. To mope over the loss, the way her life had shattered. But something stronger and more important struck Cassie—Kiew was awful chatty today. Yesterday she'd been tightly controlled and tight-lipped. Now she laughed and teased.

"What about you?" Cassie said, shifting the attention back to the woman who'd had everything back then. "What about that power player you left with yesterday?"

Kiew's smile faded. "He is not important."

Daniel Jin, partner of Takkar Corp., not important?

She squeezed Cassie's hand. "Tell me more of your life."

Cassie moved with the flow. "There is not much to say."

"What happened with this man? Tell me."

With a sigh, Cassie shook her head. "I fell madly in love with him—"

"And did he fall in love with you?"

That was the outranking question. "I. . .I think so."

"But?"

"Things changed. I did something really stupid and. . ." She couldn't voice the truth. Not to her sweet friend. Not to a friend who thought so highly of her. "He hasn't forgiven me, and honestly, he has every right to hate me."

"I cannot believe you would do anything so terrible," Kiew said. "And you still love this man?"

"I never stopped." Heaviness doused her again. She wanted to shift this conversation. "What about you? You are a corporate powerhouse, yourself. I can tell by the way they treat you here—and you have an assistant?"

Kiew inclined her head, exposing a red welt near her shoulder. "Some things. . .they take over your life, even when you do not want them to."

Concern for her friend bloomed through Cassie. Her mind bounced to the last conversation they'd had. This had eerily similar earmarks to what her mom went through with Adam. "Kiew, what's going on?"

Her friend frowned. "What do you mean?"

"You've changed—a lot."

Kiew laughed. But it was a nervous one. "You have, too."

"Yes, but you seem. . .afraid."

Kiew's expression snapped back into that cold, unfeeling mask. "I should go."

Catching her friend's arm, Cassie smiled. "Please. Don't."

Composed and stony faced, Kiew lowered herself to her seat.

"I pushed too much, and I'm sorry." Cassie removed her hand when Kiew cast a surreptitious glance around the restaurant to be sure they hadn't drawn attention. "So," she said, as she lifted her water. "You were a tech whiz when I knew you in Shanghai. Are you still?"

A blush rosied her friend's cheeks. "Yes."

"Graduated top of your class, right?" Cassie couldn't stop her laugh when Kiew's chin tucked even more. "I had no doubt."

Even as she said the words, pieces of a puzzle fell into place, revealing a canvas of deception Cassie had not realized she'd been painted into. The colors were brightly spread with a masterful touch. Slick and perfect.

Too perfect.

She'd been used. Manipulated. Set up.

RONIE KENDIG

Fifteen Klicks North of Kandahar, Afghanistan
28 March—1700 Hours

Rock and dirt clawed his shirt and arms as Sal low-crawled through the tunnel. Dust plumed in his face with each breath, tickling his nostrils and aggravating his eyes. Even with his shoulder lamp on, he had limited visual range. The temperature was at least fifteen degrees cooler than aboveground. He dug his elbows into the rocky surface and hauled himself forward. The tunnel ahead was black. Indiscernible.

Sal dragged himself forward, squinting through the gritty, cool air. Another ten feet told him why it was so dark. "Son of a. . ." He spit, the sand grinding between his teeth and digging into his gums. Wiping the sweat from his face, he keyed his mic. "Another fifteen yards in. T-juncture. Nothing else." The tunnel ended in a T with options going right and left. Again. He bit back a curse. This tunnel rat had escaped.

Static crackled through his coms. "Riordan here. Same thing."

Every tunnel branched into two. It'd be impossible to figure out which way the spook had gone. Smart tunnel rat.

His shoulder lamp blinked out. With a grunt, Sal slapped it. Though it flickered, it didn't stay on. "Lamp's out," Sal grumbled. He pulled himself forward into the T and angled to the right then shimmied backward so he wouldn't have to crawl backward to the village. "Coming ba—"

A noise severed his words. Scraping. . .no, not scraping. That was too harsh. It was like. . .breathing. Labored, ragged breathing.

Sal stilled. *I'm not alone.* Awareness erupted through his chest with a blanket of hot dread. And yet his pulse raced at the thought of capturing this spook.

He closed his eyes, listening. Homing in on the sound. Somehow, it was getting farther away. But. . .ahead? He cocked his head slightly, listening. Slowing his own breathing and thoughts.

"Falcon, you there? We're not receiving. You broke up," Hawk's voice squawked through his coms, the team monitoring his movement through a tracking device. He mentally silenced his teammate.

Scritch.

Ahead! It came from ahead.

Sal crammed his boot against the tunnel wall and launched himself forward. Punched his hand forward. The rocky ceiling slapped his helmeted head.

His fingers grazed something smooth. Hard. Rubber. Boots!

But just as fast, the boot vanished. The spook grunted, rock and dirt churning, revealing the spook's attempt to get away.

Not on my watch.

Sal scrabbled forward, using every ounce of energy and every inch to catch this sand spider. He surged deeper into the left vein of the splintered tunnel. As he reached, something cracked against his hand. Pain shot through his finger.

The spook kicked, nailing Sal in the face. He glanced away but clawed at the leg. Caught purchase.

Both feet shot into Sal, nailing him in the nose—he'd swear lights erupted in the tunnel from the flash of white that shot through his skull. Warmth sped down his lip and nose and throat. He coughed but refused to relent. His fingers coiled around fabric.

"Contact with target," Sal growled through his coms.

A scratchy *riiip* filled the air amid grunts and the dribbling rocks. In that split second he realized his fatal mistake—he was trapped and exposed to this spook. With no light to guide him, he had to rely on his hearing. And that hearing told him the spook had just pulled a weapon from a holster.

Then he saw it.

A tiny explosion that seemed massive in the confined space. *Crack!*

His head knocked to the side.

He's shooting!

Sal backpedaled into the main tunnel. He caught the turn. Yanked—
Crack!

Fire lit down his calf as he dragged into the main shaft. As he did, another sound pushed him forward—a sound that froze Sal. Warned him this fight had taken a deadly turn. The unmistakable sound of a grenade against rock.

Panicked, Sal kicked—and felt the thump of the grenade against his boot. He willed himself to move with the speed and agility of a snake in a situation where he felt trapped like food in an MRE pouch.

Boom!

Sal dropped his head, covering his helmet with an arm.

Whoosh!

Heat rushed over him in a gust of debris and smoke. Knocked the breath from his lungs as it shoved him aside. Rocks and dirt collapsed. Punched him in the back. Sal drowned in thick darkness.

CHAPTER 10

A muted boom rumbled the ground beneath his boots. Tony VanAllen glanced down then met Riordan's shocked expression. They both spun toward the tunnel entrance where Hawk waited on both knees.

Hot and thick, a plume of dirt escaped.

Hawk threw himself away from the debris field, coughing as he came to his feet.

Tony pressed his finger to his throat mic. "Falcon, come in."

Static answered.

"Get out of there—it's unstable!" Riordan shouted to Hawk, who had lowered himself into the shaft.

Hawk scowled as he went to his knees in the shaft. "Forget you, squid. I'm not leaving—"

Thud. Crack!

Hawk threw himself over the lip of the opening as the floor around them dipped and collapsed. Curses and shock riddled the air. Tony stared in disbelief as a several-foot depression spread out around them. "Out! Out out out!" He dove for the door, glad they had already cleared the woman and children out of the structure earlier so they could work.

As if on cue, the plaster wall cracked then slumped inward, as if weary from the load it carried.

"Back," Tony shouted to the team and the locals, who'd come out to see what was happening. He waved his arms as he motioned them back.

"What about Falcon?" Hawk asked.

"Eagle, you have eyes on this?" Tony turned just as the ceiling tumbled inward.

"Holy crap!" Hawk stumbled backward as the dust seemed to reach for them. "What about Falcon?" He turned back to the carnage and his hands went to his helmet.

"Ddrake might be able to find him."

"But he's buried several feet belowground." The veins at Hawk's temples bulged. "How do we get him out?"

"Easy," Tony said. "We'll find him."

"If he's alive," someone from the SEAL team muttered.

Hawk dove for the man.

Tony intercepted him, hauling him into a reverse bear hug. "Easy, Hawk. Easy. We'll find him." He looked to the mouthy SEAL. "Alive."

"How?" Hawk demanded.

—⁂—

Emptiness. Darkness. Heaviness.

Sal hauled in a greedy breath—and got a mouth full of dust and dirt. He coughed, only then realizing he couldn't move. Each breath hurt, heavy in the darkness. He blinked to clear his vision but there wasn't anything there. Nothing to see. Only darkness.

Hands wrapped around his head, he tried to drag his finger toward the coms. But his forearm was pinned, a weight forbidding movement. He grunted—and that made him cough again. His ribs hurt. His lungs hurt.

"Falc—" His own name caught in his throat and threw him into another fit of coughing. His eyes watered, burning in the dusty, airless space.

Airless.

How much air did he have?

How long before this tunnel in the middle of the desert became his coffin?

Panic beat against his chest.

Calm down. Calm down. Elevated breathing meant he sucked in more air. Which meant he could run out if this place was completely blocked.

"Falcon to Raptor," he said around a raw throat.

Silence was the only reply.

Sal sagged under the oppressive realization that he could very well die down here. If Raptor couldn't find him. . .if they couldn't dig their way through. . .

And would that be a bad thing?

He'd die in the line of duty.

Nobody would be the wiser to who he really was.

Defeat thickened the air, making it harder to draw a breath that wasn't painful. Really, suffocating to death. . .it wasn't all bad. He'd simply go to sleep and never wake up.

His parents would never know about Vida. Neither would her parents know his guilt in her death.

I'm not guilty. Cassie is.

Her face hovered behind his eyelids like a tormenting ghost.

Why? Why had things been so screwed up with them? Things had been good for a while, but then things changed. Time brought Vida to the base. Reminding Sal of his responsibility. His promise.

He'd been beaten by his own doing. Just like now.

I'll die here.

Pulling in several ragged breaths, he lay there. Unable to move a limb. Barely able to breathe what little oxygen remained.

It was wrong.

He was wrong.

It's not Cassie's fault.

He burned the thought as soon as it ignited in his brain. *"You're the best man I've ever known."*

Cassie had said those words to him more than once. And like an idiot, he believed them. Wanted to believe them. Wanted to be what she saw in him.

Then he broke her heart.

To keep a promise.

A promise he hadn't wanted to keep. Grief pushed against Sal's resolve. What kind of coward leads a girl on with a promise of marriage then falls for another woman, and yet still keeps that promise, breaking the heart of the woman he'd fallen in love with?

You are some kind of screwed up.

Right now, he just had to get out of here. He couldn't breathe. Couldn't think about these things anymore. Didn't want to die with those thoughts on his brain.

With those regrets burned into his heart.

Sal wriggled his other arm. Hope jolted through him when it gave a couple of inches. He reached, straining. . .his fingers digging around the rocks. Scraping his knuckles. Never thought moving his hand would take such a Herculean effort. If he didn't get help, he was dead.

Surprise ripped through him. How many times had he silently wished he could just die? And yet—here's a perfect opportunity. But Sal refused Death's offer. With his fingers, toward the ear mic. Pressed it. "Falcon to Raptor."

Nothing.

Darkness swam in his vision and leapt at him, dragging him into the deepest, darkest abyss. Just as he deserved.

—⁓—

Rubbing his beard, Tony glanced at the rubble. The tunnels had snaked out from the center of that main structure.

"Hey." Riordan pointed toward the rusted-out truck. A depression there gaped back.

Tony clapped the SEAL's arm. "Thanks." He walked toward the gate. "Eagle, you have eyes on this?"

"Copy that," Eagle replied, his tone grave.

"I want you to trace a path approximately fifteen meters from the structure."

"Roger that."

"You're looking for a depression. Some of the tunnels caved in. If we can find one that—"

"Got it," Eagle said. "Sixteen meters due north of the structure. Left five feet."

Tony pivoted. Hawk, Knight, and Riordan were already running toward him. They rushed around the wall. Halfway across the open rocky terrain, he spied the depression.

"Dig!"

"With what?" someone balked.

"Those things on the end of your arms," Hawk bit back, the first to go to his knees and start clawing at the dirt.

"Move!" Riordan shouted.

Tony bent down, but someone caught his arm. He glanced to the side and found an elderly man with scraggly gray-white hair holding a shovel. Relief speared Tony. "Thank you."

Another boy trotted up and passed off a shovel to Hawk.

Each *shink* of the shovel against the hard-packed earth gave Tony hope of finding Falcon alive. The sooner the better. He was short on time and air. He threw the steel into the dirt.

The ground gave way.

Tony stilled, staring into the dark hole that opened up.

Ddrake jumped in, barking. His paws rapidly dug through the dirt, exposing something.

"Boot!" Hawk pointed to the heel of an ACU combat boot. He grabbed at the rocks, rapid-fire digging.

Tony did the same, feeling the bump of shoulders as soldiers and sailors dug hard. "Falcon! C'you hear us?" He grasped the calf. Felt a twitch. He paused and glanced up the mound, imagining his buddy under there. "Falcon, can you hear me?"

Tony's heart slowed when there was no response. He resisted the urge to look at the others. "If you can hear me, move your leg." Hand clamped around the calf, he waited. Waited.

Nothing. The others shifted uneasily, unsettling rock and dirt around their feet.

"A recovery," someone muttered.

"Shut it!" Tony refused to believe this had gone from a rescue to a recovery effort. He squeezed the leg and silently willed Raptor's team daddy to respond.

Then. . .a flex.

"He's alive! *Dig!*"

Shoulders rubbing with others', Tony hauled the dirt in as big scoops as he could manage. Sailors and soldiers worked. When two of Falcon's legs were exposed, he grabbed one. "Pull!"

Hawk had the other. They tugged. Falcon's body shifted.

"Again!"

More hands clamped on to Falcon. They tugged him back. Drag straps on his pants now exposed, Falcon wiggled.

"Haul him out," Hawk roared. "On three. One. . .two. . .pull!"

The tunnel rumbled its objection, surrendering Falcon to their efforts.

They dragged him free but he lay unmoving.

Tony checked him. "He's not breathing!"

CHAPTER 11

Get him up!" Hawk shouted.

Two SEALs climbed out of the collapsed tunnel and assisted the effort to get Falcon on terra firma. The team passed Falcon over the lip of the depression onto the ground. Beard and face coated in dark red dirt, Falcon lay death-like. Mouth open. Eyes closed.

Tony watched as Harrier ripped off Falcon's tactical vest and started compressions. Hawk was there with the oxygen mask, squeezing air into the team daddy's lungs.

"C'mon, c'mon, Falcon," Hawk shouted. "You're too mean and ugly to quit like this!"

Pump. Pump Pump. The compressions continued, Harrier never breaking rhythm.

Falcon coughed, his spine arching. His legs drew up as another spastic cough overtook him. He dragged himself onto his side, heaving to take in greedy breaths. On all fours, he barked out the dust. His limbs shook with the effort of pushing himself up.

"What'd I tell you? Help him up," Hawk ordered.

Breathing hard, he shook his head, leaned back against the ground.

Tony knelt beside him. "Where do you hurt?"

Falcon tugged at the chin straps of his helmet and pushed it off. That's when Tony saw the hole—a bullet hole, right over where the man's forehead would be. A centimeter lower. . . "Dude." He lifted it from Falcon's grip. Turned it around and showed him. "You about met your maker."

—m—

Kandahar Airfield, Afghanistan
28 March—1930 Hours

Fool me once, shame on you. Fool me twice, shame on me.

Cassie should've known this was too good to be true. She'd been asking for the last fifteen months to work this region, to be near Sal in the hopes of finding reconciliation. When the assignment came through, placing her here, she'd leapt without looking. And apparently, without thinking.

She knew better than this. Knew better than to believe they would do anything in her favor. How many times had they told her it wasn't about her? That she was working for her country's benefit and safety.

But this...this was going too far.

Phone in hand, she coded in.

"Cassie!"

She looked up and froze. Brie Hastings was running toward her. *I've been discovered.* "I thought you were outside the wire?"

"Had to come back for some things. D'you hear?" Brie's face was flushed as she kept moving toward the front door.

The fervor in the woman's face pulled Cassie to her feet, the phone almost forgotten. "What?"

"Raptor—they were hunting down a spook. Falcon got buried alive."

Her pulse whooshed in her ears, her heart thudding against her ribs. "H–he's dead?"

"No. C'mon—the hospital!" Brie shoved out the door.

Numb, Cassie stood there. Sal was buried alive. But not dead. But ...needed medical attention. *God, You can't let him die. Not when I came all this way to resolve things.* She was halfway to the door before she realized it.

Outside, Cassie spotted Brie jogging toward the hospital. She raced to catch up. "What happened?"

"He was tracking a spy through some tunnels." Brie tugged open the door and hurried inside.

Cassie slowed, catching sight of the field uniforms. The SEALs hanging back, but the familiar, bulkier shape of Candyman stood out. The team stood huddled, shoulder to shoulder. Intense. A German shepherd panted in the corner, squinting as if to say he'd done his job.

"I'm fine," a voice growled.

Sal. That was Sal. And hearing the irritation in his voice made her smile. Her breath shuddered, pushing relief through her veins.

"You're not fine. You have a concussion—that bullet might not have pierced your skull but it gave it a good whack," a man in scrubs said.

"I've had worse," Sal groused.

"And the bullet in his shoulder?" Titanis asked.

"A graze—one that cost me a sixty dollar tac shirt," Sal said as he lifted his bare arm, the material having been cut away.

"He's right. It's a graze, but we want to do an MRI and make sure there are no internal injuries from the collapse."

"Just bruises and scrapes." Sal shifted off the gurney, remnants of what he'd gone through evident on his face. The beard—it was so strange to see that on him, even now—had dust and blood in it. A red, angry welt across his cheek and nose made him look like a prize fighter. And the fire in his eyes roiled.

Cassie couldn't help but smile. That was Sal. Never one to take things lying down. A man of action.

"Am I cleared?" Sal scooted to the edge of the gurney—his gaze struck Cassie's and he slowed.

"Not so fast," came a firm, authoritative voice. Captain Watters strode toward them. "Doc, get him checked out. Do that MRI. Make sure that tunnel doesn't permanently bury him."

"Dean—"

"Two hours, Sal. Meet us back at Command." Captain Watters turned to the others. "Let's debrief."

As one, the team shifted and headed out the door.

Cassie hesitated off to the side, not wanting to leave Sal and yet not willing to brave his acerbic comments.

"Get him in a gown and down to imaging," the doc said as he left the bay.

A nurse pulled a gown out of a bin and set it on the bed next to Sal.

"Change into this and we'll get you back in action ASAP."

Sal huffed. Grabbed the blue folded gown—and grimaced. He winced and tried to tug his arm through the hole. That's when she noticed the red, raw lines on his upper arm. Not scratches like she'd thought before. They were too even. To narrow. Rocks would leave jagged marks.

He tried again and growled, clearly in pain. Sal lowered his head, eyes pinched tight.

How she ended up next to him, she wasn't sure. But when those chocolate eyes flared with anger at her closeness, Cassie pushed a pleading expression into her face. "Just let me help."

"I know how you help. And I don't need that," he spat at her as he tried again to remove the shirt. "Leave."

"Sal—"

"Get out, Cass!"

"You can't shut me out forever. We need to talk."

"No. We don't." He tangled his arm in the hole and lost his balance. His foot caught the edge of a wheeled tray and he pitched forward.

Cassie caught him by the sides.

Anger exploded through his face but he was free, the shirt dangling around his neck. Sal pushed her. "What did I say?"

Stumbling backward, she tensed. Slammed against a locker unit. "Please, stop."

Sal towered over her. "How do I get through to you? I *don't* want you here. Ever since you killed Vida—"

"I did *not* kill her," she bit out, her throat burning.

"Might as well have." His words were hissed, his hot breath dashing across her cheek. His nose pressed into hers. His eyes bore into hers, his breathing hard.

Her vision blurred with unshed tears, aching for the time he'd stared at her with respect and love, not anger and disgust.

But then something shifted. His gaze. It went to her lips. Skated around her face. His expression relaxed. Amid the sweat-caked dirt and scrapes, his handsome features again beckoned to her.

He punched the locker by her head.

With a blink, Cassie sucked in a ragged, startled breath, but their eyes remained locked. Vulnerability roiled through her. Always powerless beneath his gaze, she stood there. Felt hope spring through the dregs of his anger.

His thumb slid down the side of her face as his eyebrows knotted. Each breath of his skidded along her cheek. He angled closer. The mechanism of time powered down to a microscopic pace. She saw his lips part beneath his beard. His gaze softened as he homed in.

CHAPTER 12

Kandahar Airfield, Afghanistan
28 March—2010 Hours

Her lips were soft, willing, as Sal gave in to the demons that had tormented him far too long. He curled a hand around her waist, ignoring a dart of pain. The chasm of passion that had lured him into falling in love with Cassie over four years ago gaped, swallowing him whole.

The surrender felt good. Being with her felt right. Always had.

But no. No, he shouldn't do this.

But she was perfect. Sweet. Even after—

Vida.

Vida's dead. Because of her. *What the heck are you doing, Russo?*

Breaking the kiss, Sal snapped his head to the side. He heard her heavy breath but wouldn't meet her gaze. Why did Cass have to be here? Alive, beautiful, sultry. And Vida. . .dead. Gone.

Sal punched the locker again. Pain rushed down his wrist and arm, resonating in his shoulder. It felt good. Pain felt good. He punched it again.

Cassie sucked in a breath with a whimper as his fist connected a third time. She blinked and recoiled, her chin trembling.

He hated himself. Hated that he'd fallen into this weakness again.

"What's going on here?" a male voice demanded.

Without a word, Cassie ducked and left. "H–he needs help."

More than she or anyone else could ever know. Knuckles to the locker, Sal didn't dare move. Didn't trust himself with his stupidity. His anger. His demons and self-hatred.

Weak. He was *weak* and dumb. A little pain and near-death experience and he was already willing to fall into the arms of the woman who'd bewitched him into betraying a promise he made to his high school sweetheart.

"You ready, sir?"

Sal stepped back. Drew himself up straight with tight lips and muscles as he turned toward the nurse. "Yeah." On the tray by the bed, he saw the scalpel.

One word flooded his mind at the sight of the shiny blade: relief.

—◊◊—

Kabul, Afghanistan
30 March—0800 Hours

"He has agreed to look into things."

Daniel stood at the window of his condominium on the thirteenth floor of Takkar Towers, staring at the embattled city. The crumbling city. This sandpit of a desert had nothing on the energy and vitality of Shanghai. Why had Sajjan insisted on continuing to build his empire in such a wasteland?

"He was suspicious."

At this, Daniel smirked. "Of course he was." He turned, sliding his hands into the pockets of his silk slacks. "I would be concerned if he were not." He strode to the bar and lifted a snifter from the glass cabinet.

"But if he learns of what you are doing, what you have planned. . ." Aamir scurried forward like some street rat fleeing a mangy, unclean dog. "If he learns what you are doing, he will stop you. You should kill him before he can interfere."

Fury surged through Daniel. He flashed an angry glare at the man.

Aamir drew up, his dark face going white. "You do not realize the power he has. You have not been here long enough to see how far he can reach. They listen to him. All the mullahs and imams respect him—"

"They do not respect him. They *fear* him." Daniel felt disgust at his words and let the rancid taste hang for a few seconds. "And that is what we will capitalize on. If we sever the serpent's head, the carcass will be thrown to the winds." But even he knew he could not kill Sajjan Takkar. It would betray the memory of Daniel's father. Somehow. He wasn't sure how, but the thought had kept him awake more than once.

Aamir's eyes widened. "Sever. . ." He shook his head. "No. No, you cannot do this."

After sipping the vodka, Daniel let the heat of it spill through his body. Drew strength from it and the reaction Aamir had given, convincing him he was indeed on the right path. He would not literally decapitate Takkar, but he would decapitate his ability to control the company so resolutely. And by severing that control, Daniel would also restore the power and strength to China, as his father had long dreamed. "Do you believe in our plan, Aamir?" Glass in hand, Daniel returned to the window. He lifted his phone from his pocket and sent a message.

"You know I do, bu—"

"And do you have what it takes to see this through? Or do I need to find another? One who is not so easily moved by unrealistic fears?"

Standing rigid, Aamir stared at him. "You. . .you would threaten me?"

Daniel again sipped his vodka. Held it on his tongue then slowly swallowed, allowing the warmth to permeate his being. "Consider it a promise, Aamir."

A man appeared in the hall, hands folded calmly before him.

"Ah, Nianzu," Daniel said, motioning to the new arrival. "Aamir, have you met my friend, Lee Nianzu?"

"No." The Afghan looked pale and terrified. "We—I thought he was dead."

"As you can see, he is not." Daniel smiled. "Nianzu has been with me since the beginning. There is not a part of this plan that he is not familiar with." He turned to his friend. "Please show Aamir the labs."

After inclining his head, Nianzu stepped back and to the side, holding out a hand. "This way, please."

With a disconcerted shake of his head, Aamir shot a glance to Daniel. "I would warn you not to act against Takkar. He is too powerful."

"Why would I act against the man who has allowed me into the company, the one my father and his founded?" Daniel's animosity hid behind his cloak of civility. "Good-bye, Aamir."

As the Afghan turned and followed Nianzu, Daniel saw a shape gliding across the hall. Someone had just come in. Kiew. She stopped at the foyer to the living area and watched the two men retreat. Dressed in a red-and-white top and black slacks, she epitomized grace and elegance. Beauty unrefined. Strength. Her brown eyes came to his, filled with concern.

She descended the three stairs into the living area and crossed the cream cashmere rug. Though she hadn't hurried or rushed, there was an urgency about her somehow. "Are you sure it is wise to"—her gaze slid in the direction the men had left—"take care of things?"

"You question me?"

Kiew lifted her chin and straightened. "Of course not, I only seek to protect our interests. Should some grow suspicious—"

Daniel's hard laugh silenced her. He dumped back the last of his drink and returned to the bar, where he poured another. "We have them so confused, the right hand does not know what the left is doing." He added two ice cubes, a luxury here. "What of your appointments?"

Kiew sighed heavily. "You are so confident, but I wish you would for once show some care."

He walked toward her and ran a hand along her cheek. Then grabbed her neck. She dropped her clutch, gripping his wrists as she knotted her eyebrows.

"Do not tell me what to do, think, or feel," he hissed. "You do your job and stick to that, and things will be fine. I do not need you."

"I want only. . .to help. We. . .worked so hard."

"*We?*"

Her brown eyes glossed with tears, and her face went dark red from the constriction of air.

"This is my plan. My company. My attack."

She nodded, tears bursting free and slipping down her porcelain cheeks.

He tossed her back.

Kiew wobbled on her heels but steadied herself then bent to retrieve her purse.

"Now, your appointments—how were they?"

Nostrils flaring, she took a minute to regain her composure. "I met with the hacker I told you about, in an effort to find Boris. His trailer is on the base, and I've communicated with our mole to get access to it."

"Why do we need this trailer?"

"It is where he did all his work. I believe if we can get in there, we may be able to find—"

"I am beyond this effort. Forget about it. We did the damage. Their systems have been compromised. We are one step from having the names of every ODA team. With that, the names of the men responsible for interfering with my plan."

"We must also be sure," Kiew said softly, cautiously—she was afraid of his reaction to her insistence—"that he did not have information that would compromise our identities."

Daniel glowered. "That would be very unfortunate. . .for you."

"Agreed."

But would she confess the truth? "What of your other meetings?"

Doubt flickered through her eyes. "What other meetings?"

"Our wedding is soon. Surely you have things to wrap up."

Her chin tucked again with a coy smile. "Of course, but those are all in Shanghai." She held up her wrist. "In fact, I have a video conference with the hotel. If you will excuse me." With a faint smile, she gave a courteous bow before heading toward the hall.

"You no longer kiss me," Daniel said, unmoving.

Kiew paused. Lowered her head. Then came around. "Forgive me. There is much on my mind." She returned, sat on the edge of the sofa, and bent toward him. Her lips were soft and warm against his cheek. Those almond eyes were as calm and confident as the day he chose her.

He watched her leave. Without hesitation.

From a side door, Nianzu returned. The man was cold, calculated, and efficient. He tugged on the sleeve of his dress shirt beneath his silk jacket and shrugged, adjusting it. Not a trace of his deadly deed.

"Did they meet again?"

Nianzu gave a short, crisp nod.

There could only be one reason Kiew hid the American female soldier—"I believe she intends to betray me, Nianzu." Losing Kiew would not affect the fulfillment of his father's dream—a powerful business entity that provided wealth for the family and strength and power for their country. But it would anger Daniel. A lot.

"You want me to have the American soldier killed?"

Daniel swirled the amber liquid in his snifter, still staring in the direction Kiew had left. He would need to learn more about this American. "Soon."

EAMON

His head throbbed with each step. Eamon pushed himself down the hall, crazily relieved the closer he got. Not because of the safety of being in there. But because of who waited on the other side.

Yet she'd made it clear she found his attraction inappropriate. *She thinks me a brigand.*

Shoulders taut against the pain, he slid his key card into the slot and let himself in. A lone light glowed in the corner of the small sitting area. But the sofa and chairs were empty. She'd been right to go to bed. But he wished—

Metal clanged in the kitchen.

When her gaze hit him, Brie straightened and gasped. "What happened?" She came around the L-shaped counter.

"Someone didn't like me looking around the basement."

She was within reach now. Her blue eyes shadowed with concern. Right there, he could almost think she cared. "Well, then I guess that's where we need to focus." Obviously she didn't. She had her mind in the right place—the mission.

He should get his there as well, so he nodded. "I'm going to shower then bed down." Halfway down the hall, he hated himself for cutting things so short, but he didn't want her close to him right now, and he didn't want her thinking he would use his injuries to bait her.

"Titanis?"

He closed his eyes. Turned. It was no use asking her to call him Eamon. That would be inappropriate.

She had her hands tucked in her back pockets, a pose that made her seem more like a sheepish teenager than a striking lieutenant. "Are you okay?"

There again, almost as if she cared. And she probably did, to be fair. Just because she wasn't attracted to him didn't mean she was cold and heartless. "Fine." He nodded and resumed his mission to escape her presence and shower.

—᠁—

Morning came too swiftly when sleep eluded a person. On the floor doing sit-ups, Eamon huffed through another rep, attuned to the running of the shower. He did more push-ups then sat staring at the door, an arm hooked around his knees. This wasn't going to work. They'd had a natural chemistry back at the base, which had provided a great segue into working. But his pathetic attempt to win her over had tangled it all into a maddening knot. He'd watched every word and move to make sure she didn't misinterpret it. Sitting there, breathing heavily, he realized he had no idea how to woo a woman. Truthfully, he'd never had to make an effort. With a billionaire father, a face and name recognized throughout Sydney and most of Oz, he never lacked for female attention.

And he'd never wanted it either. Shallow gold diggers were the ones throwing themselves at him. That's what he'd loved about being a commando—everyone was the same. Everyone worked for a common cause. He ran a hand over his jaw. How had he been so wrong about how she felt? His fingers itched to grab his phone and call his mom.

All these years after her death and he still sought her counsel. She would tell him what he'd done wrong. How he could fix it.

A light rap on the door shoved him to his feet. He spun and grabbed for his shirt.

The door creaked open. "Ti—oh."

Threading his arms through the sleeves, he turned. "Sorry."

"My fault." Brie couldn't hide her red face. "Sorry. Anyway. I . . ." She touched a finger to her forehead. "I—um, I was running back videos from the basement."

Eamon strapped on his holster. "Yeh?" When had she gone into the kitchen? "Did you even sleep?"

"The man who hit you. . ." Avoiding his question was as much an admission. "I think I found him."

"Show me."

In the eating area, he stood behind her as she pulled some images from the video feed. He wanted to bend closer to the screen but kept his distance.

"Here." She pointed to the screen. "He leaves and then you see him up the stairs before you."

"Eh, it's no good. Can't see his face very well."

"Right, but this morning"—her long, piano fingers struck the keys deftly—"he's upstairs on the main lobby, heading into the café." On-screen, the man walked up to another. "Look! It's Lee Nianzu."

"Zmaray—The Lion," Eamon muttered as he lowered to a chair. Stroking the beard that was no longer there, he wrangled the information. The man who'd beaten Dean to a pulp and exerted horrible influence to have Miss Zarrick raped. The snake coiled between the attacks and their architect.

"It's obvious he's working with Meng-Li."

"We see it that way, but we need proof they are connected."

"We have it—he's right there, meeting with him."

Eamon shook his head. "I've met with terror leaders, knowing full well they are evil, in an effort to get actionable intel or convince them to work with us, but that doesn't make me evil or a terrorist."

She sighed and lifted her hair off her neck with a puffy exhale of frustrated breath. "Actionable intelligence. Curse the thing!"

"We have to follow him—"

"Hold up," Brie said, brushing her bangs from her face. "Aren't you afraid he's going to come after you? No doubt this guy told Meng-Li about you."

Eamon hesitated. "Possible, but we'll have to trust the disguise worked. It's imperative we tag and track him and listen in on every conversation he has. He shows up like a festering boil after every situation. I want him undeniably tied to this attack on the American military."

She eyed him.

"What?"

"Why do you care so much about us?"

He frowned. "It's not Aussies, Americans, Brits. It's *us*—Coalition Forces against this terrorist." He hated the lines she'd drawn, ones that separated not only their military effort, but them personally. "Besides, he's attacking my mates. Killed a man I highly respected. I won't let that rest."

CHAPTER 13

Kandahar Airfield, Afghanistan
30 March—1820 Hours

One-hundred-eighty days deployed to the desert, but the heat and sand never felt more prominent than when she had a video call with her sister. The normalcy, the domestic "bliss" of chasing little ones around the house, corralling the two dogs and cats, the kiss of the husband as he swept past her on his way to work. . .

"What I wouldn't give to be there," Amanda said as she collapsed, arms folded on the granite island, in a heap in front of the camera. Though her hair was in a quick updo and she had no makeup, her sister looked beautiful.

Being away from family and exposed to the brutalities of war did that to a soul. "No, you wouldn't. Trust me on this one."

Amanda's head came up, her eyes bleeding through the feed with understanding. "What's happened?"

Cassie swallowed, stretched over her cot, pillow tucked under her for support. "I can't say much, but I. . .an officer died. He was shot right in front of me."

"Oh, Cassinator." Amanda's face etched with sisterly concern—and a heap of motherly concern. She'd been six years older and always had been like a second mom to Cassie, especially when Mom started hitting the bottle.

"I tried to stop the bleeding." Though she'd scrubbed down in the shower several times since then, Cassie could still feel the blood on her hands. She shuddered.

"Was it someone you knew?"

She fought through the tumultuous images and sensations—the

blood between her fingers. The gurgling noise of the wound...

"Oh my word—it wasn't *him*, was it?"

Cassie blinked. "What?" Her mind caught up. "Oh. No. No, it was an officer I worked with, but I didn't know him well."

"I'm glad for that, but still. That's awful. I'm so sorry for you, Cass. I'll pray for you."

"Thanks." A thick cloud of depression hung over the conversation, making Cassie wonder if she should've waited to make this call.

"Boos coos! Boos coos!" A bright, round face appeared over Amanda's shoulder with hair in lopsided pigtails.

Her sister lifted the three-year-old into her arms, laughing. "Mila's bingeing on *Blue's Clues* while the kids are doing schoolwork."

"I get all the credit," Leila's voice carried from the side.

Amanda glanced back at her ten-year-old daughter then back at the camera. "This is true. Leila dug the DVDs out of the bin in the basement and has been showing them to Mila."

Heart full as she watched the girls, Cassie felt the edge of the last week falling away, heartbeat by heartbeat.

"Malcolm, don't"—Amanda's stern "mommy" voice carried strongly through the live feed—"I'll be right back, Cass."

"Hi." Mila pressed her face almost completely to the iPad screen so that only her forehead was visible to Cassie. But her voice—so husky and sweet. "I miss you."

Oh to be back there. To hold Mila. Hug Leila. And her sister. Aching, Cassie leaned closer. "Hi, beautiful baby girl. How are you?"

"Fine," Mila said. Then she whipped her head around, watching something. She lowered her face back to the iPad. "Malcolm's in trouble." She swatted hair from her face. "He's been a bad boy."

"Have you been good?" Chin propped on her hand, Cassie soaked in the sweet face and voice. Such a glorious respite from war.

"Yes." Mila bobbed her head. "I'm an angel."

Cassie laughed at the unadulterated honesty and innocence.

"That's what Uncle Byron said," Leila popped back into the conversation.

"Okay, bye!" Mila vanished from the screen and then could be seen across the room, gathering up stuffed animals and plopping them into a small plastic stroller.

"Sorry about that." Amanda returned to her spot on the stool. "Malcolm's been a demon lately. Not sure what's gotten into him." With a frantic shake of her head, Amanda scrunched her shoulders. Then refocused. "So, still going to be there for another few months?"

"At least," Cassie said.

"I thought we were pulling out?"

"They are. But things are worse, chaotic, da—" Telling her sister things were dangerous was not the right conversation to have, especially with the kids in the background. "Anyway, yeah—it's messed up."

"I see, I see," came Mila's husky little voice.

Amanda rolled her eyes and lifted Mila back up.

Elbows on the counter, Mila pushed her dark hair from her face again. "I know my colors!"

"Let's show her." Amanda reached for something. She held up a card. "What color is this?"

"Boo!"

"Blue," Amanda corrected, emphasizing the *l* in the word.

"Buh-lll-eww," Mila said, sticking her tongue out on the *l*.

"And this one?"

"Red."

Tears welled up in Cassie's eyes. She was missing out on so much. "Good job!"

"I gotta go. Bye!" Mila made a noisy kissing sound then squirmed out of Amanda's arms.

"Bye, Mila." Cassie blew a kiss at the camera.

"She's just like you—never stays in one place very long."

Laughing again, Cassie could only shake her head. She should feel better, but after watching Mila—so full of life and unaffected by what was happening on the other side of the world. . .in Cassie's world. . .combat. . .death—that innocence seemed a lifetime away.

"Well, we'd better go. Dentist appointments in an hour."

"Okay, love to all!" After a round of good-byes, Cassie signed off. The screen went black. And a ghostlike image appeared on the glossy surface. Her heart thudded as her brain registered what she saw. Someone behind her. But it wasn't just any ghost.

Sal!

Cassie swung around.

He stood there, silently watching. His gaze flicked to the device. Then back to her. "All hands at Command. Zero nine hundred."

Including me? Since when? "You want me there?"

His left cheek twitched. "Skip it if you want. Won't bother me."

Of course.

His gaze again hit the iPad. "Who was that?"

Panic thumped in her breast. She'd been so careful. "My sister, Amanda."

He stood there for several long, painful seconds, staring at the blank screen before confusion rippled through his dark eyebrows. "Your sister named her kid Mila?"

Cassie swallowed hard. "I did. I—I named her."

He jerked back as if he'd been punched.

She knew what he was thinking. But she didn't want to go there. Didn't want to open Pandora's box. A deadly box of shattered dreams and broken promises.

Sal scowled at her. Backed up a step. Then another. "Zero nine hundred," he said in a clipped manner. And then he was gone.

She let out a breath weighted by deception and fear. If he ever learned the truth, what would he do? He already held Vida's death against her. He hadn't forgiven her for that sin. If he found out about Mila, forgiveness wouldn't even be in his vocabulary. Only murder.

Kandahar Airfield, Afghanistan
30 March—1840 Hours

Sal stalked out of her tent, hating that he'd lied to her. She'd show up tomorrow and find out there was no all-hands. But he'd needed to see her. Something had possessed him to go to her bunk. What he had in mind once he got there, he didn't have a clue. But being trapped in that tunnel unlocked something in him.

Weakness.

No. No, he was too familiar with weakness.

Desperation.

Could be. He was desperate to quell the storm in his gut. To douse the fire. Seeing her again, being around her—*kissing* her. He snorted and shook his head. He'd blame that on the painkillers, but they hadn't given him anything strong enough to justify that level of stupidity.

What pushed him to Cassie?

Habit. Having her around—had it tricked his mind into falling into old habits established back at Fort Huachuca while stationed there for training? He'd work then find her and they'd go out. Catch a meal. Maybe a movie. A hotel room.

Sal rubbed the back of his neck as he sat in a lone chair by the old Boardwalk. A real class act.

She named her niece Mila.

Had she driven a dagger through his heart, it would not have hurt as much. Scratching at his beard, he told himself it didn't matter. They weren't together anymore. He didn't want anything to do with Cassandra Walker ever again.

And yet, he'd been shackled to her on this mission. To find the one who killed Burnett and dozens of others. A mission he couldn't accomplish to save his life. They were missing something monumental. And it was his job to figure out what. And he'd gotten exactly nowhere.

His near-death experience and Burnett was gone. Dean was off liaising, working from the top down to find this sicko. The team had next to nothing on this moron who'd attacked the security protocols of the military computers. That put everything at risk and vulnerable to repeated attacks.

Failing. Again.

Why exactly did God have him on this earth? To screw up? Make others look good? To aid the Angel of Death?

Light glinted off steel. Sal blinked at the Ka-Bar in his hand, unaware of drawing it from the sheath. He leaned forward swiping his thumb over the blade. He tightened his fist around the handle and placed it on his bicep.

"Hey, got a minute?"

Sal jolted and jerked the knife away. Held it low, out of sight as he met the probing gaze of Hawk. "Isn't it past your bedtime?" Sal taunted as he slid the knife back into its sheath.

"Nah, I got hours still." Hawk slapped his shoulder. "What about you, old man? Shouldn't you retire?"

With a laugh, Sal shook his head. He only had two years on Hawk. But retiring sounded better and better every day. "How's your girlfriend?"

"Fiery, gorgeous, mouthy, puts me in my place." Hawk grinned. "Perfect."

"About time someone put a leash on you."

"What about you?"

Sal frowned beneath the lone stadium light a couple of yards away. "What?"

"You and Walker."

Sal snorted again. "I thought you had something serious to talk about."

"Very serious." Hawk's gaze burned through Sal's attempt to casually blow off the intrusion into his personal life. "You've been different since she showed up."

That was true in more ways than the one Hawk implied.

"She has power over you."

"You're crazy." Was he an open book?

"You avoid her. You won't confront her—I've never seen you do that. You're in my face all the time. Do the same to everyone. But not this chick." Hawk leaned against a post and crossed his legs at the ankle. "What's she got over you?"

"It's not your concern."

"Wrong," Hawk said, but then he crouched with his back to the post. "Her presence has altered the way the game is played." He spread his hands. "Look, I'm not here to cause trouble, but I think this needs to be in the open."

"Leave it alone."

"What happened?"

Relentless had to be Hawk's middle name. And unless Sal gave the guy something to chew on, he wouldn't let up. "How about the biggest, juiciest steak of reality, served up cold and heartless?" Just the way Cassie had served it up.

Hawk finally had nothing to say.

"She killed my girlfriend." Sal hated himself for saying those words. They weren't entirely true.

"Seriously?" Hawk punched to his feet then slowed. "No, no that's not true. I can see it on your face."

"I said leave it alone."

"I will—when you come clean."

Sal huffed. "Cassie worked at Huachuca. We met. Went out. Things got. . .heavy." He gritted his teeth, the images of those nights blazing through his visual cortex. "When my girlfriend—"

"Girlfriend? I thought—"

"When Vida PCSed there," Sal pushed on, unwilling to address any more questions, "Cassie got jealous. Used her spheres of influence to have Vida transferred to Helmand, knowing it was the most dangerous province. That more American lives were lost there than anywhere else. Vida was killed within a week."

"Dude."

Sal glanced down. "Cass sent her there to get rid of her. Permanently." His chest heaved with the volatility of saying those words.

"Dude, that's messed up."

The words vindicated Sal's feelings.

"But you were dating them both? At the same time?"

"I broke up—" Sal bit off his words. It didn't matter. He wasn't going to justify himself to anyone, especially not Hawk. "Is there a real reason you're here?"

Hawk nodded. Straightened and took a step back. "Thought I'd stop you from carving up your life." He nodded to Sal's right. "And your arm."

Sal stood.

A shadow shifted behind Hawk, freezing Sal. He took a step forward.

Hawk held up his hands. "Hey. I'm not—"

"Shh," Sal hissed, scowling as he tried to see through the two buildings that held the shadow. "Someone's there."

Hawk turned.

A figure slipped beneath a singular beam of light. He wasn't in uniform. No buzz cut. Sal sprinted across the foot-hardened path. Damp, rank air of the alley permeated his senses. He tore through it. Skidded to a stop as he scanned the road. Searched for the man.

"What'd you see?" Hawk panted as he caught up.

"A man watching us." Sal turned a circle, watching the corners and shadows. He'd seen him. Right here. "I swear, he was right—"

Hawk pointed. "There!"

Sal took off in that direction. Not toward the center of the base but toward the perimeter. Heck no. He wasn't letting this guy get away. The bruises and aches from the cave-in slowed him, but not too much.

The guy scrabbled over a cement barricade.

Sal sped up, using his momentum to sail over the obstacle like a hurdle. The move gave him an advantage. The man was only a couple of feet away. Sal spotted the hull of an MRAP that had eaten an IED. He jumped to the side. Toed the steel hull. And launched into the air.

He sprang forward. Drew back his fist. Slammed it into the back of the man's head. Landed on him. His teeth clacked as he landed hard.

The man groaned beneath him. Pushed onto his hands and knees. Then collapsed. Unconscious.

Breathing with a heady sense of vindication and triumph, he stared with a crooked smile at the man. Then grinned and turned. "Hey, Haw—"

Sal froze.

Hawk lay on the ground. A dark stain spreading over his chest.

CHAPTER 14

*H*awk!"

Sal lunged toward his fallen friend. He skidded on his knees across the dirt. "Hawk! Hawk, talk to me."

But there was nothing. No response. No movement.

Sal pressed three fingers to Hawk's thick, sweaty neck and waited, his gaze on the still-unconscious intruder.

Hawk was alive. His pulse was steady. So was the blood flow. But the heart rhythm could change at any second.

He tugged out his sat phone and dialed up Dean.

"It's late—"

"Hawk's down. Someone shot him."

"Where?"

Rocks spat at him. Dirt peppered his cheeks.

Shots! Someone was shooting at him. Sal threw himself to the ground. Snagged Hawk's drag strap on his tac pants. Keeping as low a profile as possible in the vehicle graveyard, he scooted backward, tugging a limp Hawk with him.

A squawking noise snagged his attention.

The phone!

Sal snatched it from the ground and pressed it to his ear then gave his location. He got Hawk to safety then glanced up in time to see the intruder stumbling to his feet.

"Hey!" Sal shoved forward.

Bullets sliced through the air. Pinged off the hull of the vehicles. He leapt backward, out of visual range. He tugged his weapon from his leg holster. Took aim at the fleeing intruder. And fired.

The *thwat* hit his ears the same time he saw the guy pitch into the dirt.

But the bugger climbed back up.

Sal tightened his lips. "Stupid—" Maybe if he was fast enough. If he dove ahead, like an obstacle course, beating the bullets. He was not letting this guy get away. They'd already lost a witness, an enemy combatant to a spook's skills. He was not losing this guy. Though Sal had no idea what this man wanted or what he'd done, the guy clearly didn't want anyone to ask those questions.

Sal again lurched from the protection of the truck. Fire trailed across his arm. "Augh!" He dropped back, cursing and banging the ground.

Fine. Want to play dirty? Sal lined up the weapon again. He didn't want the guy dead. But he couldn't let him get away. He fired in his right leg.

Scaling the wall, the guy howled in pain now. But didn't stop.

Realigning his sights, Sal eased back the trigger again. Hit the back of the man's left thigh.

The intruder lost his grip. Dropped.

Roaring engines and shouts joined the fray. Sal turned his attention to Hawk. His buddy lay with his eyes open, brow knotted in pain.

"Falcon!" came a shout from behind and to his left.

"Here," he said, peering out, perpendicular to where the sniper hid. Just beyond the hull, Sal spotted Dean striding toward them. "Down! Stay down!"

Dean immediately complied, as did the two MPs with him.

"Shooter—north wall. Stop him!"

With a nod, Dean and the MPs ran in that direction. A hollowness swept through Sal, realizing they were alone again. But more vehicles pulled up—and one eased right up to the MRAP. Two soldiers hopped out and rushed over, one wielding a med kit, the other a stretcher.

"Stay low!" Sal said, shifting backward. "There's a shooter." He knelt beside Hawk, whose eyes were hooded in pain. A sheen of sweat made him look sickly. "Hang in there. Help's here now."

With a smirk, Hawk slowly blinked. "I'm thinking this is your way of getting out of coming clean about Walker."

"Thinking's not your strong suit." Sal smiled. "Stick to looking pretty."

The medics had the driver bring up the armored vehicle on the other side, effectively blocking them from the shooter The four of them ushered Hawk out of the hot zone and into the rear of the MRAP.

With his buddy secure and getting the best possible help, Sal focused on the intruder. Needed to help Dean take care of this scum. He pivoted.

Two MPs scurried back toward them, running in a bent posture to protect themselves and the prisoner held between them from more shots.

Dean trotted up and slowed next to Sal. "He has a few extra holes in him."

Sal nodded.

"I'm guessing that's not from the sniper."

"He had a partner, whose job was to make sure he got out alive and unharmed."

"One out of two ain't bad." Dean nodded toward the ambulance rushing away. "How's Hawk?"

"Bullet wound to the chest. Lost a good amount of blood, but I think he'll make it."

"Means he's out of commission."

"Don't tell him that."

—⁂—

Kandahar Airfield, Afghanistan
31 March—0915 Hours

She could handle a lot of things. Being made a fool of was not one of them.

Cassie stood at Brie Hastings's desk, humiliated as she held the phone to her ear. "Seriously? There's no meeting?"

"Sorry," Brie's voice came through the line. "Even if there was, it would've been canceled after last night."

"What do you mean?"

"Oh." Brie's voice held levity. "I thought you would know. There was another incident on the base. Falcon and Hawk were involved—Hawk was shot."

"Are you serious?" She sounded like a glitching MP3. "How is he? Is Sal okay? Who shot him?"

"They don't know. Falcon saw someone lurking around the base and gave chase. They pinned him down at the northern perimeter, but the guy had a buddy working with him and started shooting our guys."

Stunned at the news, Cassie nodded. Another attack. Sal—Sal was in danger. Again. Of course he went after the intruder. He had warrior in his blood. Protector. When she'd first met him, first saw his thick biceps and quick smile, she'd been smitten. Until he told her he was Special Forces. They didn't just toe the line of danger—they crossed it and demanded it respond. Not because they were bloodthirsty but because they were sheepdogs.

"Okay. . .thanks." She had to see Sal. Had to verify with her own eyes that he wasn't hurt. "I–I'd better see how things are."

"You mean how Falcon is doing?" Brie had a knowing smile in her voice.

"He won't even talk to me."

"Give it time."

"Yeah." There wasn't enough time in the universe to change things between Sal and her. He'd made that perfectly clear. "Thanks, Brie. Bye." In a daze, she wandered back to her cubicle. She rounded the corner—and a blur of brown collided with her. "Oh, sorry. I didn't—"

Hands cupped her shoulders. Her gaze collided with warm brown eyes—eyes that more than once warmed Cassie to her toes.

"Sal."

Determination etched through his dark brows, he shifted her to the right and kept moving. Without a single word.

She watched as his broad shoulders receded down the hall. Hated herself for not ripping the bars from between them. Time to muster up. "How's Hawk?"

Sal paused and shifted toward her. "Recovering."

"And you?"

A ripple of confusion wormed through his dark brow. His stare rammed her pulse into a solid right cross against her breastbone. "Me? I'm fine."

Acute relief rushed over her shoulders like warm butter. "Good." Seconds thudded off the clock as he stood unmoving. *Say something!* "Oh, that AHOD—the one you told me about last night?—got canceled."

His expression flickered as his lips parted.

No, she wouldn't give him a chance to drive another dagger into her heart. "I just thought I'd mention it. In case you didn't know," she said, her voice unnaturally calm and soft. Deliberate. "I wouldn't want you to show up and look stupid when you find out there isn't one. That'd be cruel."

His expression went wonky-weird. Like he felt bad. Like he'd wanted to apologize. As they held each other's gazes, a smile worked its way up from her heart to her lips.

He turned and left.

So did her smile. "Right. Give it time," Cassie whispered, repeating Brie's admonishment. If they couldn't withstand a two-minute conversation, they'd never be able to talk through real problems. The ones that kept them bound in tight boxes of hatred and resentment.

Back at her desk, she pushed her mind into work. Into figuring out what was going on with the entirely-too-accurate attacks. When she'd had lunch with Kiew, a revelation coursed through her. But she needed to be sure.

Cassie powered up her agency-issued laptop and coded in. She scanned the documents. Spent hours poring over them. Verifying information. As she stared at the Venn diagram she'd scrawled across three taped-together pieces of paper, the wretched truth stared back, mocking. They are using me!

How could I have been so stupid? She shoved her hands through her hair and gripped her head. History had a way of repeating itself, especially bad history, no matter how hard she tried to change its course.

The agency knew she'd stayed with Kiew Tang in China a decade ago on a high school exchange program. They knew they had been fast friends, and they were using her to get to Kiew. They expected her to betray her friend.

Ripping up the pages, she made her way to the shredder. No satisfaction came in watching the blades shred the paper. They couldn't shred the truth. But there was some psychological satisfaction in watching the machine eat the painful facts. Her realization called everything into question, right down to her very worth. She'd wanted to believe this assignment had been given to her on merit. On her success with other missions. But it wasn't. Things were clear to her now. The timeliness too convenient.

By the time lunch rolled around, the only appetite she had was one for physical activity. Frustration pushed her out of the chair. She headed over to the showers, changed into PT clothes, and worked out in the makeshift gym until her limbs ached like her insides. She had this glorious idea of how things would work here—she'd show her mettle and through it or in conjunction with that accomplishment, win back Sal. Live happily ever after.

Ha. Just call me Pinocchio. She'd lied to herself as much as apparently her superiors had.

After a shower, she donned her pants and tank top. She brushed out her hair then tied it back with an elastic and rolled it into a tight knot at the base of her neck. Adding deodorant, she mulled what she should do about the lies her handler had spun around her. Options were few: confront them. Play along. Ignore it.

She was too mad to play dumb, and she had too much invested in making a reputable name for herself. If only she could ask Burnett. He wasn't her CO, but he'd always shot straight. Given her the facts, whether she wanted them or not. He was about the only person she knew who would.

So they wanted to play with her life? Treat her like some dimwitted blond? Well, time to let them know she was on to them, wise to their scheming. And maybe, just maybe, she could turn this for her benefit. Yes—she was friends with Kiew. Yes, they had a connection. So her bosses wanted her snooping in Kiew's business. No doubt because of Daniel Jin. And though the U.S. government wanted to use their friendship for their means, Cassie had another plan. Help Kiew escape.

It would give Cassie a lot of joy to help her friend, whom she suspected was innocently involved with the wrong man, but also on the receiving end of his anger and fists. Cassie had seen her own mom take more than her hits from losers. She wasn't going to watch a woman she once considered closer than a sister suffer that horrible fall into victimhood. Kiew was too strong. Too smart.

It just didn't make sense. What had happened in the seven years since they'd seen each other to make Kiew so subservient? What was she doing with Daniel Jin anyway? Maybe it was his power. Weren't Chinese girls pretty much auctioned off at the whim of their fathers? Mrs. Tang had always pushed Kiew toward the sons of the rich and powerful. Was this what was happening with her and Daniel Jin?

What if Cassie failed—then Daniel Jin would be ten times worse the abuser. She stuffed her feet in her boots and laced them up. When she straightened, Cassie felt a warning prickle her neck—someone was watching! She lifted her shirt from the locker and slid her arms through it, glancing around.

Brown eyes collided with hers. Sal stood on the other side of the showers, staring at her. His head cocked to the side. Brow knotted.

Cassie slid her shirt over her tank. "Something wrong?"

He scratched his thick black beard—she still wasn't used to that thing—then swung around and left.

What was that about? She added a light touch of makeup while at the mirror. Then her reflection screamed back at her. Not just her reflection, but the one in the other mirror that exposed her shoulder tattoo.

Oh no. . .

Sal would've had a perfect angle to see the heart-shaped tattoo with Mila's name in it. Dread spilled through her stomach. She was being careless and that could open the box of secrets too-many years in the making.

But right now, she had bigger fish to fry. And Sal. . .he hated her too much to even consider the possibilities.

Back at her desk, Cassie grabbed her phone and headed for the bathroom. Concealed in a stall, she coded in. Demanded a meeting.

Not possible.

Frustration tightened her muscles. The response even seemed to speak the truth—she'd been used. If they could play this game, so could she.

Now or I'm done, she texted back, her fingers nearly pushing the keys through the phone.

The phone rang.

Her heart thudded as she answered and pressed the device to her ear. "Hello."

"I think we need to establish some rules, Walker. You work for us. We don't work for you."

Hearing his flat, curt tone chased away her courage. What if she was wrong? They'd fry her and her career. She couldn't let that happen. No way would she be like her mom, working at Pick N Pack and the Bueno Nacho just to pay the bills and put food on the table for her kids.

"I thought something was urgent. You were ready to quit," his voice jogged Cassie out of her thoughts.

"What do you know about the asset?" It was the closest she could come to the mention of Kiew without divulging her suspicions.

Hesitation thickened the line. "I gave you the information on her."

Yes, they had. They'd provided a dossier that included Kiew's birthplace, family, violin training, university years, and degree path. But why didn't they mention Cassie living with the Tangs for almost a year? They would've known, right? If they had all this other information on her, and the records existed that Cassie had lived there, why hadn't that been brought up?

"Just seemed to be missing. . .things."

"Your voice is stressed, Cassandra. Would you like to explain why?"

Right. Of course. Stress-analyzing phone calls. Using her first name in a condescending tone. She shouldn't be surprised. This type of invasive monitoring and psychological conditioning had been SOP for the last year. "I just want to make sure I have all the facts."

"You have what you need to complete your assignment."

The line went dead, and so did her hope of a legitimate mission. One rightly earned. Cassie sat down, contemplating the meaning. The implications. They were using her to get to Kiew. Using a decade-old friendship.

I'm nothing more than a means to an end. They wanted to get to Kiew. That's what all this was about. The cushy—in terms of notoriety and level—assignment with top-tier brass and soldiers, in the thick of one of the deadliest attacks. They'd pulled her from analyzing phone records and digging through endless waste piles of computer traffic. . .

Why hadn't they just come clean and told her?

Because they knew I'd say no.

They were right, too. She'd never violate her friendship.

Her phone vibrated. She glanced at the screen and saw a text message: Focus on your assignment. And be careful where you step. Wouldn't want you to get hurt.

CHAPTER 15

Kandahar Airfield, Afghanistan
31 March—0945 Hours

Sleep pulled on his limbs. Pushed his eyelids. Burned his eyes. Plucked a yawn from him. The powerful enemy of vigilance warred against Sal's effort as he sat in the metal folding chair, fighting off the sandman. The world faded to black—and Sal jerked straight.

Yawned and punched to his feet. Paced in front of the cell holding the prisoner he'd shot off the fence. Stifling another jaw-stretching, eye-blurring yawn, he shook his head.

"You been here all night?"

Sal pivoted toward the voice he knew well. "Wasn't going to let anything happen to him."

"DIA let you stay while they questioned him?"

"Didn't really give them an option."

"Good." Dean nodded as he looked into the cell where the prisoner, stripped of pants and sporting bandages on both legs, lay on his side, facing the wall and supposedly asleep. "Doubt he'd get far with those injuries."

"Hey, I let the doc clean the wounds."

"Did he tell DIA anything?"

"Nothing. Not to our analysts, not to the 'terp."

Dean studied their prisoner. "If he won't talk, what do we do?"

"Let him go." Sal had worked through the scenario all night long.

Scowling, Dean said nothing but shot a questioning look to Sal, who eased closer. Leaned in toward Dean's ear. That prisoner might not have answered questions, but that was no guarantee he couldn't speak English.

"Let him go and follow him," Sal whispered.

Gaze back on the prisoner, Dean's expression waxed thoughtful. "Get you and Knight outside the wire in a native vehicle..." He nodded as he spoke.

"Have the doc change his bandage again and put the tag there. Tell him he's being let go because we treated him so bad." Anticipation of the hunt thrummed through Sal. "We follow him, find out who he contacts or who contacts him."

"You could end up waiting a long time. Remember—they have time on their side. We don't. We can't afford to just sit around with our thumbs stuck—"

"And we can't afford to take the risk that this guy"—Sal stabbed a finger toward the cell—"vanishes or ends up missing a few quarts of blood."

"And if they catch you?"

Sal shrugged. "I become God's messenger, delivering them to their virgins a little ahead of schedule."

"This sounds a lot like a death wish. Is that what this is about, Sal?"

Stepping back, he frowned at Dean. The one man he considered his closest friend. How could he think that? "This is about me sick and tired of them being a step ahead of us. I'm ready to turn the tables. Get in their faces. Shove some trouble up their—"

"What's going on here?"

Sal jerked around, ready to unleash on the intruder, when he made eye contact with General Ramsey. "Sir." He pulled up straight and took a step back from Dean.

"I hope you weren't giving Captain Watters any trouble, soldier."

"No, sir."

"That looked like a mighty intense conversation, Russo."

"Discussing the future of this prisoner."

"And disagreeing?"

"No, sir." At least not about the prisoner.

Ramsey motioned to the guard. "Unlock this door."

Sal looked to the cell, to Dean, then back to the general. "Sir?"

"I have experts coming in to talk to him."

"Experts in what?"

Ramsey glowered. "Are you questioning me, son?"

Whoa. Sal hesitated, surprised at the venom dripping off the general's words. "No, sir. I—"

"What do you hope to find out, sir?" Dean stepped into the thick tension that had erupted out of nowhere.

Ramsey gave him a stern look. "Same thing you want—answers."

Wow, that was the opposite of enlightening. Sal scratched his beard. "If you don't mind, sir, we'd like to stick around."

"What for?"

Dean squared his shoulders. "We already lost one possible witness to the CECOM attack. This man was caught with a military-issued weapon and ammo. I'd like to know where that came from, and if he gives any intel, I'd like to hear it firsthand and immediately rather than in a report two days later." He indicated with his head toward the soldier. "They're messing with a lot of intel. What if they get private, personal data on the teams, on the personnel in the area?"

"What are you saying?" Ramsey frowned.

"I'm saying personnel data would include private information—addresses, next of kin. . ."

"You're thinking they'll go after your families?"

"Yours, too, sir. It's a possibility." Dean shrugged. "I'd like to make sure that doesn't happen."

"Wouldn't we all?" The voice that boomed down the hall belonged to none other than Lieutenant Commander Riordan, who had two SEALs flanking him. He strode toward them and threw a cocky grin at Sal. "What are you growing in that rat's nest you call a beard?"

"Something you wouldn't know anything about—manhood," Sal shot back.

Riordan laughed then slapped Sal's shoulder. "Challenge accepted, Black Beard." He nodded to the prisoner. "Good job chasing him down."

Surprise held Sal's response hostage. The guy was telling him he did a good job? Since when?

"Now, let the *real* men work." Riordan delivered the slam.

"Down, boys." Ramsey chuckled. "Look, none of you need to be here. We have professional interviewers coming to talk to him."

Professional interviewers. The same thing had happened to the first prisoner. He'd been a professional all right. A professional assassin. There was no way Sal would walk out of here, not now. Walking out of here meant this prisoner could end up six feet under just like the previous one. He shot a look to Dean, who bore a similar expression.

"Sir," Dean said. "DIA already tried without success. The prisoner wouldn't talk."

"I'm sorry, did I give you the impression this was up for discussion, Captain?" Ramsey's dimpled face resembled hacked-up granite, and it'd gone stone cold with his words. "When my team gets here, I want you all to clear out."

Something was wrong. *This* was wrong. And Sal would be buggered if he would let someone walk in and slice this man's throat. If that spook got back on base and killed another asset in stopping this attack. . .

Grinding his teeth, Sal waited for Dean to object. Call the general on this stupidity. But Dean didn't do anything. He nodded. Caved. Futility coated Sal's muscles with adrenaline and a need to punch some lights out.

"Sir, I need to talk with you about contingencies for a mission," Dean said, swiftly changing tracks.

Unbelievable. Where was his sense of honor? Duty? His. . . Something in Dean's eyes stilled the anger swelling through Sal. But the captain didn't argue or stop Ramsey.

"Remember, clear out and let the team do their work." Ramsey's thick fingers wagged in Sal's face. "Clear, son?"

"Sir."

Sal flared his nostrils. Balled his fists. Told himself to wait. To not lose it. Fire spiraled through his veins as Dean walked behind the general, following.

You sorry—

As Dean walked past him, he turned his face into Sal's and breathed the words, *"Do it."*

---—ᴍ—---

Kandahar Airfield, Afghanistan
31 March—1320 Hours

Uncertainty flooded Cassie as she stared at her monitor. She wasn't uncertain about being used. Her handler's cryptic response to her questions left no doubt that they were using her. But with that knowledge came a flood of awareness that she might not be cut out for this. She might be in over her head. Right now, she couldn't even get Sal to talk to her.

But Kiew. . .she remained tight-lipped because Daniel Jin was around. And if he caught wind of Cassie's probing, Kiew could end up dead. No doubt that man would go to such extremes to protect his interests. He'd already shown his willingness to beat Kiew. Killing her was only a more *extreme* version.

She'd have to be careful. Execute the plan to save Kiew while Daniel wasn't around to stop it. So, first things first—discover Daniel Jin's whereabouts and planned trips to target the right time.

To shield her location and identity, Cassie used a ghost program to show a million different IP addresses. Her fingers flew over the keyboard as she worked to figure out Jin's travel plans. A few technology conferences listed him as a guest speaker, but they were months out. She needed more immediate dates and times.

With her secure sat phone that would also ghost her location, Cassie punched in the numbers and waited.

"Takkar Corp.," a woman answered in several Arabic languages then English. "How may I direct your call?"

"Daniel Jin's office please."

"I'm sorry, who?"

Cassie cleared her throat. Tried his other name. "Meng-Li Jin, please."

"One moment." A few seconds later another voice carried through the line. "Meng-Li Holdings."

Interesting. His own company within Takkar's. Cassie put her covert skills to work. "Yes, my employer is supposed to be doing remodeling in the building, and I've been informed that Mr. Meng-Li does not appreciate loud noises."

"Yes—"

"So, if you could let me know—"

"It is no problem. Mr. Meng-Li will be out of the country for the next ten days."

Air whooshed from Cassie's lungs. "Oh, that is good news." And much easier than she'd expected. "My boss will be so glad. Thank you." She hung up before a trace could be activated or she accidentally revealed her hand.

So, he'd be gone long enough for her to put together a plan to rescue Kiew. Now she had to find a way to get there, recover her, and get out. Alive.

If she could somehow convince Raptor to help. . .

She laughed. Like that would ever happen with Sal as team leader. But Raptor wanted Daniel Jin. And Hawk had said Kiew held a gun to his head—something Cassie struggled to believe. Maybe if she presented an opportunity for them to capture her. . .but have an asset in place to grab Kiew first.

Risky business, Cass.

First step: Think up an explanation for Raptor. For Sal, because he'd see through her like Saran wrap. Okay. Well. . .well. . .

Her desk phone rang. She grabbed the handset and answered. "Lieutenant Walker."

"*What* do you think you are doing?"

The icy tone froze Cassie but more so the voice it belonged to. "Kiew?"

"Are you so foolish you don't think he monitors all calls?"

"I—"

"Why do you want to know when he will be here?"

"I don't." *I want to know when he'll be gone actually.*

"You may think you are the smart one, Cassandra, working for the military intelligence division, but do not think so little of me to believe your lies."

Wow, Kiew was competing with Elsa from *Frozen* this time. "I don't understand."

"That is more than clear. Stay out of it. Stay away."

"Not if he's hurting you." Her heart pounded, remembering the marks. The timid actions of her friend. Classic abuse signs. "I won't let that alone. I care too much about you."

"You do not even know me," Kiew said, her words thick with chilled venom. "I will not warn you again. And your soldier friend can tell you what I'm capable of, I believe."

Accosted by the animosity, Cassie stared blankly. "You're threatening me? I just want to help."

The line went dead. Cassie let out the breath she hadn't realized she was holding. After a disbelieving glance at the phone, she returned it to the cradle. Quickly, she mentally catalogued the words, the inflections to include in her report to her handler.

Who'd be ticked as all get-out about this development.

Kiew was giving her a kick to the curb. Cutting her off. "She *threatened* me," she whispered around a weak laugh. Was it real? Was her warning about taking care of Cassie real?

What else could it be?

I got too close to the truth.

Why else would Kiew threaten her like that? Resolution carved a hard line through her soul. She had to do this—had to get her out of there. Of course, she couldn't do it by herself. If Kiew was in such danger that she resorted to scare tactics, Cassie would need an army to help get Kiew out alive. She had to convince someone.

Gearney. She should ask her handler for help in formulating a plan. Cassie grabbed her satellite phone, punching the code even as she hurried outside.

"What?" Irritation weighted the single word.

"I talked with Kiew Tang."

"And?" Not quite so much irritation. Maybe even a little respect.

Ha. Right. Keep dreaming.

"She promised bodily harm if I didn't stay away."

"That's a problem, Walker."

"It is, because it means I got close to the truth."

"Or too far from it. You need to pull out. It's too dangerous. If you push her, she might kill you."

"No, I don't believe that. I think she was concerned for me."

"Which leads to the supposition that Daniel Jin is aware of your presence in her life."

"Of course he's aware. I don't think that man misses anything. But Kiew's voice held fear, not the warning she threw at me. She's afraid. He's beating her, Gearney."

"Names!"

Cassie cringed at her mistake. "I want to get her out. But she won't walk out of there with just me. I believe Daniel has her afraid for her life. If I go in there with a show of force, I believe she'll come with me."

"Raptor is not going to help you rescue an abuse victim. And I'm certainly not going to authorize that or help."

"But what about securing a national asset? You've seen her college education and what she's capable of."

His silence screamed a small victory.

"She's a brilliant forensic computer scientist, and she's been right there with Daniel. She knows what he's doing. She can"—might need to leave out the *probably* for assurance—"help us take him down, but she has too much to lose doing it from the inside."

A heavy sigh was his answer.

Cassie fisted a hand, knowing she'd hooked him. "I just have to know how to get Raptor onboard."

"Have them think they're capturing her."

She blinked. "What?"

"Tell them what you know. Tell them you need to get her out."

"And then how am I supposed to get her out of their custody?"

"You won't. I'll have an asset waiting to take her to a safe house."

So. . .lie? Lie to Raptor team. Lie to Sal.

Again.

"I. . .I'm not sure that's—"

"Do it, Walker. That's an order."

"Sir, it will compromise me."

"You won't be there after it goes down. If we get Tang, your mission is over."

CHAPTER 16

Sal scurried up behind the guard and hooked his arm around the man's neck. He pulled him up, flexing his bicep and then adding pressure to the back of the guy's head until he went limp. He hoisted the man over his shoulder and hustled him into the supply closet. Back at the station, Sal lifted the keys and sprinted down the hall, gun aimed at the guard posted outside the cell.

He fired twice as the guard looked up. Alarm widened the guy's eyes and mouth as the two darts found their mark. His body went limp.

With a lunge, Sal caught the guard. Verifying the soldier hadn't gone into cardiac arrest and died, Sal pressed two fingers to his carotid and detected the steady thrum. "Sorry, man. Just doing my job."

He eased him to the dirt floor. At the steel-barred cell door, Sal quickly unlocked it and dragged the guard inside. He kept his head down, in case the monitors were live, though Harrier had promised to take care of it.

The prisoner lifted his head. Confusion wavered through the kid's expression.

"Don't talk and do as I say," Sal ordered in Farsi. "Understand?"

With a hesitant nod, the kid watched him. "Why are you—?"

"You speak English?"

A crimson stain bled through his face as he lowered his gaze a little.

What else did this guy know? "How old are you?" When the guy didn't look up, Sal shook his head. "Never min—"

"Eighteen," the kid said at the same time.

"Don't talk," Sal repeated as he knelt and unchained the prisoner.

English. The guy spoke English but never let on before.

"But why—why are you helping me?"

"You'll die if you stay here."

The kid looked at Sal. Intently. Eyes bright with understanding and a thick dose of confusion considered him. "Why do you care what happens to me?"

"Quiet!" He hooked an arm through the kid's and hauled him to his feet. "Can you walk?"

The kid nodded but tripped as he came upright. "Sorry," he muttered.

Sal made it to the door and pushed the kid back as he peeked out, hand on his weapon. "Okay. Stay close. Got it?"

Again the kid nodded. "He will kill you if he finds out—"

Sal yanked the kid's shirt. "Run!" He kept a fist hold of the material as they darted down the hall and out the rear door to a waiting rusted-out Jeep. Sal thrust him toward it. "In. Now!"

The man stumbled but grabbed the door handle and pulled himself inside. Sal leapt around to the other side and dove in. Cranked the engine. Gunned it. "Don't say anything. I talk for you. If they ask—you don't speak English. Got it?" Sal shouted, the wind ripping at them as he barreled toward the gate.

"It won't work."

"Got it?" Sal shouted louder.

The kid nodded.

But even as they revved northward, Sal noted the MPs jogging to the gate with their weapons. Crap!

He nailed the brakes. Slammed it into REVERSE.

"No," the kid said, touching Sal's shoulder. "He won't let me leave. I know this."

What in blazes? "No way." Not only had Sal committed to this mission by walking into the holding area, but he'd committed the prisoner's life as well.

"Even if we leave, he will kill me." Though the kid was only eighteen, he had a maturity of forty. Brown eyes bright with conviction, he fisted a hand on Sal's tactical sleeve. "Listen. Takkar Towers—you know it?"

A crazy sickening dread erupted in Sal's gut.

"The towers. Tallest buildings in Kabul." He shook Sal. "You know it?"

MPs shouted as they ran behind them. Military police vehicles pealed away from the gate, giving pursuit. He'd have a heck of a time explaining this—

Again, the kid shook him. "You know it?"

"The towers—yeah. Why?"

"There is a planter out front," the kid shouted over the roar of the engine. "To the right of the fountain. A stone is loose. You will find a book there."

"What the—?"

"It will tell you what you need to know."

"To what?"

A vehicle shot out from between two buildings. Right into his path. Sal yanked the wheel hard to avoid a collision. The Jeep tipped. Sal tried to correct. The vehicle whipped left. Lifted into the air.

Sal braced himself as the Jeep flipped. His head rammed into the door. Then the roof. He bit down on his tongue. Tasted a wash of warmth. Something hit him from the side. The vehicle flipped again.

When the world stopped smearing in myriad colors and sounds, Sal found himself bent in half, his backside almost through the windshield. He extricated himself, his mind buzzing. His vision blurry.

A large form filled the windshield with blood and broken glass. The kid!

Sal lurched toward the guy. "Hey! You okay?"

A meaty groan answered as he drew the guy free. Blood gushed down the side of the man's face, pooling in the hollow of his throat. "Easy, easy."

Eyes rolling, the kid struggled to stay alert. "You must. . ." A gurgling sound rumbled through his chest. He coughed. Blood dribbled out of his mouth and down his chin. "Stop. . .him." His hand slapped at Sal. "Book. . .find. . ."

"Hey, hey, stay with me, kid!"

His brown eyes went wild. "Gun. Give me your. . .gun."

Sal frowned.

The kid flapped his hand toward the holstered weapon. Groped at it. Did he want to kill himself?

"Please. . ." He tugged on it.

"Hey—"

The weapon came free. The kid tightened his grip.

"Hey!" Sal's heart thudded. "Don't—"

"Put it down, put it down!" three MPs shouted, aiming their weapons at the kid.

Sal's heart rapid-fired as the scene coalesced in his mind, what the boy intended. What the MPs intended. "No! Don't shoot." He thrust a hand toward the MPs. "He's—"

Thunk.

The weapon dropped against the door, surprisingly loud amid the chaos and shouting. The kid's hand flopped. His body sagged. Sal lunged for him. Checked his pulse. "No!"

"Sir, you okay?" An MP bent into the overturned Jeep.

This kid could not die. Their only possible break in this insanity where the enemy had been one step ahead—heck, he'd been a mile ahead of them and concealed in a dusty cloud of mystery. "Yeah—help me with him. He needs a doctor!"

"They'll take care of him, sir. Let's make sure you're okay." The MP assisted Sal out of the Jeep. "Pretty mean cut on your temple. You feeling it?"

Sal's hand went to the sticky spot. "Yeah. . ." Add it to the concussion-inducing headache. He watched two other MPs haul the kid onto the ground. They laid him out and checked his pulse and began CPR.

Crap. This could not happen. He'd be blamed. Get cut from Raptor. And he didn't care about that. This meant the truth died with the kid. Roughing his hands over his face, Sal bit back the frustration and a curse.

"Got a pulse!" No sooner had the words been said than the boy was being rushed to the hospital.

"Did he hurt you, sir, taking you hostage like that?"

Sal couldn't pry his gaze or thoughts away. Hostage? He finally dragged his attention to the MP. His ears rang with the word. The kid. . .the kid faked his aggression with the weapon. Why?

"He won't let me leave. I know this." Who was the kid talking about?

"Yeah—he had a gun on you. In fact, looked like your own weapon."

"It was." And in taking the weapon, the kid had absolved Sal of any responsibility—at least in appearances.

Why? Why would he do that?

The book. *"It will tell you what you need to know."*

—∞—

Shanghai, China
1 April—0925 Hours

Crossing his penthouse, Meng-Li Jin shed his silk jacket as easily as he did the Americanized form of his name. The fine apparel he could appreciate and savor the experience of wearing. But the name? Infuriating and humiliating.

A man exited the rear of the penthouse, leaving the private residence apartment. He had a black briefcase and a condescending expression. Behind him waddled the fat nurse he'd hired to tend to his mother.

Mother!

"What are you doing here?" Jin demanded.

"I am Dr. Li—"

"I did not ask your name," he hissed at the doctor. "I asked what you are doing here?"

"Please, Mr. Meng-Li," the nurse said, waddling forward. "I called him. Your mother is not well."

"I know she is not well." He shot fiery daggers at her with his eyes. "That is why I hired you!"

"Forgive me, but your mother needed a doctor. She needed more than I could do."

"Then *what* use are you? Get out!" Jin cursed himself for not having Kiew with him. He needed her, needed her calming touch.

"Sir," Dr. Liang said quietly. "Mrs. Chen is a fine nurse, but she is right. Your mother needed to be seen by a doctor. I was happy to come—at no charge, of course—to see to your mother's needs. Your father and

I were friends long ago, and it is an honor to help your family. I've prescribed stronger pain medication, and now, your mother is resting comfortably." Then his round, muddy eyes pinched together. "But I will not lie, Jin. She is not well. Her time is short. I would advise you to prepare—"

"I do not need your pity, Doctor." Jin's heart rate doubled. "Thank you for your help. Cao will see you out."

Though Jin stared down the long, gilt hall to his mother's quarters, in his periphery he saw the servant silently materialize from the side room without a word. Dr. Liang inclined his head and started for the door.

Nurse Cheng leaned forward. "I—"

"Leave us," he said as he entered his mother's room. Closed the door and stood, taking in the setting. The stench of death, a stale mixture of oxygen, antiseptic, and . . . some other odor he could not isolate.

Draped in the dim, golden light of the lamps on either side of the bed, the room lay in somber repose. As if it, too, anticipated her death. But no—he would not surrender her yet. She must stay. He went to her, brushing aside the curtain.

Frail and small in the oversized bed, she lay unmoving. Barely breathing. Coarse hair washed free of its once-luxurious ebony color and silken feel lay in a halo around her pale face. So much paler than normal.

His gaze fell on the photo framed on the nightstand of her and his father in their youth. Before Jin had been born. When dreams were simmering and hopes were high. When grief had not touched his father's dynasty. Or gouged a hollow line through his mother's heart. When they were young and believed in the goodness of others, in the brightness of their future.

If only they had known what darkness awaited. Would they have still journeyed so bravely? Could he ever rise to meet their legacy and create one of his own?

He would. He had. And though some stood in his path, he would level that opposition. His father's dreams would become reality. His mother would be honored.

He leaned against the plush mattress. *"Māma."*

"Jin," she wheezed out, her eyes fluttering but not fully opening.

"Here." He cupped her parchment-like hands and pressed his lips to their feather-softness. "I am here."

A whisper of a smile flitted across her lips as another wheeze dragged breath from her lungs. She went deathly still.

"Stay, Mother." He glanced at her chest, searching for the sign that she was yet alive. "Don't leave yet. It is almost done. Just a little longer, and it will be real. Father's dream. Your dream. It will be real. I'm making it happen. You will see. And be proud."

"Proud," she moaned. Swiped her tongue over her lips, the sound like sandpaper. "Yes." Her fingers twitched in his, and though her chest continued to rise and fall, she was no longer alert.

"I promise, Māma."

His phone buzzed against his hip, and he silently cursed the device and whoever interrupted these precious moments. The incessant vibration did not ease up.

Grinding his teeth, he laid her hand across her stomach. Then bent over and pressed a kiss to her cheek, before turning and making his way to the window. He did not want to leave. Did not want to allow the intrusion of servants and anyone else into his mind right now. Did not want to take this phone call. But as the light glared bright in the somber room, he registered the name.

He pushed open the glass french doors and stepped onto the balcony as he accepted the call. "Has she made any calls?"

"Yes. One. To the American soldier as you said she would."

The knot in Jin's chest tightened as the lights of Shanghai twinkled at him in the haze of the gloomy night. Wind tugged at his shirt and hair, taunting him. Mocking him. "And what did she say?"

"She told her to leave her alone."

The knot loosened. He allowed himself to breathe. The cool rail beneath his palm soothed the heat that had moments earlier exploded through him. "What else?" Could it be that she was faithful after all? That her heart had not been corrupted? He wanted her, for himself. Completely. He must know her loyalties were not divided.

"Nothing. She hung up when the American tried to dissuade her."

Triumph lifted Jin's chin. He looked over the city he ruled, over the lives and empires he had toppled and owned "Good. Watch her. If she does anything that would make you question her loyalty, contact me immediately. I want to know everything."

"Yes, sir."

"And Nianzu."

"Yes?"

"If that American whore shows up again, kill her."

CHAPTER 17

Kabul, Afghanistan
1 April—0825 Hours

Letting go had never been her forte. That would be why Cassie left Kandahar Airfield bright and early. Too many hours spent regretting her mother's lack of action pushed her into the government vehicle and onto the hours-long trip to Kabul. More specifically, to Takkar Towers.

She would hear from Kiew's own lips and look into her eyes before believing her friend wanted her out of the picture. Before turning her back and a few days later hearing of Kiew's mysterious death.

Okay, that might be the result of an overactive imagination, but then again, wasn't real life more unbelievable than fiction?

Cassie parked in the garage, a three-level structure crammed into the heart of the city, a cement giant towering over crumbling plaster buildings and dirty streets. Even Takkar Towers struck a dichotomous pose with its gleaming metal and glass over the smudged cityscape.

She tugged back the glass door to the building, noting the thickness and wondering if it was bulletproof. In a land plagued with violence and terrorism, it'd make sense for Takkar to take measures to protect his investment and property. Though guards were posted on the lower level, they were discreet. Not so much that they blended into the marble walls. They made their presence known. Allowed the guests to feel another measure of safety to conduct business. For Cassie, it meant another layer of security she must bypass.

She stepped into the elevator and pressed the fifth-floor button. Her pulse thrummed against her breast as the door closed and the steel contraption lifted. What would wait for her once the doors slid back—a terse dismissal or a relieved friend? Surely Kiew would see that Cassie could bring her into protection. It'd be so much better if she could walk out of here with her friend and return to Kandahar. Then, no involving Sal. No lying to Sal. And she could prove to her superiors that the task they'd assigned her—not on merit, she understood now, but on her connection to this woman—had not been a mistake.

She hadn't been to the offices before. Nor to Kiew's private residence, which intel showed to be in this building as well.

The elevator alighted. Swift and silent, the doors eased open. Cassie immediately pegged the three cameras eyeballing the reception area.

Distinctly Asian in style, the foyer held a fountain wall that broke the view of the rest of the offices. A sleek onyx desk with a high facade protected the petite Chinese woman seated and talking into a headset. Had she worn the white paint and defined red lips, she would not have looked more geisha. Except for the severe expression.

Once the receptionist raised her narrow eyes, Cassie angled her walk so she deftly avoided being captured on the cameras. "I'm here to see Ms. Tang."

"Do you have appointment?"

With a nod toward the phone, Cassie ignored the question. Pretended to answer it without answering. "Cassandra Walker," she said, eyeing the gray handset. "Tell her I'm here."

Huffing, the woman's manicured fingernails clicked on the keypad, though she hadn't removed her glare from Cassie. "A Cassandra Walker to s—" She flinched. Nodded but said nothing, her gaze now distant. "Of course."

Anticipating an affirmative response, Cassie stayed poised. Watched the woman's round face. But she never looked at Cassie again. Didn't move. She answered another call.

Rude. Just rude.

A door clicked open behind Cassie, and she turned.

Two men in black suits stalked toward her, expressions taut. One had slicked-back hair and stood an inch or two taller than his compatriot. "If you will follow us, please, Ms. Walker."

Hesitation gripped Cassie tight. "I'm here to see Ms. Tang."

Both men cuffed her upper arms in steel-like holds and guided her—quite forcefully—toward a side door.

"Hey!" Cassie's pulse thundered. She knew evasive tactics. A knife-hand strike to the throat would put these guys on their knees. But were they hauling her to a dungeon? Escorting her to Kiew? Or throwing her out on her backside? "Release me!"

"You must leave," the shorter one said around a thickly accented voice.

After jerking free, Cassie tugged her shirt straight and squared her shoulders. "I'm here to see—"

"Nobody here will see you," Slick Hair bit out as he crowded her into a stairwell. "I believe you were given that message already."

Cassie felt the cold threat run down her spine. She lifted her chin. "I will leave on my own, thank you."

"We will assure your safe exit from the building."

I just bet you will.

But she held up a hand. "I am an officer in the United States Army. I will not be treated like a prisoner by a Chinese national." She gave a nod. "Thank you for your time and courtesy, gentlemen."

Cassie took the stairs quickly down the five flights, her calves aching with adrenaline and the quick workout. She reached the first floor and slipped into the lobby, not surprised to find two more security guards within a half-dozen feet, hands on weapons, eyes alert—and staring right at her. With a sigh, Cassie hoisted her shoulder and chin then proceeded toward the front.

Sun glinted off the glass as she pushed through the doors, blinding her for a second. Cassie pivoted and headed toward the garage. Her shoes clacked with an annoying echo in the cement structure as she hurried to her car. Awareness of something. . .off. . .tickled the back of her neck. She glanced over her shoulder.

A dark blur rushed her.

Slammed her into the car. Grabbed a fistful of hair at the back of her head and rammed her face into the side of the vehicle.

Pain exploded across her temple. Her vision danced. Though panic drenched her muscles, Cassie knew this was life or death. If she went weak, she'd die. Fighting fear, she reminded herself she was trained for this. Trained to defend. Trained to kill.

She fisted her hand and plowed her elbow into the man's abdomen. He grunted but remained powerful and strong. He threw her into the car again.

This time, his grip loosened a fraction.

Cassie seized the chance and bent, whirled down and under his arm, severing his hold. Again, she thrust her other elbow into his side, aiming for that sweet spot.

And missed.

She straightened and this time drove her elbow into his face.

He angled away, giving her the opportunity to sweep his feet out from under him.

But fast as lightning, he flipped her. She landed hard on her back, her head smacking and bouncing against the cement. Stars sprinkled her vision. She blinked and found him lunging at her—with a knife!

Even as the blade came near, her hands went up. With one she nailed his wrist. With the other, she slapped the blade. It tumbled to the ground and clattered away. The stealth of the move startled—and angered—her Asian attacker.

He narrowed his eyes, determination glinting. Almost as if he'd expected her to steal his weapon, he lunged seamlessly and tightened both hands around her neck.

Air deprivation seized her with panic. She didn't want to die. She choked, the crushing force against her esophagus thumping against her temples.

Knife!

Cassie raised her right arm and swung it up and over his arms. Simultaneously, she rolled to the side, deliberately upending him. Breaking his grip on her throat. He collapsed on her, punching her face. She used a leg as an anchor and twisted, effectively reversing their positions. With a hard right, she broke his nose. Repeated. Blood spurted.

With a hard punch, he sent her spiraling backward. Her head connected again with the car.

He loomed over her.

A gun fired.

Cassie sucked in a breath. Expecting to feel her life bleeding out of her. Instead the attacker stumbled. Glanced to the side, then sprinted away. Footsteps pounded after him then slowed.

Peeling herself off the ground, Cassie squinted up at the intruder.

The man's shoes scritched as he turned to her. "What in blazes are you doing here?"

—m—

"Now, Candyman."

On a knee, Sal bent over the flower bed, his gaze skimming the small plaza in front of the two high-rises. The blue jumpsuit felt strangely baggy since he was more accustomed to his tactical gear and having a vest and weapons strapped to his person.

He squinted across the street from Takkar Towers to where Eagle and Harrier sat in a car, guiding what should be a simple mission.

Sal pushed up and lifted his bucket as he made his way north, toward the fountain. Another dozen feet. But there was a lot of firepower on the other side of that glass. And some out here.

He went to a knee again, plucked some leaves and dead grass from the flower bed—which really wasn't a flower bed. At least not what they had back home with mounds of lush mulch and a million different flowers. Things were drier here. Not as much expense dedicated to trivial things as flowers. Yet, thankfully, Takkar had a welcome area that included enough of a garden to provide Sal this quiet insertion.

"Any day now, Candyman," Sal muttered as he once again stood. He lifted trash from the ground and veered left. The stone lip of the fountain shielded it from the small bed with flowering shrubs. He eyed the brick blocking it from the path. Traced it. Saw that one pushed up higher than the others. Quickly, he scanned the others to make sure this was the one.

"Eyes on target. Candyman—"

Shouts erupted. A small crack.

Bin in hand, Sal moved swiftly toward the shrub, his chin tucked but his gaze out, using his periphery to guide him to the bricked wall that was no more than a foot high. He knelt. Plucked a few leaves from the shrub. Let his arm lower to the brick as he watched a commotion inside the lobby. Guards were running. A crowd formed.

Brick scraped his knuckles as he dug his fingers in and pried it free. A guard floated toward the windows. Sal hurried, praying the guard wasn't focusing on him. They didn't need the attention. Didn't need more trouble.

"Falcon, you have trouble headed your way," Eagle voiced through the coms.

"I see him," Sal said, lowering his head slightly and reaching with his other hand to collect some trash. His fingers dug through the arid soil. Pushing. Prodding. Where was it?

"He's outside," Eagle said.

Sal gritted his teeth. Crammed his hand into the spot. Felt the rough edges of something. "Distract him," Sal hissed into his coms as he pushed harder. His fingers closed around the corner of the package. He tugged it free. Angled his shoulder to cover dropping the book into the bucket.

"You!"

Sal stood and turned his back. Started walking. Some sixth sense told him to hide the package. He lifted it from the bucket and tucked it into his jumpsuit.

A hand caught his shoulder turned him. "What are you doing?"

With a gasp, he leapt back and dropped the bucket, feigning shock. He let out a gargled cry as the dirt and flower bed litter danced over the clean plaza.

Gunfire cracked the relative quiet—another diversion by his Raptor teammates. A contingency for exactly what had just happened.

"Keep moving, Falcon," Eagle spoke quietly. "Veer around the east side of the building to avoid another guard."

Sal did as instructed, trusting his team implicitly. As the building's shadow fell on him, he heard voices. Urgent voices that slowed him. He glanced around a jutting section of the building. And froze.

A triangular indention and trees with waxy flowers almost hid her. But not quite. Cassie. Sal stopped, backtracked a half-dozen steps to hide behind another tree as he monitored the exchange.

Hands slicing the air, the man wasn't happy. Shoulders tight, he leaned into Cassie. Her brows were knitted and she scowled as she folded her arms over her chest.

He thrust a hand toward the street, as if telling her to leave.

Cassie held up a hand and made a jerking gesture.

An argument. They knew each other. Well enough for her to be at odds with him and still speak her mind. What was she even doing here?

"Falcon, why aren't you moving?"

Sal shifted back, trying to negotiate a better vantage point by which he could identify or at least see the man's face. No good. He'd have to be on top of these two to see. "Candyman?"

"Go ahead."

"You inside?"

"Roger."

"Can you see the eastern exit?"

"...negative."

Sal tightened his lips in frustration.

"Falcon, what's going on?"

These two had history or something. This wasn't a casual acquaintance. And for her to be here, at Takkar Towers, a place that all this trouble seemed to keep coming back to...

Since he couldn't see the guy, he'd have to force the two to expose themselves. He'd have to show his hand. Get Cassie to react.

Sal stepped from behind the tree. Too intent on her argument, she didn't notice him at first, so he took another step. Waited.

Cassie glanced over, and without looking away, she said something to the man.

Come on, turn around. Show your ugly mug. Why would Cassie be with someone here? Why were the two bent on concealing the man's identity?

The man navigated around her and entered the building. Sal broke eye contact to trail him, figure out where he was going. But the man immediately turned right, vanishing through another door. Obviously trying to hide his identity.

Sal slid his attention back to Cassie. Gave her a long look.

She said nothing. Simply wrapped her arms around her waist and started for the parking garage just beyond the spot where she'd stood.

"Falcon? You turn to a pillar of salt or something?"

"Pick me up. South side," he said as he hurried down the sidewalk. He didn't know what game she was playing, who she was messing around with—*is that what it was? An affair? Wouldn't be the first time.* But she *would* tell him.

Sal vowed to drag those secrets from her or ruin her permanently.

CHAPTER 18

Kandahar Airfield, Afghanistan
2 April—0840 Hours

Dean entered the Command building with Zahrah at his side. Dating six months and he couldn't remember a day without her. Didn't want to think of a day without her. "Just remember," he said, motioning for her to walk ahead since the corridor was narrow leading to the cubicles, "you're mine."

Zahrah turned, her smile warm and inviting. She wore the hijab still, out of respect for those she worked with and for. "Why? Are you expecting trouble?"

Dean slipped his arm around her waist and tugged her aside. He couldn't get enough of her. Couldn't see enough of her. "There are soldiers around here who haven't seen a pretty woman in ages." If he could just somehow memorize her features, her smile. He tried. Every chance he had. "Then you show up and they lose their good minds."

Her hands slid up his arms, sending a rush of heat through his body. "Is that what happens to you when I'm around?"

Dean kissed her, tasting her sweetness. Savoring the beauty she was, inside and out. "Every time."

Voices drew his attention to the cubicles. There, he spied Sal at his desk, hand over his bearded mouth as he stared at his computer. He looked ticked.

"What's wrong with Falcon?"

"When isn't something wrong?" Dean sighed. "C'mon. Let's see what he's got."

They made their way over to him.

Sal punched to his feet. Smiled and nodded at Zahrah. "Double Z, good to see you again."

"You okay?" Dean asked.

"Sure." Sal frowned. "Why?"

"You looked like you were ready to take someone's head off."

His friend's expression said "I am," but Sal shook his head. "Just...trying to figure this out." He lifted a small brown leather-bound journal. "Here."

Dean took it. Flipped through it, eyeing the Arabic script, angling so Zahrah could look at it with him. Having her close, safely nearby, gave him a sense of strength he couldn't understand. Just knew that he liked it. A lot. Liked her a lot. Scratch that. He *loved* her. More than anything else.

She leaned in, her body pressed against his arm as she studied the dirtied pages. Creamy olive complexion. Dark brown eyes. Pert nose. Calm, but fiery demeanor. "Can you read it?"

She scowled, meeting his gaze, and took the book from his hands. "Of course I can." Turning, she began muttering words in Arabic.

"English, please?" Dean said around a smile.

She arched her dark brow. "In a minute." That's when she moved to the printer and tugged a few sheets of paper from it. She lifted a pen from Sal's desk. "May I?" But Zahrah didn't wait for an answer.

Dean couldn't help but notice the way the other soldiers and personnel eyed her. Watched her. Especially that SEAL who had the same fire Hawk had. The one who'd sparred with Hawk. "Schmidt."

The guy jerked. "Yeah?"

Dean shot him a glare. "Get to work."

The SEAL grinned.

Yeah. Dean needed to marry her.

"You have a minute?" Sal asked quietly.

Dean hauled his mind back to the moment, away from Zahrah. "Sure."

Sal moved to a corner and shifted to face him. "I think I might know where our leaks are coming from."

Now his friend had his undivided attention. Dean planted his hands on his tac belt. "Go on."

"Mr. Russo," charged a crisp, clear female voice.

Dean glanced to the side where Lieutenant Walker strode across the room.

The fury emanating off Sal was so thick, Dean was sure he could touch it.

"Excuse me, sir," Walker said, acknowledging Dean as she turned to Sal. "May I talk to you?" She joined them, her expression as tight as that bun on the back of her head.

"I think you're already doing that." His tight words didn't have the sarcasm normally expected. And his hands were fisted. His lips taut.

"Privately." Lieutenant Walker swallowed hard. "Please."

Sal's nostrils flared before he gave Dean a nod then stalked from the room. When Walker didn't follow, Dean tilted his head toward her. "You're losing seconds, Walker." He bounced his eyebrows in the direction Sal had gone.

She opened her mouth. Shut it. Started forward. Stopped. "H–how do I get through to him?"

Pulled straight by her question, Dean couldn't stop the laugh that shot out of his trap. "Why would you ask me?"

"You're his friend. He respects you. Listens to you."

"Maybe that's it," Dean said. "Respect." But he didn't dare say any more. This felt like he'd stuck his boots in quicksand. "Excuse me."

—✺—

"Make it good or don't say anything."

The unusually warm spring had nothing on the heat in Sal's words or the fire in his eyes. "You should remember that I am your superior officer."

Sal's left check twitched.

And instantly Cassie regretted her words. She glanced away. "Look, I'm sorry. You don't make having a conversation easy."

"So it's my fault."

"Why does there need to be any blame? I want to talk to you."

"Then talk."

She used to love this about him—his intense, direct nature. But not tonight. Not anymore. Not when it had so much venom. "Will you ever—?"

"Start with the man. Who was he?"

Something in his tone drew her gaze up. He stood there, hands on his belt, expression daring her to tell him. "You do realize that in my position, in my job, there are things I cannot tell you."

"Why? Why can't you tell me who he was?"

Cassie tried to breathe, but his anger— "Will you ever listen to me again? Will you ever give me the benefit of the doubt, enough to hear me out?"

His dark eyes probed her. Searched her very soul. A piece of the jagged cliffs of his resentment broke away. "Probably not."

The well-placed dagger of his words seared straight through her. What she'd expected, she didn't know, but it wasn't that. "Sal—"

"No." His voice went dark. "Don't go there. Leave it alone."

"How can I when it's getting in the way of us doing our jobs?"

"I don't need you here to do my job. Leave. Let me get on with finishing this."

"I have information you might want."

Sal's jaw muscle jounced.

"I was at Takkar Towers because of Kiew Tang."

Though he'd tried to keep that rocklike expression in place, he slipped. "The woman who hit Hawk in the mountains?"

Cassie gave a slight nod. "It's my firm belief that she is not completely complicit with Daniel Jin's operations."

"Holding a gun to Hawk's head makes it 100 percent complicit in my book."

She couldn't argue that, though she wanted to defend her friend. "I can't explain fully what's going on, but I think he's got something over her. I believe he's beating her. That she's not acting on her own cognizance."

His cheek twitched again but he didn't speak. "How do you know?"

"I met her when I was in high school. Exchange program—I lived with her family."

Sal scowled. "You *lived* with her? That makes me question everything you say—how am I to know you're not compromised? And you weren't in the shadows with Jin's lover. You were in the shadows with a man.

Who was he? Your lover?"

Slice and dice, straight through her heart. Mean words spoken with such anger often meant the person was invested. The subject mattered. The thought hooked a line of hope through Cassie's chest. "I have been with no man since you, Tore."

Her words hit center mass. He flinched and drew up, his expression shifting from anger to surprise and back like colliding ice shelves. And in the seconds between his flickering emotions—ones she saw as plain as writing on paper, though someone not as intimately versed on this fierce warrior wouldn't see it—Cassie stepped into the sliver of an opening in his cracked armor.

"Sal, I was a stupid, self-absorbed girl who was madly in love with you. My actions were egregious. I was desperate and didn't want to lose you, so I—"

"Sent Vida to her death."

Cassie felt her chin trembling and fought to stop it. "I..." She wanted to make an excuse. Wanted to say she didn't really think anything would happen to Vida. But back then, she couldn't see beyond her blind rage and desperation to get Sal back. "There's not a day that goes by that I don't beg God to forgive me."

"So you *did* want her to die?" He was searching, digging, a strange pleading expression in his face, as if he didn't want it to be true.

"I wanted you back. That's all I could see, all I could think."

"Even though I hated and blamed you for killing her, there was a part of me that kept saying you didn't mean to kill her." His brow knotted. "But you did." His face twisted with grief. "You PCSed her, got her sent to Helmand to be sure she'd die."

"No! I moved her away, yes. But not to have her killed. You threw me aside like a rag when she entered that base. If you—"

Hands up, Sal backed away from her.

"Sal—I was twenty-one and—" She gulped the next word, terrified it'd come out.

"I thought I knew you, Cass. I thought I knew..." He shook his head.

Anguish churned through her, drowning in this guilt. Drowning in his loathing. She fought back. Felt the rage welling up. "And what about you, Sal? Were you so great? Cheating on her all those months? Sleeping with me while calling home each weekend?" Tears broke through.

"At least I did what was right in the end. I fixed my mistake."

"Mistake?" Her voice shrieked. Cassie couldn't see for the tears. "Is that what I was? What our—?"

"Walker. Falcon."

Sal turned toward the voice.

Cassie swiped the tears, turning away.

"Inside. All hands." It sounded like Captain Watters.

A shudder ripped through her as she heard boots thud and a door click shut. She covered her mouth, fighting back more tears. More grief that she'd almost let the horrible truth out of the bag. *I almost told him about Mila.* But she hadn't. That was good. If he couldn't talk to her civilly, he didn't deserve to know about her. He wouldn't infiltrate their lives and be a constant sore.

You have to tell him eventually.

Did she? Why?

Cassie couldn't think about this. The Army was embroiled in a bitter battle with a powerful enemy. She swiped the tears away and drew in a long, clean breath. Then spun around to head inside.

Icy dread spiraled through her veins as her gaze met Sal's. He hadn't left. That meant. . .

"Why did you name your sister's daughter Mila?"

Misery wrapped its cruel talons around Cassie's heart. A lie sat poised on her tongue, ready to lodge in the wall he'd erected between them. But she was tired of fighting. She felt a spurt of her own anger. She didn't have to answer. She didn't have to respond, not after the way he'd treated her, tossed her aside, and then acted as if she alone bore guilt in Vida's death.

But she couldn't take any more of this bone-draining fighting. "Because she's not her daughter." Breath shuddered through her again. "She's mine."

Sal frowned. Stepped closer, his breath hot against her cheek as he traced her face. Searching for the answer, no doubt. The answer to the question she could almost hear screaming through his brain. "Why did you give her that name? That was "

"Our name," Cassie said, daring him to take her meaning. It wasn't like they'd talked about having kids, but they both agreed during some silly conversation after meeting someone with an awful name they'd never do that. Somehow, they found common ground, which was easy back then, with the name Mila. He'd even given her a teddy bear and said her name was Mila.

His anger washed away. Confusion replaced it. Thick and vigorous. Questions danced in his eyes.

"When you cut me off, I had no way to contact you. How was I supposed to tell you, Tore?"

His gaze penetrated the only defense she had left. "What. . .what are you saying?"

"I tried to tell you. . ." Hot tears streaked down her cheek. "You made me the one thing I vowed I'd never be. The one thing I fought against being."

"Andra. . ," He breathed her name, conflict evident in his rugged Italian-Latino features. He shouldered in closer.

"A single mother."

CHAPTER 19

Kandahar Airfield, Afghanistan
2 April—0920 Hours

The earth shifted beneath his feet, her words ringing hollowly in his ears. Sal stumbled back, disbelieving. Unable to grab on to those words. How. . . ? Nausea churned through his gut. He'd rather sit in a gas chamber than feel what he felt right now. Than be hit with the sickening truth.

"You were *pregnant?*"

Cassie swallowed and looked away.

Limbs leaden, Sal couldn't move. "With my baby." The truth coalesced in his mind. Became something of substance he had to get his head around. "Mila." He turned away. "And you never told me."

"You wouldn't let me tell you."

Sal spun back to her. "Wouldn't—"

She held up her hand, nodding. "I should've found a way. But you devastated me. I was wrong, Sal. I kept her from you and for a time, I took pleasure in the fact you'd never know how amazing she was—so bright and funny. Such a character. For the first couple of years, I saw her as something you'd never have, a way to punish you for what you did to me." Cassie shook her head. "But over time, the guilt ate at me. I sought counseling and through years of mentorship, I learned to forgive myself. And you. And to surrender what I did to Vida. And to you."

"You had my baby and never told me." It sounded stupid to repeat those words, but it was too unreal. Too unbelievable. "Mila's. . .she's my"—the word was foreign, wrong, weird—"daughter."

Cassie stood still, sagging.

"Crap, Andra." Sal threaded his fingers and hooked them over his head. "I can't believe you kept this— *my own child!*—from me. What were you thinking? How could you do something like this? First you kill Vida—"

"Hey. That's not fair or accurate."

"— then you withhold my own flesh and blood from me." A daughter? How was that possible?

"Don't do this, Sal. You left me and never looked back. I may bear blame for concealing Mila from you, but you threw me out with the trash when Vida showed up at the base. You didn't care what happened to me nor did you ask. I tried to contact you, but you severed all communication. You even had your mother tell me to stop calling." She lifted her chin. "So, I did. And I made the best life I could with Mila."

He should be angry. And there was some distant part of himself that was, but Cassie was right. He was so afraid his feelings for her would resurface that he'd gone as far as to get a new phone, block her number at home, and ask his mom to tell her to bug off.

It *was* his fault.

Just like Vida. He'd betrayed her by dating Cassie. Broke his promise to her. He cursed again. Not because he was mad but because he didn't know what else to do. Or say. "This is messed up." His entire life was messed up.

"She's a lot like you."

He considered her, a strange warmth spilling through his chest. A heady sensation in his mind. "She's. . .three?"

Cassie's face went soft as she nodded. "Quite bossy."

"It's confidence." Sal gave a soft snort, shook his head again, and turned away. Roughing a hand over his face, he groaned. "Andra. What. . .what am I supposed to do with this?"

"Nothing."

He speared her with a glance.

"You didn't want to be a part of our lives."

"That's unfair."

This time, she snorted. "Yeah, I know." Because he'd been unfair to her. "She's your daughter. I won't stop you from seeing her. If you want to."

"I'm a Special Forces operator, Andra. I'm gone nine months out of the year."

"We can make it work. I'm not asking you to make a commitment to me. But I would like Mila to know her father."

Father. Sal considered her. Remembered the firebrand he'd fallen for as soon as he hit Huachuca. "You've changed." She would've been in his face, demanding her rights. She could've come after him for child support. The Army took that stuff seriously. But she hadn't said a word.

"I had to," she answered quietly. "Life wasn't just about me anymore. I had a baby to provide for."

Though he wanted to be angry with her, he couldn't get that round face he'd seen in her picture frame on her desk out of his mind. Curiosity about Mila overrode his sense of injustice. Guilt hung an anchor around his neck. He'd made a mess of things. And in the end, he not only lost Vida, but he lost Cassie and a baby he never knew existed. "I'm sorry."

Blue eyes widened, her face washing clean of the defensive posture she'd held since their first encounter that week Hawk fled into the mountains.

He owed her that apology. "I had to keep my word to her."

"I know," Cassie said, her chin dimpling and her eyes glossing. "You hate me for it?"

"I did. Once." She swished her mouth to the side, as if to prevent herself from crying. "But there were too many things against us. And I was drowning in guilt and grief. I had to let it go and raise Mila."

Curse her—she looked so beautiful in the morning sunlight. Always had. That blond hair like a golden halo. Blue eyes bleeding with sincerity and vulnerability. Drew him in like the sap he was. "I don't know what to do with this."

"We're doing it." Her smile went all crazy soft again. That kind that made him get stupid one too many times. "It's what I hoped for."

Stepping across this line, letting go of his anger—he couldn't do that to Vida. He couldn't pretend that didn't happen. "This doesn't change things between us, though."

"Did you love her, Sal?"

"Doesn't matter. She's gone—that's what matters."

"Is it?" Cassie leaned in, her voice softening. "If she's gone, why does she hang like a storm in your eyes?"

"Because I got her killed." The words pounded with each beat of his heart.

"You didn't! Neither did I."

"I cheated on her with you, and then you sent Vida to her death because of me. I can't live with that."

"Sal, we *didn't* kill her. I know it feels that way—and for years I believed that. I was wrong, for what I did and in believing that it was my fault she died."

"If you hadn't gotten Hammonds to send her to Helmand, she'd be alive."

"Maybe. Maybe, but not absolutely. Neither of us could've predicted she'd die."

"Sal!"

He pivoted and found Dean waiting at the door.

"Now." Dean vanished back inside.

He shifted to her. "We'll talk later."

She smiled but it fell away quickly. "Sal, are you cutting again?"

That was a place she didn't need to go. And where he *wouldn't* go. Wouldn't discuss. Shouldn't have opened up to her and made her think she had a right to ask him about anything in his life.

This thing with Mila turned his brain to sludge. "We have a meeting. Let's go."

—∞—

She should be relieved the truth was out, that they'd had a face-to-face about the past, about Mila—wow, she sure never meant for that to come out, at least not right now—but feeling those ridges on his arm, remembering how he'd started cutting back at the base in the days before Vida showed up. . . What was stressing Sal now?

"All right, listen up," Captain Watters said as the team settled into seats around the briefing area. The SEALs were here with Raptor along with a couple of MPs. Why were MPs in a briefing? A large screen sported a grainy image of Brie Hastings. Where was she?

Sal stood near her at the back of the room, arms folded over his broad chest.

"We've got new intel to work and a plan to put in play," the captain said, holding up a piece of paper. "Miss Zarrick has translated a few pages from the journal we found. Much of it is encoded, so the journal will head to DIA, but we caught a few." His eyes were dark as he met the team's gazes. "They are specifically targeting the ODAs and special operators. They are looking for our identities."

"The only reason they'd want that is to take us out."

"And maybe go a little deeper," Dean said with a nod.

"Like what?" Hawk asked, hesitation tightening his tanned face.

"Address, next of kin."

Curses singed the air.

"So, more than ever, it's our mission to stop Meng-Li Jin and his minions." Dean let out a heavy breath. "Lieutenant Walker."

Cassie straightened, the heat of the gazes swinging toward her burning down her spine. "Sir?"

His intelligent, keen eyes bored through her. Intense. Determined. Like Sal in a lot of ways, but somehow gentler. No, that wasn't the right word. Subtler, maybe. "Would you like to explain this to us?" He nodded to where a grainy video footage sprang onto a monitor mounted on the wall.

"Sure." Her mind worked to decipher what she saw. Then she knew. *Oh no.*

The images were of her and Gearney at Takkar Towers, talking outside. Then switched to her entering the elevator. Exiting on the fifth floor. The camera zoomed, zeroing in on her inside the reception area waiting for Kiew. Heat wafted across her shoulders.

"What do you want to know?" Trained to act calm and innocent, she struggled to maintain a normal tone.

"I'd like to know what you were doing there. Especially when this team and its allies are in an active investigation to prevent future attacks. The very attacks we believe Daniel Jin, owner of that office space, is directly responsible for. The ones that killed General Burnett and dozens of other American military personnel on this base." No mistaking the anger in Captain Watters's voice.

Cassie considered the two paths before her—be honest about her friendship with Kiew or feign investigating just like the team. If she did the latter, they'd want to know why she wasn't open and direct with them. That would lead to more questions that she didn't want to answer.

Though the gazes locked on to her held suspicion, they had not blown into full anger. "My friend works for Daniel Jin."

"What friend?" Watters demanded.

"A friend I've known since high school," Cassie began, knowing she had to provide backstory before they learned she was long-lost friends with Daniel Jin's paramour. "I lived with her family for a year."

"I'm sitting here wondering why you're leaving her name out," Hawk said from a nearby chair where he sat stiff from the gunshot wound, turning a pen over and over in his hand.

Cassie lifted her chin. These men were at the top of their game for a reason. "Kiew Tang."

"Son of a biscuit." Sal glared.

Hawk slapped down the pen. "You're kidding me, right? The same psycho chick who put a gun to my head?"

"And *didn't* shoot you," Cassie reminded him.

"When, Miss Walker," Captain Watters's still-calm voice cut through the murmurs and whispered objections and curses, "did you plan to inform us that you were friends with one of our enemies?"

"I am not convinced that Kiew is your enemy."

Eyebrow arched, Captain Watters reached toward Riordan, who handed him a file. "What about this?"

Another image splashed over the screen. "Who is this man?"

Cassie drew in a breath and swallowed it just as fast. Gearney. She couldn't reveal that. It'd break her cover.

"His name"—Brie Hastings stared through the feed, eyes on Cassie—"is one that she is probably not allowed to mention. Because she's not with DIA."

Cassie wet her lips as she met the captain's gaze. "Can we talk—privately?"

Her ears rang with the silence and the tension as dense as

sandstorms. Beside her, she felt Sal shift to look at her. Cassie's chest heaved with the effort of trying to maintain a confident posture. But the adrenaline squirted into her throat, forcing her to swallow hard.

"You've been lying to me? Again?" Sal whispered, his words barely audible over the thrumming of her pulse.

Captain Watters folded his arms over his chest and held her gaze, not answering. Not moving. Finally, "No." He pointed around the room. "These are my men, my brothers. We've let you into our meetings and briefings, but you've concealed from us a key piece of intelligence."

Cassie said nothing. The situation had progressed beyond something she could salvage. The men here were trained to rout lies and analyze intelligence and responses. They would know—did know—that she wasn't who they believed.

"Andra, give it to us," Sal said, his voice soft but stern. Angry.

Cassie maintained eye contact with the captain but kept her peace.

"Lieutenant Walker, how about we tell you what we've been able to figure out." Watters nodded to Hastings.

The woman let out a heavy breath, glanced at Titanis for an affirming nod, then opened a file of her own. "The man you met with is a spy known as Vasily Litvenko—"

Vasily?

"—who was born in Serbia but raised in South Korea when his mother married a South Korean."

Cassie almost laughed. When had military intelligence gone so horribly wrong?

"His most recent aliases," Brie continued, "include Elias Jennings, Eric Gearney, and Edward Gaines."

Frozen at hearing his name in the middle of the list, Cassie couldn't process what this meant. No. This couldn't be right. "Call General Phelps."

Captain Watters squared his shoulders, apparently recognizing the name.

Naming him was her only recourse. Her get-out-of-jail-free card. It meant her career as an operative ended right here. But she didn't care. Not about those things. If this was true—and it couldn't be—she'd been working *against* the very people she thought she'd been helping.

I'm a traitor.

Watters's face went stone cold as he nodded to the MPs. "Please remove Miss Walker to the detention area."

EAMON

"You sure about this?"

The hint of uncertainty in Brie's voice turned him toward her. They were by the front door, still in the safety of their condo but on the verge of making some risky plays. She would attempt to tag Nianzu or his basement friend. Eamon had the task of getting to the penthouse condo of Meng-Li and planting bugs in adjoining walls. "If you aren't, then we need—"

"No." She drew in a slow, long breath. "I'm good. Just shedding last-minute jitters."

"We can wait."

"No," she said. "Raptor's been hit one too many times, and SOCOM is vulnerable after the CECOM attack." She nodded. "Just have to remember why I'm doing this."

Eamon touched her shoulder. "We're wired up together. I'll hear everything." Though he wouldn't be right with her, he'd be in the same building. Somehow, that thought didn't even give him the comfort he'd intended to provide.

"There will be a dozen floors between us," she muttered with a jut of her jaw toward the door. "But I appreciate the heroic sentiment. Let's go."

Eamon let her out then followed, locking the door behind them. He headed to the stairs, telling himself not to look back. Not to double-check that she was okay. At the quiet intoning of the lift car arriving, he turned and met Brie's gaze just seconds before she entered the lift. As he pushed into the stairs, he told himself not to take any meaning in the fact that she'd been watching him. She probably just turned because he had.

Stop reading into things.

He headed up six flights, cutting off into a sublevel of the penthouse where generators, Internet, electricity hubs, and general maintenance areas for the penthouses lurked. A heavy steel security door barred entry. To the side hung an access panel. Eamon went to work with a handheld device that worked through the security protocols.

As the seconds fell off the clock, he pushed his mind to what would happen once the door unlocked. Security cameras would automatically activate—Meng-Li was obsessive about security. It was a wonder the man didn't have an armed guard here.

A buzz snapped Eamon's nerves like a tightly wound guitar string.

He pocketed the device and reached for the handle. According to the research Brie had done, the security cameras were aimed toward the middle and around the control panels of the Internet and electrical grids.

He pushed inside, hugging the wall. Though he moved with his head down, Eamon roamed the room with his eyes. Weapon up, he swept along the perimeter until the panel stood ten paces to his nine o'clock.

Walking sideways and keeping his back to the camera, Eamon sidled up to the panel that held the cabling for their Wi-Fi. A map tucked in the pouch velcroed to his arm, he worked quickly, piggybacking a device that would allow the data to stream to his system in the condo but wouldn't interrupt the flow for the penthouse. Undetectable was the idea. He worked quickly then sidestepped back to the wall, once more hugging it. Reaching up, he planted listening devices, thankful his six-five height made the feat possible. Brie wouldn't be able to reach the ceiling beams.

The roaring din of the AC units grew as he got closer. Just a few more. . . He hoped Brie was doing okay because he wouldn't hear a cry for help right now anyway. As he tiptoed to place the final one near the beam of the floor in the bedroom, Eamon heard something. He turned. Noticed only darkness and the compressed sound of machines and the garbling of pool water.

But no. . .something wasn't right.

He snapped the bug in place and quickly made his way back to the wall. He flanked right. Scurried along the outer perimeter.

A weight plowed into him. Slammed his face into the cement wall.

Eamon bucked, throwing his elbow backward to nail the man's face. But the bruiser caught his arm, twisted it, and rammed Eamon back into the wall. He might not be as tall as Eamon, but the guy had a bulk not to be messed with.

"What are you doing here?" he demanded.

In English.

The realization forced him to look over his shoulder.

But the attacker hiked up Eamon's arm and pressed his hand against his neck, straining the tendons in his shoulder and neck. Eamon growled through the pain that forced him to stop fighting.

"I said"—he pushed harder against the arm—"what are you doing here?"

"I heard you the first time," Eamon bit out.

"Then you might want to give some answers, hot shot."

"You're American."

"And you're not."

The attacker flipped Eamon around.

He swung out, ready to pummel this man and get away, but the attacker anticipated it. Cut him off and jammed his forearm under his throat, crushing the air from his lungs.

Eamon knew how to break this hold. He'd been trained. But when he saw the green eyes, he stilled. "Candyman."

"What's it going to be, Man From Oz? Do I end you or do you tell me why you're here?"

This didn't make sense. Not one iota. Candyman working against them? That made him an enemy. That made Eamon's next move necessary.

"Don't." Candyman growled, pushing up into his face. "I see it in your eyes, Aussie. I see your readiness to cut me down."

Eamon tapped his arm, indicating his willingness to talk.

Candyman eased off.

"Burnett sent me here."

"Burnett's *dead*," Candyman hissed and let his arm fall away.

"Just because a senior officer dies or leaves doesn't mean the mission is abandoned. Or maybe you forgot something about loyalty once you got out." When the pressure lessened, Eamon shoved his arm away and took a step back. "Meng-Li Jin is the primary suspect in the attacks against your brothers-in-arms. Or do you already know that—?"

"No!" Candyman's shoulders rose, the threat screaming through his posture. "You don't get to put this off on me. You're here, on private property that belongs to Sajjan."

Eamon rubbed his neck and stretched it, making sure to emphasize how Candyman had gone against someone who had once been on the same side with him. "Sajjan. First-name basis."

"He's my wife's stepfather. I think that gives me the right to use his name. Now—"

"Does it also give you the right to change loyalty? Why aren't you with Raptor?"

Candyman looked ready to eat him alive. "I'm walking out of here. But if I find you snooping around here again"—he shook his head and shrugged—"no promises on how it ends next time." He started toward the doors. "Clear out, Titanis. Game's over."

"It's not over till someone wins. Are you helping Meng-Li win? I thought you were a Green Beret. An American patriot."

Candyman pivoted. Fists balled. "There are things you don't know about. Things that make what you're doing here deadly for everyone involved."

CHAPTER 20

Kandahar Airfield, Afghanistan
2 April—1340 Hours

I gotta say—it's buggin' me that she didn't defend herself or argue," Hawk said.

Sal slid a mean look in his direction.

"What?" Hawk lifted his arms in surrender—and cringed, his face twisting in a knot of pain. "I'm just sayin'—if you're innocent, you scream it all the way to holding."

"Unless you can't," Sal heard himself say.

"What do you mean?" Titanis settled cozy-close to Brie Hastings, his big Oz shoulders pressed to hers, as the two leaned in to the camera of the live feed from Takkar Towers.

"I mean," Sal said, wondering why he was defending her, "when we're taken captive, we're trained to say only certain things. To not give information or defend ourselves."

"So, you're saying she's one of us?" Hawk snorted.

With a quick shake of his head, Sal grunted. "I'm saying, whoever she is working for trained her well—trained her not to give away intel when she's scared or questioned." He wasn't sure if that was good or bad. And he certainly didn't like it.

"Brie—get ahold of Phelps." Dean waited as Hastings left the room then went to the table. "You want to tell us what you two were talking about out there?"

Sal could more than relate to Cassie's silence right now. "Not particularly." But that wouldn't do, and he knew it. "Suffice it to say, she and I have a past. It wasn't pretty. Still isn't."

"You still soft on her?"

Sal met his friend's gaze and held it. Dean's question wasn't about Sal's love interest with Cassie. He was testing the waters of brotherhood. "My loyalty is to the team."

Dean nodded. "Good to know."

But Sal had recognized the name Cassie flung out there. "Who's Phelps?"

"That's the bugger of it all," Dean said. "He's the Associate Director for Military Affairs."

"Is that supposed to mean something?" Hawk asked.

"It means were in a crapload of trouble," Harrier finally spoke from the corner. "He's working in conjunction with the CIA."

"More spooks!"

"Hold up," Sal said. "CIA? But you just accused Andra of working with a foreign intelligence service."

"I named the man she met with," Dean corrected. "I wanted her to explain it."

"But if you knew she was working with spies, you also knew she couldn't talk openly, yet you called her onto the carpet in front of us and outsiders." Sal met Riordan's gaze. "No offense."

"I called her onto the carpet because she's putting us at risk. If she's doing it now, did she do it earlier—is she the reason the base was attacked? The reason Burnett was killed?"

"Burnett put her on the team!" Sal shouted.

"That's a lot of anger for a guy whose history with her is ugly," Titanis said.

Ignoring the statement would only add fuel to it, but Sal had no idea how to respond because he didn't know why he was so angry. Something in him didn't want Cassie to be this person. But after all her lies, why should he even care? "I knew her, yes. And that's why I'm saying something isn't right. Andra—"

"I thought her name was Cassandra." Hawk shrugged.

Biting down on his aggravation, Sal huffed. "Lieutenant Walker and I might have our *differences*"—a nice way of putting it—"but she's not the type of person to—"

"Get someone killed?" Dean's words held challenge and

understanding. A knowledge of things past. "I need to hear you say this woman is 100 percent trustworthy. That we can put our lives in her hands and you'd be comfortable with that."

The next breath burned Sal's lungs. His defense of her fell away with the potent reminder of Vida's death. She had admitted she wanted Vida out of the way. He'd called her a killer. All these years of blaming Cassie and holding her responsible. . . He couldn't respond. What he'd felt, the names he'd called her, had been colored out of anger—at her, but also at himself.

Dean lifted his head as Sal stood there, considering the demand. Fighting himself. Fighting to understand what he felt and why he felt it.

He'd loved her. Slept with her. Apparently, even fathered a child with her. Yet he couldn't stand before his band of brothers and defend her? At her core, she was a decent person. He knew that. Believed it, once he dug past the crap and heartache piled between them.

Grumblings sifted through the room as his silence lingered, objections growing louder on a tidal wave of hesitation.

"What if she has intelligence we need to bring down Jin?" *Is that the best you can do?*

"So what?" Hawk held up his hands. "We're supposed to sleep with the enemy because she might have intel that helps us? What if our assistance helps her?"

Sal balled his fists.

"Hawk." Dean locked eyes with Sal. "Easy."

"Naw, man. She's been lying, so how do we know where that stops? How do I know the bullet I ate wasn't her fault, that she isn't working with the enemy?"

"Define enemy," Sal said. "Even if she's working for the South Koreans. . .she'd still have intel we can use."

"*If* you can get it out of her." Hawk had a pinecone up his craw.

"I *can* get it out of her," Sal snapped.

The door flung open and Hastings rushed in, her freckled cheeks flushed. "Phelps is here."

Dean turned to Sal. "With me."

—⁂—

"What happened?"

Cassie came to her feet as the stoic voice rang through the cement cell. "General Phelps."

"What happened, Walker?" He motioned to her cut-up face. "And that?"

"Sir, they saw my visit to Takkar Towers as an attempt to sway Kiew Tang from Meng-Li Jin. I think they tried to have me killed."

"Say what?" He scowled at her then at his aide. "What is she talking about?"

The lanky uniformed major shrugged. "No clue, sir."

Phelps rubbed his jaw as his gaze scraped over her. "Walker, you went MIA six weeks ago."

"What?" Cassie frowned. "No, sir. I've been right here, working my assignment."

"What assignment?" Phelps growled. "We've been trying to track you down and reestablish contact for the last six weeks."

"Sir. You sent me here, had me work with Burnett."

"Yes, then you were ordered to return to D.C."

She drew back. "I received no such order. After we determined Meng-Li was involved, I was assigned to Raptor team. It took me longer than it should have, but I finally figured out I was put in place because of my longstanding friendship with Kiew Tang. Gearney has had me working on that since."

"Gearney?" Phelps's eyes had a laser-like effect to them, narrowing in on her, slicing her words apart like a heat-seeking missile. "Walker, maybe you should start from the beginning."

Cassie gripped the bar, Hastings's words ringing through her brain like a brass gong. "Sir, I confess I'm pretty unsettled right now. Gearney—does he work for us?"

"Depends on who your 'us' is, Walker." The major, a handsome man with salt-and-pepper trimming his dark hair, smirked. He had a thick chest and his name patch read PENNER. "When did you get first contact from Gearney?"

Her stomach threatened to hurl its contents on the lieutenant general. She took a step back, reaching for the small cot. "Back when Raptor was hunting down the source of the cyber attacks. As my new handler, he told me the network had been compromised and not to trust anything that came through normal channels."

"And you believed him?"

"Watching elite special operators getting blown up by supposed communications from their own people—yes, sir. I believed that completely." Cassie warned herself to calm down, slow her breathing. She'd done nothing wrong here. "He gave me a new phone, told me to report in weekly."

Phelps sighed heavily then pointed to the cot. "Why don't you tell us what you know?"

"So, he *doesn't* work for us?"

With a shake of his head, Phelps again pointed to the steel-frame bed. "I'm afraid not."

Cassie dropped onto the mattress, springs digging into her thighs. She wrapped her arms around herself. "I can't believe it. First time in the field and. . ."

"I'm pretty sure Gearney saw you as a soft target for just that reason—your first time out." Major Penner didn't sound condescending, but somehow it still came across that way. "You were gung ho on proving you could handle the mission, as any fresh blood would be."

Phelps cleared his throat. "Just tell us what's happened since Gearney inserted himself."

The entire last month? "I. . .I made contact with my friend, Kiew Tang. Gearney seemed really interested in my reestablishing contact with her."

"Of course he did." Phelps lowered himself to the cot beside her. "If he could get you to draw her out, then they'd have a hefty anchor over Meng-Li's head."

"She's a friend, so once I realized what he wanted me to do, I tried to get her to come out without compromising our friendship."

"So, you were willing to compromise your commitment to your job, even though it wasn't a real situation?" Major Penner's green eyes held fast.

"Leave her alone," Phelps said, waving him off. "Walker, you work for the CIA. There are going to be times—like this one—that you have to do something you normally wouldn't do. What you have to believe is that we'd only ask if it was absolutely necessary."

"Wait." Cassie looked between the two of them. "You still want me to get her?"

"Of course!" Phelps laughed. "Walker, Kiew Tang isn't your friend—not in this scenario. I need you to see past that."

See past that. Like it was something nebulous or nonexistent.

The *scritch-squeak* of approaching boots on the vinyl floor made them all turn toward the door. Captain Watters and Sal came into view around the corner.

"Captain," Phelps said. "Nice of you to join us."

The four men exchanged handshakes and greetings, which were kept short. Captain Watters skidded a look in her direction. "I have questions, sir." He turned back to the general.

"Of course you do." He clapped him on the back. "First of which is to absolve Lance of any deception. He didn't know why Walker was sent here. And as it turns out, she was the unwitting pawn of a South Korean spy."

"Gearney."

"Seems he managed to convince her he was her new handler."

"Handler." Sal bit the word out. His jaw muscle popped with tension. "So she's a *spook*. She lied to us."

Cassie could pretty much hear the "again" at the end of his sentence, though he didn't say it.

"She provided the cover story she was told to give," Phelps said. "We had special interests—"

"So, this is CIA activity? Inserting this operative into a delicate Special Forces operation?" Watters now sounded ticked.

She stood, hating the way they talked around her, as if she didn't exist.

"It's activity in the vested interest of our military and protecting Americans." Phelps wagged a finger at Watters. "Don't get an attitude with me, Captain. Your men aren't the only ones trying to stop this very real threat against our military cyber security and computers. They broke through and decimated some first- and second-tier data. Thank God they didn't get to more sensitive information before we shut it down." He grumbled and scratched the back of his head. "Look, the thing of it is—Jin *did* get to some sensitive information through Miss Tang that put lives at risk."

"Kiew wouldn't harm anyone." Hearing her own words, Cassie gulped. She was out of line but couldn't take this anymore.

Phelps rounded on her, his disdain evident in his weathered face. "When was the last time you saw her—before your first encounter here, that is?"

"We send cards every year—Christmas, birthdays." But even Cassie knew that didn't mean anything. "Our last phone conversation was seven years ago." The way Kiew treated her yesterday even left her wondering if they were still friends.

"Leave the analysis to the analysts," Penner said. "Tang's activities over the last few years have proven that she is lethal, cunning, and in the right-hand pocket of Meng-Li Jin. The attack on the base allowed a breach of some very sensitive data that we were able to trace directly back to Kiew Tang's people."

"Her people?" This couldn't be true. Couldn't be right. She'd sat in the restaurant with her. Had a good conversation. Kiew had sought her out the next morning, but now Cassie wondered if it was of her own accord.

"What information?" Captain Watters asked.

Tension rippled through the cell and ran like a river of mud over her shoulders. Cassie waited, dreading the general's words.

"Names and locations of key assets in the region."

Captain Watters seemed to grow like an impending storm. "*Which* assets? My girlfriend is an asset! Her cousin, too."

"And your Miss Zarrick is on this base right now, isn't she?" Major Penner asked.

Watters went very still. "And you know that how?"

"Because we've had an agent following her since the breach."

"You have that many agents here to follow every asset?" Sal demanded.

Penner snorted. "Hardly. We put the agents on the *top* assets."

"And the others?" Captain Watters's shoulders were hunched and his fists clenched.

"Look, we do what we can with what little we have," Phelps said. "And right now, our priority is to stop Kiew Tang."

"Stop her? How?" Words shrill, Cassie tried to rein in her panic. Words like that had been used to reference more permanent means of interrupting an enemy combatant than what she wanted aimed at her friend.

"We want her extracted." Penner pointed to the ground. "Brought back to U.S. soil and questioned."

"You mean *interrogated*."

"Cass," Sal spoke softly, touching her arm.

She shoved his hand away, undeterred from plucking the truth from Phelps and his aide. "I'm sorry, but this isn't what I signed up for."

"No, what you signed up for you haven't done. In legal terms, you went rogue."

"I was tricked!"

Penner shrugged. "You still went rogue. You will work with us, Walker, or you're gone."

"You're threatening me? Because I won't threaten her?"

"Hey." Sal stepped in front of her and caught her arms. "Easy, easy."

"No!" She wriggled, but he held her fast. She bounced her gaze to his. "You realize what he means, right? What they'll do to her if they capture her?"

"Cassie." He leaned closer. "Stop."

"I *mean* that we will do our jobs." Penner focused on Sal and the captain. "We want your team to go in and bring her back—"

"Sorry, we are U.S. Army. We're not under your command," Captain Watters said. "We take orders from—"

"Me." General Ramsey stepped into the room. "Sorry, couldn't help overhearing with all the shouting." He nodded to Phelps. "Sir."

"General Ramsey."

Ramsey motioned toward the captain. "You might not take orders from him, but General Phelps is the Associate Deputy Director for

Military Support. He works in cooperation with the Unified Combatant Command." Though his tone held placating tones, Ramsey's expression seemed to ripple with something Cassie couldn't identify—anger? Frustration? He turned to Watters again. "Do what he needs you to do." And he was gone.

The captain and Sal shared stiff glances.

"I'm not trying to pull rank, son, but Ramsey's right—and this threat is big enough that we can't squabble over territorial lines."

"Permission to remind you of that when I get strung up, sir?"

Phelps quirked a smile. "Won't happen. Now back to this mission. You'll use Walker to get close to Tang and lure her out."

"I tried that," Cassie said. "It didn't work. They threw me out of the building."

"Then get back in." Penner's brow knotted.

If they let that happen, Kiew would probably not be seen again. Whether they held her in some maximum-security prison indefinitely or killed her—no one would know the difference.

"General, I appreciate your vote of confidence in me and my team," Captain Watters said, "but I'm concerned things are not being considered here."

The man stood almost as tall as the six-two captain but had more bulk from apparent years behind a desk. "Like?"

"Like the delicate relationship with the owner of those towers."

"Sajjan Takkar is no one to spit at," Sal said.

"Burnett was always very careful in his dealings with Takkar. It's my understanding that he's neither an ally nor an enemy." Captain Watters angled his head, his eyes glinting with meaning. "But we go in there and he finds out? We *make* him an enemy."

"Then make sure he *doesn't* find out."

CHAPTER 21

Kandahar Airfield, Afghanistan
3 April—1750 Hours

This is some kind of messed up," Sal said as he and Dean headed back to the briefing room where they'd left Raptor.

"Hooah."

"It's like there's this tangle of trip wire around our feet and a barrel of explosives just waiting for us to blow ourselves back to the States."

"Then let's avoid stepping on it."

Sal nodded then glanced over his shoulder. Cassie trailed them by a half-dozen feet. That she wasn't talking, fighting, and arguing told him the meeting with Phelps knocked the wind out of her.

Knocked it out of him, too. She'd lied to him, to the team about her job. Where did her lies end? Just when he'd started wondering if they could work things out, he got broadsided by another lie. Not exactly the working material for a relationship.

Dean stopped outside the Command building and reached for the door handle. "Talk to her."

"About what?"

"Make sure she knows we're not done. She has a mess to clean up with us."

"Dean—"

But he was already inside the building and the door was closing. Sal popped it with a grunt.

"What's wrong?" Cassie asked, her voice devoid of feeling. No, not devoid—*smothered*.

Gritting his teeth, he turned around. Stared at the ground. "They're not happy. I'm not happy."

"Who *is* happy, Sal?" She held fast with those blue eyes. Puddles of grief and anger. "Everything I thought I was working for has been a lie."

With a nod, he almost smiled. "I can relate—any more lies you want to come clean with before we go on?"

"It was my job, Sal. You don't tell your mom what you're doing out here on a daily basis, do you?"

"Hey. Stick to the facts, to this mission." Man, he hated her under-the-radar attack on his mom. Low blow. "My mom isn't relying on me to protect her or depending on me to be straight up in something that could mean life or death. I am—they are!"

Cassie looked away.

"My team is going to put their lives in your hands." He moved closer again, his boots crunching on the pebbled path. "And so help me God, if you have any more lies up that sleeve of yours—"

"I don't!"

"Good!" Silence snapped through the evening, chilled and desperate. He roughed a hand over his beard and groaned. "I don't know what to do you with you, Andra. I want to tell my team they can trust you, but"—he shook his head again and shrugged—"I don't know that they can. I don't know that *I* can."

She flinched and again looked away.

"I want to. Why? I have no idea." He inched closer and hooked her arm, bringing her around. She wore a floral perfume that snaked up and coiled around his brain, squeezing off oxygen. "Can I trust you? Can I believe that there aren't any more lies? That you aren't hiding something else from me?"

Her blue eyes held misery. "You? Or your team?"

Sal felt his life caving in. His resolve sinking beneath the quicksand of their past. He was tired of this fight. Tired of learning about more lies. Two doozies in one week had pretty much done him in. Yet it terrified him to let go and dishonor Vida's memory.

"Because while your team is important, I could care less about them. But you?" Her eyes went all glassy, digging through the sandy years of anger and hurt to the heartstrings he'd buried beneath. "You know I'd do anything for you." She always had a way with words that knocked his feet out from under him.

"Then give me a reason to believe in you again."

"What? What do you want me to say, Sal?"

"Say there are no more secrets, that what is there now is real and honest and true."

"It is!" Cassie said. "How many times do I have to say it? And in how many ways? What I did—working with Gearney, I did out of honest belief that I was doing my duty. It wasn't a conscious betrayal."

"But you're not military. You're not DIA, like you presented. That was a lie."

"Yes, you're right. What will it take to prove myself?"

"We don't have proving time, Andra. I have to go in there"—he jabbed a finger toward the door—"and sell the team on you."

"And you can't do that." She said it with a breathy, disbelieving laugh. "No."

Her full lips tightened. "Good thing you don't have to."

Sal let go of her arm and straightened. "Come again?"

"It's not up to them." Blue eyes flashed. "Phelps wants me on the mission. I'm on the mission." Cassie let out a long, deep breath. "While I want your belief in me more than I'm willing to admit—though I am starting to wonder why I still hang on to the hope that you'll one day forgive me and take me back. . .I guess I'm just stupid that way—I don't need their belief or yours for this mission."

"Wrong!" Sal leaned in until he felt his breath hot against her cheek. "Those men have to believe when the guns are drawn and the bombs are going off that you'll be there. I need to know that you aren't going to stab me in the back again!"

Cassie planted both hands on his chest and shoved him back. "Step off, Russo! I have no secrets left. No more lies. If you can't accept that, well, I guess that's your problem. But right now, I just want to get my friend out of a deadly situation."

"You still call her a friend?"

"Yes," Cassie hissed. "Because I believe in her."

—∞—

Watching her walk into the briefing area was like watching the devil walk into his midst. Dean didn't trust her. Didn't want her in the room. Didn't want her on this mission. But he wasn't in control. Not this time. "We clear?" he asked as Sal stepped in behind her and closed the door.

"Crystal." Sal moved to a seat at the table by Riordan, leaving Walker on her own. She stumbled to a chair that listed off to the side, away from the others.

"Brie managed to tag Nianzu, but the tracker's not working, so we're one down on that. Walker will provide intel and shadow us on this mission," Dean explained to the others. "Lieutenant—please." He motioned to the floor. "Tell us what you know about Kiew Tang, the lover and assistant of Meng-Li."

Lips tight, she moved rigidly to stand beside him. "What do you want to know?"

Her clipped question left no doubt that she wasn't happy about this, so that made two of them. "Offices, layout, hot spots—anything that will give us a tactical edge, including where we're most likely to find her. Where you expect trouble. And if she will be trouble."

"Since I don't know the mission details, it's a bit hard to say where she will be, but—"

"Night."

Her round blue eyes popped to Dean, but he gave her no more information. Less for her to spill to her sources or whatever. "Okay, night. Well, Kiew and Daniel Jin—that's his Americanized name—have the penthouse as their living quarters. It would be my guess that she'd be there."

"What about the offices?" Hawk asked.

"They're on the fifth floor, immediately opposite the elevator. There's a reception area walling off the rest of the business space. I can't say what's beyond it because they didn't allow me back there. Just inside the foyer, there's a side door that leads to a stairwell."

Dean glanced at Titanis, who had joined them for the briefing. The Aussie nodded. So far, Walker had provided accurate intel.

"What about Tang herself?" Harrier asked. "Is she going to give us trouble?"

Arms folded, Dean held a hand over his mouth and watched Walker, who seemed to stiffen at the question. "Go on."

"I—I don't know for sure."

Hawk snorted. "Make that a yes, then."

"You don't know that," Walker countered.

"Murphy's Rules of Combat state: The enemy only attacks on one of two occasions: When you're ready for them, and when you're not ready for them." Hawk grinned, his chest out. "I aim to be ready so I don't eat any more bullets."

"Hooah," Sal mumbled.

"I just. . .Kiew might best be viewed as an asset, not a target."

"You want me to believe she's an asset," Hawk said. "But I'd have to be what you get when you leave off the last two letters of that word."

The SEALS erupted in laughter, high-fiving Hawk. Sal didn't move, but a smile quirked his lips then faded as he looked down at the table. Not at Walker, whose face had probably gone ashen.

"All right," Dean said, roping in the craziness at Walker's expense. "Titanis has schematics of the building. I want each of you to take one and study them tonight. Memorize them. If things go ape down there, you might be the one leading us out of a burning building."

EAMON

You think he's. . .what? Defected?"

Having secretly slipped out of Takkar Towers to avoid another encounter with Nianzu, Eamon hunched his shoulders as he sat across from Brie in a small briefing room. "I don't know. It didn't make sense. Him confronting me. If he really had traded sides, he'd have beat me bloody. The guy has the brawn to do it."

"So, he was warning you?"

Eamon rubbed his jaw. "What do you know about Takkar? Who is he loyal to?"

"Sajjan Takkar is loyal to himself and to Afghanistan. He works heavily and closely with the Aga Khan Foundation. In fact, he's become good friends, according to intel, with the Aga Khan himself."

"Could he have bought Candyman?"

Brie laughed. "Candyman can't be bought. His own moniker speaks to his character—giving candy to children while on patrol. He's a gorilla of a guy, but he's got a soft heart. And after losing his leg to an attack"— she shook her head, brown hair swinging—"I can't see him siding with anyone close to those responsible for terrorism here."

"Then what's he doing being Takkar's heavy lifter?"

"Warning us? That's the only thing that makes sense."

"I'd recommend pulling him off the team. Cancel his contract," Eamon said.

"Sorry." She lifted a bottle of water and took a sip. "That's out of my hands. Besides, I think you're just mad he got a leg up on you."

"He slammed my face into the wall and nearly choked me to death."

Brie's eyes danced with laughter.

"What?"

"You're going to tell me, with those biceps, you couldn't have taken

188

Candyman?" Her laugh turned nervous. "Anyway, I think you held back because you know and respect him." Her gaze traced something on her laptop. A flash of confusion rippled through her eyebrows. She leaned in. "What?"

Her face shifted into a full scowl. Her eyes darted over the information.

Eamon slid to the seat beside her. "What'd you find?"

She lifted her head and angled it toward him, but never met his gaze. "This. . .according to the feed, Meng-Li's heading back to China. If he leaves, our ability to gather information leaves."

"What about Kiew Tang?"

"She's to follow a day later."

"Didn't Walker say she was a soft target?"

"Yes, but I'm not convinced." She chewed her bottom lip. "She's pretty cold and heartless for someone who's supposed to be Cassie's former BFF."

"The same could be said of Candyman."

"Ah, but see, I have an entire military career and experience to back up my belief. Candyman has a plan we don't know about. Didn't you say he warned you there were things you didn't know?"

"I don't see how that's different from Tang."

"Well, you need to see with my eyes." She smiled at him, batting those eyelashes in a taunting fashion.

Did she have any idea how pretty she was? With her shoulder-length brown hair and blue eyes, a nice complement to her tanned complexion. But her personality! It took an effort to push his mind to the topic and away from the way she sat there, amused and coy. "What does that mean?"

"I am an officer with the Defense Intelligence Agency. I'm trained to know the differences like this." She threw him another saucy smile.

"And I'm not? An elite Australian commando with—"

"—two Victoria Crosses and"—she flashed wide, fake-innocent eyes at him—"has the queen given you your knighthood yet, Sir Puffsalot?"

Eamon arched his eyebrow. "You're mocking me."

"No." She stifled her laugh, but it pushed out. "Yes, I am. I so am."

"You mentioned your credentials. I thought I should mention mine. But you call me puff—*what* did you call me?"

"Seriously?" Her mouth hung open. "You went there—I showed you mine, so you showed me yours?"

Heat scaled his neck. Shock riddled him. "That is *not* what I meant."

Now she looked mortified. Brie came to her feet. "Titanis, I'm sorry. I didn't mean it that way either. I—"

His phone buzzed. He tried to haul his brain out of the muck she'd submerged it in. He glanced at the caller ID and stilled. "Excuse me." Phone in hand, he left and slipped into a darkened office. Closed the door. "This is Eamon."

"Please hold for the prime minister," came the distinctly Australian voice.

His eyes closed as the line went void of sound.

"Eamon!" boomed a firm, gravelly voice. "How are you?"

Annoyance pinched his muscles. "Fine." He wouldn't be rude. "Your trip going well?"

"Made a diversion. Come see me."

"You know I can't just leave the Army—"

"But I'm here."

Eamon lifted his head. "Here? What do you mean—?"

"Afghanistan. I'm visiting the Aga Khan Foundation and Sajjan Takkar—brilliant fellow that one. Come see me. His penthouse. Ten a.m. tomorrow work for you?"

Bloody—

"Eamon, it's been a while. Do this. For me."

"Fine." He let out a thick breath. "Okay, Dad."

"Brilliant! Tomorrow then."

The line went dead—and so did Eamon's hope for anonymity. If his father was here, that meant Takkar knew Eamon was here. If that was true, then Candyman had ratted him out. All those combined told him they were seriously buggered.

CHAPTER 22

Pain sluiced through his arm. Sal hissed and dropped the knife, cursing himself for pressing too hard. As he scrambled to stem the flow, he focused on the pain. The release of the pain. Like opening a dam and letting the water flow, cutting gave him relief.

Nobody would understand. It was backward to them. They'd string him up on charges. But finding out about Mila. Learning Cassie was lying to them again. The whole freakin' world felt messed up beyond belief.

Fisting the handle of the knife, Sal laid the blade against his arm again, this time just below the crook of his elbow, and drew a line down the tattoo of the Special Forces emblem. He stopped, the sight of the blood-slickened blade glaring against the darkened pigment of the tattoo.

Arm cut, pain gone, he let out a breath. Swiped his thumb over the mark, though the blood rushed free.

It was wrong. Wrong to cut. Wrong to deal with problems like this. In the back of his head, nagging buzzed in his brain that he was breaking his oath as a Special Forces soldier.

Sal lifted the knife, coiling three fingers around the blade and pinching his nose with his thumb and forefinger.

Cassie.

He wanted her back. Wished to God that things hadn't gone the way they had four years ago. Wished. . .

He didn't know what. He'd made a commitment to Vida. To marry her. To give her everything she wanted. They'd grown up in a rough neighborhood. He'd protected her since their junior high days in New York. Being her boyfriend was comfortable. Easy. She was beautiful and everyone liked her, including him

He pushed the blade against his flesh, watching the skin surrender to the sting of the steel. Wincing, he drew another line down his arm—for Vida.

No. Not for her. For himself. For the grave he'd dug. Two graves, in fact. Hers. And...*mine*. He drew it farther down.

"Falcon!" Hawk's voice bounced through the shower and latrines.

He flinched. The blade flicked into his arm. Sal hissed. Dropped the blade and clapped a hand over his arm. "Can't a guy have some peace?" he called from the stall.

Hawk laughed. "Not in this country. Captain wants you on deck."

Pressing toilet paper to his arm, he wrangled the other to see his watch. "We've got twenty mikes still."

"Yeah?" He heard and saw Hawk's dusty boots beneath the partial door. "Well, he said now." Two raps on the wall. "Let's go, soldier!"

"D'you forget I outrank you?"

"You out-stink me, too, and I didn't think that was possible." Hawk hooted then started walking. "See you there, Sewer Rat!"

Rolling his eyes—since he wasn't actually using the restroom, he knew Hawk was just yanking his chain—Sal wiped away the blood from his arm, wishing it was as easy to wipe away the reasons he did this, then tugged the quick bandage cream from his pant pocket and applied it to the fresh marks. That's when he noticed the cut he made when Hawk startled him had gone a little deeper. Probably could use stitches. But yeah—that'd go over well. He'd have to watch it. He applied the cream and then covered it with tissue before tugging down his sleeve. He'd need to leave it covered for a while.

He exited, glanced around as he made his way to the sink. He scrubbed his hand and blade then stowed it. When he looked up, he didn't like what he saw. Haggard. Dark circles under his eyes. *Guess that's what happens when life screws with you.* Shame deepened like dark shadows in the night, hiding his sins and heartache.

Cleaned up, he gave himself a nod. Warrior on. That's what was expected of him. That's what he'd do.

When he made it to the JSOC building, he found Dean there waiting. Hawk sat in a chair at the table, looking over a handful of documents.

"Hey," Dean said, turning to nod at him. "Sorry to haul you out of the john, but I wanted to go over things with you."

Sal shrugged off the moments of guilty release and focused. "Sure."

"Hastings and Titanis are back. They've given us some actionable intel, so we're doing this." Dean pulled in a breath then nodded. "I want you to lead the team. I'm going to be here, keeping an eye on some things."

"*Things* sound a lot more specific than you're saying."

"That's why you're my first." Dean nodded to the paper. "Takkar is out of town for the next couple of days so we might be able to pull this off if we hit first thing in the morning."

"Fly out?"

"Negative. We'll head out, avoid the highway—"

"Better chance of staying alive," Sal agreed.

"Right."

"We'll get into position and hit before dawn."

"And we're going after the woman?"

"Kiew Tang," Dean said with a nod.

Bobbing his head, Sal felt the tremors of something else here. "And why are you telling me this before the team?"

"Because the team will include Walker." Dean's hazel eyes pinged with meaning.

"You want me to keep an eye on her."

"Is that a problem?"

"No," Sal said.

"I have no idea if I can trust her, but she's already tried to help Tang, so I wouldn't put it past her to do it again." Dean angled a shoulder in. "Sal, if she does that, she puts the lives of every man on our team in danger."

"She won't." But even as he said it, Sal had his own doubts.

"Ehhh," Dean said, his left eye narrowing. "I know you too well. You don't fully believe that."

"My reasons are personal, but I do *not* believe she'd compromise a vital mission like this."

"I'm going to have to trust you because we don't have any options. Phelps wants this done, which means the POTUS wants it done. So it's going to get done. I just hope nothing happens that will make me regret this and take action."

"You and me both." Sal knew what it meant—Dean would neutralize Cassie if she interfered. He didn't need a briefing on that. He knew how things would go down. It was his job to make sure Cassie stayed in line. Did as she was ordered. If she didn't...

"You won't be alone, Sal. Riordan's going in with his men—they're secondary, but you and I both know that Ramsey is hand-feeding Riordan orders. If they get a whiff of anything negative with Walker, I can guarantee you he's been given orders to take her out of the equation."

—ᚱᚱ—

Kabul, Afghanistan
5 April—0350 Hours

Weighted with the tactical gear, vest, and helmet, Cassie waited in the darkness with Raptor team and the SEAL team. After an "all quiet" order, they waited in the bombed-out building that had more rubble than roof and waited for the signal to move closer. Less than a klick from Takkar Towers, they'd rushed along the empty streets and sneaked in through the garage level.

But for now, they sat. In silence.

She might not have been an operative long, but Cassie could read body language and their deafening silence. These men did not trust her. And maybe it stirred a mutual distrust in her. If they decided she did wrong on this mission, would they act against her? She'd been trained to expect that. And with the wary and annoyed glances, they seemed ready to pounce.

Sal squatted against the far wall, talking quietly, marking in the dirt and strategizing with Riordan and Hawk. This was where he thrived. Among his men, keyed to the mission. Resolute focus, gifted with strategy, Sal seemed born to be a warrior. And add in his Latino heritage and Italian blood—a volatile and beautiful mixture. *Gorgeous* didn't come close to the right description for him. She'd fallen hard and fast for the gregarious Special Forces soldier when he served stateside before his second deployment.

How many times had he come over here since. . .Vida? Must've been a lot—he'd changed so much. Back then, he seemed untouched by war. Or rather, it had not taken as great a toll on him.

He reached toward the floor, brushing something aside then scratching in the dirt as Riordan and Hawk looked on, nodding and pointing. His bicep, etched with a tattoo of an inverted rifle, tugged against his black tactical shirt. She'd seen the tattoo shortly after arriving here. Was that for Vida? Or another fallen comrade? Either way, it tugged at her heart how much pain he'd gone through.

Only as she thought of it did she notice his sleeves were down now. Interesting, considering Sal's pride in his buff build. The men beside him had theirs cuffed either right above or below their elbows.

Cutting. She really hoped she was wrong. He'd always been an intense person, despite his easy laugh and jokes. Even now, she saw the lingering moodiness. It seemed much more pronounced since Huachuca.

"How long have you known him?"

Cassie flinched and looked to the side, where Harrier sat propped against the wall, arms draped lazily over his knees. "What?"

"Falcon. How long have you known him?"

Averting her gaze would only fuel the fire. "About five years." She turned her attention to the team medic. "How long have you been with Raptor?"

"Two years. I'm the fresh meat—well, that is, until Knight and Ddrake"—he nodded to the German shepherd, snoozing slumped against his handler in the corner—"joined. Took the newb heat off me."

She couldn't help the smile. "I bet that was nice."

He laughed. "You have no idea. They can be brutal."

"They?" Cassie tilted her head. "You're one of them, aren't you?"

"The Captain, Hawk, and Falcon are more intense than me. I've only been deployed three times. They've been here a half-dozen times."

"You think that's why they're intense?" She tried not to mock him. If she believed the war is what made Sal intense, he had no clue. "Sal's been keyed up since the first day I met him. But he was funny, too. That's what drew me in."

"Funny?" He laughed again. "I can't see that."

"Yeah," Cassie said softly. "Neither can I—not anymore."

"Listen up," Sal called as the nearly half-dozen warriors came alive from their relative quiet and slumber. "Eagle's in position. Guard change happens in thirty. Gear up. We're going in."

Cassie hopped to her feet and hurried over to where Sal knelt double-checking and securing his gear. "Hey." She went to her knees. "What's the plan?"

Lifting an M4 from the floor, Sal shrugged. "Just stay close."

"Stay close?" Cassie tried to keep the ridicule from her words and failed miserably. "I'm entering a building—"

"You're part of a team making a dangerous insertion." Sal went to his feet and so did Cassie. "You stay close and keep your head down. Your job is to verify Tang's identity."

"And not get in the way," Hawk murmured as he walked past, slinging his weapon over his chest.

"Sal." Cassie pursed her lips and stepped closer. "Do not do this— don't treat me like some wannabe. I'm trained—"

"I'm treating you like a part of my team. The mission is to get Tang. Get out. It's not that hard."

"And it's not that easy either," she hissed.

"Thirteenth floor insertion. Sweep the condo. Find the asset. If we make it that far, you verify the package. That's all. Nothing complicated."

"Why are you doing this?"

He lifted his helmet and secured the straps beneath his chin. "Doing what?"

"Treating me like—"

"You're a spy?" His eyebrow arched and those rich brown eyes nailed her with her own deception. "Yeah, I have no idea why I'd do that." He lifted his hand, making a group-up motion to the others.

"Sal." Cassie caught his arm as he tried to move away and noticed him flinch.

His expressive eyes hit her hand. Then her eyes. His silent warning to let go.

"Please—I'm just doing my job. And I want to be sure Kiew isn't hurt."

With a snort, he cuffed her wrist and freed himself. "And I'm doing mine." He inclined his head toward the team huddling at the door. "Which is leading this mission. Now, you're ready or you're not. Either way, we're going in." He pivoted and strode through the darkness toward the others. "Let's rodeo."

—∞—

Shanghai, China

With a snifter of vodka in hand, Jin tugged on the belt of his silk robe and made his way to his office down in the secure facility beneath his penthouse where his mother clung to the frail threads of life. He should remain at her side, suspecting these were her final hours, but the strange thing about life was that it waited for no one.

He accessed his private office, draped in obsidian lacquer and stainless steel. The cool air and atmosphere soothed the roiling acid in his veins. At his desk, he set down the crystal glass, pressed a button, and ran a hand through his hair. Steady whirring preceded a five-by-eight screen sliding from the ceiling in front of the painting hanging over the credenza. As he eased back in the chair without a squeak or groan, Jin reached for his liquor.

White glared angrily across the room as the screen sprang to life.

Ah, that word again—life. So powerful and yet so. . .fragile. It could be powerful in its force, the opposite of death. And so susceptible to a button. One flick of his finger and it would die.

The screen. And Kiew.

The resolution adjusted as the camera in the thirteenth-floor condo snapped alive. The living room lay empty and dark. He glanced at the clock and saw the early hour there. It made sense. Tapping a few keys switched the camera.

His heart quickened. He zoomed in as Kiew lay on the satin sheets on her side, her back to the spying lens. So still. So small in that enormous bed. Black hair spilled across the gray sheets that shone as white beneath the pale moonlight that streamed in through the massive floor-to-ceiling windows.

Rubbing a finger over his lip, he watched. Remembered nights of passion. Remembered the lure of the chase to secure her. That first night he'd seen her in the club with her friends she'd been small and insignificant. . .yet stunning. Her silver dress hugging her curves. He'd pursued her for months. Learned of her brilliance. Her way with computers and technology. Assets he had been searching for to exact his revenge against the Americans.

A buzzing wormed through his thoughts, his mind seeped in the past.

Jin blinked and saw the red light on his phone flashing. Registered the vibrating buzz of the handset. He lifted it. "What do you want?"

"Sir, you were right."

His nostrils flared as he finally accepted her betrayal. When had she made contact with the Americans? How could she do this after all he had given her? After the position he set her upon? But he'd listened to his instincts. Followed his—as the Americans would say—gut.

"Sir, it could have been the Sikh."

Jin lifted his chin, considering the words. It was true—the Sikh could have betrayed him. He'd left the country on business almost as quickly as Jin had. "Perhaps."

"Should we interfere?"

"No. How long now?"

"Fifteen minutes, maybe ten. No more."

He stared at her unmoving image. At what point would she rise from the bed and feign surprise? "Good. Let it happen."

CHAPTER 23

Kabul, Afghanistan
5 April—0400 Hours

Go go go!" Night-vision goggles on and M4 tucked against his shoulder, Sal scurried forward through the night-darkened streets. His boots crunched over the rocks and litter like a booming homing beacon. Ears registering every sound and rustle, Sal's nerve endings buzzed with anticipation of discovery and failure.

Ahead by a half klick, Knight and Ddrake had taken point, ready to sniff out the enemy and give the team advance notice of possible confrontation. Sal silently whispered a prayer of thanks that he'd fought to get the MWD team assigned to Raptor. Knight was sharp and Ddrake—well, the MWDs defied explanation with their thousand-word command vocabulary and their incredible instinct for trouble.

In bound-and-cover fashion, Sal led the way down the street. Hawk hustled ahead, then Sal took the lead again. Back and forth as they made their way to the multilevel parking garage huddled against Tower One.

"Nice and easy, Aladdin," came Dean's calm, steady voice over the coms as he monitored the mission from Kandahar. The Aladdin nickname for the mission was as corny as they got—rescuing a Chinese heroine called up ideas of the ancient heroine Mulan for Hawk to resist.

"Roger that," Sal whispered, throwing his shoulder against the cement parking garage and keeping watch as Harrier, Hawk, and Titanis slid by in a silent stream.

Sal felt the pat on his shoulder and knew they were in place. He rolled around and took up the lead on the team. They snaked in the parking garage. Dim lights cast strange shadows that would make it easier for the team to be seen and harder for them to remain incognito.

Sal jerked back, spine against the wall. "Genie, we have no-go on entry. It's a little too bright."

Within seconds, darkness clamped down. The half wall that blocked their direct path to the stairwell door now swam in a sea of green. Sal moved forward, pieing out and left as Hawk went right. They swept inside and made it to the center support wall. Hustled along it. He came to stop, the door three rows over beckoning to him. He waited for the signal that the team had grouped up behind him.

"Abu in position," came Riordan's firm voice. That meant the SEALs were in position to breach the tower from the south stairwell.

Bleep! Bleep!

Lights flashed on a BMW ten feet from Sal as the stairwell door swung closed after a businessman.

He dropped to a crouch as feet crunched over the ground. He heard a voice talking, sounding tired and irritated.

"Eyes on target," Hawk said.

Sal's heart rate kicked up a notch as the man strolled to his car, chatting on his phone. Between a white sedan and a gray truck, the man approached the Beamer. Opened the door and threw in a briefcase. If the guy saw the team. . .

Keep moving, keep moving, Sal willed him.

The man removed his jacket and laid it in the backseat. Shut the door and opened the driver's side door. He stopped, his voice pitching as he talked.

C'mon, c'mon.

"Aladdin, do not engage," Dean warned.

Head tucked, eyes on the man still, Sal subvocalized, "Copy."

The man snapped his head around, wary eyes wildly green in the wash of night vision. He looked to the left. Then right. He turned and faced the team.

Sal sunk into the shadows, willing them to swallow and prevent him from being discovered. His pulse punched his ribs.

With a snapped word in Farsi, the man whipped around and slid into the car. The engine revved and bright white reverse lights slapped Sal's eyes.

He clenched his eyes tight against the NVG, which amplified and seared the illumination through his corneas. Blinking, Sal watched through the spots in his vision as the car swung around and left the garage.

"Go!" Sal hissed and pushed up from a crouch. He practically sprinted to the door and slammed against the wall, M4 trained on the door. Three seconds later, Hawk patted his shoulder.

Sal stepped out and gripped the handle.

Hawk aimed his assault rifle at the door.

Sal ripped it open.

Cheek pressed to the weapon, Hawk rushed in, pieing left. Though the man had been shot and laid up for a couple of days, nobody could tell that from the way he moved. The precision with which he carried out his mission.

As Sal held the door, Knight and Ddrake hurried inside, the dog sniffing and panting, his tail wagging excitedly. For an MWD, there was no greater thrill than the hunt. Harrier and Titanis brought up the rear, escorting Cassie between them. The Aussie covered their six, facing to the rear until the last minute when he pivoted and entered the stairwell behind Sal. He ignored the panic written all over Cassie's face as she advanced with the team, wearing a tactical vest and helmet. Only her awkward body language gave her away as someone not intimately acquainted with combat.

Tension rose with each step Sal took. Not only did the iron stairs provide the worst acoustics and amplify every sound, but it was a death trap. Each floor provided an entry, but if they got trapped above and below. . .

By the time Sal hit the fifth floor, he wished taking the elevator had been an option. Hugging the cement brick walls, he rounded one level after another, muttering the level to keep Genie—base—updated on their progress.

"Abu in position."

Sal wanted to curse. The Beamer had cost them time. Riordan and his team had already made it through the mid-level maintenance floor, which had access to the balcony via an air-conditioning access room.

Eight.

He heard a soft noise behind him and glanced back. Titanis held Cassie's arm and she flashed him a nervous but thankful look. She wasn't conditioned for long hikes nor quick ones, so she was probably struggling. Tripping, by the dusty mark on the shin of her black pants. But when she looked up and met his gaze, Sal saw the mark of determination in her eyes—eyes washed green through NVGs.

He focused on the goal, getting into position to breach the condo. He palmed the next number painted on the wall. "Nine." Up a flight then a landing, another dozen steps that—if the map tucked in his sleeve was right—abutted the rear of the elevator. The one he'd have gladly taken it if wouldn't have been so dangerous.

"Ten." He took a knee at the door, gripping the handle in his gloved hand and waited.

A double-pat on his shoulder.

Sal keyed his mic and subvocalized, "Aladdin in position."

—⁂—

Electricity thrummed through her veins. At least, that's what it felt like as Cassie moved with Raptor. She'd worked with them on logistics and analysis, but never in this capacity. Her respect and admiration for the men rose exponentially. To her surprise, that included Sal. She knew him in ways most of these men didn't. Knew what he'd been like *before*.

Her muscles knotted when Sal pushed from a kneeling position and Hawk moved to the other side of the door, holding it. They looked at each other.

Sal held up three fingers.

Two.

A nod. And the door ripped open.

Light flashed into the stairwell. Not bright light, but with the darkness they'd been submerged in—darkness that had made her miss a step and ram her shin against the steel step—this amber glow felt like a spotlight. Though her instinct said to shrink from the light, from discovery, she moved with the fluid team into the condo.

If she didn't have a massive spike of adrenaline, maybe Cassie would've stopped to admire the lavish appointments. A rich brown marble floor that reminded her of Sal's eyes—minus the gold flecks. Sleek lines and stainless steel gave it a cold feel. The foyer diverged in two paths. To the right, the living room, kitchen, media room, library, and whatever else a rich person needed.

Movement jacked her pulse. Cassie sucked in a breath and experienced a dump of adrenaline across her shoulders as she watched shadows filter into the room from the balcony. Three, four men. Moving with stealth and precision. The first man—

Wait. That should be Riordan's team. The breath she'd held escaped in a quick breath.

In front of her, Sal and Hawk banked right, bound-and-covering through the corridor, one in front of the other until they reached a door. Titanis and Harrier rushed in with M4s up, night vision guiding them. When Sal yanked open a door, his weapon trained on the void beyond, her heart climbed into her throat at the very real threat he faced doing his job.

She watched, powerless if someone shot at him. Waited, scared. He moved on—and as she followed, she looked in. Coats hung on a rack. Shoes on the floor. An umbrella.

Next they came upon a powder room, flanked by two smaller closets. *How many closets do two people need?* Harrier and Titanis rejoined the other two as they made their way toward a set of double doors. Master bedroom.

Most likely location of Kiew at this hour. Cassie drew back, her mind whiplashing through scenarios. Would Kiew hate her for this?

I hate myself for this!

Why did she always believe in people so firmly? She believed in Sal—and he had pretty much hung her out to dry. And yet, she still believed in him.

And Kiew. . .who had held a gun to Hawk's head and been ruthless with her words to Cassie.

The four soldiers converged.

Cassie's stomach roiled. She placed a hand over it and leaned against the wall, her knees rubbery.

The door flicked open with a soft click. In seconds, she stood alone in the hall, straining to hear. When no sound came, when they didn't demand Kiew get on her knees, when they didn't call for her to identify her friend, Cassie peeled herself off the cool wall. Taking a calming breath, she stepped forward.

A rustle of ficus leaves behind snapped her around.

The mostly dark hall made it hard to see. But not too hard—she saw a flutter of some light color float around a closing door.

The closet Sal had checked. The one with shoes and umbrellas.

Cassie went for it, her mind screaming to call Sal. She glanced back and realized if she called out, she could ruin the whole mission. Give away their location if they hadn't been discovered.

A soft whirring pulled her to the closet.

Hand trembling, she reached for the long, thin handle. Her palm grew sweaty in the second it took her to grip the silver. She drew it back.

Coats were shoved aside. Shoes knocked over.

A light gray panel was shrinking.

No! Not a panel! A secret door.

Cassie threw herself through the sliver of an opening.

"Walker, no!" Sal's shout chased her into the dark void.

CHAPTER 24

Kabul, Afghanistan
5 April—0418 Hours

What was that?"

Sal ignored Hawk's demand and used his fingers to trace the wall. Despite his own eyes telling him there'd been an opening, he could find no trigger or depression to release the door. He slapped the wall.

"Is she helping this chick?" Hawk asked.

"No," Sal growled, rounding on the coms specialist. He keyed his mic. "Genie, we have a problem. The package has eluded us. There's a hidden access panel in a closet. Any way to tell where they went?"

"Clear the rest of the apartment. We'll work on it," Dean barked, his tone mimicking the anger Sal felt. He stormed into the living area where Riordan and his team had subdued a house servant.

The man knelt, sitting on crossed ankles as he held his hands behind his head.

"You okay here?" Sal asked.

Riordan nodded. "Go. Find her."

Sal slapped his shoulder and jogged out into the foyer.

"Why don't we ask the servant?" Hawk asked as he trailed him.

"Because Meng-Li's only other tie in this building is the fifth floor."

———※———

Cassie stood in the chilled darkness of what was a stairwell. She didn't have NVGs like Sal, but she could see—barely—the stairs. Tentatively she moved forward, listening.

Somewhere. . .distantly. . . she heard the slap of feet. Huffing.

"Kiew!" Cassie's voice bounced off the cement and steel, vibrating through her very bones.

A gasp and clang responded.

Pushing herself to brave the darkness, Cassie went for the stairs. Closed her eyes and focused on the height and length of the steps. If she could memorize that, she could develop a rhythm to move quickly. She kept her eyes closed, listening to the steps. The stairs coiled around. After eighteen steps, a platform. Probably to another floor. Then the steps continued.

Eighteen.

Platform.

Eighteen.

Platform.

After two more, she slowed. Thinking back. Looking up to the floor she'd fallen through the hidden door, though the black sea above hung thick and ominous. Wasn't it a law to have lights in the fire well? Lights not keyed to the main building? Maybe Raptor had those turned off as well.

She looked back. If she'd counted right, she should have reached the fifth floor. Sixteen. . .seventeen. . .eighteen. Cassie stopped, pressing her foot hard against the steel and noting the slight difference to the feel. Yes, another platform. Toeing her way forward, she stretched out her arm.

Her hand struck something. She traced it with her fingertips. Rough. Not a door. She moved to the left. Her foot slipped. With a yelp, she caught herself. Jerked backward. Adrenaline dumped through. Okay, not that way. Too far. She moved more determinedly. Felt the cold steel. Smiled. Angled toward where the handle should be. "Right. . .about"— metal smacked the back of her hand—"here." She smiled, twisted the knob, and tugged it open.

Light flooded her senses. She squinted and stepped into a carpeted office. As she did, as the hollowness and eerie silence of the well-appointed space rang in her ears, Cassie realized her mistake.

She glanced to the door. No backup. No weapon.

The door to the main area stood partially open. Teak desks and sleek chairs filled the office, the monotony broken by occasional trees and artwork. Somewhere, a triangle of light traced a dragon statue that coiled up and seemed to watch over the cubicles. But that light—it was an anomaly. No other lamps were on. Kiew must be wherever that light originated.

Cassie walked into the open and skated a glance around. Thirty or forty cubicles spanned the space to the wall that must have the fountain on the other side. The wall that had prevented her from reaching Kiew last week.

To her left, down the hall a bit, she spied an open door, light spilling out.

Mustering her courage, she headed that way, wishing she had a way to communicate with Sal.

On second thought, no she didn't. He didn't believe in her. Didn't believe when she said Kiew wasn't the enemy. As she stood in that padded comfort of silence, Cassie wished for once someone would believe in her with the same level of trust as she did.

She slowed as she approached the door.

Something slammed. Wood on wood, it sounded like.

Cassie peered through the narrow splice, where door and jamb met. Through the half-inch space she saw Kiew stuffing files into a leather duffel. She had a phone pressed to her ear. She was talking crazy-fast the way Chinese did. Even with Cassie's limited Mandarin from that year in China, she couldn't catch enough words to make sense of what her friend was saying.

She stepped into the doorway.

Kiew snatched something from the desk and whipped toward Cassie. In the space of two heartbeats, Cassie realized her friend held a gun on her. "I trusted you!"

"No," Cassie said. "You didn't. Otherwise we wouldn't be in this position."

Grabbing the bag handles, Kiew kept the weapon with its screwed on silencer trained on her.

Cassie took a step. "Kie—"

Thwat! Thwat!

The wall spewed gypsum at her, stopping Cassie in her tracks. She raised her hands.

"I will not miss next time." Kiew started toward her, the silenced weapon closing the distance.

"Let me help you!"

"Back up," Kiew ordered, motioning her aside with the barrel of the weapon.

Cassie did as instructed. "Kiew, please."

"You are not my friend. You work for the government."

"I work for someone who wants to help you get out of this."

Her friend laughed. "You have no idea what you are talking about."

"I know Jin beats you."

Kiew's narrow eyes flitted to the door then to Cassie. "So what?"

"So, I can help you get out of this. You don't have to stay."

"I'm not staying." Kiew's expression mocked her. "I'm leaving. As soon as you get out of my way."

"We can help you!"

"You are a sweet woman, but this is so much bigger than you."

"Then tell me," Cassie said earnestly as she leaned toward her friend. "Come with me and tell me then. We can sort it out."

"You Americans have a traitor in your midst and you want me to trust you?" Kiew's caustic laugh stabbed Cassie.

She was going to lose her friend, and who knew what would happen then. Desperation pushed her on as Kiew made her way down a hall. "Please, Kiew. Talk to me. Let me help you."

"I will not go with those soldiers."

"Then come with me." Heart thundering, Cassie advanced. "I'll sneak you out of here and we can get you to safety."

Kiew considered her, expression wary. "How?"

Right. How? How would she get them out with the U.S. monitoring the entire complex? "We'll figure it out. You know this complex better than I do. Show me how to get out then I'll get you to safety. I have contacts."

Who weren't talking to her at the moment, but she'd get them to help her.

"You would do this? Betray your lover and country? For me?"

Mind blazing, Cassie tried not to think of Sal or his team. They'd hang her out to dry. "I want to help you."

A noise erupted behind them. Sounded like the stairwell. Cassie glanced back, terrified Sal would find her talking with Kiew. Helping her. When she returned her attention to Kiew—she found an empty passage.

Cassie threw herself down the gray-lined walls to a T-juncture. She checked right. It dead-ended and went left. She turned in the other direction as the clang of a door slammed shut.

Cassie pivoted.

Something slammed into her back. Threw her into the wall. *Crack!* Her vision blurred and went black.

CHAPTER 25

Kabul, Afghanistan
5 April—0430 Hours

Disbelief stabbed Sal as he watched Cassie take a bullet in the back. She pitched forward and collapsed. Heart in his throat, he sprinted forward, right up to the opening into the T-intersection and threw himself against the wall.

"Falcon," Hawk hissed, padding up beside him.

Sal went to a knee and then whipped around the corner, ready to nail whoever had shot her. The gray hall lay empty. He jerked right, reaching for Cassie as he did. He caught the drag strap on her vest and hauled her, bent in half, into the safety of the other passage.

"I got it," Hawk said, covering them.

He reached around in front of her and nudged her back into his arms. She flopped, her head lolling against his chest. Sal adjusted and cradled her head in the crook of his arm. "Andra."

No response. No movement. Two fingers to her carotid verified she was alive. He held his hand to her nose. A whisper of breath skated across his skin. Relieved she was breathing, he laid her down. Traced her body for blood. Nothing. No visible wound. A million thoughts fired through his brain—she could've been paralyzed if the bullet had hit a few inches left of the mark. Her heart may very well be in jeopardy. He couldn't lose her.

Sal patted her face. "Andra!" He did it again, this time harder.

She sucked in a hard breath, arched her spine upward, and reached for her back with a strangled cry.

"Easy, easy." Relief speared Sal. "You took a bullet. Knocked you out."

A red knot swelled over her brow. "Nearly put a hole in that wall, Walker."

Tears pushed from between her lids.

"We need to move," Hawk said

Cassie rolled onto her side, pain etched into her soft, dirt-smudged features. She grimaced and pulled upright.

Sal held out a hand and tugged her to her feet. When she swayed, he held tighter and braced her back. "Okay?"

"I need to find her." She wrangled against his hold.

"We will." Sal tightened his grip, dark meaning tucked squarely between those two words.

"No, she's not—" She shook her head. "Kiew's in trouble. I have to help her." She slapped his arm and barreled into him, pushing him aside.

Pain sluiced through the spot she'd hit, but he focused on Cassie. "Easy, we do this according to plan. Stay on plan, Walker." On keeping her from doing something stupid.

But she seemed hell-bent on doing just that. Though she walked like a drunk, wincing with each step, Cassie started for the hall.

"No." He caught her arm. Twisted her around. With a death grip on her, he nudged her back against the wall and pinned her.

Her head thudded against a framed print with a crack. She winced and stilled, chaos swirling in the blue ocean of her gaze. "What—?"

Tweet.

"Just stop. Listen to me. We need to regroup. This isn't about you and your friend, Andra. It's about—"

Bleep.

"This is *bullcrap*," Hawk snapped. "I told you she was helping that chick."

"Quiet," Sal said. What was that noise?

Beep. Beep. Sal's gaze rose to the ceiling. To the sprinkler set there. To the red light. *Beep-beep.* It flashed in cadence with the noise. What. . . ?

"She's working against us. How can you not see that?"

"I am not working against you. I—"

"You're aiding our enemy, trying to help her escape."

"Falcon, you okay?" came the calm, steady voice of Dean through the coms.

Sal grabbed Hawk's vest and jerked him up straight. "Stop," he growled into his face.

"Is there a situation?" Dean didn't waste time with politeness.

"No," Sal said, still honed in on Hawk with one hand and Cassie in the other. But he sent as much fury as he could work into his expression to warn Hawk to stand down. "We're good." With a wag of his eyebrows, he dared Hawk to contradict him.

Though Hawk's nostrils flared he relented, giving a nod.

Beep–beep.

Sal again checked the smoke alarm. A dark feeling crowded his thoughts. "We need to move." Instead of voicing his ominous thoughts, he focused his energy on Cassie, on getting the mission done and getting out. That's when he noticed the pale sheen to her face. The graying around her eyes. Her wound was taking its toll. "We have a lot of moving around to do. Are you going to be okay?"

Beep. Beep. Beep.

Was it his imagination or was that beeping getting faster? "Genie, we may have a problem."

"Go ahead," Dean said.

"I think they activated something."

"Alarm or bomb?" Dean's voice hardened.

Sal looked at the two with him. "Yeah," was all he could say since he didn't know which had been set off.

"Clear out," Dean ordered.

"We can get Tang," Sal insisted.

"Negative. I want my team alive."

With a huff, Sal weighed the options. Defying this order could mean they all died. Obeying meant a complete mission failure.

"RTB. We'll sort it out here," Dean said, his words edged with defeat.

Sal watched Cassie. Her eyes widened. And curse it all—with each shake of her head, she tugged the thin threads of their relationship. Threads he'd severed the day Vida died, sealing the cauldron of his feelings for her. Feelings that were intense. Fiery. And if she tugged once more. . .

Why did he even care? Because his mind was still lodged in his throat back at the instant when he thought the bullet had ripped Andra from his life, too.

It bugged him. He shouldn't care. Shouldn't let it affect his decision. His resolute commitment to his team and commanding officer. But it was one thing to lose someone you cared about, and another to lose someone you loved.

He hated himself for that. For not smothering that weakness completely the way he'd convinced himself. But this wasn't about Cassie and him. He didn't want to make the wrong move, and the setup of this mission seemed to have the fate of the American military in the balance.

"You can't," Cassie pleaded. "She has to be found. I can help her."

Burnett had said Cassie could read a situation unlike any other person he knew. So if that was true, then was she seeing something he wasn't?

"Do you copy, Aladdin?" Dean once more penetrated Sal's thick skull.

Everything in Cassie's Swiss features begged him not to comply. "Yes," Sal said, his mind bungeeing back and forth between terra firma and reckless, intentional abandon of protocol. "I hear you."

But even as he said the words, Cassie threw herself around and sprinted into the hall, no doubt expecting him to follow protocol. "Walker!"

"Falcon, what's going on?"

"Holy cow," Hawk hissed, muting his mic. "For once, I'm with the chick. We need Tang."

"Walker's gone after Tang," Sal replied to Dean, his mind raging.

Sal nodded, his mind snagging on the fact he wouldn't put it past Meng-Li Jin to blow the place if he felt compromised. But without Tang, the mission was a bust. A failure.

"Hawk, Falcon, clear out," Dean made the call for him.

"Sir, we have to get Tang," Hawk said.

"It would do you well," spoke a voice thick with accent and intensity, "to leave immediately. You have four minutes before the bomb detonates."

"No way. I'm going to bring her Chinese butt in." Hawk sprinted into the hall.

"Hawk! Wait!"

CHAPTER 26

Kabul, Afghanistan
5 April—0438 Hours

Steel clanged as Cassie rushed down the steps of the stairwell, determined to catch Kiew. She had to be here—it was the only logical course of action. To go down, to the garage, away from the team. And Kiew had said she wanted to leave, which meant she'd find the nearest exit from the building.

Panting as she leapt down to the landing, scaling four steps, Cassie grabbed the rail. Swung herself around.

Knocking steel echoed from below.

"Kiew!" She leaned down to see the maze of stairs. "Kiew, wait!" Hurtling down almost guaranteed she'd get hurt, but Cassie didn't care. Her friend's life was in danger.

Again, she hooked the rail and swung herself around.

Right into a booted foot. Kiew swung a round kick straight into Cassie's face. Connected. Cassie flung backward, shock and pain riddling her body. Her head cracked against the cement wall. Pain jarred her, vibrating her bones and rattling her teeth. A fresh explosion of fire tore through her shoulder and warmth slid down her back. Shock choked her—Kiew attacked her as if she were a threat. Numb at the realization, she almost didn't see the next kick.

Cassie threw her right arm up and out, shoving Kiew's foot into the incline of steps. Though adrenaline doused her body and ignited the fight or flight mechanism, Cassie couldn't think past the fact that her friend was attacking her.

"Kiew, please." She hopped to her feet.

And came face-to-face with a silenced weapon. Cassie skidded, her boots slipping on the steel floor that offered no traction. Her legs went out, but her grip on the rail prevented her from a bone-jarring fall. She scrambled upright, chin up.

"What will it take to get you to leave me alone?" Kiew's round face betrayed nothing but the cold, unfeeling words she'd spoken.

Hands up, Cassie eased back a step. "Listen, I know you feel you have—"

"You know *nothing* about me!" Eyes slit, her friend kept the weapon aimed at Cassie's face. "You have not seen me in ten years! Christmas and birthday cards do not mean you have any idea who I am or what I want."

The emotion behind those words betrayed the cold, heartless ones spoken earlier. "I do know you, Kiew. I know the girl with a soft heart who couldn't get enough of *Neon Genesis Evangelion*. Who was outraged when Shinji's father disowned him. You were as strong and outgoing as Mari Makinami, and I was—"

"This is not a manga, you idiot!" Face red, Kiew inched forward.

Affronted, Cassie shuffled back, her boots thudding against the step for the stairs she'd just descended. She struggled to keep her balance.

"This is real life and you are where you do not belong. Now." She waved the weapon toward the door.

"Kiew—"

"Out! Or I will shoot you. And trust me, you are not the first American I have killed and you will not be the last either."

Cassie's hand went to her aching shoulder, wondering if Kiew had shot her as Sal had asked. "But—"

"Tang, stop right there," came a deep, booming voice. Hawk.

Kiew jumped back, out of view from the center well of the stairwell.

"Please, Kiew," Cassie said, her aching body warning her to be wary. "I can help you."

Dark brown eyes lit with intensity. "Yes." Her nostrils flared. Lightning fast, before Cassie could react, Kiew grabbed her by the collar. Hauled her up against her. "You can help me by being my insurance."

Cassie went cold. Was this really Kiew Tang? The woman who had shared her room, laughter and love of anime and manga with her a decade ago? A girl who had an amazing career in front of her?

Hooking an arm around Cassie's neck, Kiew dragged her backward. A fumbling of a handle then they were passing from the stairwell into the eerie silence of a floor of professional offices. By the smell of paint and new carpet, she wasn't even sure the spaces were occupied.

Kiew shoved Cassie into a wall. Riddled with pain, throbbing in her jaw and fire in her neck and shoulder, Cassie stumbled. Used the wall to gain support and catch her breath. She wanted to scream that she didn't understand how her friend could do this, how this could be the real woman named Kiew Tang, but she'd seen too many movies where the clichéd line only brought on criticism and ridicule.

Click. Tink.

Beep.

Cassie glanced to her frie—*Kiew*—and froze. She pressed buttons on a small, round device she'd set on a steel girder. Charges! "What are you *doing?*"

Kiew pivoted, only then the messenger bag slung over her body draped to reveal a half-dozen more. She lifted her weapon again and motioned with it. "Go. Toward the atrium."

"No." Cassie drew straight, her spine suddenly intact and not weakened by the delusion of a friendship long-since dead. "No, I'm not—"

Kiew lifted the weapon. Before Cassie even heard the *thwat*, gypsum spat at her. "Next one will not miss."

How. . .how had she read it so wrong? Read Kiew wrong? "You're going to kill us. All of us."

"It is not my fault your team chose to ignore my warning."

"It was you with Hawk. You nearly killed him."

"And when I didn't," she said as she moved hurriedly down the corridor, "he repaid the favor by knocking me out, killing my associate, and leaving me as raw meat to Jin."

When they stepped out into the atrium that stood open to eight floors, Kiew clung to the inner wall, apparently nervous Raptor would spot her.

Safety net of belief ripped away, Cassie walked outward, not a lot, but enough for Sal to see her.

Kiew grabbed her arm and yanked Cassie to the wall. "Do not think I am stupid."

"I don't know what to think of you." Her words hit their mark. The mask of anger and heartlessness slipped. Just a little. But enough for Cassie to see.

The gun pushed against her temple. "The last person who tried to betray me dropped several IQ points."

Cassie swallowed—hard. Maybe she was reading into the situation instead of *reading* it. Reading Kiew. Shouldn't she have seen this cold-blooded killer the day they had lunch, rather than the manga-loving friend who went to cons and cosplayed with her their senior year?

"I never thought you'd try to kill me."

"I never thought you'd be so stupid to push my hand." Kiew stepped back, and for several long, silent seconds she stared at something behind Cassie.

Unsettled, Cassie glanced back. What? What was Kiew looking at? She only saw a teak door with a gold plate with the word PRIVATE etched into it.

"Sit." She waved the gun to a teak bench with lines as hard and unfeeling as the woman motioning to them.

"You're setting charges and you want me to sit?"

Kiew reared and slammed the gun into Cassie's face.

The unexpected move spun Cassie around. Her feet tangled. She pitched forward and down. She shoved out her hands to break her fall. Her forehead rammed into the protective glass barrier. Her eyes glued to the marble floor three floors down. Though her brain told her the glass barrier had broken her fall, her ears rang with dizziness that overtook her.

"Andra!"

The hollow shout of her name pulled her away from the glass. Wobbling, she came to her feet and turned to find Sal and Hawk jogging out from the same stairwell door Kiew had dragged her through.

But she pushed herself to the right. After Kiew. Where had she gone? They had to get her. Stop her. The gloves were off. Cassie's strength

RONIE KENDIG

and balance grew with each step.

She made it to the next juncture and heard feet clapping on marble below. Cassie ran to the barrier. A blur of black raced toward the lower exit to the parking garage. "Kiew!"

The door flapped open. And for a second, Kiew paused. Her expression went wide with terror. Then she was gone.

"Cassie!"

She pivoted back to Sal. "I'm going—" Her gaze snapped to blinking lights on the right side of the corridor entrance, just above a silver control panel. Her heartbeat detonated within her chest. Charges.

The instant powered down into an agonizing slow-motion nightmare. She sucked in a breath, the sound a hollow *whoosh* in her ears. Her pulse thundering—*boom*. Her breath as if she stood in a protected environmental suit, shielded from the terror, but also forced to witness it.

In a blink, she looked at Sal.

Whoosh. Boom-boom!

Another blink revealed two lights *behind* him as well.

Boom-boom! She couldn't breathe. Couldn't move. Powerless.

Hawk leaned over the barrier, shouting something she couldn't understand over the *whoosh-whoosh-boom* of her vacuous world. Just over his left shoulder. . .another charge. This one on the cement pylon supporting the overhang of the balcony section of the floor.

Charges. They were surrounded by charges. Kiew had rigged this whole level to blow.

"No!" She threw herself forward, her legs leaden like a sick dream. "Sal! Back!"

CHAPTER 27

Men who live by the sword, die by the sword.

The sick thought zapped through Sal's brain in the microseconds that had hit the freeze button on this moment. When Cassie looked toward the wall, her fair skin went white. Deathly white. And forced Sal to look in that direction.

He saw the charge. The same kind disguised as a smoke detector in the corridor. And by the terror gouged into Cassie's face, they were going to detonate.

Throwing himself toward Cassie, Sal twisted to the right. To where Hawk stood. "Hawk, ruuunnn!"

Hawk jolted. In frozen animation, he hunched his shoulders. Threw himself forward, toward Sal. Toward safety.

BooOOOOOooooom!

An invisible fist punched Sal backward. Though he blinked. Though the fireball torpedoed toward him. Sal somehow saw Hawk lift into the air and get thrown.

Sal smacked hard into something. Dropped. A gust of searing air snapped over him. Followed by an orange-and-red fireball. The concussion of the explosion clapped its mighty hands over his ears. The world cracked and rained black.

A warbling noise tugged Sal from a heavy darkness.

Pressure against his shoulder. Pain on his cheek.

He grunted.

Again the warbling noise.

He blinked. Grit fell into his eyes rubbing. Gritty. Burning.

But he saw her face—Cassie her blond hair coated with ash—peering down at him. "Sal?" Black smudged her face, mingling with the blood from where Tang had cracked open her cheek. "Sal!"

The warbling was her voice. She pushed against his shoulders. Only then did the world coalesce into a semblance of clarity. Fire licked the walls and crackled as it snaked through the building.

He'd been thrown into Cassie, who lay beneath him. He pried himself off the floor, feeling as if he'd been clobbered by Thor's hammer. Immediately he noticed the gaping hole in the floor. The spot where—

"Hawk!" Sal popped to his feet, coughing. *"Hawk!"*

"Falcon!"

Sal hurried forward, eyeing the damaged floor for vulnerabilities. "Where—?"

"Here!"

The explosion had bitten a crevice off the balcony, devouring a section of the glass barrier and several feet of carpeted floor. Clinging to a stretch of mangled steel that had held the glass, Hawk dangled precariously over the several-story drop. Below, glass, cement, and debris littered the ground floor. If a drop didn't kill him, it'd break his back or legs.

"O God—" Falcon choked on the rest of his desperate plea and threw himself forward. The floor trembled beneath him, threatening to pitch him into the depths.

"Sal!" Cassie cried out behind him as a section of the far floor gave way, widening the chomp it'd taken out of the balcony earlier.

Sal scrabbled backward.

"No," Hawk shouted. "Stay back—it's unstable." His hands shimmied along, closer to Sal.

Sal ignored him, skirting toward the crevice, hoping to reach the small handspan that eased out. With the floor and the gaping hole, it resembled the ying of a yang. Sal went to his knees. Crawled gingerly.

Tremors of the explosion and fire, eating through the walls and building, taunted him, vibrating against his palms and fingertips. Sal ignored it. Focused on saving his friend. "You are one pain in the butt, Bledsoe."

"Reckon that's so, sir," Hawk said, shifting.

The compromised area rattled.

"Whoa whoa whoa." Sal swallowed the adrenaline pumping through his body. "Easy."

"Yeah," Hawk said, his voice shaky and his eyes filled with dread. "Was thinking the same thing."

Sprawled on his belly, Sal eased forward.

"Coms," Hawk said.

Only then did Sal realize he couldn't hear anything through his earpiece. "I think mine's blown."

"Sal, where's Hawk?" came a shout from somewhere behind. Titanis.

"Stop," Cassie shouted. "The floor is compromised."

Sal shifted forward. His shoulders reached over the emptiness. Sal locked on to Hawk. Slid his arms down and coiled them around Hawk's wrists and forearms—and that's when Sal noticed the man's arms trembling. "We're going to come this way. It's more solid. Less damage."

Hawk nodded.

"Are you hurt?" Sal asked, concerned at the gray pallor taking over Hawk's face. He searched his friend for a new wound.

"Got shot— several days ago. Should've been there. Pretty"—Hawk's face screwed tight in pain then he let out a breath—"awesome."

Not what he meant. But Brian was failing fast. "Hawk?"

Green eyes met his. "The wound tore. Bleeding." He shook his head. "Not sure how much longer I can—"

His fingers slipped.

He dropped a couple of inches.

Sal gripped tighter. "Hawk!" Clamps fastened around Sal's ankles.

"Got you, mate." Titanis's firm grip and voice helped. A lot.

"Pull, Titanis. Pull me back!" Sal stared into Hawk's eyes. "Do. Not. Let. Go."

Sweat beaded Hawk's brow and upper lip. He nodded—but much weaker this time.

The weight of the bulky guy strained Sal's arms and shoulder muscles. But he would not let go. A streak of pain darted through his own arm. Almost as quick, he felt blood slide down his inner forearm from beneath his sleeve. Sal cursed himself, cursed his own weakness. Where he'd cut—too deeply—had torn open.

Blood raced down his arm.

Over his palm.

Across his fingers.

Hawk sucked in a breath.

The blood diverted some, but the more his cut leaked, the more it managed to seep between their arms.

"*Augh*," Sal growled. He threw every bit of himself into this. Ignored his pains. The blood. Building crumbling around them.

"Building's coming down," came another voice. Then an expletive.

"Need an anchor," Titanis growled.

"Right."

Hawk dropped two more inches. "Look, man." Hawk grunted, grimacing. "I know we don't. . .get along, but. . ."

"I'm losing—" Sal ground his teeth together, growling, and reached with his other hand.

With a gust of warm air, Cassie sank to his side. She reached forward to help. But even as she reached for their arms, Hawk slipped.

He groped for a hold, his fingers dragging against metal as he fell away.

"*No!*" Sal launched forward.

But something anchored him back.

He struggled, his gaze riveted to the image of Brian Bledsoe falling three floors. . .down. . .down.

Thud!

Dust plumed up, enveloping Hawk's body like a cocoon.

"*Haaaaawwwwwwk!*"

CHAPTER 28

Kabul, Afghanistan
5 April—0455 Hours

That did not just happen. Stunned, Cassie stared down without seeing. Her mind, like some sick, looped video feed, kept replaying Hawk's fall. The way he screamed—not like a girl, but a howl—as he fell. The sickening thud of his body hitting. The way the dust encased him, as if shielding them from witnessing the brutality gravity exerted. Frozen by the terror, she couldn't move. Couldn't react to the danger threatening her and the team. Her stomach roiled, the sound of his body hitting repeating over and over in her mind.

Sal lunged toward the opening.

Cracked and dribbling chunks of cement, the floor dipped down beneath Sal's boots. Cassie sucked in a breath and scrabbled backward.

"Hawk!" Sal remained at the barrier. "Hawk, talk to me!"

Crack! The blue carpet swayed like an undulating ocean.

Two large, thick arms encircled Sal's waist. Titanis dragged a writhing, shouting Sal backward. Away from the widening gap in the floor.

"Get off me!" Sal hitched his legs forward and yanked free of the Aussie, who half tossed Sal to the right, away from the danger of the collapsing floor.

Titanis held up his hands. "Easy, the floor—"

With a roar, the ground gave way. Doubled the gap that Hawk had fallen from.

"He's down there," Sal said. He spun around, fists balled. Wild panic spiraled through his eyes. "We have to save him."

The floor beneath Cassie tilted, threatening to give way. Threatening to deliver her to the same fate.

"Agreed, but not at the expense of your life." Titanis cuffed Cassie's elbow and hauled her to her feet. He nudged her toward Sal. "Stairs are blocked. We need an exit strategy."

Sal spun around, as did Cassie. Because charges had been set on either side, both walls had tumbled inward. A wall of rubble and collapsing upper offices sealed off the hall to the stairs. Heartbeats passed as Cassie stared, disbelieving. Their only way out and it was blocked? Her gaze skipped to the elevators. They'd be stupid to try those in a compromised building. But how else would they get down?

How. . .how would they get out of here?

Titanis tapped his ear. "Captain wants us out of here."

"How?" Sal growled. "Exit's blocked. Hawk is down there. And I'll be hanged if I'm leaving him down there." Gripping the steel girder, Sal shook it. As if testing the weight.

Mind blitzed, Cassie jerked toward him. "Sal, no. You can't."

He didn't respond. Just moved a little farther down, testing again. This section wobbled but not as bad as the first. He rounded the area and went to the other side, almost completely opposite.

"Sal, please." Cassie jogged after him. "Please don't do this. It could collapse."

He shrugged off her comment and touch. Focused on his mission—saving Hawk.

"Falcon," Titanis said. "Captain wants us to get to the roof. He's sending a chopper."

Fury snapped through his brown eyes, so voracious that Cassie took a step back as he stalked toward Titanis. "I need coms." He motioned for Titanis to hand over the piece.

Men in tactical gear streamed out of a darkened hall. The SEALs. Riordan led the way, grim faced but determined. "We have exactly zero options."

Tucking the earpiece Titanis had loaned him, Sal turned toward the newcomers. "Why?"

"Came up two flights—charges set at every level. They haven't detonated, but I have a feeling we're out of time. We can't go down."

"And we can't go up," Titanis said, flicking a hand at the barricaded stairwell.

Kiew. Why had she done this? Given them no way out? Had she really wanted to bury them here? Why? Betrayal. . .

Cassie turned a slow circle, eyeing the rest of the atrium. There had to be another exit, right? Granted, this wasn't America with strict building codes, but surely Takkar took precautions to protect his investments. She trekked around as far as she could go. One hall seemed okay until she rounded the corner and found a pile of cement, plaster, and tinkling lights popping at the far end. She turned and made her way to the opposite side, staring over at the crumbling shelf.

"Hey, I think Ddrake hit on something." Knight stood before a door.

Cassie stilled as she recognized the door. The one marked *PRIVATE*. The one Kiew had stared at. She hurried forward. "That—that's it!"

"Locked," Knight said.

"Open it," Cassie insisted.

"What'd you do? You stupid witch!" a meaty yell carried through the chaos.

Cassie turned, her mind numb.

One of the SEALs shouted something else, but she was too numb to realize that his venom had been directed at her. His expression twisted as he shook a hand at her. *Why is he so angry?* Then his words caught up with her. "How stupid could you be—you killed him!"

Stunned, Cassie sat there, blinking. *I killed him?* How could he think that? The accusation lasered through her heart, singeing her with its cruelty.

"Oy, ease off, mate." Titanis was at her side, nodding to the door. "Why'd you say this is it?"

"Kiew stared at it right before she bolted." Was she being stupid just as the SEAL claimed, by thinking maybe whatever was here would save them? What could possibly be in there?

"Watch out." Titanis jutted his jaw at Knight, who moved back and had Ddrake heel. The Aussie lifted his boot and thrust his heel into the door.

It snapped back, hit the wall behind it, and flapped closed again, then open.

Weapon up, Titanis inched forward sweeping back and forth. "Just an office."

Cassie entered, glancing around. Spotted another door. She rushed to it. Tugged it, but again—locked.

"Here." Titanis nudged her aside and repeated his breaching maneuver.

The door flung off the hinge—right into a private stairwell. Heart in her throat, Cassie rushed around the SEALs, who were heading to safety into the stairwell. She stepped out. "Sal—" Shock choked her words.

He had roped up and was about to rappel over the side of the hole. "*Sal*, no!"

A wall of muscle sprinted past her. Titanis. "Falcon, no! It's—"

Crack! Boom!

Fire burst up from a lower level. The floor rattled. Cement, glass, and plaster rained down from above, the lower explosion rattling the upper section.

Sal slipped. Dropped hard against the glass barrier with a thud.

Titanis caught him. Reached over and grabbed the drag strap of his tactical vest. Hauled Sal over the barrier.

"Go, go!" Titanis waved at her as they both lunged in her direction. "Stairs!"

Cassie felt as if that nightmare state had come again. Legs felt like rubbery noodles. Her arms like anchors slowing her. She reached for the doorjamb, to propel herself into the office. Fingers groped wood.

A weight plowed into her back.

She went flying. Straight into the stairwell. Panicked, desperate to survive, she pushed herself to her knees. Hands shoved. Cassie tumbled forward. Down the stairs.

The world rumbled. Groaned. The cement staircase vomited cement. Fire snaked down the steps.

—⁘—

Sal threw himself on top of Cassie, ramming into her with no way to break his momentum. He heard her head smack against the wall. Her cry was no more than a stunted whelp. He rolled, tightening his hold and dragging her with him. They tumbled down the stairs. He held the top of her head, to protect her from cracking her head against the steel steps or cement wall. Sal shouldered into the roll, determined to deflect as much as he could from her body.

Cassie's fingernails dug into his side and arm—the same bloody arm that had caused him to kill his friend.

They thudded onto the next landing. Sal flipped once more, shoving her into the wall, and pressed in on her. With her sealed between himself and the wall, he hunched as cement crumbled like a potato chip. The fury of this explosion roared in their ears, angry and violent, as if livid they were still alive.

"I don't want to die. I don't want to die." Her whimper barely found his ears.

Sal glanced down at her, blinking through the gritty air. Her blue eyes shone with the panic she'd confessed. "I won't let you die."

Hawk. He couldn't be dead. *Please, God. . .please don't let me have killed him. Not another.* He had to be alive. And Sal would save him. Make things right. Expunge this guilt from his soul.

Quiet exploded through the so-called safety area. More like a death trap.

Sal lifted his head, listening, glancing over his shoulder. Dust and marble-sized chunks of cement littered his arm and shoulder. But it seemed the building had settled some.

"Sal, talk to me!" Dean shouted.

"Here. . .here." He grunted and scooted back, eyeing Cassie's blood- and dirt-stained face. "You okay?"

Her pained eyes met his and the fear seemed to melt away, but her fingers were wound around his drag strap, and she wasn't letting go.

"Where are you?"

Sal glanced up, coughing around the dust-entombed area. "Private stairwell in the. . .north. . .northwest—"

"Northeast," Titanis corrected.

"Northeast," Sal repeated with a nod. "Secondary"—or was it tertiary?—"explosion took out lower levels."

"Get out! Riordan said the whole thing is an inferno."

Sal started. Hawk. He couldn't leave Hawk there. His friend couldn't be dead. Not at his hand. Not because of him.

"Sal!"

"Yeah." He cleared his throat. Tried to dislodge the wad of truth stuck there.

"Get out. Now. That is an order!"

A crack splintered the wall straight down the middle.

"Go!" Sal fisted Cassie's sleeve. Thrust her down the stairs. With Titanis on his tail, Sal threw himself after her, making sure Cassie kept moving. Rocks pummeled them. The ground shook.

One flight down. One to go.

He rounded the corner, sweeping an arm out to hook Cassie's waist. He pulled her with him. Focused on the steps. Not on falling. A pressure against his back told him Titanis was doing the same. Pushing forward, staying close. They'd escape this.

Cassie jumped down the last set. Her boots twisted against a foot-high pile of rubble. She pitched forward, but Sal caught her again. Hauled her toward the door propped open by debris.

He dove forward, stumbling as he went.

Titanis caught his drag strap again, pulled him on.

They rushed into the predawn morning, air cool and coated with dust. "Keep moving," Sal shouted as they sprinted into the blue haze.

Groooaaaannn!

Whoosh! Boom! Whoosh!

Superheated air punched them into the ground.

CHAPTER 29

Kandahar Airfield, Afghanistan
5 April—0715 Hours

Onboard the helo back to Kandahar, Sal dumped ibuprofen down his throat and let Harrier wrap gauze around the cut in his arm. What kind of messed-up person cuts up their arm right before a mission?

I killed him. I killed Brian. The guy's visage wouldn't leave his mind. Sal was sure it'd never leave. Just like the sound of Vida's laugh echoed in his head like a daily reminder—a taunt.

First Vida, now Hawk.

A slap against his shoulder startled Sal. He jerked and found Harrier waving him off the bird, which sat on the tarmac already. Robotically, Sal hopped out and stalked away from the rotor wash. They climbed into a vehicle to head to the Command center.

He had to get back there. Hawk had to be alive. And if he was, then he was lying there on that floor as the building came down.

How could he survive that?

Because Hawk was thickheaded and never gave up.

The Jeep lurched to a stop and doors flung open. Sal moved with the flow of traffic into the Command building.

"Hey, you need the hospital?"

Sal turned, his mind half engaged in the question. Eagle reached over and held up Sal's arm streaked with blood. "No." Sal tugged free. "I'm fine. We need to debrief."

Get your head in the game, Russo.

As he strode down the hall, gathering up the broken pieces of his psyche, he spotted Dean through a glass window. The Command room. Sick to his stomach, Sal didn't let himself stop or slow or turn around, though he would've taken any or all of them right now. Anything not to face telling his friend and CO what happened.

He pushed through the door and dragged his unwilling gaze to Dean's.

Hands on his tactical belt, Dean nodded and moved away from the man next to him. "Grab a chair and get comfortable. Coffee's on the way."

The gloom of the team was as palpable as thick goo. Sal tugged back a chair and lowered himself into it. Though pressure lifted from his knees and back, the one surrounding his heart didn't ease.

He leaned forward, elbows on his knees, waiting. How exactly did one confess to killing a teammate? Sal slumped back in his chair, hand over his mouth. He stroked the beard, finding no comfort in the motion this time.

Dean shut the door. Locked it.

Interesting.

The captain moved to the boards and folded his arms over his chest. "Okay, I'll give a rundown of what's on the logs, what happened, then I'll open it up. If anyone has ideas on what went wrong, what could've been done better, we'll hear that then. Understood?"

A chorus of "hooahs" filled the room.

He had to come clean. Tell Dean about the cutting. About being responsible for failing the team and Hawk.

"First, the most obvious—we failed to meet the mission objective," Dean said. "Kiew Tang evaded our capture."

"Sir," Harrier spoke up. "I. . .on two occasions, with the long-range microphone, heard Lieutenant Walker dialogue with the objective."

Sal lifted his head, glanced from Harrier to a now white-faced Cassie.

"What kind of dialogue?" Dean asked.

Harrier hesitated, skating a glance in Cassie's direction but not really making eye contact with her. "*Personal*, sir."

Someone on the SEAL team cursed. "That explains it all." Schmidt.

Sal pushed straight in his chair, hackles raising. "Explains what?"

"I saw her—she dove into you when you were holding Hawk, trying to pull him to safety." Schmidt's white-blond beard and curly-wiry hair made him look like a biker. "It's her fault Hawk went down."

"Now, hold up—"

"It didn't make sense. Everyone knows how precarious things are in a situation like that. One wrong move—and well, I guess we know what happens now. A man dies." He stabbed a finger at Cassie. "If she—"

"You need to back up," Sal said, coming to his feet. "That wasn't Cassie's fault in no way."

"Sal," came Dean's voice of reason and warning.

"Cassie?" Riordan snapped. "First name—that sounds personal. What, were you two hooking up or something? That'd make sense, why you're defending her."

"Hey!" Dean snapped. "Enough. Riordan." He nodded from Riordan to the other SEAL. "Get him in line." He pivoted to where Sal stood—now in front of Cassie.

His hazel eyes had darkened beneath that stern brow. "Sal?"

"She tried to help me. I was losing my grip." *Now or never, chicken.* "I—"

Cassie pushed in front of him. "Schmidt is right," she bit out.

Sal started. "Cassie."

She turned to him, her cheeks bright. Her determination brighter. After sliding him a sympathetic smile, she faced the captain again. "What I did was stupid. But it wasn't meant to harm anyone."

"Doesn't make Hawk any less dead."

Sal lunged.

Cassie stepped into his path. Hands on his chest. "Stop. Don't listen."

"Why are you doing this?" he whispered around a tight voice.

"Stand down!" Dean shouted. "Walker, finish what you were saying."

She angled around. "I saw Hawk slipping, and what I did was done out of instinct to try to stop him from falling. The floor gave way then. That broke Sal's grip." She tucked her head. "Hawk. . .fell."

"Because of you!"

"Yeah? And what about you?" Sal couldn't take it anymore—not Cassie taking the blame or this puke of a SEAL blaming her. "That's a lot of smack you're talking, but where were you when Hawk was dangling for his life?"

Challenge hung in Schmidt's eyes, which eventually found the floor.

"Captain Watters," Riordan said as he patted Schmidt's shoulder. "I need to talk to you."

Scratching the side of his face, Dean huffed. "Raptor, get cleaned up. Sal, Walker—get to the infirmary to check those wounds."

—⁘—

Cassie emerged from the hospital with stitches on her cheek and a patched shoulder. The doctor warned her she'd have a few new aches in the morning, compliments of the bruise in her back—which would've been a bullet had it not been for her vest—but should have full range of motion in no time.

It was a lie to make her feel better. Once Penner and Phelps got wind of this, she'd be out of action. And she might just make that decision on her own. She'd wanted to get close to Sal, to make amends, and it seemed the divide between them just grew and grew.

She'd prayed he'd open up to her. That they could reconcile. She'd greedily accepted this assignment believing it was God's answer to her prayer to provide a way for her to talk to Sal. And here she stood, with him trusting her less than ever. Hating her more.

She snorted. Hadn't thought it possible.

She stepped into the morning and started across the rocky path. Her stomach growled, sending her in the direction of the chow hall for lunch.

"Hey," a voice hissed behind her.

Cassie glanced back, surprised to see Sal. And despite the storm in his expression, her heart betrayed her with a wonky *ka-thump*. "Sal."

He clutched her arm.

She winced.

And he immediately relented, his rich brown eyes flicking to her arm. "Sorry." He let go. Stepped back. "What did you do that for?"

Cassie frowned. Looked at her arm.

"No," Sal said, inching closer, his words barely audible. "In the debrief. You lied to them. Said it was your fault."

Swallowing didn't help dislodge the lump in her throat. "It's true."

"You and I both know that's a lie."

She wet her lips and glanced around them. She didn't want to admit why she'd done that. "It's a peace offering."

This time, Sal frowned. Stared down at her with a mixture of confusion and—dare she believe it?—admiration. The why question lingered loud and proud in this soldier's eyes.

"Even if you hadn't lost your grip because of the blood, you would've eventually. There was no way you'd have hauled him up. Gravity, his injury, and the explosions were all against you." She touched his bandaged arm. "Sal, you're oozing agony. I see it in your everyday life as much as in the blood that slipped down your arm."

"What do you know about what I feel? It's been four years—"

Cassie shook her head, her eyes glossing. Then she nodded. "You're right. It has been. But I stare into your eyes every day I'm home because Mila has your eyes. She's a reminder of the man I fell in love with."

Sal muttered something and spun away from her then dropped onto a picnic bench tucked in a corner. He steepled his fingers and bent over, huffing out heavy breaths. "It's all so screwed up."

Cassie went and sat beside him, their knees touching. "Sal, you probably don't want to hear this, but you have to let go of Vida."

His head came up.

She held out a hand. "Hear me out. Bitterness rots the soul. And it's clawing its way out of you. Blame me if you want." Again, her eyes glossed. "But let go. And Hawk—"

"I can't believe you lied about that. I have to tell Dean."

"No—"

"We have a code to live by, and I can't let that lie stand." His chest rose and fell unevenly. "I can't let that go. It was my fault he died. Not yours."

"You believe it's your fault because of the guilt you feel for cutting." When his gaze narrowed, Cassie rushed on. "Don't lie to me or try to hide it. I know you're doing it. And you haven't told anyone, have you?"

Sal's lips flattened.

"No, of course not, because they'd put you out."

She didn't want him cutting anymore, and if that meant extending him some grace and mercy he desperately needed, some that might cost her a little, she would go there. "I was there, Sal." She leaned closer. "I threw myself across that floor. As soon as my stomach hit, I heard the crack."

His gaze swung to hers. Desperation resonating from him to be freed of the noose he'd hung around his own neck.

She touched his cheek. Smoothed her fingers over his beard. "Please, let it go. Your soul can't take any more of that poison you're feeding it. The self-condemnation." She smiled, tears slipping down her cheeks. "You're a good man, Sal. An amazing soldier. A loyal friend."

He punched to his feet, the raging storm back. "No. That's not true. I'm not loyal. I'm not a good man. It's my fault Vida died."

Surprise drew Cassie to her feet.

He rounded on her, dark brows drawn together. "I had no business getting involved with you, and that's what killed her. Now my inability to deal with the nightmare life keeps serving up killed one of the best soldiers I've ever known." He pivoted, rocks crunching beneath his boots. "How can you call me good when I've done all that?"

"Because I know you. Not the horrible circumstances."

"*Circumstances?*" His voice pitched. "Vida and Hawk were *people*! Friends—my girlfriend. And now they're both dead because of me."

"Fine. You want to play the blame game, I'm in." Cassie's pulse sped as she held out her arms. "The entire freakin' mission is my fault."

He glared at her.

"I broke rank and went after Kiew. When you found me, I'd been talking to her, trying to convince her to come with me." *Oh, man, what are you doing?* "I wasn't there to capture her. I wanted to help her get free."

Sal drew up short.

In the seconds of that moment, of seeing how deeply she'd disappointed him, wounded him, Cassie felt a blow to her gut.

"Tell me that's not true." His tone went deadly.

Why had she told him that? It was true, but. . .she would lose her job for admitting it.

He muttered an oath and shifted away, holding his head.

"Sal—"

"No." He held out a hand to her in a severing fashion. "No more, Cassie." He held a hand over his mouth then dragged it down his beard. "I can't do this anymore. I think I'm about to let go of it, and then you punch me in the gut with something like this. You were *actively* working against my team?"

His words, the truth of those words, stunned her. She'd had an assignment. "I thought she needed a way out. I thought. . ." Wow, it sounded so lame now, especially remembering the horrible things Kiew had said. The bombs she'd set off.

"It's over."

"Sal, I came here to fix this between us because we have a daughter. I prayed God would provide a way for me to see and talk to you, and I got this assignment. It was screwed up and they manipulated me, but I came. We need resolution. You said you wanted to get to know Mila. . ."

"Is that your get-out-of-jail-free card? The way you thought you could drag me back to your bed?"

Cassie sucked in a breath. Snapped back as if he'd slapped her. "How dare you! I had no intention of telling you about Mila. You know what, you don't deserve to be a part of her life! Or mine!"

"You can't stop me from being a part of her life."

Fear squirreled through her chest at the threat that hung in his words. She didn't want it to go this way. Things were supposed to be smoothed over, at best, between them. She'd never expected to win him back. Oh, she'd hoped—a fool's fancy, she understood now—but she knew Sal hated her. "Why can't you put as much effort into working this out as you do into hating and blaming me? If there's a way to fix this, tell me!"

Sal angled in a shoulder, the scent of iodine and antiseptic shielding his normal smell. "You want to fix things? Then *fix* this."

"Fix what?" She flashed her palms at him. "Ya know what? I'm not doing this. You want to be ticked off and keep hating me, then fine. But don't drag me through this."

"You just said Hawk's dead because of you, so how is it *I'm* dragging you? First Vida—"

RONIE KENDIG

"Stop. Blaming Me. For. Vidal" Her breath shuddered from the emotion. The ping-pong of their relationship. The yanking of each others' chains. "I can't take it anymore. It has to stop."

He studied her for a minute, his left cheek just below his eye twitching. "Neither can I. And you're right—this stops. Right here. Right now. We're done, Cassandra."

CHAPTER 30

Kandahar Airfield, Afghanistan
5 April—1335 Hours

You stupid, idiotic sons of—" Ramsey flung a metal chair across the briefing room, his ruddy face a mixture of rage and combat exhaustion.

Dean threaded his fingers together on the table. The men with him included Sal, Knight, Eagle, and Harrier. Riordan and his team had joined them, but the verbal lashing didn't have the weight it carried for Raptor. Nothing like getting flogged when you're already missing a limb. Hawk.

Even thinking the man's call sign pressed heavily on Dean.

"Do you realize the delicate relations you have completely upended tonight with your harebrained, failed operation?" He careened around the room, his arms writhing and lashing out. "And not just any building because that would be too easy."

Eagle folded his arms over his chest, his feelings about the general's tirade clear.

"You have compromised years of intricate political maneuvering with one of the most important assets this side of the Atlantic." He let out a growl and threw a punch in the air.

Sal sat with his head in his hands, his expression awash with grief. Shock. Fury. His fingertips whitened as he pressed them against his closely shaven head.

They'd lost two men—Burnett and now Brian.

"What brand of stupidity possessed you to think you could just go off half-cocked and do that?"

"It wasn't half-cocked," Riordan countered.

"What?" Ramsey roared.

Face blank, Riordan didn't back down. "We had a plan. We executed the plan."

"You executed one of your own!"

Sal shifted, dragging his leg in and extending the other. His breathing was growing heavier. More agitated.

"There is *always* risk." Riordan sure didn't care that he was arguing with a general. Then again, he reported to Admiral Rosen. "And every man in this room's aware of that."

"So that gives you the right to screw with lives and wreck—"

"No, but when a mission goes south as it did tonight, it means we deal with it, learn from it."

Ramsey bent toward Sal. "How are you doing with Bledsoe's death, Russo?"

Dean about came out of his chair. "Sir." That was uncalled for, shoving that down Sal's throat. And if he knew his friend, a physical confrontation could ensue.

Ramsey met his gaze for a moment then moved away, apparently seeing the storm brewing in Sal's expression. "This piece of dirt is racking up lives like they're candy, and what in the name of all that's holy have we accomplished? Except to get our butts handed to us time and again?" He pounded a fist on the table.

Harrier flinched. Shook his head and sagged under the verbal lashing.

"Do you have any idea the political damage you've done, how much this will cost the government? You can bet your sorry butts I'll find a way to take this out of your hides."

"Sir," Dean finally spoke up. "We had actionable intelligence that told us Kiew Tang was an asset. One we needed to secure. We put a plan in play."

"And did you succeed in that mission, Captain?" Ramsey's blue eyes blazed as he whipped around the table pressed in on Dean, who stared him down. "I should've been fully briefed before you went out."

"With all due respect, sir, our team is granted autonomy under the direction of General Burnett's—"

"Who is dead! Did I mention it? The man we're supposed to be chasing down killed him. And over thirty soldiers and airmen on this base in the attack last month. Or have you bumbling fools forgotten that, too?"

"No, sir." The growl came from Sal. Fire roared through his eyes as he glowered at the general.

Dean wanted to warn off his friend, but wasn't sure he could with the kindling that had been ignited. When he managed to catch Sal's eyes, he pushed as much "go softly" into his expression as possible.

"You got something to say to me, soldier?"

Nostrils flared, lips pinched tight, Sal huffed. "No. Sir."

"Good!" Ramsey barked. "'Bout time you idiots grew brains!" He pivoted to Dean. "Full report. My desk. First thing. Maybe by then I can figure out what punishment to dish out to you imbeciles!"

As soon as the door slammed shut, muttered curses filled the air right along with a hefty dose of defeat.

Sal slumped back in his chair, one leg out to the side, staring at the bandage on his arm. No doubt reliving the tragic moment he lost hold of Hawk. Would he ever be able to live that down? Forgive himself? Falcon had always been hard on himself. Demanded the best. Found his flaws inexcusable. Failings unacceptable. Dean would need to corner Sal and make him talk it through later. Would probably be the only time the guy would speak it out loud.

"They knew we were coming," Sal said, his voice low. Intentional.

Dean sat a little straighter. "What do you mean?"

Sal's gaze darted to his. "The charges—there were too many for Tang to have set them herself." He thumbed the angry welt on his cheekbone. "She didn't have time to set enough to bring the building down like that."

"I think he's right," Riordan said. "It came down too fast."

Sal poked a finger at the table. "Meng-Li knew we were coming." His breathing seemed a little slower, more deliberate this time. "He knew and he intended to bury us there." Grief twisted a knot through Sal's face. "He succeeded with Brian."

Silenced pounded the room, pushing their thoughts to Hawk.

"Let's call it a night," Dean said. This night had been too hard and bloody already. "Get some rest. We'll talk tomorrow."

The other nine men filed out, each giving Sal a pat and offering their apologies, telling him he did his best. When the door closed, Dean leaned forward and rested his forearms on his legs. "Fekiria should be told."

Sal's jaw muscle popped. "Take me to her. I'll do it."

"You're in no shape—"

"*I'll* do it." Sal pushed up and lumbered out of the room, the tragedy pressing his wide shoulders down. The growled words he'd spoken carried a deeper, darker meaning: *It's my fault he died.* Sal wanted to tell Fekiria because he wanted to punish himself. Apologize to her for failing the man she loved. Dean wasn't sure he could let that happen. Sal was too haunted.

Kandahar Airfield, Afghanistan
5 April—1445 Hours

"We need to talk."

Sal entered the Command briefing room where Dean sat with Riordan. Should've known Dean would figure things out and call him out. Just as well. He'd come here to come clean with the higher-ups anyway.

"Have a seat," Dean said, as he angled a laptop so the screen was visible. "Chris and I have been talking about the mission."

"That's why I came," Sal admitted. "I—"

"Well, hang on." Dean pressed PLAY.

The grainy, bumpy video seemed to be nothing more than a village foot patrol. "I. . .don't understand."

"Keep watching," Riordan said.

Shadows and voices clogged the feed as the camera bobbed along. Angled around a corner then steadied out. The cameraman must have stopped. Sal leaned in trying to make sure he didn't miss something. "I. . ."

A man emerged from a structure. He went to a car. Left. A woman and two children emerged.

Sal shrugged. "Not following. Sorry."

"What'd you see?" Riordan asked, his tone speculative. Not condemning or demanding.

Resisting another shrug, Sal sighed and glanced again at the screen. He really just wanted to get this confession over with. Pack his bags and head into anonymity. Instead he complied. Thought through what he saw. "The man who emerged—his uniform suggests American military. Feed was too far to see his face or rank, but he walked as someone with authority. Head up. Straight on. Wasn't afraid of being seen."

Riordan gave a firm nod. "Good."

"Who is it? Who else is in the house?"

"Why would you ask who else was in the house? You saw the woman, I take it?"

"An American soldier in a home with a woman, alone?" he snickered. "Not if you don't want to get strung up by your manhood by both the ISAF and ANA."

For several long seconds, Riordan studied Sal. "Before I answer your question, tell me what else you saw."

First—that Riordan had an answer and withheld it bugged Sal. Had he missed something on the video? "Sorry, I only saw the soldier. And the woman and kids."

"Surroundings?"

He shrugged. "Typical village." And yet— "But not average."

Eyebrow winging up, Riordan said nothing.

"It's pristine. Intact. No damage. Plaster's been painted recently—not dilapidated like most buildings out here. And it's a multilevel structure. Most are one stories and bombed out. Curtains are bright colors, so they're new. Wood door—a luxury."

"The people?"

"Woman, kid—boy." Something nagged at the back of his mind. He pointed to the screen. "Can I look again?"

Riordan gave his consent.

Sal tugged it toward him. Wound it back. Watched the feed—soldier exits. A woman and child emerge just as the soldier gets in the car and leaves. Watched it again. There. He magnified the screen. "Yeah." That's what he'd seen. "There's someone shadowed in the doorway."

"What about the people?"

Sal wasn't up for mind games. "If I'm supposed to know something—"

"Her nationality?"

Irritation clawed its way up his spine. "Is there a point?"

"Would I ask if there wasn't?" Riordan threw back.

"You're a SEAL. Your brain gets waterlogged."

With a smirk, Riordan eyed him. Amused. But still waited, insisting Sal answer his query.

"Woman is typical Afghan. Hijab. Maybe midthirties. Boy's about eight. Traditional local dress. The person in the shadows—can't tell." Sal sent Dean a silent message, warning him this was getting old.

"You know how to zoom in, right? Check out the soldier who left."

"Look—"

"Sal, indulge us." Dean finally stepped into the walk-through.

Sal yanked the laptop toward him again. Went back in the footage. Found the soldier. Zoomed. The agitation he felt washed away as the face came into focus. "Ramsey." He glanced at Dean then Riordan. "This makes no sense. Why was he there? Who was he meeting?" A thought struck him. "Is this where our terrorist lives?"

"Yes and no," Riordan said. "But nobody else was there. Ramsey was alone."

Nobody? "That. . .that's not—he wouldn't do that. It'd be a colossal mistake for appearance sake to be alone with a woman in a house." He stared at the video feed, his mind tripping over a possibility he did not want to utter. It wasn't just a home. It was the nicest home in a nondescript area. The woman wore clean, new clothes. The child, too. "I'm not following." He wasn't sure he wanted to follow, especially into the dark places his mind was taking him.

"Neither were we," Riordan said, "until my team inserted with Raptor and that mission."

"Sorry?"

Elbows on the table, Riordan held up two fingers. "I was tapped for a two-part mission since JSOC teamed my SEALs with Raptor."

"Tapped by who?"

"Burnett."

Surprise quieted Sal's questions.

"He had suspicions about Ramsey."

"Burnett had suspicions about Ramsey and didn't tell us? How is that possible when we were the team most affected?" Sal pinned Dean. "D'he tell you?"

Dean shook his head.

"Things didn't add up," Riordan said. "So Burnett threw fresh meat—me and my team—to the wolves—Ramsey. Convinced him we were there to keep an eye on Raptor. We had to get into Jin's systems to verify Ramsey's involvement."

Sal's mind had just jumped into reverse. "Hold up. You go from implying Ramsey's sleeping with a native—which is bad news, but I can handle it. . .maybe." Sal scratched his beard. "But now, you're suggesting. . ." *Oh crap oh crap.* "You're suggesting Ramsey's the mole?"

"Might explain why he crashed down on us last night, wouldn't it?"

Sal tried to digest the idea.

"Right now, we have little to back that up. No evidence. That's why we had to get to the Towers. My team's objective was to breach their systems internally—from within the Tower. We'd tried for months, as have many experts. But it was time to penetrate."

Of all the. . . "You used us as bait to distract anyone who went in there."

"No," Dean said, sitting straight. "Raptor's mission was legitimate. We needed—*still* need—Kiew Tang."

"Unbelievable."

"I had to get into Tower One and into Jin's system. That's why my team didn't show up in time to save Bledsoe. I'm sorry, Russo. Truly." Riordan pointed to the laptop. "We went in search of evidence to prove that Ramsey is feeding intel to Meng-Li."

Sal couldn't speak for the shock. He pressed his fingertips to the table and stared at the screen. Riordan was spying on his own boss. A one-star was the culprit behind the attacks. . . "No. You're kidding me, right? He's a brigadier. He's invested decades to the Army."

"You're right," Riordan said. "It makes no sense. But that woman—her name is Nawal Al-Bayati. I believe she's the key."

"To what?"

"Unlocking Ramsey's airtight vault of alibis and secrets."

CHAPTER 31

Kandahar Airfield, Afghanistan
6 April—0945 Hours

The cool of the morning burned off fast in Afghanistan and made Cassie miss her native Virginia. After a jog around the base, she showered and had breakfast, which consisted of a protein bar and a cup of black tea. Since Sal's severance of her hope that things would work out, she'd refocused on her job. What she should've been doing all along. But being near him had knocked the good sense right out of her, just as it always had. Even now, sitting at her temporary cubicle, it was hard not to wonder where he was and why he wasn't at the desk. If Raptor had been sent out on patrol or assignment, it meant he was in danger. Any venture outside the wire put lives in jeopardy.

It amazed her. All her life she'd worked hard to do the right thing, keep the peace so people liked her, but her entire existence seemed hardwired for backfiring and disaster. Like Midas with his golden touch, which killed his own daughter. But this, it was like the world was allergic to her. Why? What had she done to get dealt such a hand?

She could make herself crazy analyzing it, or she could lay it all at God's feet. Since her path intersected with Salvatore Russo five years ago, Cassie had been forced to become adept at the latter, at surrendering things. They wouldn't get better, so she had to leave them to God.

"Okay, God," she whispered. "Help me do that. My fingers in that pot just made it worse. That's what I'm good at. You're my champion, so. . .defend me, Lord." She closed her eyes and hunched her shoulders. "Please."

She couldn't deny it. She wanted things between them healed. She wanted Mila to know and love her father. Cassie wanted to know and love Mila's father. But she had to accept that God's plans were always better,

"Right, God?" Her gaze hit the computer screen, but something in her nose-dived. She didn't want to be here anymore. In fact, a fire burned through her veins, compelling her to leave the base. Go home. She didn't have any friends here anyway. Raptor, probably because of Sal's reaction to her, viewed her as the enemy. Losing Brian in that tragic explosion made her the villain. No friends. No reason to be here.

So, why not? She could talk to Phelps. Pack her things in a box, set them to post, turn in her Army-issued weapons. By tomorrow, she could be cuddling Mila and reading her bedtime stories. Her heart ached for her daughter. Yes. That's what she should do. Her mission had failed—both the official one with the CIA and with Sal.

But even as she considered it, something nagged at Cassie. A quiet whisper against a storm of accusation and condemnation. Pastor Marjorie, who had counseled her through facing pregnancy alone, delivering Mila as a single mother, and working through the abandonment she felt from Sal. . .she'd taught her to listen to those small whispers. Just as Cassie had trained herself in intelligence to pay attention to the little things. When she focused on those, God tended to reveal pretty big things. "Show me You're here, Lord. If I know You're here, I can do this. I can keep going."

A swirl of floral perfume came in a rush of cool air as Brie Hastings slid a tall cup of coffee toward her. "You look like you could use this." Taking the chair next to the desk, Brie sipped her own caffeinated brew.

Cassie wilted. "Seriously? You're awesome."

"Well, don't think I'm too awesome. It comes with strings attached."

Cup halfway to her mouth, Cassie hesitated and peered over the plastic lid. "What?"

Brie held her gaze for several long seconds then in a rush said, "Talk to me about guys."

Cassie blinked. Then laughed—hard. "I am the last person you—"

"No, I see the way you hold your own."

Surreal was the only word that came to mind. She wasn't holding her own. She was sinking in a vat of her own making.

"Look, I need advice." Brie bustled in closer, tucking her chin.

"About what?"

"Titanis."

Cassie couldn't help but smile. "So, I wasn't imagining the chemistry between you two."

"He terrifies me."

Laughing, Cassie shook her head. "What? Why? He's totally into you."

"That's why!" Brie ran a hand through the auburn fringe framing her face. "Have you ever had a bigger-than-life guy focused on you. Pursuing you?"

Cassie swallowed. "Yes, actually."

"Russo, right? You and he—"

"Are over." Cassie saw the way Brie flinched and felt bad. She touched her arm. "But talk to me about Titanis."

Brie laughed. The striking, intelligent lieutenant seemed more like a sixteen-year-old with her first crush than a field officer who handled a team of special operators with more skill than many men Cassie had seen. Seeing her giddy excitement stirred an ache in Cassie's breast. She'd felt that once. Been so convinced it was because Sal was "The One."

"We were at the Towers, and he told me I intrigued him. He said he wanted to know how I felt."

"And?"

Brie looked sheepish. "I told him the conversation was inappropriate."

Cassie felt stunned. She said nothing. Couldn't think of anything to say.

"See?" Brie groaned and dropped her head on the desk, thumping her forehead against a stack of papers. "I have flirted with the best of them. I wrangled wild and woolly special operators. I give what I get—they don't scare me. Never have."

"Until Titanis."

"Yes!" Brie sighed heavily. Dramatically. "He's gorgeous. Has that sexy Australian accent. And hello—have you seen him? Broad shoulders.

He's an elite commando. He's a gentleman. He's respectful." She gripped the sides of her face. "What more could a girl want? And yet, when he makes a move, I throw up blast shields and repel him!"

Laughing, Cassie could think of nothing to say. She wasn't a love expert by any stretch of the imagination.

"What do I do?"

"I really think you're asking the wrong person. If you'll notice, Sal hates me."

Brie waved at her. "That's what his mouth says. But that's not what the rest of him says."

"What do you mean?"

"Look, I've worked with Raptor since they were an ODA team, before Burnett pulled them from black ops. Sal has never given a girl a second look. He has never been so. . ." She wagged her fingers as if that would drum up the right word. ". . .agitated—flustered!"

"Sal is not flustered."

"Oh but he is." Brie scooted to the edge of her seat. "Look, Sal is intense."

"Tell me about it."

"But he's also intensely personal. He considers mission failures as an indication of his worth. Whatever happened between you two, I think he believes he failed."

"No, *I* failed. I was jealous when his fiancée showed up, so I convinced the base commander to transfer her to Helmand. She died one week later in an IED attack."

Brie blanched. "Whoa. That's awful." She straightened. "Wait, so you dated him while he was engaged to her?"

"I didn't know about her at first, but yeah. And I'm not proud of that." Cassie sighed. "He's never forgiven me."

"That makes so much sense."

Cassie frowned but held her peace.

"Sal doesn't hate you. He hates himself." Brie nodded, as if agreeing with herself.

"I'm not sure I agree with you—"

"Of course not. You hate yourself, too."

Cassie's gaped.

"Sorry. I just mean—what you've said to me shows you're remorseful. So you want the blame. I think you both need to bury that pain."

"Trying," Cassie admitted, "but just when I think Sal might, something explodes in my face. I'm like hardwired det cord of life." She cleared her throat. "But you came here about Titanis, not my problems. I say go for it."

Brie's eyes glittered with anticipation. "I want to. But I was so scared when I was alone with him that I pushed him away. Now, he won't come near me."

"Then go near him."

"Yeah?" Brie chewed the inside of her lip. "I don't know if I can. I've never really. . . I've never been afraid of relationships, but one with Titanis terrifies me."

"Because you want it so much?"

"More than anything."

Cassie grinned. "I think you know what you have to do." Her phone buzzed.

On her feet, Brie nodded. Tapped her shoulder. "Thank you. I'll let you get back to work." And she was gone.

Cassie let out a long breath, realizing as her phone demanded attention and Brie wandered back to her office that God had shown her He was here. She'd needed that talk. Needed Brie's perspective.

Her phone stopped ringing, and the caller ID showed no name. Her computer dinged, indicating an e-mail had arrived. Her hand froze over the mouse as she stared at the sender: Gnat Weik.

A tremor started in her fingers and wormed up her arm, across her chest, and squirmed into her heart. Anticipation hung rank—that name. It surged from her past like a heady concoction. She clicked on it, half afraid the message might vanish. It opened.

You were foolish to be at the Tower. I do not know how to say it more clearly, but you must leave me alone. If you value your life or the lives of those working with you, stay away.

*Time and people change. Do not take this personally. I am
not who you believe me to be. I have a career and a life.
Grow up. Move on.*
—K.

Cassie stared, dumbfounded at the acerbic note. Kiew had never been
so hateful. Pointed, yes. Confrontational, almost always. But not mean.
Not like this.

But something at the back of her mind, something buried beneath
years of hardship and heartache, something tender and fun kindled
against the crush of pain.

"Wait." Cassie hit SELECT + ALL over the e-mail body.
Disappointment chugged to a painful stop in her veins. She hit the
FONT COLOR button. Chose black.

A single line appeared between the two paragraphs she'd read.

*Forgive me. My hand brings death. Afghanistan is just a
distraction. Leave before it's too late.*

CHAPTER 32

Afghan Village
7 April—1115 Hours

With seventy pounds of gear, a tactical vest, and helmet, Sal hated that the heat of the desert invaded like a quick-reaction force, ensuring soldiers and civilians alike yielded to its might.

He ignored the sweat tickling its path down his back and temples as he climbed out of the MRAP. Coming here, guns blazing, was an attempt at normalcy. A routine patrol to insure the safety of Afghans. They'd work this village like any other and tell the locals, especially the woman and her family, that this was a search for terrorists, for Taliban.

"You realize," he said to the captain, whose gaze and muzzle aimed away from the vehicle, "we have less than ten minutes once we clear out before she's on the phone with him—assuming intel is accurate."

"It's accurate," Riordan muttered as he came around the side. "That's why we play nice and easy. Don't tip our hand. The question is," he said, squinting at Sal, "are your language skills enough to converse with the boy in a natural manner?"

Million-dollar question of the day. Though Sal had a moderate working grasp of Farsi—five years in the desert made that possible—he wasn't fluent. All operators were given piecemeal language school. But Sal pushed that, determined to know whether the ISAF and ANA operators were plotting his demise right under his nose. Wouldn't be the first time.

"Eagle, sitrep," Dean asked as he walked a slow circle, assessing threats and possible problem areas.

"Quiet, normal," Eagle responded from his position a half klick away, perched atop a hill that gave him prime oversight. "No visible or suspected threat."

Which meant nobody knew they were coming. That wasn't unusual but Sal had expected a kid to go tearing out of the village to report to some Taliban or worse—Ramsey—that American soldiers were in the village. Again, wouldn't be the first time. Nor the last.

"Knight." Dean indicated with a nod to the handler-and-dog team, who'd clear buildings first. Search for explosives or hidden, trigger-happy Taliban.

Riordan's SEALs announced the joint-team's presence and called all the villagers into the open. An annoying but routine method of rounding everyone up so the teams could search homes without threat of injury. It wasn't fair. But then, the Taliban weren't about fairness. They were about body count. Coalition body count, but they didn't care if they took innocents with them.

With the muzzle of his M4 pointed down and the stock propped against his shoulder, Sal kept his finger close to the trigger as he paced Knight and Ddrake. The sleek German shepherd stalked from one structure to another, sucking in scents better than one of those expensive vacuums.

Roughly thirty locals gathered in the middle of the cluster of homes. Most were your average Afghans, looking to make a living, to survive in a country hostile to anything thriving. Clothes dusty and torn, the men bore evidence of hard labor in the brutal terrain. Weathered faces etched with wrinkles and determination were a hallmark of the people. Americans with their five-buck drinks and impatience when a fast-food line took more than five minutes could learn a lot from these hardworking villagers.

Of course, assuming they were hardworking villagers and not a group of backwater villagers populating the next Taliban rally. That was the thing of it—Taliban were young, old, weathered, soft-skinned. Couldn't tell them apart—until you looked into their eyes. Hatred. Pure, unadulterated hatred poured out like a fire hydrant. Almost tangible. Sal had yet to meet one that he didn't hear a bell clanging in his head.

As he patrolled, Sal searched the crowds for their targets.

"Anyone got eyes on Al-Bayati?"

"Negative," came a steady chorus of responses from the team.

Still unable to locate the woman and children, Sal kept moving. Casually made his way toward the hut from the video, not wanting to draw too much attention. Maybe the woman had been tipped off somehow. But if Ramsey was the mole, and they'd avoided telling him where they were going, then how—?

"...warned them. They won't be taken alive."

Sal slowed, angling away from the two men standing at the back of the crowd talking excitedly in Farsi. As much as possible, Sal made himself appear bored and unable to understand them as he stood off to the side but within hearing.

"It is wrong," one man hissed. "Killing the children—for him?" He spat then whispered something Sal couldn't decipher.

Kill the children?

Heat rushed down Sal's spine. Pushed him away from the two men. "Captain, I think we have a problem." He moved to a structure and eased inside, out of earshot of the men.

"Go ahead," Dean said.

From his position, Sal could keep an eye on the men but also see the captain, who was looking for him.

"Just overheard two men talking about killing the children. Anyone got eyes on the kids we saw?"

Just then, Riordan shouted for all the children to move to the side.

"Negative on the boy and girl with the woman," Eagle reported from his bird's-eye view.

After a few more of the same, Sal moved back into the open. He noticed the strained expressions. Noticed a woman glance over her shoulder, a hand to her mouth. Another woman did the same.

A teen girl silently wept in her mother's arms. Sal had thought she was afraid of the search. Now he worried she knew what was happening.

"Sir, I think we need to find those kids." The urgency carried through his voice despite his efforts to contain it. He pivoted toward the grape huts. "Knight, what's your location?"

Ddrake trotted out of a building, Knight trailing.

Sal headed toward them.

A man broke from the group as Sal moved toward the rear where Knight entered one of the nicer homes. Sal eyeballed the man—and nearly tripped. "Captain"—even as he said it, the man broke into a run—"jackrabbit!"

Sal sprinted after him. Straight into a house. Ddrake barked and snapped. Sal rushed into the house, skidded to a stop, sweeping right and left.

A flash of light vanished behind a curtain.

Weapon to his cheek, Sal hurried forward. Reached for the curtain, anticipating getting riddled with holes. Heart in his throat, he jerked it back.

An open field met him.

He hiked his leg up, weapon out, eyes out, never breaking stride. Scanning, he searched for the man. A copse of almond trees to his right. He glanced away—but a tan movement jerked him back. Sal scurried forward, weapon and heart rate up. "Captain, we have movement on my location, south of the village."

"Titanis and Harrier en route," Captain said.

Sal jogged forward, listening. Expecting to be gunned down at any second. Thudding behind him warned of Titanis and Harrier pulling up the rear.

"What've you got?" Harrier asked.

"Runner, went into the trees," Sal said as he ducked beneath a low-hanging branch and felt immediate relief from the sun's barrage.

A scream knifed the tension.

Sal stopped. Not because someone screamed. But—

"That was a kid."

Pushing himself forward, Sal felt his heart pounding against the possibilities. He sidled up to a stone wall and hooked a leg over, scanning and searching. His boot had no sooner hit the ground then he saw a blur.

He snapped to the left.

A man stood there. *Holy*—not just a man. The same teen they'd had in lockup back at Kandahar Airfield. The one who Sal helped to escape. And the teen had guts. He stood there waving.

A moan rose through the rustling canopy of leaves. Branches scratched out a mournful note. The wind kicked up and sounded like a howl.

"Hurry!" the teen yelled.

"Stop!" Sal shouted in Farsi to the guy.

But he pivoted and vanished over a rise.

Son of— *"Here!"* he called to Titanis and Harrier who grouped up on his location. The three of them made their way toward the crest of a small hill.

"I don't like this," Harrier said. "That moaning. . ."

Sal just moved. Quickly. Methodically. Expecting trouble. Knowing they were about to get it. He hunched as they reached the top. A thicket shielded his view. He angled to the right and—froze.

A woman sat on the ground in a red-and-white tunic, cradling a small boy in her arms, weeping silently. Just beyond her and between two almond trees, the kid knelt, waved Sal over frantically. That's when it registered—blood. Blood everywhere.

A glint of steel in the woman's hand had him diving hard at her. He barreled into her shoulder, grabbing for her wrist. They went backward hard. She screamed out, but Sal pinned her, holding her arm out so she couldn't stab him or turn the blade on herself.

Outweighing her, he flipped her over, leaning down so her face pressed against the rocky terrain, as he wrangled the blood-slickened blade from her grip. When it came free, she cried out.

Riordan was there as Sal secured the woman's hands to be sure she didn't do any more harm to anyone.

"God, help us." Harrier's whisper drew Sal's attention. He knelt over a small girl. A girl, no more than three or four, lay on the ground, her stomach a mash of blood and chopped tunic. Face pale and hair matted to her forehead with sweat, she lay there, crying out in agony. The teen hovered back a little, his white face telling of the shock he suffered.

The woman pushed against Sal's hand.

He turned his full attention on her. Saw agony twisting her features. Man, she's young. Definitely not Ramsey's age. She seemed just a little older than Sal. And she had an eighteen-year-old son?

Sal's stomach knotted. He looked to Titanis. "Take her to the captain. Keep her secure. She's suicidal."

Drawn by some unseen force, he went to the girl. Dropped to her side. Brushed back the mat of black hair and sweat on her forehead. Her cries quieted as she met his gaze, her lower lip wiggling. Exhaustion seemed to crowd her body and demand surrender.

"Hi," he said, palming a hand over her head and sweeping the hair from her eyes. "It's going to be okay."

A tear slipped down her olive-colored cheek as wide, chestnut eyes went to the teen. *God...* He choked on a raw realization—this girl was the same age as Mila.

"We need a medevac!" Sal shouted to the SEALs.

Riordan nodded. "Already en route."

Sal turned to the youth. "What happened?"

"She killed them," the teen mumbled, his tone devoid of emotion.

Harrier's grim expression told Sal how bad this was. He worked feverishly to pack the wound. "IV," he said to Sal as his lips went thin with the restraint of anger and frustration.

Sal grabbed the bag and drew out the wide-bore needle and tubing. He slid the needle into her arm, his periphery stuck on the pulses of blood from her abdomen that seeped around the bandaging. "IV's in." He turned his attention to the weeping wound and pressed a hand against it.

Harrier saw the same spot and grunted as he added trauma foam to stop the bleeding by packing it in. The *thwump-thwump* of rotors grew closer.

"PJs incoming," someone shouted.

Sal pushed his gaze to the teen. "What happened?"

The eighteen-year-old only shook his head, eyes locked on to the blood.

"Why'd she do this?"

"Gentle but firm pressure," Harrier ordered as he pressed the top of Sal's hands back over the sticky, warm wounds.

Swallowing, Sal stayed focused on the teen. "Talk to me! What happened? Why'd she do this?"

Titanis joined them, nudging Sal's shoulder. "Go. Talk to him."

Sal glanced back at the little one's face. Eyes now closed, she seemed at peace. He froze. Waited for the shallow breath that barely pushed her bloodied chest upward. She could be Mila. Small, brown-skinned...

What if Mila died and he never got to know her?

He punched to his feet. Though he wanted to throttle someone, wanted to scream and rage over the brutality against these children, Sal hooked the teen's arm and pulled him away.

The teen blinked, his mouth hanging open.

He wanted to beat the crap out of him and ask why he didn't stop her, but you got more with honey than a baseball bat. "What's your name?"

"F–Fariz."

"Fariz, who is that woman?"

The teen seemed to see Sal clearly for the first time since they made it to the clearing. "My mother."

"Okay. Good. Thank you." *Breathe, bring it down a notch. Don't scare him off.* "Thank you for alerting me."

The teen started.

Sal put a hand on his shoulder. "I'm glad because you saved the lives of those children—your brother and sister."

Something in the boy seemed to melt at those words. "Do you know why she did this?"

The shock snapped away, replaced by a bloody rage. "Him. He told her if any soldiers came to the village, they would take them—us. Take us and torture us. They'd rape her and then she'd never see him again."

"Him?" The tremor raced through his veins, twitching his fingers. "Who?"

Fariz lifted his head. "My father." The way he said that last word curled his lip.

"Your father?" The words knocked him for a loop. "Why would he—?"

"My father is General Ramsey."

CHAPTER 33

§ir, I really think we need to look at this seriously."

"I am *seriously looking* at the disaster you were heavily involved in at Takkar One." General Phelps's displeasure couldn't be clearer. "You've inadvertently handed a rogue operator information and access—and now he's vanished again. And now, this. Do you realize the cost of the damages we'll have to cover?"

"Sir, we were there, but we did not set the explosives."

"No, that was the very woman you're now claiming is communicating privately with you." His caustic tone poked at her courage. "Am I right, Walker?"

"I believe she—"

"Am. I. Right?"

Deflated, Cassie cradled her head in her hand. "Yes, sir."

"Then until we have proof of clear and present danger—"

"She told me herself they're going to kill everyone!"

"'Everyone' is both vague and nondescript. When? Who exactly?" he barked. "Until you can hand me those answers, this discussion is closed. In fact, why don't you start packing up. You're heading home."

Jaw hanging, Cassie stared at her keyboard. "Sir—"

Buzzing grated through the connection. He'd hung up. The general hung up on her. Fired her, for all intents and practical purposes. She tossed down her phone and placed her other hand over her head. "God, I know You sent me here. . .I just didn't think it was to mock me and tear me down."

And it wasn't. She knew that. But for the life of her, she couldn't figure out why He had sent her. At first, she'd thought It was to reunite with Sal.

So not happening.

Then she thought maybe it was Kiew.

Phelps said it wasn't happening.

What do I say?

The question bubbled through her, warm and powerful. Not her own words. She looked around. Glanced back at her computer. Kiew's message seemed to glow and leap off the monitor. Kiew. She had to do something.

Discouragement might have a fist around her throat, but God had a mighty hand around her life. He'd placed her here for a reason. Maybe for both Sal and Kiew, though the reason and understanding might never occur to her in this lifetime.

But she wasn't going to tuck her tail and scamper away. She'd go boldly and intentionally. Starting with Sal first. So, he wanted to be a part of Mila's life. Accessing a website, she downloaded a power of attorney form and a form to alter Mila's birth certificate. She filled them out then retrieved a manila envelope. She'd find a notary, but first. . .

Kiew. . .Kiew. . .what could she do about that? Talk to Sal. She laughed. Right. He wouldn't talk to her. He told Cassie to fix things. Well, okay. She would. But how. . .

Takkar.

Another laugh plucked from her. She'd been in his building chasing Kiew. Would he listen to her? He might be many things, but she'd never seen him vengeful. Reasonable. Thoughtful. Well-connected.

Yeah. She had to talk to Sajjan Takkar. If she called the corporation, she'd probably get blown off by some admin. That wouldn't work. Time was of the essence, if Kiew's warning was right. And she didn't doubt that. She knew Kiew's heart, even beyond the terroristic things she'd done. Kiew could be doing all these things because Meng-Li held something over her head.

You have no proof of that.

Because it was a gut instinct that Kiew wasn't evil. Who would listen to her? Help her talk to Mr. Takkar, one of the most powerful men, politically, in the world?

Candyman!

Cassie's fingers flew into the system until she found the personnel file for one James Anthony VanAllen III. She lifted the phone and dialed. Erratic and frantic, her heart beat double in between each ring.

"This is Tony," a voice finally said.

"You're Candyman, right?"

Hesitation screamed through the line.

"I'm Lieutenant Cassandra Walker with—"

"I know who you are."

Cassie sucked in a breath. Swallowed. "Then you know if I'm calling—"

"What do you want?"

Okay, so no we're-all-fighting-for-the-same-team camaraderie. "I want to talk to Mr. Takkar."

He laughed, a nice, deep one that vibrated against the line. "Sorry, you seriously want me to ask the man whose building you about blew up to let you come here and do more damage?"

Cassie breathed, reminded herself to stay calm.

"See, maybe you people are forgetting, but this man is part of my family now."

"What family is that? Because the men I'm with, the ones I'm fighting alongside, they were your brothers once."

"Wrong approach, Walker."

The line went dead.

Cassie stared at the phone. Then gripped it hard, wishing she could crush the thing with her bare hands. "*Augh!*" She pitched her phone into her purse, snatched it up, and grabbed the manila envelope before heading to Brie's office.

"There has to be a way," she muttered as she made her way down the hall. She banked right into the small office.

Brie looked up from her computer. "Hey."

Holding up the envelope, Cassie sighed. "Who's a notary on base?"

"I am," Brie said, lifting a stamp. She set it on her desk then pulled out a logbook. "I notarize stuff all the time for the brass. What do you need?"

Finally. "Something finally goes right." Cassie handed over the documents. "I need to get these in the mail ASAP."

"Okay, I can do that for you. Sign the book." Brie opened the flap and drew out the envelope as Cassie bent over the log with a pen. "Are you serious?"

Cassie glanced up. Saw Brie's white face.

"You—Russo. . .you two have a kid?"

There were no words nor an explanation. Cassie sighed. "I really would rather—"

Brie held up a hand. "Forget I said anything."

"Sorry, I just—"

"Nope. It's your business. And obviously a painful one." She stood and took the documents into another room then returned and finished logging and stamping. "Here you go."

"Thanks." Cassie resisted the urge to flee the building and race to the mail center before she lost her nerve. Giving Sal this much legal right terrified her. He could take Mila away. But he wouldn't.

Right?

Her phone rang, jarring her. She fished her phone from her purse. The caller ID was blocked. "This is—"

"Tower Two, tonight at six."

—⁓—

Leaving the base on her own and with nothing more than strong willpower and determination. . .well, it sounded good in theory. But not so smart practically. The route to Kabul was long and arduous, and at times—as in when people were alive and breathing, so pretty much every hour of the day—a deadly conduit for ambushes and attacks.

Three hours in and she'd had plenty of time to consider the stupidity of her adventure. Maybe it was a good thing she'd signed the POA for Sal with Mila. If anything happened here, at least she'd be taken care of. Not what Cassie had had in mind when she'd printed and filled it out.

Ahead, grape huts jutted out of the desertlike area. Life and people defied the elements to oppress them, much as the terrorists had defied innocents to cross their paths. She couldn't help but wonder if they would dare her to enter. Statistics had shown that terrorists favored villages where roads cut through, so they had a high vantage point. And multiple ways to hide and surprise attack the passerby.

White-knuckling the steering wheel, she whispered a prayer and didn't slow as she approached the village. No people out wandering the streets. Wind swept dirt in a cloud, making it appear as if dancing.

"So," Cassie muttered, her gaze tracing the rooftops. "A dance of joy or dance of death?" She searched the shadows between the structures. "Right. Be morbid. That helps so much."

Her phone buzzed in her purse, but there was no way on earth she would take her eyes off the road and this village now that she'd spooked herself.

A ball bounced into the street.

Cassie yanked her foot from the accelerator to the brake—then second-guessed herself. A ball but no child. Her toe hovered between the two, the vehicle still rolling onward. No child. She hit the accelerator. "Not going to fool—"

A boy burst from an alley.

Cassie nailed the brake. Rocks crunched and popped. Dust plumed, pressing against the windows like some phantom trying to blind her. *Go, go,* she urged herself, but moving forward when she couldn't see? What if she wasn't in the middle of the street? What if she hit a house or the little boy?

She let the car roll forward.

Thunk!

She hit the brake again. The dust started clearing, and with it, her breathing leveled out. A little. She wasn't sure she could breathe easy until she reached Takkar Two.

Four men stood several yards ahead, assault rifles in hand. Threatening but not moving.

Cassie froze.

Her side window shattered. Cassie screamed as the door flopped open. A man leaned in, grabbing her by the collar. She slapped and scratched, but his grip was made of steel. He hauled her out of the car. With a jarring thud against her shoulder, she hit the ground.

Something sharp hit her head. She ducked as another pecked against her neck. Though she tried to stand, someone shoved her back down. Another rock. And another. Rocks dribbled around her—they were stoning her!

Feet closed in. One swung into her ribs. She cried out, fought against the urge to arch her back and instead, curled in to protect herself. Shouts went up as a mob set upon her.

A fist swung at her face. Though she dodged, she wasn't fast enough. Something cracked against the back of her head. Cassie whimpered and held her head. Dust puffed into her face as sandaled feet connected with her face, her chest, her back—everywhere!

They would beat her to death and leave her for the vultures.

She would not die easily! She pressed her hands against the dirt, but another well-placed kick sent her sprawling. Tears slipped free as she struggled. But then. . .then she noticed something.

Vibrations wormed through the ground, tickling her fingers. It grew stronger. The noise louder. The chaos and frenzy of the crowd lulled.

Cassie seized the moment to search for an escape.

But as the roar increased, the bloodthirsty mob broke up. Rushed for houses as the growl of an engine roared up alongside the left of her vehicle. A black SUV. Sleek. Clean. Amazing how a vehicle could look fierce simply because it was black and had tinted windows.

Another one followed. And another.

On her left as well—three more.

Two large Hummers lumbered up on her six.

Cringing at the pain that exploded when she stood, Cassie scrambled for her car and dragged herself inside. She shut the door. Numbly stared at the shattered window. Still, she punched the lock. Tucked herself—painfully—behind the wheel.

Phone. She had to find her phone and call for help. She spotted it on the floorboard and grabbed for it. When she swiped her thumb across the surface—the thing flung free. Dropped.

Thud. Thud!

Cassie jumped.

A man stood at the driver's window, armed. Heavily. And the man had more muscle than Sal and Titanis combined. "Move!" He swept his arm forward. "Drive."

Cassie groped for the phone, staring ahead. Ignoring the man's broken English orders. It was stupid, but she felt safe in here. At least safe enough to make a call. To get help.

Right. You're three hours from the base and you think they'll magically appear?

Still, phone in hand, she managed to hit a button. Heard a tinny ring of the phone through the speaker. She had no idea which person she'd autoselected and she didn't care.

Thud-thud. Thud!

"Move!"

A Hummer tapped her rear bumper, forcing her car ahead a foot. Cassie's foot slipped from the brake and the car lurched forward.

The man outside her door, banged heavily on the roof. "Move move move!"

A voice squawked through her phone. She lifted it to her ear. "Hello?"

"*. . .leave a message and I'll—*"

Cassie groaned at the sound of her own voice. She'd called her own desk! She hit the END button then tried another number.

The Hummer revved behind her then another bump.

Cassie yelped, losing her phone. She gripped the wheel.

Her window cracked. She screamed and ducked, but when she looked up, she saw the bullet hole. Eyes wide, she looked to the man.

He jogged back to one of the SUVs, waving her on. "Hurry! Move!"

Even as she accelerated, the first two black Suburbans slid in front of her, completely encasing her vehicle. The more she accelerated, the more they accelerated, until she glanced down and eyed her speedometer. Sixty! Where were they taking her? And why?

Kandahar Airfield, Afghanistan
7 April—1620 Hours

Arms folded, Sal stood at the foot of the gurney watching the little girl breathe. Fighting for her life. Muznah—that was her name, according to her much-older brother, Fariz, who went with Dean to answer questions. They had to keep Fariz off the radar before Ramsey got wind of him and the little girl.

Which was good. Because Sal was sure he'd put his fist through the guy's face if he saw him. What kind of sicko convinces his paramour to murder their children if people start asking questions?

One with something to hide.

Muznah whimpered in her sleep, the pain probably overwhelming. The mattress seemed to swallow her frail form as Sal reached for her hand. Black hair spilled across her shoulders and pillow. Tubes snaked in and out of her body. First operation had gone well, but the doc said another was scheduled later today, once her body had built up its strength and blood supply.

Mila. He didn't know a thing about her. Not her favorite color. Not her favorite ice cream flavor. . .nothing. Did she even like ice cream?

"You okay?"

Sal flinched and looked to the side where Dean stood in the curtained doorway to the medical bay holding the girl. "Yeah, fine. Just wanted to check in on her."

"Doc says you've been here since dinner."

"After," Sal tossed to the side. "Ate, showered, then came here."

Dean sauntered in, glancing down at Muznah. "Fariz said Ramsey met his mother in Iraq."

"The kid's eighteen. That had to have been Ramsey's first deployment. Not much happened before OEF/OIF."

Dean nodded. "It was. Apparently, they wrote letters. When he got deployed and assigned here, he brought them over. Resumed their affair."

"Explains the age gap between Fariz and these," Sal said, nodding to the bed. "He must have had something really big to hide to convince her to kill them."

"My thoughts exactly, but Fariz shut down when I opened that conversation."

Dean sighed. "Hits a bit close to home, doesn't it?"

Once again, Sal looked at Dean, who cocked his head toward the exit. "Let's talk."

Though his gut coiled and he knew this was the day of reckoning, Sal said nothing as he followed Dean out into the arid evening. Lights hadn't come on, but the calm of night was already settling in around camp.

Dean turned and faced him. "When you sought me out before we told you about this family, you said you had something you wanted to talk to me about."

With a nod, Sal folded his arms. "I did. Do."

"Let's get it in the open then."

Another nod from Sal, this one to convince himself to talk. To get it off his chest. Come clean. "Not sure if it's the right time, considering what we're facing—"

"It's always the right time for the truth."

"I'd agree with you on most days." Sal grinned but didn't feel it. "You've been on my case about what's eating me. You were right—something is eating me. My girlfriend died over here."

Dean narrowed his eyes. "Sal—that's in your record."

"It is?"

"But that was four years ago."

He bobbed his head. "Yeah, but two years ago, her brother Mario died out here, too. They followed me into the Army. Vida came so we could be together. Her family was poor, so was mine. We had a plan to graduate then join up. I was two years older but did it. But. . .by the time she signed up. . ."

"Things had changed?"

"She and I were a habit," Sal admitted with a shrug. "It's awful to hear myself say it, but it's true. We dated through high school. I'd made so many promises to her about getting married, and she desperately wanted out of her family and New York City, that by the time I realized

I didn't love her in that way, I felt obligated to her.

"I met Walker when we were assigned to Huachuca for training I'd never felt that way about anyone. Things got pretty serious, hot and heavy. . .but when Vida got assigned there, I broke it off. Had to keep that promise."

"Did you know about your daughter then?"

Sal scowled. Stepped back. "How—?" How did he know about that when Sal just learned about Mila himself?

Dean handed over a paper. "Walker had this notarized this morning. When did you find out about Mila?"

"A week ago, maybe two. She never told me."

"How could you not know?"

"I refused to talk to her after Vida died. Cassie arranged to have Vida PCSed to Helmand, knowing it was the most dangerous. When Vida died, I blamed Cassie."

"Because you couldn't handle the guilt?"

Swallowing hurt. Sal nodded. "If I hadn't slept with Walker. . .Vida would never have gone to Helmand."

"You don't know that." Dean tapped the paper. "She's giving you POA over Mila."

"Why?"

"That's what I wanted to know, but I can't find her."

Sal shrugged. "She's probably working."

"After mailing the official documents and a box with the entire contents of her locker, she left the base four hours ago."

Something about those words, Cassie's movements in the preceding hours left a hollow feeling in his chest. Granting him POA over Mila. Packing and sending her stuff home. Getting fired but leaving the base anyway. "Crap."

"And it gets worse. I called Phelps to find out what was going on. He said he'd told her he was bringing her back. Basically yanked and tanked her."

His pulse thrummed. "You said she left the base. What'd she put on the exit log?"

"'Offsite meeting.'"

"Check her logs," Sal said. "Phone and e-mail." It felt as if someone ripped his heart out of his chest.

"Phone goes to voice mail. I can get someone to pull her last dialed number."

"Good. Do it."

"What do you know that I don't?"

Sal had to face the truth. "We had a fight. She said she wanted to fix things, but I was too mad at her for lying to you."

"Lying to me?" Dean frowned. "About what?"

Tugging up his sleeve, Sal exposed the marks.

A storm rushed into Dean's face.

"This is how I've been coping."

"That looks like *not coping* in my book. That's enough for me to rec a psych eval, to send your butt home."

"It's kept my head in the game. But this"—he thumbed the large one that now held eight stitches—"*this* is why Hawk died. Because it ripped and made it impossible to maintain a grip. Cassie saw it and tried to help. But it was too late. *I* killed Hawk."

Dean shook a finger at him. "We'll deal with this later—I promise. But right now, we have to find Walker."

—⁓—

Darkness swam, coiling and spinning. Disorienting. Submerging. He pushed upward, swimming toward the surface. Toward the light.

Gotta get out of here.

The effort was brutal. Agony rushed over with every move of his limbs. Every contraction of his lung and heart. Searing pain like fire spread across his chest. Thin air repressed him. Suffocated him.

Yes. Suffocating. He couldn't breathe.

Can't breathe.

He focused every muscle on dragging in a breath. But it resisted. Fought him as hard as an insurgent. His pulse screeched in his ears.

"Augh!" He arched his back. Balled his fists, demanding air.

"Rest," came a firm, gentle voice.

Can't. . .breathe. . .Help!

The world condensed, sliding in to a pinprick. Then vanished.

268

CHAPTER 34

Kabul, Afghanistan
7 April—1705 Hours

With her close-up-and-personal escort navigating and determining Cassie's movements, she lost all sense of direction and bearing. Except she knew with the sun falling into shadows behind and to the left that she was headed north. At least for a little while. Then they'd banked right. Buildings whipped past, rushing her through a city. Every now and then she saw blurs of people. But nothing to guide her as to where they were taking her.

What happens if I run out of gas?

Even as the thought hit her, the light blinked out.

Cassie resisted the urge to hit the brake and get rear-ended. Instead she let them deliver her into an underground parking structure where the lead vehicles slowed, forcing her to do the same until they came to a stop.

The man who'd yelled at her in the village to get going hopped out of the black SUV and came toward her. He rapped on the window.

Cassie rolled it down.

"Out," he growled, flicking his wrist and motioning her out of the car.

Gathering what little courage she had left, Cassie shut off the engine, unlocked the door, and reached for her purse. She climbed out, clutching the purse to her chest.

Tall and fierce, the man hooked her arm, shouting in Arabic to the others as he hauled her around the cluster of vehicles to a wide steel door. An elevator. He slid a card in then pressed his thumb against a pad. A light flickered and a camera behind a shiny black dome whirred.

Unsettled, Cassie frowned at the man.

When the door slid back, he tugged her into the elevator. Two men followed, silent and stiff.

This was usually where the woman tells them she doesn't know what they want or why they'd kidnapped her. But this wasn't the movies. And Cassie did have something they wanted. As an intelligence officer, they could pry a lot from her thick head.

Should've stayed at the base.

She just needed to be prepared for when that door opened. If it was a hall, she'd try to catch them off guard and sprint away. But if—

She felt the steel box alight and settle. The doors slid open.

Cassie stilled. Brown marble spilled out in a rush toward a luxurious living room with floor-to-ceiling windows overlooking a city. A sunken living room boasted three white sofas and a glass table. Above it, a bar and grand hallway with a stunning chandelier glittered in the glow of what seemed like a thousand crystals.

Her escort pushed her out of the elevator as a man emerged from a doorway on the right. "Mr. Takkar." With a breathy whoosh, her fear and trepidation dumped out of her system, leaving her chilled and borderline giddy.

Another man appeared behind him. Candyman. He looked ticked.

Sajjan Takkar stood tall, lean, and proud—and a lot disapproving. His white turban made him seem noble and impressive. And dangerous. Murderously dangerous. He came toward her. "Forgive the manner of your delivery here. I am sorry for the delay in coming to your aid, but we did not think you were foolish enough to attempt such a journey on your own."

He let the reprimand hang in the air for a few seconds. "When I heard you left the airfield alone and most likely unarmed, it became apparent you did not understand the lands you operate on or its people."

Duly chided, Cassie knew she could only do one thing. "You are right. I wasn't thinking—my only thought was to find someone who could help me. So thank you for your quick thinking and your protection. General Burnett trusted you implicitly, and I know that was not a lightly placed trust."

He lifted a hand toward a rear area. "Miriam will attend you."

Cassie shook her head. "I don't need—"

"Fresh clothes and a bath."

The words pushed Cassie's gaze to her clothing. Torn. A part of her shirt hanging loose and exposing her strap. She covered it, darting a look toward the men hovering behind her.

"When you are refreshed, we will talk." Without another word, he spun on his heels and disappeared behind a set of double, ornately carved doors.

A portly woman appeared from a hall, hands clasped in front of her.

Cassie went toward the woman, who turned and headed down a dimly lit corridor. She pressed the handle on a door and stepped inside. Cassie did the same, surprised to find a bedroom, clothes laid out, and a shower already running.

The woman shooed her into the bathroom and shut the door, clearly expecting Cassie to undress and shower, so she did.

The heat of the water soothed the aches and scrapes that littered her body. She savored it. No sooner had she turned off the water than the door opened and the woman entered, gathered up the dirty clothes, pointed to the thick towel hanging on the wall, then left.

Cassie dried off and wrapped the towel around her. Back in the room, she quickly changed into the clothes—a tan tunic and gray pants. Both fit, thanks to the elastic waist and almost one-size-fits-all styling of the tunics.

When she opened the bedroom door, voices floated from the other end of the hall. From the living area, if that's what you called an enormous space like that. She couldn't help but wish Mila could see things from here.

Back in the living area, she was surprised to find it set for dinner.

"Better?"

She jerked to the left where Sajjan, genie that he was, appeared again from the other room. "Yes. Thank you."

He came to her and reached for her.

Cassie froze, surprised as he took her chin in hand.

His trimmed beard, etched with silver and white, almost made him appear younger, but here, this close to him, she saw the lines of age scratched across his face and at the corners of his sharp, dark eyes that probably didn't miss a heartbeat happening in the world around him.

He turned her head to appraise her face. "Bruising will go down. I don't think stitches will be needed. Dizziness? Blurry vision?"

Still stunned at the apparent concern he displayed, Cassie shifted uneasily. "No."

"Good." He released her and walked to the table. "I would hate for anyone to be injured or leave here injured."

Cassie's ears rang with the obvious point—Hawk. "I take your meaning."

He arched an eyebrow as he and Candyman stood next to the seats, watching her. "Do you?"

They were waiting for her to sit, so she eased closer and tugged out a chair. They moved in unison with her. "I was involved in the mission that. . .took place in your building, but I was there for a different reason."

A servant approached and began serving an appetizer.

Struck with the man's civility and luxurious life, Cassie waited until the servant left. "I came to convince Kiew Tang to leave."

"So, you were working against Raptor," Candyman said, cutting into a thick steak.

Cassie hesitated. "Yes, I was."

Candyman snorted and shook his head. "Why am I sitting here?" he said to Sajjan, who slid a hand toward him in a placating manner. With another shake of his head, Candyman stuffed the piece of meat into his mouth.

"Look, wrong or right—I don't know. But I felt it was right at the time. Things went very wrong."

"Yeah," Candyman said around the steak. "She blew your theories to pieces, right along with a close friend."

Cassie sat there, fork in one hand, knife in the other, trembling. "Appearances can be deceiving, Mr. VanAllen."

His gaze bore into hers. "Tell me about it. Here we thought you were this nice, patriotic American officer."

She absorbed his verbal attack. "You mean to malign me. I understand."

"Do you?"

"Tony," Sajjan said, his hand reaching to the young man.

"Look." Cassie put down her utensil and focused on Mr. Takkar. "I need your help. Kiew contacted me. I believe she reached out because I am one of the few people who believes in her. I can't explain the horrible things she's done, but I think she might be acting under duress or. . ." *C'mon, Cass, think!* "Maybe she's not working for Meng-Li at all."

Sajjan set down his fork. Folded his hands in his lap and sat back against a richly carved chair. "Go on, Miss Walker. You have my full attention."

Kandahar Airfield, Afghanistan
7 April—1705 Hours

With Brie Hastings and Fariz at his side, Dean entered the unconventional holding area—the back room of a now-defunct shop along the Boardwalk—the only place they felt would be out of sight from Ramsey. Holding cells would draw attention.

Dean couldn't shake the reminder of the other person who'd been in a holding cell—Hawk. His chest squeezed at the memory, unwilling to believe the guy was gone. They had to get to Fekiria and tell her. He'd take Sal later and visit her. Late but it had to be done.

Two of Riordan's SEALs stood guard.

"How's it going?" Dean asked as they approached.

"I think she stopped crying," Schmidt said. "But she's not eating."

"Open it up." Dean turned to Fariz. "Just remember—tell me what she says and tell her what I say. Do not add anything. Understood?"

The boy nodded. "I do this, but I can leave after. Yes?"

"I'll escort you out myself," Dean promised. Keeping Fariz on base only guaranteed Ramsey would find him.

In the holding room, the woman shifted nervously as Dean stepped in. When Fariz scooted in behind him, his mother howled something at him.

Head down, Fariz looked angry. "She says I have no honor. That I betrayed her, my brother and sister, too."

"Tell her your sister is alive because of you." Dean watched the woman's face as the boy repeated the words.

Nawal Al-Bayati froze. Her gaze bounced to Dean's. She whispered something quickly.

"She asks if she is truly alive. If Muznah is alive."

"Tell her very good doctors are still fighting to save her but that every day she lives increases her chances of surviving."

Once the teen translated, the woman gripped her head. Wailed. Laughed. Wailed some more.

"Ask her why she did this now. Why she tried to kill Muznah and your brother."

Fariz did, a stream of Farsi flowing quickly and freely.

Nawal shook her head, crying, muttering something.

"She says he had told her to do that if soldiers came. But he'd said something about not coming back. He said he couldn't. That things were dangerous for him." But then Fariz's words turned hateful and furious.

Dean glanced at the kid, realizing he wasn't translating anymore but shouting at her, chewing her out for something. "Hey." When Fariz didn't reply, Dean hooked an arm across his chest. But the boy continued his tirade. *"Hey!"* Dean nudged him back until their gazes met. "What happened? What's going on?"

"She said when he said he wasn't coming back, that she said it wasn't worth living. That is why she hurt Muznah. I told her a woman was no good who could kill her own child." He spat in his mother's direction. "She and my father"—he spit again—"they are nothing to me. I do not claim them!"

Dean pushed into the kid's face. "Hey. I get that. I do. What she did was awful. And no father should ever leave his kids just because things turn ugly. But I need your help. She won't talk to me without you." He eased back. Patted the kid's chest. "Can you do that? Can you talk without getting angry?"

"Without getting angry? No." His dark eyes flashed with unrequited anger. "But I can. . .will help you."

Dean nodded. "Good."

"If you promise to kill my father."

"Sorry, that's not how I operate, but I will promise that he will see the full extent of our justice."

"I want his head chopped off!"

"There are days I want my enemies' heads on platters, too. But that's not justice. That's vengeance." He took a few measuring breaths. "Okay back to the task at hand. Ask her why he was leaving."

Voice cold and unfeeling, Fariz obeyed. "He told her he'd done things and if they found out, he would be killed."

"Ask her who would kill him. Who he's afraid of." Was it the Americans finding out? Was he afraid of losing his career? If he was going to abandon his family so easily, then what *was* important to him?

Fariz turned to Dean. "I do not have to."

"Please." Dean cocked his head to Nawal. "We need to know."

"I do not have to because I know. He was working with one man sometimes, a man who came to our home."

"Who?"

"He is known as Zmaray."

CHAPTER 35

You sure about this?"

Sal pushed a sidelong glance to Dean but didn't answer as they made their way up the steps to Fekiria's apartment. They'd waited this long so Zahrah could fly down and be here with her. A kindness. An obvious alert to what was happening, no doubt. He strode down the hall, feeling the battering of the storm brewing inside him.

But as he turned the corner, he saw Fekiria through the window sipping a cup of tea and reading something...in her silk pink hijab. Fiery. Beautiful. Was there any other type of woman for a special operator?

Sal slowed to a stop. *I can't do it. I killed her boyfriend.*

Behind him, he heard Dean's shoes. "You don't have—"

"I do," Sal bit out, hating himself for being weak. He pushed on. Crossed the two yards that separated them from the front door.

It opened easily and Zahrah smiled. But then it fell, and only then did Sal realize Dean hadn't even told Double Z about Hawk. "Come in." She gave a concerned look to them then received Dean's kiss on her cheek.

Fekiria's face brightened and with it, the tiny pink scar she got from the last mission. "Hello, Captain Dean." She nodded to Sal as she set aside a binder—flight manual from the diagrams. "Falcon."

That's right. They'd never really been on a first-name basis. And with the way he and Hawk had always butted heads, it wasn't a surprise she didn't even know his first name.

"Miss Haidary," Sal said, his voice tight. "Can we have a word with you, ma'am?"

"I cannot help but think something is wrong with Brian," Fekiria said, skating them both a nervous glance. "I tried to call him but he did not answer."

Sal sat across from her. "There was an. . ." How could he call it an accident when it'd been his fault?

"An accident," Dean put in, nodding to Sal.

"I–Is he okay?" Her voice tremored.

"No," Sal said, looking down. Then back to her. "He. . .died." They couldn't tell her much because of security and protocols. And because they didn't have much to go on. They hadn't even recovered his body yet.

A shaking hand went to her mouth. Brown eyes glossed beneath tears. She shook her head. "No." Tears spilled over her cheeks. "No!" Her shoulders shook. "*No!* He's strong. He doesn't quit. Don't you tell me he's dead!" She punched to her feet.

Sal rose with her, miserable. "I'm sorry. I wish it wasn't true. He—"

"No!" Fekiria pushed against him. "Get back." She waved her hands. Then clapped a hand over her mouth. Looked pale as if she'd vomit. But she gulped, lifted her chin. Pushed him again. "No, it's not right!" She thumped his chest with a fist. "He's a fighter! He's—"

Sal wrapped his arms around her. She crumpled against his chest, sobbing. "I'm sorry." He held her like she was a fragile cup. "I'm so sorry."

Zahrah was there and pulled her cousin into her arms then lowered her to the sofa.

"No!" Fekiria shoved Double Z back, stumbling toward the door. She held out a hand, again looking like she'd be sick. Then she darted to a room and slammed the door, her sobs carrying like agonizing howls.

Numb himself, Sal stood there. He hadn't even told her how he died. That it'd been his fault. He shifted and noticed Dean holding Zahrah, who cried as well.

"I'm sorry," Dean said. "I couldn't tell you until you were here for security reasons."

Alone and guilty, you miserable creature. Sal stalked to the door. Yanked it open and threw himself down the steps. At the vehicle, he threw his fist into the door. Once. Twice. He gripped the hood and wished he could dig his fingers through it. Dig through until he could find some ounce of hope that his life wasn't completely and utterly cursed.

—∞—

Dean cupped Zahrah's face in his hands. He thumbed away her tears. "Hey."

She looked at him, blinking away more tears, their moment suffocated by the gut-wrenching sobs of her cousin.

"Look, I know—it's an awful time, but I have to do this." He reached into his pocket, sensing an urgency. That any day someone could deliver news to her about his demise. He held out the box. "I wanted a romantic dinner and time alone, but—"

Zahrah's tears burst anew.

Was he wrong to do this? He glanced to the door of Fekiria's bedroom.

Warm hands held his, wrapping around the box.

"I want to marry you, Z. I don't care when, but I want you to wear this. I want you to know there is no doubt I want to marry you. This world is so messed up, and we can't know when our lives will end—but if I ever leave before. . .I want you to know how much I felt. How much I wanted with you." He opened the box, revealing the sapphire-and-diamond engagement ring. "Will you?"

Zahrah's eyes were slits as she cried, still holding a hand over her mouth as she nodded.

Dean slid the ring on her finger. Pulled her close. Tight. "Losing Brian made me see how much time I've already lost. I don't want to waste any more." He kissed the top of her head. Then kissed her. "I love you, Zahrah."

CHAPTER 36

Kandahar Airfield, Afghanistan
8 April—0830 Hours

According to records, Cassie had been missing for approximately eighteen hours. Reports had come from a village north of the base about an attack against a female journalist. Sal couldn't detach his mind from Fekiria's reaction. How else had he expected it to go? But nothing could've prepared him for the rawness of it.

Ashamed as he was to say it, he didn't even feel that level of loss when Vida died. Regret, yes. Guilt—heckuva lot. But all-out grief? No. He'd mourned her. They'd been together for years, but more like friends.

Truth was, he was experiencing more grief right now, thinking of Cassie. Wondering what happened to her. Feeling as if his chest had been ripped open, knowing full well what jihadists and terrorists did to captured American females.

"There aren't any female journalists in the region," Dean said. "At least, none on record."

"It's possible," Titanis began slowly, "that these villagers thought Walker was a journalist."

Sal sat. Listened. Worked through the churning ache in his chest. He threaded his fingers and squeezed them, turning, rubbing. Fighting hands that had warred on behalf of innocents for years. But now he couldn't do a thing for Cassie. Yeah, he'd given her heck for the situation at the Towers. For lying to Dean. But he didn't mean it.

He wasn't sure what he meant. What he wanted.

No, that wasn't true. He knew what he wanted. And it scared him.

He'd be lying if he didn't admit he wouldn't mind a chance to see if he could fix things with Cassie. Even though he'd thrown her own desire to fix things back in her face.

Why?

Didn't make sense. She was right there. Willing and open to him.

And Mila—man. Every time he thought her name, he saw Fariz's bloodied, dying little sister.

"Sal?"

He looked up, surprised to find the team's eyes on him. He straightened. "Sorry?" Planted a hand on his leg. Played off that he'd been distracted.

"Want to go out and recon?"

"Recon?" He straightened. "Cassie's missing and you want to recon?"

Titanis grinned. "Yeah."

But then. . .everyone was grinning. What'd he miss?

"Thought we should check out some villages. Do what Ramsey ordered—play nice with the locals. See if they're okay on supplies."

"See if they need a brute squad," Schmidt said.

They wanted to sit in a field and converse with locals while Cassie was God-knows-where. Whoever had snatched her probably holed up in some—wait. Out there. "Yeah." His brain finally caught on. "We should check some villages. Make sure they're okay."

After the way Ramsey had breathed down their necks, and with them on the verge of busting his infidelity and collusion with an enemy into the open, they needed a wide birth around the brigadier. "I'm more than ready to get out of here and stop sitting on our thumbs."

"Hooah!"

―⚊―

The heat annoyed him almost as much as trouncing in the Humvee for three hours over unfriendly roads and with men who chatted—which required a hefty amount of shouting over the din of the vehicle—and taunted Dean for finally proposing to Double Z. But right now, Sal figured pretty much everything would annoy him. Cassie was missing, and somehow, that tormented him.

Probably because he knew he'd treated her wrong. He'd placed blame on her that belonged right on his own shoulders.

"Heads up," Dean shouted over his shoulder. "Village is less than two klicks north. Five mikes."

The men donned their helmets, double-checked their weapons, and tightened up the loose camaraderie that'd existed for the last few hours. Sal bounced his legs, anxious to get out there and track down any sight of Cassie.

Dean headed into the village and Riordan's team pulled up the rear.

"Nice and easy," Dean said before he pushed open the door.

"I'll just take a stroll." Sal climbed out, patted his brain bowl, then drew his weapon around in front and held on as he walked a circle around both vehicles. Watching how the locals reacted to their presence should tell them a lot. Nervous was one thing. Silent was another—indicated defiance. And trouble. Clamoring would tell them the people were angry about something and needed help.

His boots crunched over the rocky road as he paced.

"Ghost town," Harrier muttered as he sidled up.

Sal nodded. "Too quiet." None of the people had come out, though he knew plenty were here. A ball rolled along a side alley though there was no wind. Where was the kid who'd been playing with it before they rolled in?

"Eagle," Sal subvocalized as he made his way back toward the Humvee. "What're you seeing? Where is everyone?"

Dean's expression mirrored the unease roiling through Sal.

"Thermals show a full house—but that's it. They're all inside."

"Let's round 'em up," Riordan said as he trudged over.

Sal nodded.

"Ok—"

An expletive shot from the coms.

Sal stopped, listening. "Eagle?" He shared a look with Dean that said this was bad. Eagle was the strongest Christian he'd known. For him to curse, things had to be bad. Sal pivoted, stalked back down the road, weapon up and ready, as he looked toward the mound Eagle had set up on. "Eagle! What's going on?"

"I didn't see them. Have no idea"—*huff, pant*—"where they came from. Or"—*pant, pant huff*—"Augh! They've got me." The words sounded grimaced.

Sal knew a painful truth in that second. Eagle had run not only to save his life, but to buy time to tell the team they were in trouble. No sooner had Sal made it to the last hut than he saw it. Air trapped in his lungs. He stared at the line of SUVs barreling at them from the north side of the village. Were there more? Either way, Raptor was in trouble.

"Incoming!" Sal spun back and sprinted toward the vehicles—and running with all his gear proved as difficult as trying to run in water. "Three SUVs headed our way."

The team scrambled and took up defensive positions, avoiding the vehicles that could become boiling cauldrons if hit with an RPG or an IED.

Sal threw himself around the corner. Past Dean, who knelt with his weapon trained out. He whipped around and went to a knee, covering Dean's six.

"This smell like an ambush to anyone else?" Riordan shouted. "Thinking they grabbed your girl, Falcon, because they knew we'd come after them."

Your girl. He wouldn't dignify that with a response. Because he wasn't sure if he liked it or resented it.

"Well, lookee here," Harrier said. "Suddenly the locals come out to play."

True enough, a half-dozen men and boys peeked out the door. They were talking and pointing. Nodding. "They know something." Sal shimmied closer, wanting to hear.

"Yeah, like we're all about to get blown sky-high."

But the locals didn't look afraid. They seemed. . .curious.

One of the men said something about a girl. That made Sal's pulse surge. They were in the right place then! But then he said something about "same one."

"What're they saying?" Riordan asked.

"Not sure," Sal shouted. "Said something about a girl and the same one. But I can't hear or make out the rest."

"Sounds like we're in the right place, then," Titanis said.

"Right place, wrong time?" Harrier asked.

The vehicles lurched into the U-shaped village and swung their big black SUVs around. And not just the three he'd seen, but five. Before they came to a full stop, men were falling out, weapons up, faces dark with forbidding intent. Shouting, they rushed toward the team.

"Get down, get down!"

The men wore keffiyehs and standard dirtied tunics. There had to be twenty or twenty-five. Outnumbered and outgunned, Raptor hesitated. Looked to Dean, who waved for them to cooperate.

"You gotta be kidding me," Schmidt muttered.

"Easy," Dean said.

Sal tensed as two men came toward him. His nature was to resist. Fight these terrorists off with everything in him. But he saw something in Dean's expression that restrained him.

A lanky Arab stalked toward Dean with a burlap sack. He met Dean's gaze evenly, calmly.

Dean stared at the guy. Nodded.

Nodded? Why was he nodding?

The man stuffed the sack over the captain's head, secured it, then turned to Sal. He scowled at the man. "Who are you?"

The leader shouted at Sal then jerked him forward and bagged him, too. Darkness swam and the heat of the desert smothered him with the burlap over his head. Somewhere he heard the squawking of brakes and the crunch of an axle. The grumbling noise of a diesel engine growled to a stop nearby.

Iron grips clamped around his arms and yanked Sal forward. Dean didn't want them to fight, so he wouldn't fight. He'd learned to take the lead from him, but this. . . Walking himself to his death?

"Just move," came a heavily accented voice near his ear. "Soon it be okay."

It'd be okay? In what way?

He heard the pleading in the voice but couldn't piece together this puzzle. Maybe Dean had seen or known something. Sal's foot hit something. But the men urged him forward still. He found himself climbing an incline of some sort.

A ramp into a truck!

No no no. He'd seen this before. Men herded like cattle off to a butcher shop.

The thought put a boulder in his path. Sal hesitated. His muscles twitched in resistance. One of the goons hauling him off shouted at him.

Which only made Sal more resistant.

Pain exploded against the back of his shoulders, pushing him forward. He stumbled. Used the momentum to dive to the left. Into the man who'd struck him.

Men pounced on him, wrangling him. The more force they applied, the more it forced Sal to apply pressure, too.

His feet went out from under him. He fell forward, pain scoring his palms and knees.

Darkness thudded into the back of the truck.

Sal froze. Was this it? He'd die in the desert? What about Cassie? And Mila—she'd never get to know him. He'd never find out if she liked ice cream.

The truck shook back and forth, bouncing.

Sal bumped against something solid.

"Sorry, mate," came a grunt.

"Titanis?"

Light snapped through the bed of the truck.

Sal stilled. What the. . . ?

"Forgive us for the roughness," came the thick voice who'd reassured him earlier.

Someone fumbled with the sack over Sal's head. Then ripped it off. Light blinded him and he blinked feverishly to gain his bearings.

A man stood at the front of the truck. With Dean.

Sal came to his feet, the vehicle trouncing them. "What's going on?"

"I am Waris. My friend invites you to his home for a meeting."

"A meeting?"

"Who's your friend?"

"Your friend has a sick way of inviting people over for tea and scones."

Sal made his way to Dean. "You knew. . . ?"

Dean shook his head.

"But I saw you—"

"I recognized Waris."

Wait. Waris. Right hand of— "Takkar." When Dean nodded, Sal felt sick. They'd infiltrated the man's building. Left it heavily damaged. And left Hawk, too. "Think this is about payback?"

—∞—

Kabul, Afghanistan
8 April—1215 Hours

"I'm proud of you." Delicate arms wrapped around his waist as he stood in the kitchen getting a glass of water.

Sajjan encircled her small waist, tugging Nina closer. "And why is that, my bride?"

Nina wore elegance like a fine diamond. With her platinum blond hair and expertly applied makeup, she was in a class all her own. "You are extending patience and peace when your hand has been slapped by these men."

He gave her a quick squeeze and nodded. "They will know of my displeasure."

She smiled up at him, with eyes that had dazzled him since they first met at a premiere for his friend's movie. "Ah, but not your rage."

He kissed her. "You make me too soft, Nina."

"No, my love, you have a good heart and you know when justice must be meted out. You are a fair and honest man. It is why you are so well loved and respected wherever you go."

Her words were as honey on his ears. But Nina only saw the side she wanted to see. The side she'd fallen in love with and married. He must also be the strong arm of a law bringer if he was to be taken seriously. Swift justice showed those who only spoke with bullets and swords that he knew how to play that game as well.

It was why he did not fit completely in either world—not the civilized, nor the barbaric. It was why he had gained this position. He knew how to deal political cards with a quick hand.

"I must go." He kissed her again.

"Timbrel's not happy that you've involved Tony." Disapproval hung on her lips.

"He hasn't *involved* me in anything," Tony said as he appeared from the hall. Then nodded to Timbrel who had followed him. "She's ready to head to Dubai for that trip."

"How did you convince her?"

"Promise of a vacation alone, just the two of us."

"Far away from anything combat." Timbrel shot Sajjan a fiery look.

As Nina's son-in-law joined him, Sajjan walked toward the elevator and gave her a good-bye look over his shoulder. They entered the elevator and he pressed his access button.

As the car carried them to another level, Sajjan shifted roles. Shifted his mind-set. "You sure you can handle this? They are your brothers."

"They won't understand at first, but in the end. . ." He nodded, his beard once again scraggly. "They'll know they would've done the same." He shrugged. Then he cast a speculative look back. "You going to tell them?"

"About my guest?" When Tony nodded, Sajjan almost smiled. "That depends."

"On?"

"On how receptive they are to my demands."

―⁓―

Head throbbing from the whack they'd given him, Sal strode with the team through the parking structure and into the steel trap. Waris had said little since his brief apology and seriously lacking explanation of what was going on. Did Takkar plan to chew the team out? Take the damages out of their backs? Or turn them into slave labor to repair the building?

None seemed likely, and yet, knowing the elusive and mysterious Takkar, all were likely. The guy hadn't earned a reputation by being soft. Show favoritism to one side and another rebelled.

That was why Sal hated politics. Action—give him action over cheap talk any day. Crammed into the elevator like cattle, the team said nothing. Tense shoulders and wary glances spoke enough. Half unsettled, half angry, they all wanted answers just like Sal.

But Cassie.

Pinned at the back of the steel box, he wondered where she was. Where the kidnappers had taken her. There'd been no word of a ransom video, so he had no choice but to believe she was still alive. And he was glad to believe. Wanted to believe 100 percent.

Mila needed her mom. She didn't even know her dad.

My fault. Totally his fault. But it didn't change the fact that life would be really hard for a little girl put in that situation.

Why on earth did he keep thinking about Mila? Why. . .why was she so important? He didn't know her. Hadn't met her. Hadn't even spoken to her. Yet somehow. . .she seemed like the most important thing. An urgency filled him to fix the things he'd just mentioned—talking to her, meeting her in person, getting to know her.

But not without Cassie.

"Holding it together?" Dean asked as they filed down a long hallway with no doors and too many flickering lights. Like some really bad horror flick.

Sal tried to nod, but he wasn't sure it happened. "I don't have time for this. Cassie—"

"We'll work it out," Dean said. "I promise."

A set of double white doors swung open. They stepped into an entrance with some serious security protocols. Fingerprint, eye, voice. All coded in before what Sal thought was a wall whooshed up out of the way.

Waris held a hand toward the opening. Sal noted the others hesitating. He didn't blame them. That area beyond the vanishing door looked an awful lot like the often-nondescript warehouses where men are tortured and left for dead. Or worse—left alive with festering wounds that turn septic and kill them slowly and excruciatingly.

Sal moved forward, the nerves in his body thrumming in anticipation of an attack. Of finding himself waking up hours later with a few body parts missing. But inside, he only found moderately cooled air, a half-dozen bulbous cameras dangling from the ceiling. But no chairs. No people. Just an empty cement area.

A clink sounded beneath his boot. He lifted his foot and stared at the hole with a metal ring encircling it. His gaze rushed the room, noting a dozen more. Evenly spaced. He looked up and his power bar curdled in his stomach.

He swung around—right into the others filtering into the room—and took a step toward the door. "Hey! What is this?"

"It's a freakin' torture cell," Schmidt announced.

As if answering Sal's question, the door whooshed back down, sealing them in. Waris hadn't joined them.

"Son of a—"

"No doors." Dean noted as he joined Sal. "Think they plan to have some fun with us?"

"You know what they say about payback," Riordan said. "And I can promise Takkar didn't take our incursion into One lightly."

"So, what?" Schmidt turned a slow circle. "He's going to punish us?"

Dean muttered, "I wouldn't put it past him."

"He should talk to us, find out why—"

"I agree, Mr. Russo," a mechanical voice boomed through the cement prison. "But you did not extend me that courtesy when you and these men raided and damaged my property."

Sal held up his hands, acknowledging the point but not agreeing or apologizing. War was tricky territory. Admitting to a grievance like this could get the entire U.S. military hung up for weeks. Limit their operational capabilities. Raptor had bypassed Command for a reason.

"We appreciate your position," Dean said in a clear voice. "Unfortunately, we are on an urgent mission. One of our own has been taken hostage. We do desire to sort this incident out with you, but we request—"

A hissing noise in the far corner silenced Dean as their attention focused on the sprinkler head spewing water over the heads of the SEALs and Titanis. The men instinctively moved out from under the spray.

Just in time, too.

A crackling noise chased the water. Hissing. Popping.

Electroshock therapy.

"Holy. . . !" Eagle and Titanis shuffled farther back, the men pushing for dry ground to avoid getting shocked.

"I find your lack of respect and consideration for me and my business quite shocking. Have I not worked as an ally with you, cooperated with you, and even helped you in many ways over the last few years?"

Dean held his hands out again, glancing to the water racing toward them. "You have. Burnett saw you as a friend. He worked hard to preserve that relationship."

"And Captain Watters? How do you see me?"

Dean hesitated. And every second that he wavered, the water didn't.

"Dean," Sal hissed as the team crunched together, cursing.

"I see you as a man who must establish boundaries. One who knows what levers to pull to gain cooperation. Are you a friend?" Dean shrugged and indicated the water. "That remains to be seen."

"You would tell me how to conduct my business?"

"I would encourage you toward diplomacy and friendship."

Sal balled a fist. The captain was a far better negotiator than him. This Sikh was threatening the team. If an enemy had pulled this stunt, Sal would've thrown himself at the guy. But there was no visible enemy. Just four walls, spigots, drains, and zapping electricity.

This was ridiculous.

Crack! Pop!

"Augh!" Schmidt hopped around, shaking out his hands. His team tugged him back and they all huddled away from the water, grateful for the drains that diverted some of the electricity conductor.

The clatter of teeth followed a meaty thud. Eagle lay, head in the water, thrashing as currents tormented his body.

CHAPTER 37

Eagle!" Titanis lunged and dragged Eagle off his feet. Hoisted him up over his shoulders.

Son of a— "Look!" Sal shouted at the ceiling. "You got us. You made your point. But you know us. You know these men. We wouldn't have entered that building if we hadn't felt it absolutely necessary. Now—now we have someone missing. And we want her back." His mind zigzagged back to the village. To their words. "And I can't help but think you can help us there." He palmed the air. "Tell us what you want, but cut this crap out. These men were doing their jobs. Just like you're doing yours. We get it. Point made."

Dean gave Sal a "really?" look then shook his head. Silence hung in the air.

The water pipes groaned and stopped.

"Your first isn't very diplomatic, Captain Watters."

"That's why he's my first," Dean said.

Silence fell on the room, the hiss of electricity gone.

"Who are you looking for, Mister Russo?"

"An intelligence analyst."

"You mean a spy."

Sal didn't reply. Didn't that just prove that Cassie was here or that Takkar knew where she was? "I mean we want her back."

"What are you willing to do for her life, Mister Russo? From what I've heard, she's told a great many lies and endangered your men. In fact, some around you believe she killed your compatriot, Brian Bledsoe."

"And according to some liberal-leaning Americans, I'm a baby killer and murderer just because I'm a soldier. Perspectives get skewed."

"Then you don't feel she's lied?"

"Haven't we all?" He shrugged. "I want her back. Are you going to help us or just get your thrills off trying to electrocute us? Aren't you better than that, Takkar?"

Click.

A rectangular area punched out of the wall.

Cassie stepped through the portal-like opening. Hair down and wearing a cream tunic, she stood there with an ethereal smile. A tear slipped down her face.

Relief flooded him. "Oh, thank God!" Three large strides carried him to her. He pulled her into his arms.

—〰—

Sweet release! Cassie fell into his warm embrace, tightening her arms around his waist. Hearing his words, hearing the vehemence in his mission to get her back—it'd filled in every hole the last few weeks had stabbed into her heart. She pressed her hands against his back, clinging for dear life.

"I'm sorry," he muttered.

"Not even a thank-you?" A deep, resonating voice asked.

Sal shifted but didn't let her go. "Thank you."

Sajjan Takkar stood with Waris and Candyman just inside the same door she'd passed through. Cassie felt Sal jerk when he saw his former teammate with the two men.

"Tony," Dean whispered. "What are you doing?"

"Please forgive him," Sajjan said. "I've asked him not to respond to your questions. For now, he's indulging me."

"Traitor," whispered through the thick throng of operators more than once.

"I expected you would see it that way, which is why I've asked him not to speak." Sajjan turned to Dean. "Your men infiltrated my business, without the courtesy of speaking to me first or warning me." His eyes ignited with the injustice.

Cassie shifted, but Sal's arm tightened around her. He wouldn't let her move and he wouldn't look at her.

"I cannot discuss missions with you," Dean said, but then held up a placating hand, "but I will tell you that a woman occupying an office and residence there was viewed as a high-value target."

"You would play these games with me?"

"You've given me no reason to trust you." Captain Watters didn't sound angry, but he also wasn't yielding.

"What of Miss Walker?" Sajjan pointed to Cassie and she was sure she looked like a candy cane with the cream tunic and beet-red face. "I returned her to you safely."

Dean's eyes glinted with resolution. "Why did you even have her?"

"Ah." Sajjan nodded.

"Wait," Cassie said, stepped out of Sal's grasp. "That's my fault."

"Miss Walker, I appreciate your effort to defend me—"

"No, it's just an effort at the truth." Cassie turned to Captain Watters. "I knew nobody here would listen to me, so I contacted Mr. Takkar."

"About what?"

"About Kiew Tang."

The captain studied her for several long seconds then looked to Sal and nodded. His focus returned to Takkar. "Still not seeing how you ended up with her."

"I learned she was headed north. The roads are dangerous. I feared for her safety, so I sent my men to escort her."

Sal gripped Cassie's chin and angled her toward him. "This how you escort a woman? Just like your men did me?" He jabbed a finger to the back of his head.

"What? No," Cassie said, tugging free. "The villagers beat me. Takkar's men escorted me, just as he said. They never touched me."

His eyes dropped to hers and he frowned, his gaze skipping over her face. "You're sure?"

"You think I'm lying?"

"Well, you went to him for help. . ."

"Because you told me to fix things!" She waved her hand at Takkar. "So I am fixing them. Kiew Tang is not who everyone thinks she is, and I'm determined to help her however I can."

"Help her what?" Captain Watters asked.

"Help her stop what's happening."

"And what's happening?"

Cassie took a deep breath. Looked to Takkar who gave her an affirming nod. "She's being forced to orchestrate a devastating attack against us—but I think—she told me that what's happening here is just a distraction. However, she also told me to go home before it was too late."

Sal lifted a shoulder. "So, we're expecting another attack."

Sajjan stepped forward, hands in the pockets of his black slacks. "This is where I extend an olive branch."

Vibrations wormed through Cassie's shoes. She glanced around, staring at the floor and automatically reached for Sal. He stepped closer as a strange glow filled the room.

Men uttered curses and oaths.

Sal pulled her to himself, a protective move that made her look at him. His expression went like granite to something behind Cassie. She shifted and glanced over her shoulder. The entire wall had receded, revealing a—

Cassie sucked in a breath. The contents of her lunch climbed up her throat.

"No." Holding her tight, a hand on the back of her head as he pressed her face into his tactical vest, Sal said, "Don't look."

—⁓—

"How can you be okay with this?" Sal demanded of Candyman.

He stalked forward, stabbing a finger at the trench-like cell of the prisoner. "That man? That coward"—Candyman's chest rose and fell unevenly—"he's responsible for ratting us out. For revealing our locations, our plans to Meng-Li. It was his expertise that sent us ghost messages. Faked military protocols."

Sal glanced at the prisoner chained to a wall, fingers missing and face bloodied beyond recognition.

"You want someone to be mad at, someone to take out your anger on? Him!"

Cassie pushed back a little, and Sal gave her some room, his attention still on the gruesome reveal.

"Your government limits you, ties your hands on extracting information," Sajjan said as he walked toward the pit-like area. "We won't play diplomat here. In war, the game changes. Gloves come off. If they don't, lives are lost—and at the hands of this man, hundreds of lives have been lost."

"You can't put that on me," the hefty man snarled, spitting blood as he talked.

"That is what you would have us believe, but the information you withhold sends innocents to their graves."

"What's he doing?" Cassie whispered to Sal, reaching for him.

He caught her hand and lured her closer. "Ticking him off."

"Innocent." Sneering, the prisoner craned his neck forward. "And I suppose you think the grunts around you are innocent, too."

"Ah, and herein lies the irony." Takkar paced before the prisoner, hands in his slick pant pockets. "You see, these men probably don't see themselves as innocent, not completely."

Sal wouldn't comment. Wouldn't feed whatever sick game Takkar was playing here. But he was right. War demanded high costs of those who stepped onto the field. It wasn't a cleaned-up romance novel where hands and consciences were never bloodied.

It was raw. Brutal. Bloody.

No one hated war more than the soldiers involved. At least, the ones with honor and a moral code binding them to humanity.

"They often refer to themselves as the sheepdogs. They protect the sheep. Protect those who won't or can't protect themselves. But that inherent meaning is that the sheepdog will do whatever it takes to protect the sheep—including neutralizing the wolves that prey on their flock."

Sal had thought those very words. Hawk had spoken them before. Dean lived it. But hearing Takkar refer to them like that, especially considering the situation, made Sal's gut tighten.

"Who is he?" Dean asked, his tone clipped, his posture tense.

"He is often known simply as Boris, or Boris Kolceki." Takkar watched the prisoner for several long seconds. "But his real name is Michael Donnelly."

The prisoner jerked.

"Yes, Mr. Donnelly, I know your true identity, and that is why you will cooperate with us."

The man shook the chains. "What do you mean?"

"Your parents. Your sister. Your brothers. What of that pretty niece you brought chocolates to last Christmas?"

The man strained against the chains, steel clanking against cement. "You piece of dirt! Stay away from them!" He tugged hard then collapsed with a yelp, leaning to the left.

"Are you in pain, Mr. Donnelly?"

Cassie turned and allowed herself a brief look then jerked away, easing behind Sal as he and the others watched the two dialogue.

"What do you think? You seem to have all the answers."

Cold and hard as an ice cube, Takkar squatted before the man. "You wouldn't want that pain visited on anyone you know, would you, Mr. Donnelly?"

Wait. What? Was Takkar threatening the guy's family? Not even his direct family but— "Hey." Sal nudged Cassie toward Dean then started toward Takkar. "Hold up."

And Takkar did. He held up a hand.

Two men caught Sal by the arms and restrained him. He struggled but figured out quickly they weren't going to release him. "Fine, fine." Sal motioned with his hand and relaxed. When they released him, he remained where he stood.

"I believe I have made my point clear, Mr. Donnelly."

Bloody spittle ran down his double chins. "What do you want?" he asked through gritted teeth. Tears slipped over puffy, bruised eyes.

Takkar stood. Kept his back to Raptor and the SEALs. "It's right up your alley, Mr. Donnelly."

"What?" the man screamed. "What do you want?"

"In two days, Kiew Tang and Meng-Li Jin will be here for a fund-raiser I'm hosting. While Tang and Meng-Li are away from their nest, you will get me into Kiew Tang's system."

CHAPTER 38

Unknown Location
8 April—1925 Hours

Mister! Mister Soldier!"

Eyes open, he saw the face hovering over him riddled with concern, and like a flood, pain rushed in over him. Strangling. Blinding.

"Augh!" He arched his back, the cold hard table digging into his shoulder blades and tormenting him with fire-like air in his lungs.

The young man clapped a hand over his mouth. "No! Shh! You must not make noise." He glanced down the length of his body toward something. "They hear you, they come."

Hot tears squeezed between his eyelids. He grimaced, the weight of the man's hand even painful against his face and neck.

"Okay?" The young man stared at him, expectantly. "You quiet?"

A grunt was all he could manage.

"Good. Good. We get you out of here."

Move? Are you freakin' kidding me? He could barely breathe without passing out! "No," he croaked out.

The young man froze. Frowned. "We must. They kill you if you stay."

"Can't," he whispered.

"Must," the man reiterated. He lifted his hand. "Pills. They help with pain, yes?"

The pills felt like rocks in his mouth, but he did his best to work them to the back of his throat. "Water. . ."

"I brought some!" The man seemed pleased with himself as he helped coax water into his mouth.

A miracle that he didn't choke.

"Now." The man bent forward and slipped an arm beneath his head.

Teeth clamped together, he tensed against the knifing sensation in his lungs and spine. The man hoisted him up.

The room spun, crazy and carnival-like.

"Whoa," he breathed as the earth tilted.

A hand pushed against his ribs. "Got you."

The young man guided him off the table. His toe struck the cement floor. It felt as if an IED went off. His body railed against the explosion of pain. Everything hurt. His ears rang. Stomach roiling, he felt his legs give.

The man pushed up under him, supporting. "Hurry. They will be back soon."

Hurry? He wasn't even sure he could stand up, let alone walk. But if it meant staying alive, he would. Had to. If he couldn't stand, neither would the terrorist's attempts to silence him.

—∿—

Kabul, Afghanistan
8 April—1925 Hours

The words she'd ached to hear for four long years had been spoken. Well, almost. Sal said he wanted her back. But even she knew it wasn't meant the way she'd hoped. That he wanted her back in his life. He was a soldier and an American had been taken hostage.

But he'd held her. Protected her from the awful brutality exerted against that man. Now, he stood with his teammates in what looked like a bunk room, twenty or more bunk beds lining the wall.

She didn't expect him to cuddle with her and croon over her. But she had thought he'd at least talk to her. But as soon as the doors closed and the team was shut up in here, Raptor huddled and had been talking among themselves. Strategizing. Mind-numbing dialogue about options, contingencies, retaliation—their soldiering on exhausted her.

And that man. She wasn't ignorant. Real-life situations and war scenarios weren't prime-time TV fodder. Nobody wanted to admit it happened, nor did they want to look on it. Least of all her.

She scooted back on the bunk and braced her spine against the wall. Hugging her knees, shadowed by the upper bed, she watched Sal. She'd promised herself no more pining, and she wouldn't break that promise now. No matter how he'd acted a few hours ago. She let herself lie on her side and closed her eyes. Sleep hungrily pulled her into its viselike grip.

Cassie flinched awake. The room hung in semidarkness, quiet chattering flitting from various bunks. She blinked and yawned—

A face turned toward her, not a foot away.

She started. Blinked again.

Sal sat on the floor beside the bunk. Legs up, arms over his knees, he looked at her. "Good nap?"

"How long—?"

"Forty minutes."

She shook her head but stayed prone, liking the closeness to him. "What's happening?"

"Takkar came in, said he wants us to stay. He can't afford word to get back to the base—"

"To Ramsey?"

Sal nodded. "Gala is in two days. Team will report in as if we're on recon in the field."

"Are y'all okay with that?"

"It's some downtime." He smirked. "Who would be against that?"

Cassie nodded. What did it mean that he was here, talking to her like she was a normal person rather than avoiding her as if she were the plague itself? Though everything in her screamed to embrace this change, she didn't dare trust herself. She'd wanted this too long, and she'd once already read into a situation and created a wider divide.

Was she weak to want him back? Pathetic? Or was she strong because she saw the good in him and knew his heart, knew the man he really was, not the one beaten down by war, grief, and self-condemnation?

"Did you hear about Ramsey's daughter?"

Cassie stilled. "Daughter?"

Sal exhaled long and loud. "He has a four-year-old daughter with some Arab woman."

When he didn't go on, Cassie shifted to look at him better.

"Ramsey convinced the woman that if soldiers came to ask questions, she should kill the children before soldiers could."

Cassie sucked in a hard breath. "What?"

Sal lifted a hand and ran it over his head and down his neck. "That is some sick crap. It was awful. The girl was bleeding out. Dying. Because he wanted to save his own butt. How could he do that to a kid?"

Swallowing, Cassie forbade images from conjuring in her mind what that would look like, because she knew invariably Mila's face would replace the little girl's.

"Working with Harrier to save her life," Sal whispered, his gaze vacant, lost in the memory. "All I could think of. . ." He shook his head. Tears welled up in his eyes. "All I could see. . ."

"Mila?"

He looked at her, haunted. "I kept thinking—she'd die and I'd never know her." He craned his neck. "Does she like ice cream?"

Cassie lifted her head. "What?"

"Does Mila like ice cream?" He shrugged, his brow knotted. "I don't even know that. I don't know her."

I will not cry. I will not cry. Cassie bit her lip and gulped the urge to defy her own commands.

Sal dropped back against the wall, thudding his skull twice against the cement. "I've screwed up so much. Been too angry for too long at too many people, including myself." He shook his head. Met her gaze once more. "I want to change that."

Darn tears were too powerful. Her vision blurred and Cassie ducked, pulling herself upright and turning her gaze out to the open. Away from him.

Sal was on the edge of the mattress. "Let me, Andra."

She shook her head, not trusting herself to talk without a sob choking the word. "You know how long I've wanted you to say that?" Liquid drops of relief rushed down her face.

Calm down. He's not asking to marry you. He just wants to know Mila. Right.

Right, Mila. No, this was good. The way things should've been— well, mostly. He wanted to be a part of her life, and wasn't that what Cassie had prayed for so hard?

Sal took her hand. "I—"

"Stop." Cassie couldn't believe she was doing this. But the thought of him being soft one minute and hard the next terrified her. "I can't do this—I can't have you tell me you want this and then you find some reason to be angry again."

He let go and bent forward, arms on his knees. "I know." He scratched the sides of his head. "You're right. I'm tired of being angry. Tired of holding grudges." Soulful brown orbs, the gold flecks glinting with grief and exhaustion, shifted to her. "I'm sorry, Andra. Really sorry."

Stunned didn't come close to expressing what she felt. Because along with it went elation. Shock. And even fear—what if he changed his mind, or realized once he got some distance between him and the Afghan-girl experience that he'd just been hyped or PTSDing. "What brought all this on, Tore? I'm glad to hear it, but I have to admit, it's a little. . . I don't know whether to trust it."

Hurt rippled through the rugged lines of his face. "Seeing that little girl. . .it ripped apart something in me." Intensity radiated off his taut muscles as he cocked his head to the side. "No." He gritted his teeth and pursed his lips. "It ripped something loose—as if something had been stuck inside me."

Salvatore Russo had never been one to wax poetic, so Cassie held her tongue and questions. Being this reflective charged the air around them and made her listen better than she had ever before. This was important. Very important.

His chocolate eyes searched hers, wrought with fervency and yet question. He looked lost, which stunned her silent because Sal had always been centered—and the center of her universe.

Suddenly he twitched. Glanced at her then away. "Sounds stupid, I bet." He pushed to his feet and dusted his backside off. "I'd better talk with Dean about the plans for tomorrow."

—✺—

Kabul, Afghanistan
10 April—1615 Hours

Something had been knocked loose all right—his good sense.

Sal shrugged off the foolishness creeping along his shoulders as he and the team ran through scenarios and contingencies for the gala, for drawing Meng-Li Jin or Daniel Jin—whatever you wanted to call him—into their web. Painters tape on the cement floor provided a layout of the event setup for the team to rehearse lines of sight and strategy.

"Sal, wrong position," Dean's stern voice carried loudly through the basement.

Sal stopped. Glanced where he stood.

"Unless you like sitting in the punch bowl."

Chuckles released some pent-up tension as Sal shifted to his left a foot. Might seem silly to some, but getting a feel for the layout would make the difference between a successful op and a total screwup.

"Group up," Dean said, stepping toward the middle of the room.

Sal moved toward the team captain and bumped shoulders with someone. He glanced to the side. "Sorry."

"No worries, mate," Titanis said.

"Takkar wants everyone out of sight well in advance of the gala, so we'll head topside. Sal, Titanis—anyone else who'll be in view—shower up. Rest, check weapons and gear. Walk through the plan in your head until you can chant it in your sleep." Intensity radiated off Dean as he considered the team. "This is our chance to not only capture Kiew Tang, but the mastermind. We can't screw this up."

"Think Takkar has something else up his sleeve?" Sal asked. "While I appreciate his help and cooperation, I'm finding it hard to believe he's just letting us in on this." Hands on his belt, Sal gave a one-shouldered shrug. "Last I knew, we were on his hit list for our attempt to take down Tang."

Riordan, who stood a half-dozen inches shorter than Sal's six-three, sauntered closer. "Agreed—something's off."

"Does Takkar have plans we don't know about?" Dean bobbed his head firmly. "Absolutely. Do I know what they are? No. Will he deliberately act against us or put us in jeopardy?" He pursed his lips. "I don't believe so."

Schmidt grunted. "That sounds a lot like 'probably' in my book.

Look, the guy's given us no reason to trust him."

"Gentlemen," came the thick, stern voice of Sajjan Takkar as he entered the basement with his never-far-away strongman, Waris Singh, and three Asian men in suits. Also with them, Cassie. "If I might have some of your time. I've asked Miss Walker to join us because this information and her cooperation are integral."

"To what?"

"The successful completion of this attack against you. The fundraiser I have asked you all to attend will be the endgame, the point at which your thirst for justice and my desire to protect Afghanistan unite to take down a common enemy."

"Meng-Li Jin," Sal said, noting Cassie had made her way around to his side.

"Indeed." Sajjan took a minute to meet the gaze of each operator in the room. "My sources say that Meng-Li will be here tonight to obtain a final high-level code."

"To what?"

"While we have all been scrambling to stop the extensive breach of security, while your soldiers have stopped to lick their wounds and tend the injured, your government quickly shifted all security protocols and efforts to a new security program and software—Evangelion."

"Are we supposed to know that?" Harrier asked. "I mean, Brian—Hawk would know it. But we're not geeks."

Cassie breathed a laugh, and Sal glanced down at her. She leaned closer and whispered, "It's the name of an anime—her favorite."

"It is also a program designed and created by none other than Kiew Tang." When muttering and cursing singed the air, Sajjan nodded. "It is exactly as they planned—attack, expose the underbelly of the American cyber network, and they'd get your government to dive headlong into their very hands. With the code he will obtain tonight, Meng-Li and his rogue organization will have unfettered access and control to American troop location and movement."

Riordan frowned. "I'm sorry, but don't they already have that? I mean—that's why the brass pulled in our operators and teams. Right?"

"The breach of data was much more extensive than that," one of the

Asian men said, his words thickened by his accent and his eyes narrowed slits beneath his buzz cut. "It is one thing to ping a network and glean information, but with the implicit trust placed in Evangelion, the American government has, unwittingly, provided Meng-Li with that access. Troop movement, ships, contacts, covert operatives."

Ah now it made sense. Sal gave a soft snort. "You have compromised Chinese assets. If he can get into that information, your double agents and your spies are exposed as well."

"Yes. Unfortunately, his intention was one thing—to get the American government to shift security programs. In doing so, he exposed the covert operators of many countries," the other said. "Mr. Guo and I are here, however, for one asset."

"I'm sorry." Dean stepped forward. "Who are you?"

"Yeah," Riordan said. "And why do we care about your assets when we're trying to save our own?"

"I am Mr. Song. We are with 61398."

"Yeah?" Schmidt sniggered. "I'm with 90210."

More snickers skated through the room.

"It's the Chinese organization renowned as hackers. There's no one in the world better." Cassie angled her head to the side. Wet her lips before asking a question she probably knew the answer to already. "The operative you're looking to protect? Is it Kiew Tang?"

—⁘—

Kabul, Afghanistan
10 April—1815 Hours

As the elevator climbed to the penthouse, Eamon adjusted the tie on the tux in the mirrored walls. There were benefits to being rich and powerful, or at least having a father with those "qualities." He couldn't help but wish Brie were here to guide him and talk him through the thoughts crowding his mind.

But she hadn't been with him and Raptor when they'd been "rescued" by Takkar, so she was tucked away safely back at Kandahar Airfield. For that, he could be thankful. The vibes about tonight's fund-raiser for the Aga Khan Foundation hung thick and rancid in the air.

Or maybe it was just his nerves.

Nerves about the fund-raiser.

Nerves about the cryptic message from his father to meet with him and Takkar. Would they try to sway his loyalties from Raptor the way Takkar had done with Candyman?

With a quiet tone signaling his arrival at the penthouse, the elevator settled. The doors glided back and Eamon entered a grand foyer with marble floors, gilded stands supporting vases and busts that looked as ancient and expensive as the ones lining his father's mansion. The chilled air and austere-yet-museum-feel to the penthouse were cold and forbidding.

"Ah, Mr. Straider." Dressed in a silk suit, Waris Singh approached him and inclined his turbaned head. "Welcome."

Eamon nodded. "Thank you."

"Your father—"

"Eamon, my boy!"

Boy. As if he didn't dwarf his father by at least a head. As if he hadn't even graduated uni yet. But Eamon kept it civil, as was expected and as he'd always done. "Dad."

After passing through a tall doorway, Eamon stepped into a slightly sunken living area. The arrangement of the living space gave him a perfect line of sight on the seating area, the dining area, and even the bar.

"I was surprised you asked me to meet you here," Eamon said softly as they moved to the bar where his father lifted a half-full snifter of bourbon.

"Indeed, I was surprised to find you not at the Kandahar Airfield but living in a condo with a woman." Thick, disapproving eyebrows lifted. "Thought you knew better than—"

"You would assume the worst."

Anger flashed through his father's blue eyes. "I assumed you were actually doing your job to your country and being an honorable representative of the cross you bear so proudly on that big chest of yours."

"I was and have." Eamon would not be goaded, not this time. "Just because you fly in on your jet and find out I'm not where you think I should be doesn't mean I'm doing something wrong. Special operations are clandestine—"

"I don't need a lecture from you. In my position—"

"Yeah, it always is about your position, your reputation, isn't it?" Eamon growled, his voice low. Hating himself for letting the words come out. Lowering himself.

Approaching steps silenced the verbal war.

Eamon turned and found Takkar and Candyman coming down a hall toward them. At one time he respected both men. Now he wasn't sure about either one. Without a word to Takkar or Candyman, Eamon faced his father. "What did you want to talk with me about?"

"Actually, I asked your father to invite you," Takkar said, head high, as he joined them.

"Why?"

"Because once Lance died, the list of people on that base whom I could trust all but disintegrated."

"You know about Ramsey."

"I know about Ramsey," Takkar confirmed.

"I'm sorry. I'm still trying to ascertain the point of this meeting." Eamon pulled his attention back to his father and Takkar. Strange bedmates, those. One ruled a country as political leader. The other seemed to rule the world as a *deus ex machina*.

"General Ramsey will be in attendance tonight."

"That's why you wanted Raptor here," Eamon voiced his thoughts.

"Among other reasons," Takkar said. "I wanted the team here because. . . First—will you tell me the real reason you were assigned to Raptor team, Mr. Straider?"

Eamon betrayed nothing. He knew he hadn't. If Sajjan asked the question, then he probably had the answer.

Takkar slid a hand in his pocket and moved to the bar, where he lifted a decanter of gold liquid and a snifter. Candyman remained positioned between them. "Let me settle a debate going on in your mind right now. You wonder if it is a betrayal, what you have done. The men you've worked with for the past nine months count you as a brother. It would bother you if they viewed you as a traitor." Ice tinked in the glass before Takkar poured the liquor. "Let me dispel those fears. Once they know why you've done this—they are warriors. They've done their own deceptive trade practice." He sipped the drink. "Is that not right, Mr. VanAllen?"

Candyman's green gaze had locked on to Eamon. "It is."

"So, are you willing to divulge your true purpose?"

Eamon didn't speak. Knew he couldn't.

"Or have you been so long in the skin of that Special Forces team that you forgot what you were doing?"

"I haven't forgotten anything." Eamon remained calm.

"Then let me spell it out for you—tell me if I'm right."

He wouldn't. Couldn't. Not without—

"You're probably clinging to some misguided notion that speaking now would violate your own allegiance to the SAS. But I will reassure you—what is said here stays here." Takkar smiled as he lowered his crystal glass. "You are in fact reconnoitering for your government. They believed there was a Chinese asset so deeply implanted in the American military hierarchy that they tapped one of their finest operators."

There was only one place that information could've come from. The records had been sealed, the operation blacked out. Eamon slid a glowering look to his father.

"Well, since we are all out in the open with secrets," Takkar said, then took a gulp of his drink. "Let me come clean with one of my own." He motioned for Eamon to follow him.

Sajjan strode toward the rear of the penthouse and accessed a panel in the wall. A door receded from the wall and slid back, revealing a private room. He glanced back at him. "Please."

Eamon checked his flanks and found his father and Candyman. A beeping noise pulsed out of the room followed by a hissing noise. With no little amount of hesitation, he stepped inside. A wall of white cabinets consumed his view. To the left a blue curtain shifted. Medical?

He frowned at Takkar who crossed the room and thrust back the thin divider.

Eamon pulled straight at a man seated in a tall, straight-backed chair. A wheelchair. The gray pallor wasn't normal. But the features were easily recognizable. "Sir!"

CHAPTER 39

Kabul, Afghanistan
10 April—1830 Hours

Never before had so many die been cast or knocked around on such a vast game board. But with good men, honorable men, Sajjan remained convinced they could tear down this tower of evil power that had been erected on the bodies of innocents and patriots.

He folded his arms as Eamon Straider took a knee beside a worn, weathered general. A man he'd long counted among his closest friends. A hero to thousands.

"I think Sajjan just gets a kick out of parading me around in a hospital gown."

"Lance, you're wearing a two-hundred-dollar robe," Sajjan said with a smile.

"I—I don't understand," Eamon said, then rose and pivoted to Tony. "This is why you—"

"This is why," Tony said, vindication emanating from him. "I've been an intermediary since Sajjan brought him here."

Eamon's gaze roamed the general's body. "But how—are you—?"

"Yes. Paralyzed from the neck down. When they tried to kill me, they hit the right vertebrae. I sit in this chair for a while then lay in the bed until my body recovers from the strain. One heckuva life, eh?"

"But you are alive."

"Yeah, that's about the only thing VanAllen keeps saying."

"It'll matter to your wife."

"Oh shut up," Lance groused. "Go on. Get on with it. Tell him what he needs to know so he'll stop looking at me with that pathetic look."

"Sorry, sir. It's just a relief to see you're not six feet under. I know

Raptor will be very happy to see you."

"Then they'll kill him," Tony said.

"Who needs your mouth, VanAllen?" Lance's gaze had always been as fierce as his gravelly voice. "I can bust you down a rank."

"Sorry, sir." Tony crossed his arms over his thick chest and grinned. "No longer under your command. Private contract."

"Well," Lance groused, "I can make your life miserable."

"Have for the last two weeks, sir."

"Yeah, yeah," Lance said, but a smile tugged at the drawn lines on his face. "Man, it's good to be alive to make someone else miserable."

Eamon pivoted. "My father—"

"Your father is a great friend and asset. His role is complicated, even beyond yours." Sajjan held his shoulder. "I'm afraid I have more news that you must quickly accept and adapt to for this night to succeed."

The man was a veritable fortress of strength. Legends were written about men like Eamon Straider. "You've withheld more information from us? That's not a smart tactical decision."

"Perhaps not tactically, but it was imperative that this information be kept close to the heart until the very last minute."

"Fact was," Lance said, his speech slowing.

Sajjan motioned to the nurse, who moved toward the bed and raised the safety bar.

"No, give me a minute."

"You must rest," Sajjan said.

"After this is done." Lance shifted his gaze to Eamon, who took the meaning that Lance wanted to talk to him and drew closer. "Ramsey will be here tonight."

"Yes, sir. We're making arrangements with the FBI to take him into custody."

"Good." Lance's eyes drooped. "But. . ." Breathing seemed a chore. "There's more. . ."

"Why tell me, sir? Tell Dean or Falcon. They're team leaders."

But Lance had fallen asleep. Sajjan had the nurse adjust the bed to a prone position.

"Raptor team needs to be told about General Burnett," Eamon said.

"Not yet."

"Why?"

"Sir!" Waris rushed into the room.

Sajjan held a hand up to his associate. "As I said, this secret must be kept close. Too many people know, and. . .tonight could be for naught. And I must ask that you not speak of this to anyone. Not to a single person." He speared him with a look until he was sure Eamon's mind landed squarely on Brie Hastings. "No one."

"Sir, sorry—the Aga Khan's car is arriving now."

—◆—

"I'm not sure about this," Cassie whispered, staring at her reflection in the mirror. A mocha brown gown hugged her body, and while the neckline wasn't plunging, she had cleavage showing. Hair swept up, she looked more like a movie star than a soldier on a mission. She glanced at the beautiful brunette standing behind her. "You said the point was to blend in."

"It is." Timbrel reached around in front of Cassie and draped a multistrand necklace with chocolate pearls and crystals.

"How am I supposed to blend in when"—Cassie glanced down—"certain parts are standing out?"

Timbrel laughed. "Believe me, girl. There will be a lot more standing out in that gala. "There is nothing wrong with what you're showing. It's still very modest."

In front of her now, Timbrel twined a lock around her finger and let it curl along Cassie's neck. "Besides, I hear a certain soldier is having trouble remembering what he felt for you."

Surprised, Cassie looked her new friend in the eye.

Timbrel laughed. "Yeah, I think it's endemic of elite operators. Maybe too many bumps on their brain bowls."

There was a rap on the door. "Okay, ladies. Showtime."

"Coming," Timbrel called over her shoulder. She made one more adjustment to the dress then gave her nod of approval. "Now let him act like he's uninterested."

"Look, this is great 'n all, but seriously—tonight, I just want to get to Kiew. That's my goal."

"You keep telling yourself that, sweetie."

"I'm serious."

"So am I. But when you see that look in his eye, the one that says he is totally *into* you, that he could devour you—yeah, tell me how good your mission focus is then." The timber of her laughter carried them both into the hallway.

"Okay, I'm changing."

Timbrel caught her hand and kept walking until they were in the living area. Candyman turned and his gaze completely feasted on Timbrel. He let out a long, low whistle and pulled his wife into his hold. "I think we need to skip the fund-raiser."

With an arched meaning, Timbrel looked at Cassie as if to say, *see?*

But there was one difference—those two were married. She and Sal had gotten the cart before the horse before. And it'd been completely messed up ever since.

Tony turned to Cassie and nodded. "Yeah, that's how to knock a guy on his butt."

Timbrel slapped him.

A growl came from the side—her dog lying there, lifted his head and upper lip in a snarl.

"Hey, not *me*. I'm talking about Falcon," Tony explained. "Let's go before I get in trouble."

He escorted them into the elevator and down to the second floor, where the entire level served as a banqueting area. Heavy security stood along the sidelines, appraising each attendee waiting to enter. Two eight-foot tables were draped in luxurious linens and floral arrangements.

"Audrey! Darling, there you are!"

Timbrel groaned. "I swear she calls me that on purpose."

"Any time she can," Tony said.

"Mother." Timbrel approached the table, bypassing the long line. She glanced at her mother. "*Timbrel* and Tony VanAllen. We're on the list."

The platinum-haired woman waved a dismissive hand. "Oh, you know I can't get used to that name."

Nina Laurens. It was *the* Nina Laurens standing right there big as day! Timbrel nodded. "This is Cassandra Walker. She's on the list."

"Of course she is, darling. And such a pretty name for a beautiful woman."

"Thank you," Cassie said. "And I just loved you in *Evening Love*, Miss Laurens. But you're awesome in any movie." As soon as the words escaped her lips, Cassie cringed.

Timbrel groaned. "Do not feed this woman's ego," she said and threaded arms with Cassie.

"Oh, aren't you sweet. Thank you, Miss Walker." She flitted her hands toward the wall of doors affording entrance. "Go on. Enjoy the event."

Timbrel led her through the wide doors.

"I'm sorry," Cassie mumbled. "I can't believe I did that."

"Happens to the best of them."

But Cassie's mind had already shifted into work mode. Into seek and find—Sal that is. She wanted to see him. Ached for him to look at her the way Tony had, as Timbrel said, devoured his wife with his eyes. As if he couldn't get enough of her.

"Hey," a large, dark blur moved in front of them. "Here's your coms piece."

It was Sal. Right in front of her. Angled sideways and he hadn't even seen her. Not two feet away. And he stood there, talking with Tony about the coms and the mission and who was expected.

Cassie's heart plummeted. So much for standing out. Timbrel had been right—she *was* blending in. So much that Sal didn't notice her.

"Excuse us." Arms still threaded, Timbrel barreled with Cassie right between Sal and Tony.

"Sure. Sor—*Andra?*"

He hooked her arm, pulling her around to him. And it seemed every breath he took soaked up more of her strength because her knees suddenly felt like Jell-O.

"Booyah," Timbrel muttered in Cassie's ear. "Sorry, I need to dance with my man." She and Tony vanished.

Sal smiled at her. Really, deeply smiled. "You look amazing."

She probably matched the royal-red curtains draping the space between the massive marble columns. "It was Timbrel's doing."

He hadn't let go. He just stood there staring. For a very. Long. Time.

CHAPTER 40

Kabul, Afghanistan
10 April—1855 Hours

Falcon. *Idiot*. Ask her to dance," came a taunting voice through his coms.

Sal gritted his teeth, half embarrassed. Seeing her all dolled up, those curves taunting him. Curves he'd once been intimately familiar with—and now off-limits. A beauty of a woman—inside and out.

"Dance?" he finally managed to ask.

"Hooah!" came a chorus of cheers through his coms.

"Shut up," he hissed.

Cassie frowned then her blue eyes noticed the small plastic piece in his ear.

He guided her onto the dance floor and took her into his arms. He turned off his mic. "This is really unfair." Though he stood a head taller than her, she always fit so perfectly against him.

"What?"

"You, that dress. . .the mountain between us."

Hand on his shoulder and one on his arm, she met his gaze. "Why is it still there?"

"Good question." He could not get enough of her. The oval face. Her full lips—not pillow lips like a lot of Hollywood and plastic women, but natural, taunting ones. The long, graceful slope of her neck and—

Sal lifted his gaze back to her eyes. Safe territory. "You look beautiful."

"Thanks. You clean up pretty good, too."

"Heads up," a voice said as they swirled past a small crowd.

Sal reached up and turned his piece back on.

"You back on, Falcon?"

"Yes," he subvocalized.

"Kiew Tang is on-site."

"Tang is here," Sal said, and immediately felt Cassie go rigid. He pressed a hand against her back. "Easy. Keep it natural."

Cassie hauled in a breath. "I see her." Her gaze locked on to something. "I don't see him. Seems she's alone."

"Confirm," Dean's voice came through the coms. "Tang arrived alone."

"She came alone," Sal repeated for Cassie's benefit.

Cassie nodded, tucked her chin, and let out a breath.

"You ready?" Sal asked, suddenly unwilling to let her go. To release her to try to connect with a woman who turned out to be a much more highly trained operative than they could've imagined. More than just a high school roommate.

He let go, but Cassie clung to him. "Andra?"

Her fingers tightened against his biceps. "The reason I did the POA—"

"No," Sal said. He cupped her face. "Just focus on tonight. Don't let your mind go there."

"If anything happens to—"

"It's not."

"But if it does—"

"Andra."

She clutched his arms as he held her face. "*Promise* you'll take care of Mila."

"*Move!*" Dean growled through the coms.

Sal glanced to the side. Saw Dean and Titanis navigating the thick crowd. But then he saw the willowy, elegant figure of Kiew Tang. She'd narrowed in on Cassie, but worse—on him. "She's watching us."

Cassie slapped his face.

Sal jerked, stunned as she stalked off.

"Nice save," Dean whispered. "Falcon get lost in the crowd."

Carrying his wounded pride off the floor, Sal ignored the smirks of the team, who were littered around the massive event hall and interwoven among several hundred guests.

Sal pushed around one clique after another to take up position by a marble pillar. Had she slapped him because he hadn't answered? Or because she wanted Kiew to think them at odds? "Where is she?"

He surfed the crowd, searching for her. She'd been headed in Tang's general direction, but with this many people finding her would be a challenge.

"Anyone have eyes on Walker?" Sal asked, pushing farther back toward the windows to more easily move through the hall.

"Negative," Eagle said.

"Just lost her," came Titanis's reply.

"We need eyes on her at all times." Sal reminded the team. "Find her!"

"Easy, Falcon," Dean said quietly. "She's not the only bird in play."

Maybe she wasn't but she was the only bird he cared about.

—∾—

Might as well put her through a clothes wringer. Cassie held her breath as she pushed through one tangled mob after another, heading in the general direction she'd seen Kiew.

A shoulder bumped hers.

"Sorry."

A hand wrapped around hers, passing something to her. "Coms," a voice breathed.

Cassie stopped, rolling the small piece in her hand as she looked around, searching for whoever from Raptor had handed off the communications device. But strange, unfamiliar faces glanced back. One or two men smiled, and another started toward her, innuendo clear in his posture and pace.

Great. Cassie turned and ducked, grateful she wasn't tall and could bob through the crowd without too much notice. Irritation clawed her partially from the claustrophobia choking her but also because she'd told Raptor she didn't want a coms piece. It'd stop Kiew from contacting her.

Through a cluster of tuxed-out men, she saw Captain Watters trolling. Cassie aimed for him. Caught his arm.

He turned, his expression stern. "What—?"

"No." She held out the coms. "I told you, I'm not wearing one."

Slowly, he looked down at the coms. Then back at her. "It's not ours."

Cassie blinked. "What?"

"Ours are clear and long range. It's shortwave." Captain Watters

314

stared at her for several long seconds. Though he looked at her, he wasn't *looking* at her. His expression firmed with what looked like determination. "Put it in."

"What if it makes my head explode?"

He smirked. "It won't."

She nodded to his coms. "What'd they tell you?"

He didn't answer quickly. "That it's safe."

With a huff, Cassie moved away from him, wandering to a table that provided an array of drinks—water, punch, liquors, and sodas. There, she casually let down her hair and slipped the coms piece into her ear, rubbing her scalp and reveling in the way her scalp no longer throbbed from the updo.

"My friend."

Cassie inhaled, her gaze skimming the crowd as she turned and breathed, *"Kiew."*

"I hope slapping him was not for my benefit."

Cassie smiled, still searching for her friend. "Completely my benefit. He wouldn't make a promise to me. Where are you?" Probably shouldn't have asked that, but it'd come out before she could think it through.

"Remember the OVA when Shinji was in the robot and Asuka was in one as well?"

Cassie's mind whirred to a stop, trying to extract that long-ago memory card. "I. . .barely." Yeah—she recalled the original video anime. It was called *You Can (Not) Redo.* "Sorry. You loved Shinji more than I ever did." Where was she? Why wouldn't she talk to her face-to-face?

"Remember that robots sometimes went rogue."

The words turned Cassie's stomach into a knot.

"Asuka's robot went rogue and started killing?"

Nausea roiled through her.

"And Shinji was forced by his father to shoot and kill the robot Asuka was in?"

"Kiew—"

"Remember how angry and upset Shinji was?"

"Kiew, please talk to me. Where are you?"

"I'm afraid, Cassandra, that you may have to be my Shinji."

CHAPTER 41

Tides were shifting. But with tides, when one thing shifted, another invariably got knocked around. For Sal, the tides had started with the little girl.

No, no it was before that. Seeing Cassie again. All those old memories and images catapulting to the front of his mind. But he'd taken control of them, managed them. Contained them with bonds of determination.

Until the little girl obliterated those bonds, unleashing a flood of revelations that had tethered him to new determination—to change.

Then Cassie had to go and show up in that hot little number tonight. Way to mess with a guy's focus. He'd lost sight of her for a few minutes earlier, but once he reacquired her location, he hadn't let her vanish again. She stood very still, her expression taut.

When her eyes widened, Sal tensed. What was she seeing? He tried to follow the direction of her gaze but only saw dozens of guests. Nothing discernible. She whipped around and her eyes locked on to him.

Something in those baby blues yanked him forward. Sal was halfway across the room in a purposeful stride before he knew it.

What did his heart good was that she was heading his way, too.

She met him. Caught his arm. "Kiew—she'sgoingtodosomething-butshewantsmetostopher. Idon'tknowwhatitisbutIhavetofindher."

"Cass—"

"Shetalkedtome, toldme."

"Slow down." Sal held her bare shoulders. "You said something's going to happen?"

She nodded, her hair loose and curling around her shoulders. "Yes, she"—Cassie touched her forehead—"it's a long story, but she told me to stop her." She licked her lips. "I think. I mean—"

"What's happening?" Dean came up behind her.

Cassie yanked around. "You were right—it was Kiew. I put the earpiece in and she was there."

"What'd she—?" Dean froze. His face washed white.

"Captain?"

His nostrils flared, lips pressing into a pinched line.

Sal slowly glanced around. "Dean, you okay?"

"Nianzu—the Lion," he said through gritted teeth.

Over his shoulder, Sal spotted the Asian who'd been responsible for torturing Dean. Enabling the rape of Double Z. The visceral response from Dean set off alarms in Sal's head. He shifted to block Dean's view of the man. "You got it together?"

Dean balled his fists. "I knew he'd be here, but I didn't expect. . ." His words tremored with pent-up anger. "I didn't expect to want to take him down."

"Then you weren't thinking," Sal said. "Because any normal person would have. Once Meng-Li and Ramsey are on deck, we'll be ready to put the game in play."

"Ramsey's here but keeping a low profile," Dean said. "I've narrowly avoided him twice. He's too full of himself to think we might actually know what he's up to." Venom coursed through Dean's words. "And Nianzu—I'm going to make sure he sees justice for what he did to Zahrah."

"Hooah," Sal said. "Be nice to have that resolution before you marry her."

Dean sighed. Shook his head then shifted—saw Cassie. "Sorry." He blinked. "You—what did Tang say to you?"

Cassie launched in a hurried explanation of some anime with rogue robots and how one character had to kill the other to prevent what the rogue forced it to do.

"She told you that—to kill her?"

"Well, she told me I might need to be her Shinji." Cassie looked up at him, her face awash with the pain.

"It won't come to that," Sal said. "We're stopping them. Tonight." No way did he want her living with the torment of taking her friend's life.

Relief rushed through her pretty features. She leaned into him.

"But where is Meng-Li? If Tang is here, why isn't he?" Dean sought an answer from Cassie. "Do you know?"

"She only spoke to me through the earpiece." Cassie touched the device.

"Keep it in," Dean said. "She might reach out to you again."

"It's more important now than ever that I get to her, stop her. Let Kiew know we'll help her."

Across the room by the ice sculptures and drink fountains, Kiew Tang in her cream gown stood out as a lily placed on black lacquer. The suits around her stuck close. Not business acquaintances. Security. "I doubt they'll let you get anywhere near her."

"Agreed. Meng-Li might not be here, but his security team is—and they're attached to Kiew. They haven't left her once. Even when she used the restroom, they stayed outside."

"Look," Sal mumbled with a nod as Nianzu entered the protective perimeter around Tang without a glitch. Expected and accepted. "If that's not proof he's complicit..."

"He's mine when it goes down," Dean growled.

"Who's the American with them?" Cassie asked.

"Where?" Sal shifted closer to follow her visual line. "Son of—that's Slusarski!"

"Who?" Cassie turned—and their noses nearly touched.

"Okay, team, we have a full deck except Meng-Li." After giving him a slap on the shoulder, Dean started away, speaking into the coms, "Stay eyes out and ready."

"We have a problem."

Could things get any worse? Sal pivoted, hand going to Cassie, who stepped into his touch, and found Takkar standing shoulder to shoulder with Dean. "My team believes Meng-Li is not coming."

"Why?"

"Tonight was a distraction—"

"Right."

"No, Meng-Li also used tonight as a distraction just as we hoped to do. My team monitoring his facility said he has not left."

"So, he has us here to. . ."

"Keep us distracted." A storm had moved into Takkar's eyes and morphed into a full-on hurricane. "He is manipulating me. It has been his way from the beginning, but I believed I could turn and control things. My attempts to forge cooperation and unity were tossed aside like a dog "

"Then why is Kiew here?" Cassie had singular focus where her friend was concerned. "Oh, look. Brie is there. She's going to talk to Kiew." Cassie started forward. "If she can—"

"No." Takkar cuffed her by the elbow. "Stay." His word came out like a hiss. "Watch."

Once more, just as with Nianzu, the security detail parted. Brie walked over to Kiew Tang and greeted her. Not entirely unusual but—

"The hands," Takkar said.

The fingers did a little dance. Then Brie walked away.

"Brush pass," Dean muttered, disbelief coloring his words.

Immediately, Sal searched the crowd for Titanis. No doubt, just as Sal had kept tabs on Cassie as quietly as possible, the Aussie had done the same with Hastings. Sure enough, Titanis had the fury of being betrayed all over his face.

"Ramsey," Dean breathed. "He's with them."

"My friends," Takkar said. "I believe this is the most opportune time to realize your goals. Meng-Li will not be coming. You have three of the four targets in one circle."

"One heavily armed circle."

"I have but one request," Takkar said.

Sal and Dean waited.

"Slusarski is mine."

What? Since when did Takkar get rights to American soldiers? "But he's—"

"*Mine,*" Takkar said.

Dean didn't seem to like the situation either. "Meaning you want to kill him or you own him?"

"Meaning, he's not to be harmed." Takkar strode off.

"Get ready," Dean said as he started for the corner. "Alpha and Sierra teams, we are a go. Move into positions."

CHAPTER 42

Kabul, Afghanistan
10 April—1945 Hours

Eamon did as ordered, but his mind and thoughts were hung up on seeing Brie pass something to Kiew Tang. Instead of moving toward Ramsey, Eamon cleared a path straight toward Brie.

"What'd you do?" he growled. "What was that?"

Brie's face blanched. Her lips parted.

"Yeah, I saw it—and so did the team. What'd you do, Brie?"

"How dare you—"

Eamon closed a hand around her wrist.

"Let go of me!"

"What'd you do?" He hated it. Hated what he'd been thinking. The pieces had fallen into place when he saw her enter the building tonight. Tracked her moves. He didn't want to believe this, not of a woman he'd hoped to bring home to meet his dad. She was the one handing off the codes to Kiew Tang. Brie had been the mole. Then what. . .what about Ramsey?

She struggled against him. "Release me!"

With a twist of her arm, he anchored her against his chest. Had her tight. "It's you—you're the mole."

Her lip lifted in a sneer. "You have no idea what you're talking about."

Anxious to believe that, to believe she wasn't really betraying her own country or friends, he searched her face. Searched for a sign of shock at being accused of something so terrible. But there was no fear. Just flat-out panic at being caught. "I think I do."

He hauled her toward the door, toward the FBI waiting on the third floor, monitoring movement with Takkar's men.

"Do I still intrigue you, Titanis?"

"I'm intrigued to know how you can live with yourself."

"Easy to say coming from someone who could buy his way up any ladder he wanted. Try fighting it."

"So, what? They offered you money?"

"A butt load. And respect—"

Eamon let out a laugh.

"Five years as Burnett's lackey and no promotion."

"Promotions are earned, not handed out. Maybe you didn't get one because he saw through your facade."

Surprise flickered through her blue eyes.

"Burnett might've been gruff, but he wasn't blind."

"Yeah, and what good did it do him? They killed him."

"*You* killed him, you mean."

"No." Her eyes flashed. "That wasn't me. That wasn't supposed to happen."

"Hmm, maybe you should've told them. They would've listened, right, with all that respect you earned."

—⚌—

"Go go go!" Dean rushed forward, weapon cradled in both hands as he approached Nianzu's men.

The man had unbelievable instincts. As if something in the air alerted him, Nianzu snapped straight. Three men closed around him.

"Lee Nianzu," Dean called.

The circle of men herded the man toward an exit.

"You don't want to do that," Dean said, his heart thudding. "Authorities are waiting out there."

The bubble swung around. "I thought you better than this," Nianzu said, his British accent present even now.

"Yeah, well, I guess you ripped the 'better' out of me." Dean closed in on him, weapon at the ready.

Guns faced him, but Dean noted in his periphery as Riordan and his SEALs formed a protective arc behind Nianzu and his men.

"You have wanted this," Nianzu spat, realizing he was cornered.

"I want justice."

"What man wants justice when he can have vengeance?" Nianzu shifted, looking around, probably for a safe exit.

"I don't play to that tune." Though he had to admit the only tune he'd wanted for a long time was a death march for Nianzu. His mind became clogged with images of Zahrah lying in the hospital bed, hair butchered. Body butchered. He'd broken her. And yet. . .he hadn't.

The gun in Nianzu's hand wagged, as if he itched to open fire. To shoot his way out of this trap.

"Game's over," Dean said. "Put the weapons down. Hands up."

Tense minutes clicked off the clock, but Dean refused to budge. Refused to talk their way through this. The order had been laid out there. It was up to Nianzu to comply now.

The men in front of him hesitated, lowered their weapons.

Relief soaked his muscles.

But the men raised them again.

Which forced Dean to do to the same. "You can't win here. It's over."

The men bent at the knees, slowly, and lowered their weapons.

A peaceful resolution. Nianzu hadn't surrendered his weapon yet, so Dean maintained vigilance, though he could see the defeat scrawled over the Asian man's face.

Dean nodded, chiding himself for the small fraction of him that had hoped—

Nianzu's weapon snapped up. Straight at Dean.

Instinct crackled. Dean eased back the trigger.

Crack!

CHAPTER 43

Kabul, Afghanistan
10 April—1945 Hours

Nianzu fell.

"Augh!" Dean shifted. Swayed. Went to a knee, grabbing his arm.

Sal surged. "Dean!"

He shook his head. "I'm good. A graze." But pain pinched his features. Blood turned his sleeve dark. He scooted closer and pressed two bloodied fingers to Nianzu's neck. Let out a breath and sagged. "He's gone."

Sal breathed a little easier, knowing the slick Asian guy wouldn't make like a serpent and slither away this time. Seeing their leader taken out, the men around him raised their hands and moved away from their dead boss.

"Hold up," Sal said, turning around and searching the chaotic room. Nianzu was down. Hastings was with Titanis. "Where's Ramsey?"

"And Tang," Dean said, coming to his feet.

Though Sal didn't look directly at the doors, he knew security protected them. "Feds have the exits."

"Which means Ramsey's still in here," Dean muttered. "Fan out—find him!" So the general was hiding like the chicken spit he was.

The crowds had split wide open, with a thick throng crowded near the windows and pillars. The rest huddled near the kitchen, where Takkar's men guarded the doors.

Sal stalked the crowd, determined to end Ramsey. Not exactly acting like a general now.

"Spotted him," Takkar's people spoke through the coms, having the benefit of security cameras for an aerial view. "Heading toward kitchens, right side."

Crack! Crack!

"He took the guard. Right side," Takkar's man said.

Just then, Ramsey was in view. Arm hooked around the guard's neck and holding a gun to the man's head, he dragged him through the kitchen door.

Sal launched himself toward the crowd, pushing through, using his size and speed to bowl them out of the way. Like the fool he was, Ramsey attempted to run. Stupid move. They had guns on all doors leading out of the building. He wouldn't get far. But then, Sal didn't want him getting killed. He wanted the guy to suffer in a federal pen for the rest of his life.

Crack!

The sound of a gunshot echoed out from the kitchen. Metal clanged and a woman's scream pierced the room. The crowd roared in response to the shot, like a herd of buffalo rushing for exits. Trampling each other. He grew less concerned about being polite to the people and more about protecting them.

As he made it to the swinging door, Sal noted a sea of suits rushing through the other door.

"We have two people," came Dean's words. "Footage is grainy. Crowds are making it impossible to decipher—"

Sal stepped into the crowded kitchen. Stainless-steel refrigerators lined the wall on his three and a similar island spanned the length of the room. Metal shelving cut into the layout, packed with tubs of vegetables and fruit waiting to be served.

Movement drew Sal. "They're at the back," he said, gliding forward. To his nine, he twitched at the sight of someone. He snapped to neutralize the threat.

And veered off, a curse flinging through his mind that registered *friendly*! Harrier. Pulse leveling, Sal resumed course.

He eased around a corner and spotted a man. With about twenty feet between him and the swinging doors, Sal saw him. The youth they'd arrested and questioned. The brother of the little girl. Sal's shoulders tensed. "Fariz is here." What was he doing here? Had he lied to them?

"Come again?" Dean asked.

"Fariz—Ramsey's son." Sal inched closer. "How did you know?"

"I hear my father talk on the phone. He also took me with him one time. I saw this and wanted to help the man he wanted to kill."

Sal shook his head, trying to believe this. It seemed far-fetched. Should they trust him?

"What is he—?"

"Oh crap!" someone else—Harrier?—said.

Fariz reached for someone beside him. Sal tensed, expecting trouble, but he turned and spotted a huddled form, bent beneath the weight of pain, leaning heavily on Fariz for support. A weapon dangled from his bloodied hand.

At their feet lay a writhing Ramsey, clutching his leg that blood gushed down.

The shooter's head lifted. Dirty brown hair and beard.

"Hawk!" Sal surged forward, throwing himself past the last lines of onlookers. "Move!" he shouted. This was worse than a nightmare. His legs weren't leaden, but the guests refused to budge. "It's Hawk! Hawk's here," Sal shouted into his coms. "He's alive!"

Sal shoved between two people and broke into the clear.

Gray-green eyes met his. A beard crusted with blood twitched as a smirk hit. "'Bout freakin' time."

—w—

Kiew was gone. Somehow in the chaos of the shootings, Ramsey's escape, Hawk's return. . .she'd seized the confusion and used it to her benefit.

Cassie pushed into the kitchen area where Raptor and Riordan's teams had gathered up around their back-from-the-dead team member.

"I'll give Fekiria a call. She'll have my head if I don't tell her you're alive."

Hawk groaned but said little else. He'd been on his feet, and he'd managed to disable Ramsey and prevent him from running. But all that had been done with reserves of energy he probably didn't really have. He'd told them of being held by Meng-Li's men, aided largely in part by

Ramsey, who had been loaded on another chopper in critical condition. Though the operators had been betrayed by a man they'd trusted with their lives, they'd treated him as if he hadn't visited evil upon them.

"Take care, Hawk." Sal squeezed his hand. "We're glad you're this side of dead."

"That must've hurt to say," Hawk chuckled.

"You have no idea." With a grin, Sal stood back as the team of PJs moved in to carry Hawk out to the chopper, which would ferry him to a hospital for reparative surgery and recovery.

"Make a hole," a voice barked.

Cassie shifted from the scene toward the booming voice. Her breath caught in her lungs. Sajjan Takkar steered one Lance Burnett into the room in a wheelchair and tubed with oxygen.

"General!" Two large strides carried Sal to Lance Burnett. "Holy—how in—what—?"

Captain Watters was at his side, taking a knee. "Knew you were too mean to die."

Sal stood covering his mouth. Then ran his hand over his head. His expression went from shock and awe, to anger.

Burnett grunted. "Don't get your pants in a wad, Russo. Couldn't get rid of me that easy."

"Apparently, sir," Sal said with a smile. "How and why?"

"Takkar's men got me out of there—in cooperation with Phelps and Ames."

Cassie pressed a hand to her chest. "My boss?"

"He knew what he was doing planting you with the team, Miss Walker. But we knew Ramsey wanted me out of the way to finish his deal. To take care of his mistress and illegitimate children. Meng-Li had him over a barrel."

Cassie shifted back as the men of Raptor gathered around their general.

"Besides, Takkar brought in the best surgeons and doctors to tend me here. Better than the hack-jobs working on me—and not knowing if they were in Ramsey's pocket."

"I can't express how relieved I am," Captain Watters said.

"That goes for me, too." Sal nodded to the team. "And all of us, I'm sure."

"Now that we've got the feel-good stuff out of the way, you all need to know I'm paralyzed. Can't move my arms or legs—"

"Remember, my friend, that may be temporary," Takkar put in.

"Maybe. But right now, it's not. Right now, I have no use of my body." His eyes glinted with determination. "Meng-Li turned our world upside down, gentlemen. We need to take him down."

"Kiew Tang fled the building," Takkar said.

"How did that happen?" Sal asked. "Thought your men and the FBI—"

"We let her leave."

Sal scowled and Cassie felt the fury of his expression. "Why?"

"Because we know where she's going," Takkar said. "And she must return to Shanghai to keep Meng-Li in play. If she didn't return to him, he would know we have the upper hand and would vanish. Then we would be against him again, more fierce and deadly than ever."

"But now she has the code."

"And we have a contingency," Takkar said.

"One Brie didn't know about," Burnett added.

"Wait," Cassie asked. "So you knew about her?"

"*Suspected,*" Burnett corrected, "which is why I pulled her under my wing—so I could monitor her moves."

"So, what's the contingency?" Sal asked.

"Our nightmare from the earlier missions—the ghost in our mikes." Burnett shifted, cringing and clenching his eyes closed.

"Ghost?"

Takkar squared his shoulders. "Boris Kolceki, the man spying on you and Raptor for the last year. He's cooperating and will be vital to getting us through the building and once in, he will wage a virtual war against Meng-Li seizing that information."

"A cyber duel." Hawk grinned.

"Yes." Takkar inclined his head. "As we well know, there will be a winner and loser. Since we don't know which one Boris will be, we need the team there."

"So, we're going to Shanghai?" Sal muttered, shaking his head.

"I want to go." Perhaps she'd overstepped with the demand, but Cassie couldn't just sit idly by.

"What? No!" Sal snapped. "No way. You stay here. You're not trained—"

"I am, actually. I have weapons training and—"

"You haven't been in combat. You haven't killed anyone," Sal argued. "It's going to be too dangerous."

"Kiew told me I needed to be her Shinji. She's being forced to do something she doesn't want to do. I have to be there for her."

"No—"

"Enough!" Burnett wheezed.

Sal cocked his head in that angry way of his, tightening his lips.

"Russo, we need her there," Burnett said.

Again Takkar spoke up. "We'll access Meng-Li's system, Boris will do his magic, but we need Walker there for Kiew Tang." He pointed to the door. "My jet is waiting."

CHAPTER 44

Shanghai, China
11 April—1945 Hours

It was a trap."

Phone to his ear, Jin left the safety of the elevator. "Of course it was."
He'd expected no less. In fact, he had planned on their attempt to end
his campaign. "You escaped."

"Of course."

Jin almost smiled, but her question held not only confidence but
defiance. He tossed his keys on the table by the statue and red cloth.

"Lee is dead. He died honorably, fighting. He did not surrender."

"He has always been a warrior. You could learn from him, Kiew."

"We land in two hours," Kiew said.

Jin stilled. Glanced at the statue on the pedestal draped in red silk.
He pivoted, looking back to the god in the foyer. Then his pulse slowed
as his gaze traced the other statue in front of the fire pit, also covered
in crimson. The mirror above the mantel had been turned. "No!" He
dropped the phone and keys, hurrying toward the bedrooms. *Māma!*

His heart beat harder with each step, with each statue of the gods
draped in red cloth. The mirrors turned so a soul could not escape.

The maid stood outside his mother's bedroom door, hands clasped,
gaze down. "I am sorry, Mr. Meng-Li."

He threw open the door and ignored the maid's gasp. Rushed to his
mom's bedside, where she lay in quiet repose, her frail body wrapped in
muslin to keep her soul intact. Her face protected.

He reached for it, to rip away the veil, to break this nightmarish
curse that had consumed his life. "No," he breathed. "No, Māaama!" He
clung to her, feeling her brittle bones beneath his hands. "Come back

to me. You must see me win! You must see what Father began and I finished!"

But she did not answer. Did not move. Did not breathe.

"Please!" Tears choked him. It was not good for him to cry. It was not right, in front of others.

"Sir," came a soft voice. "You should—"

"Get out!" Spinning as he rose to his feet, Jin shouted. "Leave me. Lock the doors. Nobody comes in!"

The maid fumbled backward, her small eyes wide.

"Get. Out!"

She sprinted down the hall.

Pulling himself together, Jin reached for the doors. Closed them. Secured the locks. He rested his head against the mahogany and let his eyes slide shut. How could the gods do this to him? The family gods who had served his mother? The ones that had carried him this far to avenge and honor his father?

He moved to the armchair and eased himself onto the cushion, staring at her ghostlike form.

This was not supposed to happen. She was not supposed to leave him before his plan had been fulfilled. She needed to see him succeed, needed to see all that his father—her husband—had worked to achieve come to life.

In that dark hour as he sat alone, Jin promised himself he would visit on the Americans tenfold what they'd done to his father or die trying.

When he emerged, he knew not how long he'd sat with his mother, but it must have been at least two hours.

Kiew stood before him, her face carrying the pain he bore in his heart. "She is. . ." She started forward. "I am so sorry. She was a wonderful woman."

Jin said nothing of his mother. "You have the codes?"

"Should you take time to mourn—?"

"Do not think to tell me what I should do."

"Forgive me, I am not. I only meant—I know you want to honor her—"

"I grow tired of your attempts to ply me to your will, Kiew."

She drew back. "No, you misunderstand."

"It is you who does not understand, my pearl." He sensed his man behind him. "I've allowed you to roam free too long, you who would tear me down from within."

Kiew shook her head. "I don't know what you're talking about. I was there at the fund-raiser. I got the codes."

Jin sneered. "The wrong codes. Do you think I am so stupid that I do not know the codes are the wrong ones?"

"No," she said, holding out a piece of paper. "They are right. They came from the same source."

"Compromised!" He threw his hand up and stalked down the hall. He heard the click of her heels as she trailed him, with his man behind her.

He passed the array of blades he'd collected over the years. Signs of strength. Power. He ran his fingers along the steel. He drew one free. Admired the razor's edge.

And in his periphery, he noticed Kiew straighten. Grow more poised. Tensed.

"Takkar has been meddling too long and too deep. And he did not think I would know. That I am too weak or stupid to see what he has done to me. So, I will finish not only these Americans but Sajjan Takkar."

"I can help with the codes! You brought me here for this reason. Let me—"

"All are compromised." With that he turned and thrust the sword through the one who had betrayed him. "You would have been a beautiful pearl."

—∞—

Shanghai, China
11 April—2245 Hours

Rotors *thwumped* as Raptor raced to stop a maniac. A five-hour flight had given the team time to prepare a plan and one contingency. They'd rappel in, locate Tang, and stop Meng-Li from accessing the very lives of soldiers and operatives around the world. If he could access that, then not only were the soldiers' and operator's lives in danger, but so were the lives of their families. He'd have access to their entire personnel files.

Geared up and adrenaline jacked, Sal sat in the jumpseat, watching the glittering lights of a thriving metropolis. Cassie would be ferried in after the insertion team. Once immediate threats were neutralized.

But that put the onus on him to make sure he did his job and did it right. If he didn't, Cassie could die.

God had lifted one burden from his shoulders by bringing Hawk back from the dead, so Sal didn't want to wreck that.

"Two mikes out," came the pilot's voice through the coms. "Going silent."

The heavy *thwump* of the rotors vanished, but the numbing vibration worming through his boots, legs, and backside didn't. Sal lowered his night-vision goggles then caught the rope, readying himself to fast-rope onto the rooftop of the high-rise that housed Meng-Li's private lab.

The bird raced up to the building and swung around, his side exposed.

Boots propped on the edge, Sal coiled the rope around his arm and a leg. Dangling out into the cool, rank air, he pushed off. Sailed through the night, feeling the burn of the rope in his hands as he sped toward the tarred surface. On the roof, he snapped up his weapon and knelt, taking up a position to watch for unfriendlies.

Behind him, came the soft thud of six more pair of boots.

A pat came to his shoulder and he pushed up and rushed around a main AC unit. Dirt and pebbles crunched beneath his boots, the view before him awash in a monochromatic green. Ten yards to the door. The team hustled up and even as he advanced on the point of entry, he heard the telltale *whoosh* of the second chopper arriving.

Sal sprinted to the door, expecting trouble. Why hadn't they already had some? Meng-Li *had* to know they were coming.

Even as he thought it, Sal saw the wiring on the steel door.

He held up a fisted hand, bringing the insertion to a halt.

Dean sidled up.

So much for a stealthy breach. Sal pointed to the explosives. Dean patted his shoulder, held up a finger, then jogged toward the three-foot-high cement ledge rimming the rooftop. He peered over, obviously looking for a quieter alternative. If there was a balcony. He rushed farther down then jogged back.

He pointed to the door and nodded.

Do it. Sal looped a rope to the handle and the team backpedaled a half-dozen paces to take cover behind that AC unit. He yanked the rope.

Booom!

The building shook. The door flipped outward, blasted free amid a fireball.

A little more noisy than a flash-bang. Nothing more. As Sal made his way into the building, he knew Meng-Li didn't expect to kill them. He just wanted a little warning. One they'd had to oblige him with.

"Boris has cleared the motion sensors and rerouted video footage to keep security from rushing up there," Takkar spoke from his seat back in Afghanistan.

Snaking into the building, down the stairs from the roof, Sal heard the crack of thunder outside. Unbelievable. A storm.

They moved quickly down the steel steps, which amplified their movements. Still, with a half-dozen men in the well, it amazed him how quiet they were. At the first level, they grouped up. Sal waited, hand on the door, until he had the telltale pat on his shoulder indicating they were in position.

Dean shouldered the wall in front of him. Mouthed, *"Three. . . two. . .go!"*

Sal jerked open the door.

Gunfire peppered the walls. Dinged and vibrated against the steel barrier.

Dean jerked back.

Sal held the door. Eagle and Harrier fired back, advancing as a coordinated strike effort. They flanked right and left, still firing.

Dean moved out, shooting until the cacophony of weapons' fire consumed his hearing.

A clap of thunder snapped off the electricity.

Enemy fire hesitated.

Raptor didn't. Within seconds, silence fell on the foyer as did the bodies of three of Meng Li's men. Sal and Titanis were in position with the rest. In the stairwell, they heard boots thudding. Riordan and his team were on time.

Darkness gave them the advantage, but Sal knew that wouldn't last long. Generators would kick in.

They moved quickly toward the midlevel entry lab. They had to stop Meng-Li from decimating American forces. As they moved through the high-end penthouse, Sal couldn't help but feel creeped out. Something was wrong here. Really wrong.

His gaze hit something on a table draped in a cloth. Another by the fireplace. What the. . . ? Why were things covered and mirrors turned?

Freaky.

"Chinese custom," Titanis said, "to protect the souls of a loved one who has died."

"Who died?"

"Probably his mother," Takkar said. "She was ailing."

They hurried through the living room and down the corridor. There they found the access stairs.

Someone sat in the corner.

"Hands, hands," Sal shouted, his heart thundering.

Slowly, much slower than he would've preferred, hands came up. Bloodied. And as he stepped closer, he saw the face. "It's Tang. She's injured!"

"Me," she breathed. "You need me. . ." She cringed and hissed, holding her side where blood stained her blouse. "Codes—me, take me—"

"Biosensor locks," Dean shouted from below.

The pieces clicked together. Sal knelt and eyed Titanis. "Help me get her up." After hoisting the petite woman to her feet, they carried her down the stairs. She gritted her teeth, and he knew that injury in her side had to hurt. It wasn't a bullet wound.

She waved a hand toward the three-by-five-inch panel. Sal aimed her at the pad. She pressed her hand against it. When the light flashed green, she punched in a code.

Pressurized, the wall hissed and then slid back.

"Leave. . ." Her eyes fluttered shut.

"Titanis—"

"Go. I'll stay," he said.

"No." She snapped her head up and cried out. "No, you need me. He's in the contained room. My passcode. Only my pass. . ."

"Kiew?"

Sal glanced back, agitated that Cassie and the SEALs had already caught up.

"She said we need a code to get in." Sal keyed his mic. "We need a code. Tang says we need her code, but she's in and out of consciousness." He looked at Cassie as the others headed into the den. "Stay with her. Get her to talk. Tell you that code. We need it, Cass."

"Boris is working on it from here, too," Takkar said through the coms.

Sal trailed Dean, Eagle, and Harrier into the corridor marked with blue lights. They moved like a machine, the well-oiled machine he'd come to love and appreciate. With a threat against not just his brothers-in-arms, but their families, Sal felt the stakes had never been higher. It was one thing to kill soldiers in war. It was another to go after their families, children. Innocents.

But moving in on him wouldn't do any good unless Cassie got that code.

CHAPTER 45

Shanghai, China
11 April—2315 Hours

Kiew?" Cassie cradled her friend in her arms. "Kiew, I need your help."

Eyes fluttering were the only sign that Kiew fought to live.

"What's the code?"

Kiew's head lobbed. "Bio. . .both. . ."

Titanis met her gaze. "The first one was a biosensor—they'll need her."

Cassie glanced down at her friend, hair askew and life seeping from her. "Can you carry her?"

"Whatever it takes." Titanis hooked his arms beneath Kiew and lifted her from the ground. "Stay close."

They rushed through the darkened area and Kiew fluttered awake and back into preservation sleep demanded by her body.

Cassie followed behind and to the right of Titanis. Ahead, she saw the SEALs bounding from side to side down the hall. Clearing the way. Titanis stopped each time they entered a room and then returned.

Somewhere ahead, shouts went up. Gunfire erupted. It took everything in Cassie not to rush forward. The air crackled with a firefight. In the darkness it seemed like a small fireworks show.

"Tango down," came a call. One that gave Cassie a little more room to breathe. But she wouldn't relax, wouldn't breathe easy until they were out of this skyscraper. It was hard not to think of 9/11 and the towers that collapsed. They were taller like this one. Not like Takkar. Even now, she could feel the natural sway of the building and it knotted her stomach.

Cassie had her own weapon, but she was to help Kiew. To make sure they stopped Meng-Li from getting that information, from terrorizing and killing more Americans.

"Bring Tang," came a shout.

Titanis nodded and Cassie finally saw Sal at the far end of the narrow space, waving them closer. She ran toward him, glancing back to make sure Titanis was doing okay with Kiew. When she looked forward again, she faced not Sal but an Asian man.

Cassie jerked back to a stop, her feet skidding out from under her as she screamed. The man bucked, twitched then collapsed.

Past the man, Sal had his weapon up, trained on the spot the man had been. "Move!"

Yanked out of her panicked stupor by his growl, Cassie bolted toward him. When she reached Sal, he swirled her around behind him. "Panel," he pointed to Titanis, who hoisted Kiew closer to the panel.

Sal pressed her hand against the pad. "Tang, we need the code again."

Kiew lay limp in Titanis's arms.

"Tang! The code!"

Only as Sal shouted and glanced backward, did Cassie see Meng-Li poised at a massive computer system, hacking away at a keyboard. Was Boris holding him off? Or had Meng-Li already won?

"F–five. . .three. . .two. . .seven," came Kiew's soft, labored words.

Sal punched in the numbers.

Captain Watters, Eagle, and Harrier—and all the SEALs grouped up, weapons trained and ready.

"Boris said to hurry," Sal said, holding his ear mic. "The codes are uploading and Meng-Li has almost fully accessed the information. If he does—"

"Quiet," Dean said slowly and low.

The door lumbered aside.

The team flooded in.

Titanis set Kiew down and nodded to Cassie, who hovered at her side, torn between being with the team and helping somehow—and staying with her friend.

"You are too late!" pronounced Meng-Li Jin as he yanked the keyboard free and cracked it in half. "The codes are in."

"It's over," Captain Watters said. "Away from the system."

"It does not matter if you kill me. The codes and the system are set to send this information to the Chinese government. And the Russians after that."

"Down. On your knees."

Cassie couldn't tear her eyes from the scene. Sal and Captain Watters flanked the crazed man, both aiming their weapons at him.

"Ahhhh!" someone shouted and sprinted into the room, firing.

The SEALs neutralized the newcomer, who tumbled to the ground.

Somehow Meng-Li produced a gun. Aimed it at Sal.

Cassie's breath backed into her throat, frozen.

The detonation of that bullet in the barrel punched her in the gut as she watched Sal's head jerk back. As he flipped around then thudded to the ground, Raptor brought down Meng-Li in a firestorm of bullets.

"No!"

Something tightened on Cassie's collar, squeezing her throat.

Kiew had her shirt, pulling her. "Help me."

Cassie frowned, her gaze diving back to Sal, who wasn't moving. "No, no..."

Eagle had rushed toward Sal while Harrier squatted next to Meng-Li and dipped his brown head, verifying Meng-Li was dead.

"Bomb."

Cassie jerked. "What?"

"Raptor," Takkar said, "Boris detected a rogue code that looks a lot like a destruct code to the main building."

"What about the codes?"

"He's crippling the system, but a well-placed grenade would help."

Heavy glass walls slammed into place, sealing off the team in the main systems room.

"My terminal," Kiew said, her gaze hitting something. "Hurry."

Cassie glanced over her shoulder. Saw a desk-like area. The men were sealed in the room, banging on it. Captain Watters knelt over Sal. Shook his shoulder. But Sal didn't respond. Cassie's mind warped into panic.

"Code...Shinji..."

Leaning forward, Cassie lifted Kiew over her shoulder in a fireman carry. She trembled as she pushed to her feet, her legs unwilling to support the extra weight. But she would, doggone it. She would do this. With one last glance, she prayed Sal hadn't been killed.

Captain Watters shook Sal again, and this time, he shifted.

Thank You, God!

Cassie focused on getting to the terminal. Saving his team and Kiew. All of them. For once in her life, she'd be the answer, not the problem. She'd stop this insanity.

The first several steps were made, not with ease but firm resolution. But her knee buckled. Cassie thrust out a hand and caught herself against one of the system tables as Kiew shifted. Cassie counterbalanced. Pushed herself up. Hauled her and Kiew the last few steps.

Kiew tumbled off.

Cassie cried out, catching her friend. "Sorry. So sorry." She adjusted Kiew so she could reach the system keyboard.

Her friend's fingers groped for keys. She shuddered and bobbed forward, about to collapse.

She clicked something and a dialogue box popped up.

Thuds drew Cassie's attention around. Sal and Dean were shouting something. Hand on Kiew, she kept her place and tried to figure out what they were saying.

"Shin. . .ji. . ."

Cassie glanced back. Realized Kiew wasn't moving. "Hey, you—"

Head down, arms limp, Kiew wasn't breathing.

"No!" Cassie pressed her friend back and glanced at the box. She hadn't entered the code. "Kiew! Kiew, no! I need you." Terrorized, she looked at Sal and shook her friend. "Please, Kiew! Don't do this. Don't die. Not now."

Tears blurred Cassie's vision, the dose of panic acute.

"God!" She cried out to her Maker, desperate. Frantic. She clapped her hands over her head, turning to see Sal and Dean banging. They pointed to something.

She looked and saw a red display with numbers. Countdown.

Bomb.

Cassie couldn't breathe. Couldn't think. Kiew warned her a bomb would go off. Warned her. . .

You'll have to be Shinji.

How? How could she be her Shinji when Kiew was already dead? It didn't make sense. Why bring her here? Why have her. . . ?

Cassie gripped the edge of the desk. "O God. . ." Desperation made it impossible to think or pray. "Help me!" she screamed, the words scraping the very marrow of her bones. "They're all going to die!"

Shinji.

"What does that mean?" Cassie screamed again. *Okay. Okay. Stop it. Panic doesn't help. Screaming doesn't help.* "Oh, Jesus, please. . .please please please. . ."

Shinji. A reload movie. *You Can (Not) Redo.* 2.22.

Cassie hauled in a breath. "Two point two two!"

Codes couldn't have non-numeric digits. Could they? She punched in the numeric digits. Glanced back at the display. Still going. Panic vaulted over hope. She glanced at the screen. Saw she'd typed 2.23. She reentered it, more carefully—slower—this time.

A buzzing roared through the level.

Behind her a cheer went up. She looked back, thrilled to find Sal and the others rushing toward her.

Sal's eyes widened, he bolted around the corner. "No!"

Cassie turned to see what he was doing and then noticed the main door to this area dropping into place. Sal dove and rolled into the room, narrowly avoiding losing a leg as the wall slammed into place.

"No! What are you doing?" she screamed at him.

"Secondary explosion," Sal said. "Meng-Li must've had a trigger on the main floor. Look!"

Cassie checked the monitor in the corner—of the penthouse. Flames engulfed it.

"Go, go!" Sal shouted to the team. "We'll find a way out."

Dean scowled at him but the others were already hustling out of the sub lab.

"How are we going to find a way out?" Cassie demanded, her childhood fear of fire suffocating her thoughts.

"Go!" Sal growled as he rushed over to Kiew and lifted her off the chair.

Cassie couldn't help but feel a suffocating pressure against her chest as she watched the team vanish, leaving them alone in a burning building. "What are you doing?"

But he didn't answer. He rushed toward the panel. Pressed Kiew's hand against it.

"Code! Code," Sal demanded.

Cassie froze. "I don't know—"

Sal punched in a series of numbers.

The blast shield lifted.

Cassie gaped. "How—?"

"Her passcode—she used it earlier with my help." Sal grabbed her hand. "C'mon!"

CHAPTER 46

Shanghai, China
11 April—2335 Hours

They barreled through the lower lab, feeling the concussive boom of the bomb that had been set off after Cassie deactivated the first one. Sal caught her hand and flung her toward the door, which was sliding closed.

"Falcon, report!"

They shimmied past it and up the stairs. His boot hit a slick spot and he nearly ate it, realizing too late that's where Kiew Tang had lain when they found her.

"En route. Two mikes."

"Time is short."

Fire roared and surged, licking the ceiling. Devouring the furniture.

Sal pushed Cassie forward, willing her to run faster. They threw themselves at the stairs. Cassie stumbled.

"Fire has engulfed the three levels below you."

Sal's heart vaulted into his throat, hearing the secondary boom. "Move, move!"

The explosion shot into the stairwell. Punched him forward, right into Cassie. A scorching wave rushed over his back. He dove over Cassie and protected her, toeing the door shut with his boot.

Catching her drag strap, he hauled her up. "Go!"

"Falcon, you're out of time! Supports are crumbling."

Cassie fumbled but finally got on her feet. Sprinted up the stairs two at a time. She flung herself around the next flight and Sal overtook her, reaching the door seconds before she did. He yanked it open and pushed her onto the roof.

The chopper hovered and swung toward them.

A rope rippled down.

Sal sprinted and caught it. He waved her toward it. Even as he did, he felt the building groan.

Cassie's eyes widened as the entire roof tilted.

Sal wrapped his arm and leg in the rope. "Hold on to me!"

She frantically shook her head.

The building pitched and tossed Cassie at him.

"Now!" Sal hooked her waist and snapped her tight against himself. Almost instantly, they were yanked up. Over the building. Bright white light exploded below them, chasing their legs with its furious heat. With a massive groan that sounded like a freight train, the building surrendered the fight.

Cassie's arms clamped around him, her face pressed into his neck. Her legs coiled around his hips, her entire body rigid. The frigid air tore at them. Threatening his grip and their very lives.

He would not drop her.

Wind tugged hard, actively trying to punish them for defying gravity.

Cassie's frame trembled. He couldn't hear her for the roar of the air, but he was pretty sure she was crying as they trailed behind the big bird.

Sal saw another rooftop rushing up at them and breathed a sigh of relief when the rope lowered them from a horizontal position over the road to vertical. They touched down on the roof.

"You okay?" Sal shouted, now able to feel her hot breath on his neck as she still clung to him.

"No," she managed.

"We need to climb up. Can you?"

Cassie released him and stepped back. Stumbled and plopped hard onto her backside.

Eyeing the rope dangling overhead, he held out a hand to her. Sal hauled her back to her feet. "We have to go up," he shouted. "Have to get out of here."

She nodded and he rigged her up. The team hoisted her into the bird and then Sal scaled the rope and climbed aboard. Cassie sat on the steel deck and leaned against him. It was nice to have her cling to him.

The chopper zipped over the city and then out across the water until it rushed up over a gleaming white yacht floating in the moonlight and landed on a helo pad.

Sal hopped off and bent against the rotor wash, reached for Cassie, who dragged herself off. They hurried away to give room for the rest of the team.

Titanis motioned them toward a door. They stepped into a lavish but simple seating area. Once the team and SEALs grouped up, Titanis slid a door closed and the helo vanished back into the night.

"What is this?" Schmidt asked.

Sal hovered beside Cassie, the strain of the mission, of losing her friend, unmistakable.

"Pretty sure it's a super yacht," Riordan said.

"Cute."

"Mates, welcome to the *ViCross*." He motioned to the seats. "My home is your home for as long as needed."

"Come again?" Eagle asked. "This is *your* ship?"

Titanis gave a curt nod.

"Why are we here? Why did that helo take us—?"

"Until the dust settles, we need to stay out of sight." Dean removed his tactical vest, and the rest of the team followed suit, shedding gear, along with the physical and emotional weight that went with it. All except Cassie. "It was decided that we'd lay low for a while, once we finished the mission. As far as anyone knows, we're in the field."

"Who decided this?"

"Burnett," Dean said. "The mission didn't go as planned, but we accomplished our objective—stopping Meng-Li and that code. We don't have a lot of answers about the explosions nor if he managed to get that software out to our enemies, but we did good." Dean's gaze hit Cassie. "Walker, good job. You saved the lives of every man in this room. Thank you."

A round of applause went up and Cassie's head went lower.

Sal rubbed her back.

"Titanis will tell you about the ship, but I want everyone writing up their reports before grabbing rack time. This is crucial. We can't lose details to groggy minds in the morning. Clear?"

"Captain," Harrier said. "I need to check your arm."

"Probably should check Falcon's head," Schmidt said. "He ate a bullet through that brain bowl. Look at the hole."

Sal held up the helmet, still stunned that the Kevlar helmet had stopped the bullet that nearly ended it all. "Thick skull."

Hooahs answered, and Titanis led the men below.

"How are you doing?" Sal asked Cassie, holding her back.

Chin dimpling, she ducked. Covered her face with her hands. Sal wrapped her in his arms and held her as she cried. As the tears grew in intensity, Sal tightened his arms around her, hooking one around her head and another around her waist, his lips against her hair. "You were amazing tonight."

She shook her head, shuddering. "She's dead. I couldn't protect her."

"She knew that, Andra. That's why she told you about Shamu."

Cassie snorted through her tears. "Shinji."

"Same difference."

Her wet and red eyes came to his. "I saw him shoot you. Saw it flip you off your feet."

"Yeah, not a graceful swan dive on my part."

With a slow swing of her head back and forth, she tried to fight the tears. Then she shook her head faster. "I thought you were dead."

Her choked sob tugged at heartstrings he'd forgotten he had. Sal tugged her close again. "Imagine how I felt—with you on the other side of the blast shield after you freed us and ended up trapping yourself.

"That door about cut you in half."

"Better in half that losing the best half of me."

Cassie eased back, her dark lashes wet with tears brightening her azure irises.

"Yeah." Sal cupped her face. "You."

"Don't tease me," she said. "I can't—"

Sal captured her mouth with his, gentle at first. Testing the waters. Testing whether she'd shove him away. But when she softened against him, Sal deepened the kiss. Her surrender charged his desire. His craving. His memories of their times years ago. Times that had gotten them in trouble. That had created Mila.

"This going to be a problem?"

Sal eased off, keeping Cassie close but looking at Dean, who stood with his arms folded. "What?"

"You two on the same ship. Think you can respect boundaries?"

"I think I should guard her door," Eagle said, his thinning red hair cut short, as if he'd buzzed it after showering this morning. "To protect the lady."

Sal scowled. "Nobody's protecting this lady but me. And yes—I will be on my best behavior."

"Which has us worried," Harrier said. "We've seen your best before."

"Hey." They were ganging up on him, enjoying it way too much.

"Walker," Dean said, motioning her toward the stairs leading up.

"You can have my room," Titanis said. "It has a lock on the door."

"Oh for crying out loud."

EPILOGUE

Sal strode toward Cassie, who sat on the upper deck. He passed her a military-grade iPad as he sat beside her on the padded bench.

Cassie smiled but the dance her eyebrows did told him she was confused. "What?"

"Can I see her?"

Her lips parted with a deep smile. "Mila?"

"Yeah—you Skyped her, right, that night I saw her face from a distance? Can I see her? Maybe. . ."

"You want me to tell her—?"

He touched her hand. "Just let me meet her. This thing is knocking me off my feet. Let's go easy on her." He wrapped an arm around her as she accessed the app for a video conference. "We'll tell her I'm her daddy when we get back home."

Cassie's gaze flicked to his. "Home? We?"

Sal gave her a sheepish grin. "You didn't think I'd let you leave without me a second time, did you?"

She jabbed his side. "Let's remember, you left me."

"Well. If you want to be technical. . ." He homed in on her lips and kissed her again.

"Ahem," said a voice from the device.

Sal leaned back to find a face staring back.

"Amanda," Cassie said, blushing.

"Seems you've been busy." Amanda glared at Sal. "Want to explain this?"

"A long story," Cassie said. "Promise the full story later, but is Mila there?"

"Yes," a sweet, soft voice called from somewhere off screen. "I'm watching *Blue's Clues*."

"I can't tear her from it."

"Look what I drew!" A piece of paper blurred and blocked the view.

"Back it away, Mila. It's too close."

Sal eased forward as the paper vanished and a cherubic face filled the camera. "It's me and you watching *Blue's Clues* when you come back, Mommy."

Heart full, Sal soaked in her face. Her brown eyes. Her light brown hair, a diluted version of his.

"Mila, I want you to meet someone," Cassie said.

"I know him. He's my daddy."

Sal froze. "Why would you say that?"

"Because, your picture is in Mommy's purse."

Sal smiled at Cassie.

"Are you finally going to come home?" Mila asked, her elbows propped on the granite island as she took over the conversation.

"Well, maybe." Sal shifted, not wanting to push too hard too fast. "But I have to ask you a question."

"What?"

"Do you like ice cream, Mila?"

"No." She pouted then propped her chin on the heels of her little hands. "I *lub* it!"

East China Sea
16 April—1012 Hours

Dean stood aboard the *ViCross* with Raptor team and his new band of brothers, the SEALs who warred with him and relaxed with him over the last four days. He'd watched the approach of the private helicopter from the moment it'd been but a glint in the sunlight. Now the bird whipped the ocean water as it landed on the helo pad.

Last night, watching Sal and Cassie, he knew he was ready. More than ready to make things final. He grabbed a phone and made the arrangements.

Hawk had flown out last night with Takkar to debrief and now hobbled with his leg in a cast to hold the helo's door against the slapping wind. He leaned heavily on the cane. Resplendent in a simple white dress, Zahrah alighted from the chopper with her cousin Fekiria and, of course, her father—the infamous General Z-Day Zarrick.

They disappeared into the sun again, and Dean waited on the lower deck with his brothers. Men he'd fought and suffered with. He shifted on his feet as General Zarrick walked Zahrah toward him at the makeshift wedding altar.

As captain of the ship and since they were more than two miles offshore, Eamon officiated the wedding.

Their words were simple, their vows profound and deep. He prayed the others who had not taken the plunge of committing to the women who'd supported and loved them would follow suit.

Sealed with a kiss, Dean took Zahrah as his wife with all the promises to protect and love her. They celebrated with a feast and more relaxation.

"Hold up." Hawk propped on a cane. "I'm not letting the captain show me up."

Laughter trickled around the boat.

"Fekiria, FlyGirl," Hawk said as he tugged something from his pocket. "Will you marry me?"

"Hold up!" Schmidt laughed. "That's an O ring!"

"Shut up!" Hawk waved his cane at the SEAL. "It's all I have. I've been trapped on this fish tank with smelly squids." He turned and held out his hands. "Well? Will you have me?"

Fekiria laughed. "You're not putting a gasket on me. I want a real ring! A big one!"

"Well, crap." Hawk looked to Titanis. "Got any cash I can borrow?"

They were brothers. Warriors. Friends. Men who fought when others couldn't. When others wouldn't. Soldiers braving the face of evil, standing up when others cowered. And while it might seem they'd gotten off easy with no immediate loss of life among their number, Dean knew the toll would leave indelible scars and the men would warrior on. The next mission. The next enemy. The next victory!

"The soldier above all others prays for peace, for it is the soldier who must suffer and bear the deepest wounds and scars of war."
—Douglas MacArthur

ABOUT THE AUTHOR

Ronie Kendig is an award-winning, bestselling author who
grew up an Army brat. After twenty-plus years of marriage,
she and her hunky hero husband have a full life with four children,
a Maltese Menace, and a retired military working dog in Northern
Virginia. Author and speaker, Ronie loves engaging readers through
her Rapid-Fire Fiction. Ronie can be found at www.roniekendig.com,
on Facebook (www.facebook.com/rapidfirefiction),
Twitter (@roniekendig), and Goodreads (www.goodreads.com/RonieK).

THE QUIET PROFESSIONALS

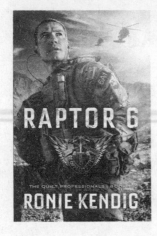 

Other books by Ronie Kendig

DISCARDED HEROES SERIES
Nightshade
Digitalis
Wolfsbane
Firethorn

A BREED APART SERIES
Trinity
Talon
Beowulf

Operation Zulu: Redemption